REPATRIATE

Praise for Jaime Maddox

Bouncing

"Jaime Maddox, Jaime Maddox. She always seems to start out with these feel good lesbian romances. You're reading along, enjoying the fun and light ride, and then—BAM—you get hit with the twisty and suddenly the light ride turns into a twisty, turney awesome mess."—*Danielle Kimerer, Librarian, Reading Public Library (Reading, MA)*

"This book has a little bit of everything: opposites attract, sports, and mystery. But it doesn't feel overly crowded, rushed, or lagging in any way. I was pleasantly surprised by how much I enjoyed all aspects of this story, and I was rooting for all of the characters because Maddox did an amazing job by writing characters that you want to succeed, as well as characters you want to fail (the bad guys). And, I can't say enough about it, the theme of honesty that is so important in this story is written in such a great way. That alone is worth picking up this book."—*Lesbian Review*

The Scholarship

"We are introduced to the killer anonymously in the first few pages, and his motive is hinted at, but Jaime Maddox has done an exceptional job at keeping the reader guessing. This story is a perfect example of a small-town setting, where everyone knows everyone, they all have shared history and experiences, yet they all also have secrets. *The Scholarship* is easy to read, it flows nicely, and it is perfectly paced as a thriller. The last 25% of the book, you will not be able to put it down."—*Lesbian Review*

"This is a sweet slow-burn romance wrapped up in a cold case mystery. Or the other way around. It's not important, what matters is that Ms. Maddox found the perfect balance between mystery and romance with multi-layered characters and a well developed plot. As the main characters' relationship grows, the author drops clues into the mystery to keep the reader guessing until (almost) the end. Maddox manages very well the introduction of so many secondary characters and murder suspects. The appearance of a character with Down Syndrome is welcomed in the genre and done thoughtfully."—*LezReview Books*

Deadly Medicine

"The tale ran at a good, easy pace…It was one of those books that is hard to put down, so I didn't…Very, very well done."—*Prism Book Alliance*

Hooked

"[A] compelling, insightful, and passionate romantic thriller."
—*Lesfic Tumblr*

"[Maddox] did an excellent job of portraying the struggles of addiction, not the entire focus of the story, but informative just the same…All the characters are deep, bringing them to life with their complexities. An intricately woven story line adds credibility; life leaps from the pages."—*Lunar Rainbow Reviewz*

Agnes

"The events around Agnes cast a dark pall over the whole book and Jaime Maddox succeeds in creating, very skillfully, a dark, brooding, almost gothic atmosphere including a grave digger and sinister relatives. It was a pleasure to read until in the end a radiant light dispels most, if not all, darkness."—*C-Spot Reviews*

"At its core, a tale of love and conspiracy, this debut work by Maddox, set in the Poconos, is a literary amble through the family history of Sandy Parker, a lesbian whose secret life is destroyed and remade in the flood that changes the lives of her and the people she loves."—*Publishers Weekly*

By the Author

Agnes

Bouncing

The Common Thread

Deadly Medicine

Hooked

The Scholarship

Love Changes Everything

Paris Rules

Repatriate

Visit us at www.boldstrokesbooks.com

REPATRIATE

by

Jaime Maddox

2023

Credits
Editor: Shelley Thrasher
Production Design: Stacia Seaman
Cover Design by Tammy Seidick

Acknowledgments

The women at Bold Strokes Books who work so hard to help authors such as me to publish our work are truly wonderful at what they do and the reason so much lesbian fiction is on bookshelves across the world. Thanks to Rad, Sandy, Ruth, and everyone else for an amazing job. My editor, Shelley Thrasher, is always spot-on with suggestions that make my manuscripts better novels. My alpha readers have expanded exponentially: thanks to Margaret, who has read every manuscript, sometimes twice, and to the newbies, Barb, Gina, Maria, Mary, and Danelle, who provided helpful critiques. Finally, thanks to each of you who has chosen this book to spend a few hours with: enjoy.

Carolyn, Jamison, and Max are my one constant and give me a reason for everything I do. Thank you, my loves.

This book is a work of fiction based on a tragic bit of history. One early morning more than thirty years ago, following a night of St. Patrick's Day revelry in the city of Boston, two thieves robbed the Isabella Stewart Gardner museum of thirteen pieces of priceless art. The heist remains the largest property theft in US history. Here's hoping that someone, such as the home health worker in this novel, notices those masterpieces somewhere, and sends them home.

To Jamison:

Your writing inspires me. Your patience and sensitivity make me a better human being. Your insight makes me think. I am so proud that you are my son, both for what you give to me and what you give to your world. I love you more than Max loves ice cream. Keep on knocking it out of the park.

CHAPTER ONE

Busted

The summer morning was magnificent—warm, with a bright, cloudless sky that made Ally Hamilton wish she had a job that took her outside. Maybe that was her problem—too many hours indoors, taking care of sick people and not taking care of herself. Maybe. Or maybe it was just her. Lately, that idea had been growing stronger, making it harder to blame her troubles on everyone else. Yet she felt so powerless to do anything, to make changes, to get help. She didn't know where to begin. Most of the time, she felt overwhelmed.

Pushing the thoughts aside, she locked her car and headed toward the ER, nodding politely toward people loitering by the entrance, greeting the security guard by name. The halls were already lined with stretchers, the patients lying in them hooked up to monitors and IV bags, wearing neck collars and little else. It was not a promising sign.

In the locker room, Ally opened her purse and pulled out a small pill holder, then spilled the contents into her palm. Four white tablets, just enough to get by. She looked at them, studying the details. The white, shiny finish. The round shape. The size. The size amazed her. How could such a tiny thing, about the size of a mini-M&M, hold so much power?

She didn't want to take it. She didn't want to need it. But no way could she make it through a twelve-hour ER shift without it. No way could she go through another day like yesterday. She'd run out of medication, and a third of the way through her twelve-hour shift, the withdrawal symptoms had started. Yawning, runny nose, sweating, anxiety. Before the shift ended, her heart was racing, and her bones ached so badly she could barely stand to finish suturing a trauma patient.

Afterward, instead of unwinding at home and regrouping for today's adventures in ER Land, she'd had to go to the ATM and withdraw the last of her savings. She'd made an emergency stop to see her source, only to be chewed out because it was so late. Yet she'd walked out with a few oxycodone and a sense of relief. She'd make it through another day. Tomorrow she'd worry about tomorrow, because today, she just didn't have the energy.

Ally knew she was running out of options. She was nearly broke. The people she could turn to for money were starting to ask questions. And one of her most reliable sources for pills, a friend of her late grandmother, was starting to get a little anxious about their arrangement.

Drugs were always available in the ER, and the temptation to steal her patients' medication sometimes overwhelmed her. Somehow, she was always able to resist that urge. Even though she was out of pills, even though she'd have to spend her time after work making calls and desperately cruising the streets of Scranton, looking for someone who'd sell her what she needed, she didn't cross that line. She would drive and call, and suffer, because diverting medication from her patients was a criminal act, and even though she'd already broken the law hundreds of times because of her drug problem, she wasn't *that* desperate. Hopefully, she'd never reach that point. She was trying to wean herself off, cutting back a little at a time, but the withdrawal symptoms kept sucking her back in.

Her physician's assistant license had taken her five years to earn. She'd spent grueling hours in the library and the operating room learning and honing her skills, time she could have been relaxing or having fun. She refused to jeopardize all she'd worked for by stealing controlled substances.

Was she jeopardizing it by being impaired? She didn't think so. The pills barely fazed her anymore. She experienced no high, no euphoric feeling after taking them—just relief. She'd avoid the agony of withdrawal for another four or five hours. Then the fear would begin again.

After popping a tablet into her mouth and swallowing it dry, she returned two to the holder and tucked another into the zippered pocket on the fanny pack she wore at work. Patting the bag and sighing with relief, she changed into scrubs and her work sneakers, fastened the fanny pack, and looked at the clock. A quarter of eleven. She was early, but that would give her time to scout the ER, to figure out who was doing what and where she needed to begin. Being early put her in control in a place that was typically so out of control she couldn't rein it in.

Before she could take a step, the door to the staff lounge opened, and Ally met the squinting eyes of Dr. Reese Ryan, the ER director, as she stepped into the room. Behind her, Dr. Jessica Benson, the director at another local ER, wore a somber expression.

Instantly, Ally tensed, on high alert. "Hi. What's up?" she asked as she took half a step back, glancing from Reese to Jess with a small smile, trying to disguise her fear.

Jess closed the door behind her as she stepped in and leaned against it.

"Take a seat," Reese said with a wave of her arm. Ally backed into a recliner, while Reese pushed a rolling desk chair toward Jess and leaned into the counter along the wall.

Reese bit her lip and raised her arms as she spoke. "Ally, this is really hard for me. I brought Jess with me because she has a lot of experience with matters like this, and I thought she could help." Reese paused and nodded toward Jess, and then she gazed at Ally again.

Ally felt her blood draining, but she fought to remain still on her perch at the edge of the recliner, waiting for Reese to continue. She knew exactly what was happening, and she didn't even care. In fact, she was almost happy. Reese was going to fire her, and Ally was relieved. She could finally stop pretending, let go of this burden she'd carried for so long. She audibly sighed as Reese spoke.

"I'm concerned that you have a problem with pills. I'm assuming pills, because of your shoulder. Opioids of some kind. I've seen it, and some of the other staff members have too. You start off your shift okay, and then three or four or five hours in you start yawning and sweating and running to the bathroom and looking like total crap. A few minutes later it's all better. I've seen you slip a pill out of your pocket and pop it into your mouth, and fifteen minutes later things seem to be back to baseline."

Reese was rambling, her nerves obvious to Ally, who knew her well. That somehow made Ally even sadder than Reese's confrontation. Reese, whose nerves of steel made her a phenomenal critical-care doctor, was on edge over this conversation.

Even though Reese was anxious, she was a professional. Reese had a job to do, and Ally sat back and waited for the knife she knew was coming.

"Probably twenty years ago when I started practicing, I wouldn't have recognized the signs. I wouldn't have been suspicious about this at all. Now with all the problems with overdoses, we've all become more aware. We've had training to look out for things like this, and I'm suspicious, concerned about you. It looks like something's going on."

Reese stopped talking and stared for a moment. Ally swallowed her anxiety and was about to speak when Reese started again.

"If I'm way off the mark here, I apologize. I'm not standing here in front of you to insult you or anger you. I'm standing here because I've known you well for a long time. I consider you a friend, but I'm also the director of the ER, who has to make sure that every single person who puts on a white coat and drapes a stethoscope around their neck is mentally and physically competent to do the job, every time they walk through the door. So I'm looking at you as your friend and as your director, and I'm asking if you have an opioid problem."

Looking from Reese to Jess, Ally could see they knew. It was in their eyes, in the slight challenge of their posture—leaning forward, arms bent. As if suddenly sensing this revelation, Reese lowered her arms. Jess remained still but studied her. And who knew better than Dr. Jessica Benson, who'd been in the same position Ally was in just a few years ago? In addition to working in the ER at Garden Memorial Hospital and directing the department, Jess lectured on addiction. Her specialty was addiction in professionals.

Ally could argue with them, make excuses, try to convince them what they knew in their hearts was a lie. Or she could just tell them the truth. Tell them and lay down the terribly heavy load she'd been carrying for months.

Ally sat back in the chair, looked from Reese to Jess and back again, and nodded. The tears rolled down her cheeks, but she couldn't find her voice. Reese handed her a tissue and, kneeling beside her, squeezed her hand.

Ally sniffled and wiped her eyes, then cleared her throat. "It's gotten out of control. I need help."

Jess joined Reese on the floor. "That's why we're here."

"I don't know what to do."

Jess hugged her. "That's okay, Ally. I do."

CHAPTER TWO

You've Got This

Six Months Later

Ally was already awake when the alarm began its obnoxious beeping. She rolled over and gently tapped the button to silence it and then stayed in that position, staring into the blackness of her bedroom. Dawn was breaking, and the outline of the morning was creeping around the drawn shades.

A new dawn, a new day. A new job and perhaps a new life awaited her on the other side of the thick comforter that protected her from the February frost. Yet even though she'd been staring at that same ceiling, that same wall, that same window for hours, talking herself into getting out of bed, she wasn't quite ready to face it all.

Arching her back, she stretched, and an involuntary groan escaped. It had been six months since that fateful day when Reese and Jess had confronted her in the staff lounge, since she'd admitted she had an opioid problem. The days after that—all one hundred and eighty-four of them—had been surreal. Days and nights of a medical detox program, meetings and counseling, art therapy and psychodrama and psychoanalysis. She'd experienced things she could never have imagined when she'd been just a normal young woman living her average life.

Now, like most people in recovery, she'd been measuring her sobriety by counting sunrises and sunsets, focusing on the positive instead of the body aches and anxiety that had taunted her in the beginning and the cravings she battled still.

Every day was different. At first she had focused on the physical aspect of her disease, on all those miserable withdrawal symptoms that caused her to continue seeking drugs long after her doctor stopped prescribing them. Supervised withdrawal in the hospital was no easier, but at least she had support there—IV fluids to keep her hydrated, and medication to settle her stomach. Shoulders to cry on and people to support her and encourage her, to tell her to hang in there and it would get better. Next came the mental anguish—embarrassment that her friends and family and coworkers knew about her problem. How could they ever trust her again? How could she face them, carrying around this shame?

She still faced the stigma, the real and imagined, but she'd been learning to deal with it.

Next, she had to confront the spiritual issues of her recovery. How she'd fallen so far and how she was going to prevent herself from another stumble. And what the fuck she was going to do with the rest of her life.

This day presented an even greater challenge than the previous one hundred and eighty-three. Today, she had to leave the womb of recovery—where she was buffered from temptation by amazing people and a sterile environment, surrounded by positivity and kindness—and return to the cold, heartless world.

You've got this. She repeated the mantra in her head, and again out loud, several times. Her father had been telling her this since she was a toddler, encouraging her—sometimes goading her—toward her goals. Ballet, golf, school projects, work—the subject area didn't matter. Her father had taught her she could do anything. Most of the time, she believed him. Sometimes, she wondered if that was good or bad. That thinking had caused her to ignore her pill problem by telling herself she was different. Not like *those people*, the ones who came to the ER after hours begging for pills, telling her their doctor was off for the night and they just needed a few pills to last until morning. She wasn't like the ones who couldn't stop, who were weak or broken and disgraceful. Not until she was.

Perhaps if she'd been weak and admitted her pain instead of pushing through it, or asked for help instead of trying to fix it on her own, the past year of her life would have been different.

You can't go back, though, she thought. Only forward, and today forward meant starting a new job, which meant she had to get out of that bed.

You've got this.

Throwing back the blankets, Ally scurried across the cold floor and into the bathroom, where she flipped the switches for the lights and the heat. As she stood on the thick rug, brushing her teeth, she eyed herself in the mirror. She'd cut her blond hair when she'd left the halfway house the week before, and the look still startled her. Her hair had been down her back since she could remember, and now the tips perched on the tops of her shoulders. She still wasn't sure if she liked the new cut or not, but she couldn't do anything about it except give it time. Her blue eyes were dulled by lack of sleep, so she smiled and looked for some hint of life in them. She supposed it was there, if she stared hard enough, but she wasn't worried. Happiness was not the priority right now. Staying alive, working on herself, and working on her new job were the goals. Happiness would come. She hoped so, anyway.

It had been a long, long time since she was the happy, carefree Ally she'd once been. Three hundred and ninety-eight days, since she was now in the habit of counting. Just over a year since her family's Christmas ski trip to Utah, where a tree and multiple broken bones in her shoulder joint had ended her former life. The woman who was born of that accident had pain, and anger, and frustration, and addiction, and she hadn't had any room for happiness with all those other feelings crammed into her consciousness.

Slowly, with her therapist's help, she was purging the negative feelings. Hopefully, some positive energy would fill the void they left behind.

When she finished with her teeth, Ally pulled on comfy sweatpants and a T-shirt, then headed to the gym in the lobby for her morning workout. Taking care of her body was a good habit she'd worked on in recovery, and the proximity to a gym made it easy to stick with it. An hour later, after an invigorating cardio routine, she hopped into the shower, then wrapped her hair in a towel and her body in a long, soft robe. Retracing her path, she crossed her bedroom and entered the living room, and a few steps later she was in the kitchen of her tiny apartment. Technically speaking it was just two rooms, since the living room and kitchen were combined, but it provided six hundred square feet of peace and quiet, her own haven. The apartment was one of the penthouses in a building her father owned, and she was the superintendent. For tax purposes, she could live there rent-free, and considering the current state of her finances, that arrangement was a godsend. Buying oxycodone on the street was like sending twenty-dollar bills through a shredder, and she was broke.

Prior to the injury that had splintered her world into chaos, she'd been contemplating buying her own house. It had just made sense. She had spent her whole life in Lackawanna County, with its rivers and mountains, and didn't see a reason to ever leave. The four seasons were amazing, and she could do things outside in every one of them. Approaching thirty, and with a good job, she needed to invest some of her salary, and what better place than a house? Thank Goddess she hadn't made that leap, because by now it would have been in foreclosure.

Pouring water into the Keurig, she stared through the etching of frost on her kitchen window. It was the first of February, and Mother Nature had obviously been following the calendar, for she'd dusted Scranton with an inch of snow. Across the Keyser Valley, Ally saw chimney smoke dancing in the air. In the distance, the sun had cleared the mountains to the east and chased the darkness away. And just to the south of that sunrise, the ski slopes on Montage Mountain snaked down from the peaks, the paths lit by muted trail lights. Ally shuddered at the image and closed her eyes.

Too late. For an instant she was transported across the country, to that other ski slope. In her mind she saw the child cut in front of her and pictured herself turning evasively, losing control, tumbling as her skis flew one way and her body the other. She had stopped with a crunch, and a bolt of white-hot pain had seared her shoulder, ten feet off the slope and against a rather large tree.

Shaking off the memory, she poured her coffee and added cream and honey, then returned to her bedroom. As she opened the door to the walk-in closet, she shook her head. A class on organization would be helpful. The space was stuffed full, with everything from sporting equipment to schoolbooks, and even some clothes, though not as many as most of her friends owned. Since she wore scrubs to work—at least she had in the past—she didn't have much need for things other than jeans and sweats and a few sweaters.

Looking in her closet the day before, she'd placed a frantic call to her mom, who picked her up for an emergency trip to the outlets. Pulling one of her purchases from a hanger, she removed the tag and pulled it over her head. The shirt-dress, in a dark blue corduroy, complemented her eyes, and Ally smiled at herself in the mirror as she tied a colorful scarf around her neck.

There it was. A little life, a little joy from one of life's simplest pleasures—looking good in a new dress.

"You've got this," she told her reflection. "Maybe if you say it often enough, you'll start to believe it. It sounds like a reasonable plan."

After pulling on boots, she finished her hair and makeup, then spun before the mirror, assessing herself. She'd regained most of the twenty pounds she'd lost during her ordeal, and her skin looked healthy. Time would tell about the new hair, but she had to admit it looked okay, parted to the side and hanging straight down. Maybe she'd try a new look and cut it all off. She wasn't out at work, except to a few people like Reese, but she knew there were rumors about her and a paramedic she'd dated for a few months in the fall before her injury. If she buzzed her hair, that would probably confirm the suspicions. It would give people something to talk about besides the drugs, though, so it might be worth it.

The thought made her laugh, and she chuckled all the way to the kitchen, where she toasted a bagel to eat with her yogurt. Pulling up *The Scranton Times* on her iPad, she read the news while she ate, and when she was done, she found herself suddenly filled with dread. Her heart pulsed wildly, the kind of panicky rhythm she could feel in her throat, and her head spun.

"C'mon, Ally," she said, again and again, as she closed her eyes and took some deep breaths. She'd practiced a ton of yoga during her recovery, and she repeated the breathing technique she'd perfected. Finally she gained control and opened her eyes.

It was twenty after eight. She had forty minutes to make a fifteen-minute drive, but the thought of staying in the apartment threatened to bring back the panic, so she grabbed her purse and her warmest coat and headed out the door.

Her phone beeped as she waited for the elevator, and she checked the text. *How's it going?* Reese Ryan asked.

Ally hit dial, and Reese picked up immediately.

"Coming or going?" Ally asked.

"I just left. I'm in the long line at Dunkin' so I can stay awake for the next few hours. Ella has a meeting, and I'm in charge."

"How is your family?" Ally asked as she abandoned the elevator and headed down the wide, central staircase to the lobby.

"That's a very good question. One I would have expected you to ask a week ago, when you were released."

Ally knew she should have called Reese, but she'd been avoiding it. With a sigh, she apologized. "I just feel weird."

"Oh, really? About what?" Reese asked lightly.

Ally laughed. "You're a jerk."

"Right back at you."

"It's so safe when you're in there. Not much temptation. No judgment. Tons of support. Now, reality's setting in."

"That's why you have friends, Ally."

Ally had lost touch with most of her friends when she'd been using drugs. There weren't enough hours in the day to search for drugs and use them and foster relationships. But Reese had always been there, and she still was. "I know. I'm so grateful to you for the intervention. And for hooking me up with Jess. She's been such a lifeline."

"She says you're doing great. Starting your new job today."

Jess had been calling Ally since the beginning. Daily for a while, and now at least a few times a week. Ally went to meetings Jess chaired and listened to her podcasts on impaired professionals, learned how to meditate and practice mindfulness with Jess's help. And she was in so much better shape than when she was admitted to rehab.

She supposed what was bothering her was the mess she had to clean up.

"Yes. New job. Today. I've got this."

"A journey of a thousand miles begins with one step."

"I know. And I've taken a lot of steps in the right direction. Maybe I just don't know where to go from here."

"Back to the ER?"

Ally sighed and asked a question whose answer she dreaded. "What are they saying about me, Reese?"

"Ally, no one's even mentioned you in months."

Ally wasn't sure if that was good or bad. "I can't imagine anyone will let me live this down."

"Fuck them."

She was sure Reese meant that remark to be affirming, to tell her she didn't need anyone's approval. All it did was affirm that they disapproved.

"Yeah."

"We're having a birthday party on Sunday. Steph turns three."

Ally laughed at the image of Reese's little girl. "Wow." Then she realized she'd missed a significant chunk of this child's life, someone she really adored and loved. "Do you think she'll remember me?"

"Only one way to find out."

Ally smiled into the phone. "I'll be there."

"Stop avoiding the people you love."

Ally reached the lobby and crossed the marble foyer without seeing another soul. At the front door, she paused and looked through the glass. The world awaited her. It was good she didn't have to face it alone.

"I will."

Their landscaping crew had shoveled the walk and plowed the lot, but Ally picked her way across anyway, mindful of falling. Her shoulder didn't need any more trauma. In a minute she was at her car and deposited her bag on the seat. After turning on the Jeep's engine, she scraped the snow and ice from her windows and sat behind the wheel for a moment while the engine warmed.

"A garage," she said aloud. "That's my new purpose."

The traffic was awful, made worse by the slushy roads, and Ally found herself saying a prayer of relief when she arrived at the headquarters of Hart Home Health and Hospice half an hour later. She'd made it safely and was five minutes early.

The office was in an old mansion in the Green Ridge section of Scranton, one that had been converted for commercial use before the zoning laws had changed. Ally glanced at the sign, which consisted of four overlapping *H*s, and winced. That was at least one *H* too many. Beside it was another very familiar sign. *This House Protected by Hamilton Security Systems.* Her father's company was everywhere.

Someone had shoveled the sidewalk in front of the building, and Ally had no trouble with ice as she made her way to the massive front door. It was at least ten feet tall, made of wood and surrounded by a frame of leaded-glass panels. After ringing the bell, she glanced around. The porch was empty, but she could imagine a rocking chair or two placed here in the summer months. It would be a great vantage point to watch the children from the neighboring houses enjoying the play sets Ally noticed in every yard.

She had no more time for contemplation as the great front door opened, and a man who nearly filled the space looked out and grinned at her. Greg Hart was almost as wide as he was tall, and he had more hair in his long, gray beard than on his head. Wearing a baggy sweater and khaki pants, he didn't look the part of the savvy businessman Ally knew he was. At first glance, he was intimidating, until she noticed the twinkle in his eye and that radiant smile.

"Ally! Good morning! I've been waiting for you."

Ally knew she was a few minutes early, and he couldn't have been waiting long, but she didn't take the comment critically. "Good morning, Mr. Hart. Chaos on the roads this morning," she said as she followed him into the vestibule, where he took her coat and draped it on an ornate coat tree in the corner beside a half dozen other pieces of outerwear.

"Don't I know it!" he said in his booming voice. "I've had calls from a dozen caregivers already, and I haven't even finished my coffee! I'm afraid our patients will have to have a little...*patience* this morning. As good as we are, Four H cannot control the weather!"

Ally smiled politely, even though his back was to her. "That would be a feat," she replied.

"Maybe in the next stage of my life I'll work on that," he retorted, then waved his huge arm. "Follow me. I'm going to show you around the office and introduce you to the staff. Even though you'll be here for only a few days of orientation, these are the men and women you'll be talking to every day. They'll do your schedule, help you with billing, stock your car with supplies, and, in general, help you get the job done. They're here for you, so I want you to know who they are, and I want them to know you."

"Sounds great," Ally said, trying to pepper her reply with enthusiasm. It was hard, though. She'd been a PA in the ER for almost six years, taken part in codes and emergency surgery, assisted with placing IV catheters and breathing tubes, and sewn broken people back together hundreds and hundreds of times. It was hard to build excitement for a job where she'd be doing what she did back in school, but she had to start somewhere. Breathing in, she put on another smile. *You've got this.*

The building was massive, once a grand old house that had been transformed. Discreet signs pointed to offices and restrooms, and a large, not-so-discreet sign indicated the emergency exit. There were plants and statues, and every wall was adorned with some inspirational quote. In the fifty feet they'd traveled from the front door, she'd been reminded *The Man Who Never Made a Mistake Never Made Anything*—one of her personal favorites—and *Just Before Sunrise There Is a Dark Night* and to *Be the Change You Wish to See in the World.* Between and around the words of wisdom were equally inspiring works of art. Paintings and drawings and tapestries lined the walls, and along the wide hallway, Ally noted three large statues.

Greg paused before a grand staircase, waiting for Ally to catch him, then proceeded up. For a big man, he moved gracefully and with an abundance of energy.

On the landing, before a half-wall of glass, Ally noticed a small collection of plants, decoratively arranged in beautifully painted pots, surrounding an ornate waterfall made of wood and copper. The plants all looked healthy, definitely a good sign. People who let their plants die shouldn't be trusted with other humans.

On the second floor, what probably had once been a sitting room was now an open-area break room, with all the appliances of a kitchen, a spacious wooden table and chairs, and a water cooler. No couch, no lounge chair, no artwork. Four H was all business, even on break.

"This is our lunchroom," he informed her as he paused. "Feel free to use any of the condiments in the fridge and cupboards. Please label anything you bring, and throw away whatever you don't want. On Friday, everything gets tossed."

"Great idea," Ally said. She never put food in the fridge in the hospital break room, for fear of contamination from the things left to rot in there. Reese was forever threatening to throw everything away, and on the last day of every month, she did. But it didn't matter. The ER fridge was still a health hazard.

"This way," he said and began down a great hall to his left. Stopping before the first door, he knocked. "Desiree?" he asked.

"Come in," sounded a deep, sultry voice from within. Greg stepped into the room, and Ally followed him into a fifteen-by-fifteen-foot box with twelve-foot ceilings, crown molding, and a faux fireplace crackling in the front corner. Near the back wall was a large desk. The walls, like all the others in the building, were covered with art, in this case, decidedly more feminine works. Every single painting depicted a nude woman.

The woman behind the desk stood and leaned forward a few degrees, and Ally couldn't help noticing the breasts that threatened to break free of her low-cut sweater.

Wow, she thought with delight. *I'm alive after all.* It had been a long time since she noticed a woman, and it took an effort to avert her eyes as Desiree offered Ally a man-sized hand that seemed to fit her six-foot frame.

"I'm Desiree Hart," she said, "the office manager. Please have a seat."

Ally did as instructed, and when she looked over, she couldn't miss the wide grin on Greg's face as he stared at his wife. She was certainly a catch for the frumpy older man, and Ally felt happy for him. She liked Greg and admired the work he was doing, even more that he'd married a trans woman whom he so obviously adored.

Desiree hadn't been with Greg on the day of Ally's interview, so they spent a few minutes getting to know each other. Desiree's background in business had made her a perfect fit to join the company when she and Greg started their personal relationship. She shared that she, like every other employee at Hart Home Health and Hospice, was in recovery. "Fifteen years of sobriety," she said with a kind smile and a pointed look.

"Congratulations," Ally said with sincerity. She was proud of her own six-month accomplishment, but it was nothing compared to Desiree, who by all appearances seemed to be doing fabulously.

Desiree shrugged. "If I didn't work with so many people in recovery, I probably wouldn't even count the years anymore. But I think it's affirming for you, at your stage, to see people like me on the other side of it."

Ally sensed Desiree was someone she should pay attention to, that she could be brutal if she needed to be, but right now she was kind, and Ally appreciated that fact.

Ally turned to Greg, who'd shared his personal history of drug abuse during her interview a month earlier. That had been at the halfway house, where he'd come to speak with her about the job at his home-health agency. He employed people like her, men and women who'd lost their licenses to practice medicine or nursing but had the skills to work in the field doing something that didn't require certification. Some people moved on just as soon as the state granted permission, but others stayed. He'd told her about one doctor, a trauma surgeon, who'd turned to pills and booze after his family was killed in a car crash. He couldn't look at trauma patients without seeing his own broken loved ones, but he could do wound care, and he worked for Four H doing just that. Another doctor had stress and anxiety issues but did well as the company's medical director. Dozens of people, just like them—just like her—worked here, and Ally suddenly felt a change of heart at the opportunity she was being given.

"Thank you. Both of you. I appreciate you taking a chance on me."

"You have a great background for this job, Ally. We're lucky to have you," Greg said.

"You'll do us proud," Desiree added sweetly.

"Let's finish the tour, and then I'll send her back up to you for the orientation."

Desiree came out from behind her desk and hugged Ally. "At most companies, I'd be fired for hugging you. Here, we require hugs."

"Good for the spirit!" Greg boomed.

Ally felt it. It *was* good for the spirit. "Thank you, again," she said softly as she slipped away from Desiree and followed Greg farther down the hall, feeling a sense of optimism that had been elusive in the past months. It carried through her meeting with the medical director, then the billing director, and finally the director of nursing, until forty minutes later she was back in Desiree's office.

Des, as she preferred to be called, presented her with a two-inch-thick white binder labeled *Hart Home Health & Hospice Employee Manual.* Ally chuckled when she opened it and read the first page. Orientation checklist. They certainly were organized at Four H.

After introductory meetings with department heads, Ally had to complete payroll forms with Des, watch HIPAA videos with Des, and obtain her physical exam and drug screen paperwork from Des. That was day one. Tomorrow, she'd spend the day learning billing and coding procedures. On day three, she'd meet briefly with the medical director to discuss the SCOPE OF PRACTICE FOR MEDICAL ASSISTANTS. The item was capitalized, and Ally thought perhaps that was a good thing, considering the former job descriptions of the Four H employees. It probably wouldn't be good if one of the physicians removed a gallbladder or an appendix on someone who was scheduled for just a flu shot.

Finally, after she learned what she couldn't do, she'd meet with the director of nursing, who'd teach her exactly what she would be doing as a medical assistant.

The binder pages that came next were divided into sections, and it seemed they had a policy and procedure for every conceivable situation Ally might encounter in the course of her job. From needle sticks to patients making unwanted sexual advances, Four H was prepared.

She spent the morning reading the policies, signed off on them, and then had lunch with Greg. Over sandwiches from a local deli, he shared his story. He'd been a paramedic before his fall from grace and decided on home health for his second career because he thought the work would be easier on his bad back. He quickly saw opportunity in both the need for services he could provide and in employment of people who desperately needed jobs. That had been twenty-five years ago, and Four H was more successful than he'd ever imagined it would be.

"Sometimes we're forced to take a detour, Ally, but that doesn't mean it's the end of the road."

Ally nodded. "I can see that," she said as she looked around. "You've got an amazing story."

"You will, too," he said sweetly as he stood and patted her on the shoulder. Ally was right behind him, and she headed back to the conference room, where she met Des. Ally signed a few more forms and spent the afternoon watching HIPAA videos on the company laptop. After an hour she wanted to poke her eyeballs out, but somehow she made it through without suffering any self-inflicted injuries.

Unsure when her workday finished, at four o'clock Ally walked out of the first-floor conference room and knocked on Greg's office door. He beckoned her to enter.

"Had enough for the day?" he asked with a chuckle.

"Is it obvious?" Ally asked with a sigh as she sat in one of the large leather chairs placed before Greg's desk.

"I may have heard a complaint or two in the past about the first day of orientation."

"It is monotonous."

"Agreed. But tomorrow will be a better day. More work and less bullshit."

Ally laughed as she studied his office. Like his wife's, the room was large, but this one had built-in shelves lining the walls. They held dozens of color-coded binders and a few books, but also small statues and carvings. Ally asked about them.

"A hobby of my wife's. She supports a charity that imports art from a village in Africa. These are hand carved by the residents, painted, packed up—they do it all. The profits provide all their needs. One carving can support a family for a year."

Ally swallowed. "A year?"

He nodded and stared at her, before looking around. "Our excesses here are shameful."

Ally thought of her own situation, and she related. Yet she also knew she'd been using her abilities to make the world a better place, for a while, anyway. Greg still was. "I see you like inspirational quotes. I think one of the greatest is biblical. 'To those whom much is given, much is expected.'"

He smiled. "Luke 12:48."

"I think you're giving, Mr. Hart. Quite a bit."

He cleared his throat. "Call me Greg."

"Greg."

"When I started out, I was so sure I was going to save the world. And I realized pretty quickly that the world was too screwed up to save. The things I saw as a paramedic were awful. No disrespect to the ER, but much worse. You get it filtered, cleaned up a little. Out in the field it's nasty. And I'm not just talking about the accidents—those are a different tragedy. I mean the violence that human beings inflict on one another. On their children. On other people's children."

He paused and sipped from a fancy glass bottle filled with water and fruit.

"I saw that stuff, and I cringed, and after work I started drinking a little. Then I started drinking a lot. Then pills. It made it easier, especially when I started taking them at work. It wasn't just the tragedies I witnessed, but the feeling of helplessness, seeing the same victims again and again, because they just didn't have the ability to get themselves out of those situations. Knowing what I did couldn't make a damn bit of difference."

Ally remained silent, listening and watching, even when he grew silent.

"Here, I make a difference."

"I'll say you do."

"I'm glad you like the statues. I can give you the information about them, if you'd like."

"I like art. My mom is an artist."

His face lit up. "Really? Mine, too. Mine is small-time, but I enjoy it."

"That's what makes it priceless, Greg. You enjoy it."

He smiled at her. "I like you, Ally."

"Same," she replied.

"I'm not sure I mentioned it, but we host a seven a.m. group here, every day of the week. Even on holidays, just not on snow days. It's only staff, but it's an inclusive, nonjudgmental bunch of folks who are all dealing with the same issues. No pressure if you want to do your own recovery program, but if you want to join us tomorrow—or any day—you are certainly welcome."

Ally had been thinking about a meeting since lunch. She'd been discharged from treatment only a week earlier, and she'd been to five different places for meetings, trying to find a good fit. Her favorite place, in downtown Scranton, didn't have parking, and she'd decided she could handle that situation only in an emergency. Jess Benson's group met only once weekly, not nearly enough for someone so freshly out of rehab. Maybe she'd try the Four H group. What did she have to lose?

"Thanks, Greg. I'll let you know."

"See you tomorrow, then. Seven, eight, whatever."

"See you."

"And, Ally," he said as she stood, "congratulations on your first day."

She couldn't help smiling. "Thanks."

You've got this, she thought as she walked out his office. *You really do.*

CHAPTER THREE

Art Therapy

Instead of a meeting after work, or even heading back to the gym, Ally decided to indulge in her own personal bit of therapy. Art. Ally had tried every known artistic medium on the planet, and while she wasn't particularly skilled at sculpting or painting, that didn't stop her. She simply loved to create and build things. That had been her favorite part of rehab, and since her mom—a renowned local artist—had a studio in the carriage house behind their home, Ally thought the plan was perfect.

The early morning slush had been ground into water by car tires, and the road conditions were not an issue as she made the twenty-minute drive from Scranton to her parents' home in Waverly. Traffic thinned as she traveled farther into the suburbs, and the water once again turned to snow. This area hadn't been plowed, and she drove carefully through the curves of the winding country road that led to their home.

It sat back from the street, on acres and acres of lawn surrounded by trees and a stone wall. She could just see the top of the ceramic roof over the top as she approached the drive.

After pressing the remote that opened the gate, Ally waited until the tall iron doors opened, then headed up the drive and parked by the kitchen entrance. She rang the bell before she walked into the mudroom and yelled to her mom as she collapsed onto the bench seat and wiped off her boots with a towel kept for such purposes. Cricket, her parents' Yorkshire terrier, leaped into Ally's arms before she could even start on her second boot.

"Hello, little girl," Ally said as the dog lavished her with kisses. She'd missed Cricket during rehab, and the dog had obviously missed her so much her parents had begun calling her Benedict Arnold because she'd stayed at Ally's side since her discharge.

In the kitchen she found her mom fussing over dinner. Janine

Hamilton put as much artistic effort into cooking as she did into painting, and Ally and her brothers had grown up eating family dinners more elaborate than those served at the best restaurants in town. Ally had never enjoyed the kitchen, but during her time in the halfway house she'd had to cook and had started sharing simpler recipes with her mom.

Wiping her hands on a towel, her mom looked at her expectantly, and she appeared to be holding her breath. "Well?" she whispered.

"It was a great day," she said honestly, saddened by the look of relief on her mom's face. Of all the bad things that had resulted from her drug abuse—losing her license, losing friends, embarrassing herself at work, being financially devastated—the worst consequence was the effect it had had on her parents.

Unlike her two older brothers, Ally had always been the perfect child, the one with the great grades who never stayed out past curfew or stole the booze from the liquor cabinet. She played tennis and golf with the rest of the family, helped in the gardens, and did her share of chores around the house. They hadn't been surprised when she came out to them, and her sexuality had never been an issue at home. The only issue, ever, was this little problem with prescription drugs.

She wasn't sure if the disease of addiction would have been easier on her parents if it plagued one of her brothers, but it had devastated them when they learned about her. The havoc continued, as they worried about her constantly—her sobriety, of course, but also her finances and her mental health and her personal relationships and on and on. They were her parents, and they loved her, and she'd caused them tremendous anguish, and it made her feel just awful.

The hug her mom offered helped.

"You're early," Janine said a moment later as she let go.

"I thought I'd go out into the studio for some art therapy before we eat."

Her mom's face lit up. "Do you feel like refinishing a frame for me?"

Ally's mom often found old, battered art and restored it. Sometimes, the restoration meant cleaning and touching up paintings, and sometimes that meant just using the canvas and frame to create something brand new. The old pieces, even ones that weren't valuable for their canvases, often had magnificent, ornate frames. Ever since she was young, Ally had been sanding and stripping and refinishing them to complement whatever her mother was putting inside. She'd also learned to make her own, from simple one-inch frames on small pieces of art, to large, textured, and carved pieces for the grander works. She'd first started this hobby to keep busy when her mom dragged her out to the studio, but it became something more. It gave them time together, of course, but it also gave Ally time alone, when she could unclutter her mind and do something creative. And she enjoyed it.

"What do you have in mind?" Ally asked.

"Sid Sandon hit a hole in one on number four, and his wife asked me to commemorate it. It's nearly done. There's a ton of brown in the painting, so I think a dark frame would look magnificent. A frame's hanging near the painting that will work fine. It just needs a little TLC."

It was just what she'd had in mind when she'd decided to come to dinner early and work in the studio. She could lose herself in the creative process and walk out of the studio refreshed. "Let me get changed."

Ally bounded up the steps to her childhood bedroom, with Cricket barking and chasing her. She passed Ally on the landing, and when Ally entered her bedroom, the dog was lying on her back on the bed, awaiting congratulations on her victory. Ally leaped onto the bed and smothered Cricket in a hug, then paused a minute to take it all in. To feel. This was love. This was happiness.

After a few minutes, the dog wiggled free. Ally rolled onto her back and studied the closet doors, imagining the contents. Even though she hadn't lived with her parents since she'd graduated college, she still kept clothes and toiletries there. Often, she'd stay the night after dinner when she didn't have work the next day, just to spend time with her mom or work in the studio. And she was the house sitter during her parents' frequent vacations. It was just easier than having a stranger in, and her two brothers, with wives and families, couldn't manage the chore.

Pulling off her dress, she eyed her choices. Just like at her apartment, her closet was filled with simple things. She had more golf clothes here, since her parents' house was so close to Mountain Meadows, the club where they played, and also more ski clothing, since she so often went up to the mountain with them. She pulled a sweatshirt and jeans from their hangers and slipped on a pair of paint-splattered sneakers before heading back down the stairs.

"I turned the heat on for you," her mom said by way of greeting when Ally reached the kitchen.

"Thanks! And good thinking. It's frigid out there."

Janine made a point of looking at the clock. Ally tended to get caught up in whatever she was doing, and her mom knew her well. "An hour?" Ally asked.

"Make it forty-five. I don't want you smelling like paint stripper at dinner."

Ally nodded. "I'll set an alarm on my phone," she said as she pulled up the clock icon and walked out the door.

Heat was blasting from all ducts as Ally entered the carriage house, a two-story structure large enough to hold three cars. They'd kept the original doors when they'd converted it to a studio, because they were old and wooden and beautiful, but they'd sealed them off to help with climate control. They'd replaced some bricks with glass to allow in light, but overhead hung row after row of fluorescent bulbs, reminding Ally of an operating room. They crackled as they came to life, and she quickly shut the door behind her to preserve heat.

After hanging her coat on a wall rack, she took stock. The room smelled of paint and varnish and home, and she smiled with joy as she audibly sighed. The three walls that weren't garage doors were lined with shelves, and in front of the doors, worktables ran across the width of the building. Any space that wasn't functional was covered by art, reproductions of masters that stoked her mother's creativity. Ally's too, really, she thought as she silently studied a portrait of Madame Monet staring back at her from between the garage doors.

In the center of the space, facing an uninspiring collection of old frames hanging precariously from shelves along the back wall, she spotted her mom's easel.

Ally walked toward it, easily recognizing Sid Sandon as he stood on the tee box, his club in hand, the fourth green at Mountain Meadows Country Club in the distance behind him. It was a magnificent landscape, and her mom had captured Sid's joy as he posed for the photo on which she'd based the painting. She was sure he'd be pleased with the work, and once framed, it would be a treasure in the Sandon family for generations to come.

Her mom was right. The stand of trees behind the green had a prominent mass of trunk—a glob of brown in the landscape of greens and blues and yellows—and a frame to match would be best. Ally grabbed a measuring tape and jotted down the dimensions. Turning, she walked toward a rack that held dozens of frames. She laughed when she got closer. Already sitting in front was one labeled *Sid Sandon*. She was sure her mother had built the canvas stretcher to the specifics of the frame, but she checked to be sure. It was a perfect fit.

Ally took the frame back to the workbench and sat down with it in her lap, studying the construction. Because of the pitting, Ally guessed the wood was mahogany, and it had been painted, but the original finish of varnish was still evident on the back. It had some dings, but nothing that wouldn't smooth out with wood filler and sanding. The corners were loose, but she could easily tighten them. Overall, she was pleased. This would be a simple project, and her mother's choice would look great with the outdoor scene.

Using her phone, she snapped a few photos, then grabbed some tools and got to work. First, she removed the finishing screws from the frame's corners. To her delight, the frame easily came apart with this simple step, saving her the work of dissolving the glue that had held it together when it was first made.

She quickly had four pieces of wood in her hands, and she glanced at her clock before going any further. Only ten minutes left on her timer. Best not to do any more tonight, because the next step—deep cleaning with a solvent—would be a long, messy process.

Humming to herself as she worked, she put away her tools and wrapped the pieces of the frame in an old canvas to protect them. A moment later, with a bounce in her step, she shut off the lights and walked across the yard to the kitchen.

Her father was leaning against the island when she came in, and his relaxed pose and instant smile told Ally her mother had shared the news about her orientation at Four H. His first words confirmed her suspicion.

"Mom tells me you had a great day."

Ally took a deep breath and remembered how much they loved her. They couldn't help worrying. They'd wanted her to stay with them after her discharge from the halfway house, so they could help her transition back to the real world, but she'd insisted on going back to her apartment. She'd lived alone for eighteen months before entering rehab, and three months of living with a bunch of strangers was enough to motivate her to stay sober for eternity. She needed some space. And besides that, she was still a little angry with her dad, and she needed to process that feeling.

"It was a great day," she said with a smile and told him all about Greg and Desiree Hart, and the others she'd met at the office. "It's a positive place, and I felt comfortable there." She paused as she chose her words. "There was no stigma. I wasn't an addict today. I was just a nurse. A caregiver. I felt like I fit in."

Her dad's broad smile mirrored her mom's, who'd joined them in the center of the kitchen to listen to what Ally had to say.

"That's important."

Ally nodded and spoke aloud what she'd been worrying about for ages. "I don't know if I'll ever be able to go back to the ER."

They both started. "Don't you think it's a little soon to make that decision?"

Ally shrugged. It wasn't soon at all. She'd been dealing with her shame since the moment Reese had walked into the doctors' lounge to confront her six months ago. Everyone in the ER knew what she'd been doing, and she'd worked with them long enough to understand how they felt about addicts. Back in the day, they'd kept a log of "drug seekers." That was before HIPAA and electronic medical records and the Prescription Drug Monitoring Program gave instant updates on the controlled-substance prescriptions patients had filled. Now, instead of being thrown to the street because their name was on the blacklist, patients were confronted by staff who thought they were Sherlock Holmes, solving some great crime. All the education about the disease of addiction, all the sensitivity training, all the changes hospitals and courts and society had made had not softened the hardest hearts, and Ally wasn't eager to put herself back into that environment.

"Reese called," she said, and told them about the conversation.

"She and her family and Jess are good for you. I'm glad you're going to the party. It'll be good to talk to ER people again."

"We'll see," she said, still unsure of the situation. "I'll work for Greg, at a fraction of my former salary. But I was thinking about the future. Weighing options." She looked directly at her father, into the eyes that she saw in the mirror every day. "How would you feel about me coming to work at Hamilton?"

Her dad bit his lip. Her brother already worked at the home security company her father had founded before any of them were born, but Ally had never been interested. She'd been enamored with the ER since she'd watched the show on television years ago, and until recently, it was the only job she'd wanted. But she needed to figure out a way to support herself, and work as a home-health aide wouldn't do it. Her review with the medical board was months away, and even if she did get her license back, unless she went back to the ER, who would hire her?

Based on the large house he'd bought and the fancy sports car he drove, her brother was apparently doing well in the family business. Maybe it would be the solution for her.

"What do you think you'd do?"

"I'm not sure. What does Jimmy do?"

"He's the director of our installation division. He orders the parts, assigns the work orders—everything that has to do with installation."

"Okay," Ally said. "Then I don't want to work in the installation division." Of the five members of her family, Jimmy was her least favorite, and she was sure the feeling was mutual.

"Sales and Service? Monitoring?" he asked. "Administration?"

Ally didn't hesitate. "Sales and service. Maybe monitoring. And a little admin."

"You're hired."

Ally laughed, and her mom suggested they eat before her coq au vin cooled.

They spent the dinner catching up. Cell phones were banned in the halfway house, and even though she'd been free to leave toward the end of her stay, she'd been fifty miles from home, deep in the Pocono Mountains, and she'd had no car. Her adventures had consisted of cross-country skiing and snowshoeing, and the occasional group outing. Her parents had visited for a few hours a week, and they'd gone to dinner, but the conversations had been strained, and talk was mostly about Ally and her progress.

"Do you want to hear some really juicy gossip?" her mom asked as Ally took a bite and moaned. The flavor was savory, the chicken delicate as it fell apart in her mouth. "Oh, Mom, this is so good. And, yes, I'd like to talk about someone besides me, so give me all the juicy gossip you have."

Her mom's eyes twinkled. "I ran into Lynn Jacobson at the market."

Ally stopped chewing and looked up. Gretchen, Ally's former girlfriend, was Lynn's daughter. Even though Ally and Gretchen had lived together for several years, Lynn never acknowledged Ally or her family. They belonged to the same country club and moved in the same social circles, but Lynn acted as if they'd never met. She didn't say hello or even offer an uncomfortable nod. She simply held her snobby nose in the air and marched straight past every Hamilton she passed, as if ignoring them would change the reality that one of them was screwing one of hers.

"And?" Ally asked.

"She spoke."

"What? Wait, like *to* you? Like, 'Hey, Janine, how's it going?' Or was it more like 'move out of my way so I can get to the imported cheeses'?"

"She spoke directly to me. As in, 'Hi, Janine. How are you? Did you hear Gretchen is engaged? She and Paul decided to make it official. They'll be married in May.' "

Ally dramatically dropped her jaw and looked from one parent to the other. How many times had Gretchen cried on their shoulders, wishing she could talk to her own parents the way she could talk to the Hamiltons? They'd told her the best advice about coming out ever: parents know. You just have to get the words out of your mouth so you can go on with your life. As long as Gretchen and Ally had been lovers, those words never came. It was all a charade, and the game had worn Ally down. When she found out Gretchen had been "occasionally," secretly taking men home to her parents for dinner and parties, it was the last straw. She'd ended it, and she'd heard from her very lesbian friends that Gretchen was still at it. Men on her arm and women in her bed. Ally had never thought it would come to this, though.

"Good thing you called it quits when you did, Al," her father said.

"I…yeah," Ally said with a laugh. "I don't know what to say. This is unbelievable."

"Maybe she was just experimenting with you, honey. Or maybe she realized she's bi." Her mother, the eternally kind optimist.

Ally had spent eight years with Gretchen, and much of that time they'd been horizontal, except when they'd made love in the shower, or in the car, or other exotic places. Gretchen had never slept with a man, and the sexual energy she had with Ally didn't leave much for the hairier sex, but Ally was not going to share that opinion with her mom. "Maybe," she said as she bit into a pearl onion and felt the flavors on every surface of her mouth. "Wow, Mom, is this good."

Her mom took the cue and changed the subject to their neighbor whose portrait sat on her easel.

"He's just beside himself. So happy," she said of Sid Sandon.

Ally had known the Sandons her entire life and had played golf with his daughter in the junior league. She knew he'd not been happy when his little girl used a driver on a par three and rolled the ball up and into the hole. He'd been harassed about his daughter outshining him for years. "I'll bet he didn't even need a driver," Ally said, and they all laughed.

"The poor man. He's been teased about that for twenty years."

"Well, now he can die in peace," her dad said.

"Russ, that's terrible," her mom said.

"Maybe we can display the portrait on the patio on opening night. If anyone at the club hasn't heard, they can see."

Her mom chuckled. "Actually, he did ask if it would be ready by then."

Ally spoke of the frame for his portrait and her plans for it. "Your choice is perfect," Ally told her mom.

"How long will it take you?"

"When do you need it?" Ally asked with a smile that evoked laughter from both her parents.

"There's time," her mother said. "A month?"

"You got it," Ally said as she popped another piece of chicken into her mouth. *You've got this*, she said to herself. Each time, the phrase sounded a little more convincing.

CHAPTER FOUR

Orientation

Unsure what to expect at the office meeting, Ally was up early and made a simple batch of chocolate-cake cookies using a box cake. When they were cooling on her counter, she hopped into the shower and then quickly frosted them before getting dressed. Finally, she carefully lined them up in a large plastic storage container and headed to work.

Work. What a strange idea after all these months. And stranger still, work was at a home-health agency and not the ER where she'd been since graduating college.

She'd get used to the strange idea, though. She was alive. She wasn't in jail. And while she'd probably always have the disease of addiction, she was managing it. *You've got this.*

What a difference an hour made, she thought when she arrived at the office. At ten of eight the previous morning, few cars had sat in the small lot behind Hart Home Health and Hospice. At ten of seven, Ally counted twenty. Pulling into the last row, she grabbed her purse and her cookies and took a deep breath before heading across the macadam to the large front door. She hesitated, then tried the knob. It turned easily, and she walked in, following the animated sounds of conversation coming from the conference room.

Ally didn't pause, didn't allow herself a moment to question who would be there or what they'd think of her fall from grace. Those fears had once plagued her, but after all these months she had come to accept that the recovery world was judgment free. The people there were either suffering from the same affliction or closely involved with people who were, and they were focusing on building people up, not tearing them down.

And, as she expected, when she did take stock of the people in attendance, she saw a few familiar faces. A paramedic who frequently brought patients to the ER. Another PA, one a few years ahead of her in school. A nurse she'd met during her clinical time. And the chief of surgery at her hospital. She swallowed and smiled and presented the cookies, and without that plate full of sugar, no one would have even noticed her. She was just one of them, and that realization was both humbling and a relief.

The meeting was interesting. It began with a prayer to a generic god, asking for strength in the battle against substances, for patience and tolerance of others, and then it devolved into something like an office party, with everyone talking about the *other* common denominator that brought them together: patient care. It was a fantastic experience for Ally, who realized more and more as the meeting went on just how very much she missed her work. She hoped she'd find the job with Four H to be fulfilling. Or at least fulfilling enough to sustain her until her license was reinstated. And based on the animated stories her new coworkers shared, she thought she'd like it here.

Like a loving father sending his children off, as the meeting broke up, Greg patted backs and wrapped people in hugs as they prepared to leave, and Ally couldn't help liking him. She'd been cautiously reserving her opinion of him, after her interview and before starting work, thinking he was almost too good to be true. Yet in the twenty-four hours since she'd met him, he'd done nothing but impress her.

He seemed to sense her studying him. "Did you enjoy the meeting?"

Ally nodded. "Probably the best meeting ever."

"Our shared passion for blood and guts is one addiction I'm never going to try curing."

"I never grow tired of hearing the stories."

He nodded, then beckoned for Ally to sit back down at the table they'd just vacated.

"I'm happy you came back."

Ally felt her brow arch. "Are you surprised?"

"Some don't. And for you…this job is a big demotion. So, to answer your question, I'm not surprised that you came back, but I wouldn't have been surprised if you didn't show up, either."

Ally laughed and he joined her. It felt good.

"How long do you think I'll last?"

He grimaced and shrugged his massive shoulders. "Des and I talked about it last night, and we agreed that you'll stick it out until you get your license back."

Ally thought of the plans she'd made for the evening. Her tour of the Hamilton offices. Would she like it enough to work here until the medical board made its decision about her? Of course, a letter of recommendation from a man named Hamilton probably wouldn't carry as much weight as one named Hart, and she'd need a good letter to make a favorable impression with the board. Her best shot of ever getting her professional life back was to stay in health care, and her best shot in health care was sitting before her.

She told Greg as much.

"Yes. You have a great deal to lose—or to win, depending on your perspective. So I'm betting you'll be here for the duration."

"Have you had many PAs come through your…" Ally didn't know what to call it. Was it a program? It really was, sort of, complete with morning meetings and inspirational wall hangings.

"Office. I prefer to call it my office. Program sounds so cut-and-dried. Like there's a beginning and an end. And we both know it's not that simple."

Ally nodded. "So…any PAs?"

"Well, I'm sure you recognized Melissa. She was in school with you. And there have been a few others, too. We take everyone, as long as they're not actively using."

"How do you make room for people? I mean, isn't there a demand?"

"Sometimes we're overstaffed, and sometimes we're under-staffed. Occasionally Desiree and I even go out on calls. I'd like to get you started as soon as possible. We have a caregiver leaving at the end of the week, and you can step right in with her clients."

"How do you assign cases?"

"Some of it is based on skill set. For instance, you probably could manage wounds well. Insert IVs and run infusions, that sort of thing. Some people are more suited for personal care, like bathing and light housekeeping. We even do shopping for some clients who are homebound, or transport to doctor visits and such. So we have all sorts of opportunities for people who want to work. And since my staff is constantly transitioning back to the real world, an opening is always looming. In fact, that's how you were able to step right in. One of my nurses just got an incredible offer and is leaving early, even though she doesn't have her license yet."

"How can she work without a license?"

"Just like here. She'll be doing a job that requires her knowledge and skills, but not that little piece of paper. I'm sorry to see her go but happy to have you."

Ally nodded. "How long do you think it'll take to get *my* license back?"

He looked toward the ceiling and seemed to think about the question, but Ally was sure someone as sharp as Greg knew precisely how long she'd be available to him. "Six months or so."

Ally nodded. That's what she'd heard as well. Since she'd voluntarily relinquished it, she wouldn't have a terrible time getting it back, but she'd still need to navigate some hoops.

"Well, if I want to get back in the game, I'd better finish this orientation. What do you have for me today?"

"An exciting day! You're going to play around with the electronic medical record, and then Linda will assess your nursing skills. You'll be given a travel case, and since I'm paying for the contents, you'll be signing everything out. It all has to get billed. If your car is robbed, I'll replace it. If your car is robbed again, or your house burns down, or your dog eats a bag of IV catheters, it's coming out of your pay."

It was the first time she had heard Greg sound like a businessman, and Ally sat a little taller and paid attention. He smiled in response. "And if today goes well, tomorrow you'll be out on the road with one of our staff."

Ally seemed to remember an additional day of training on her schedule, but she didn't argue. The sooner she was in the field, doing her job, the better.

A minute later, Ally was seated beside Carlene, the director of the billing and coding department. After learning how to turn on her laptop computer, Ally logged in, changed her secure password, and they began playing with the medical records.

Because she'd be doing her work in remote areas, she wouldn't really be using the system much. Instead, she'd document on customized Four H paper templates meant to make the process simple. She'd fill in the patient's name, date of birth, and the date and time of her visit, give a few sentences in the patient's own words about the state of their health, write in vital signs, then check a bunch of boxes to indicate what sort of care she'd provided.

The form not only served as her patient note, but it was also an invoice of sorts. Each box she checked corresponded with a billing code, which Ally would manually enter into the computer AT THE END OF THE BUSINESS DAY.

Carlene explained that simple rule a dozen times, so Ally figured it was either very important or some of her colleagues had difficulty following directions.

It was not much different from what she'd done in the ER, only there the note was integrated with the billing. With the Four H system, the note was scanned, but it wouldn't make much difference as far as Ally was concerned.

After she'd practiced on a half dozen theoretical patients, Ally thought she had it down. "And if you have any questions, you can call me any time." Carlene repeated *any time*, so Ally took a moment to save her contact information to her phone.

"I put you in my favorites," Ally said, and Carlene looked pleased. "Just say, I don't know, we have a blizzard or something like that, and I can't make it back here after my shift…"

"You are carrying confidential patient records. Confidential. In a catastrophic situation, where you couldn't return those to this secure location, I ask that you put them in a locked safe or fireproof box and bring them here just as soon as possible."

Her expression was so severe, Ally had to bite her lip to keep from laughing, but she nodded in understanding.

"Is that clear? I hope it is, because those forms are confidential. Confidential medical records."

"That is crystal clear."

If Carlene wasn't in recovery, Ally would have prescribed her a modest dose of Xanax, but she was, and so Ally just took deep breaths until Carlene finished with her and passed her along to Linda, the nursing director.

By that time, Ally's stomach was growling, and they talked in the lunchroom while they ate. The conversation was an interview of sorts, with Linda using the time to get an idea of Ally's skills and comfort level with the various procedures the home-health aides routinely did.

Ally loved procedures. She'd thought of surgery for her career, but she'd learned rather quickly that it wasn't much fun at 5:30 a.m. rounds, and most of the suturing in the OR was assigned to the residents. The physician's assistants on the surgical team did paperwork and changed dressings, but not much else.

In the ER, however, Ally could do just about everything. Working alongside the ER docs and trauma surgeons, she could jump in to do whatever was necessary when a patient was crashing. Ally put in IVs and airways, sutured, reduced fractures and dislocations, drained pus-filled abscesses—anything bloody and gross was basically within her domain. And she loved it.

In high school, she'd thought of majoring in pre-med and heading to medical school. But the idea of all those years of education sort of intimidated her. Now, she wondered if she'd made the wrong decision. Going to rehab had forced her to take stock of her life, and she realized she still had most of it ahead of her. A career change now was still possible, and a little change might do her good.

"This should be a breeze for you, Ally. I'll take you out for the next few days so you can learn how it's done. And then I'll sign off so you can start on your own on Monday."

After finishing their lunch, they cleaned up and returned to the conference room, where Linda had paperwork and supplies spread out before a large black case that resembled a tackle box, but with soft sides instead of hard plastic.

"Your kit. It's empty, for you to arrange how you'd like."

Ally nodded. Great idea.

They started with the paperwork, with Linda showing her how to complete it for a variety of different services Ally might provide her patients.

"Okay. Now the paperwork is complete. What will you do with it?"

"I'll bring it back here," Ally replied, remembering the warning from earlier in the day. The paperwork was confidential. "Immediately," Ally said as she bit her lip.

Linda suppressed a laugh by biting her own lip. "Yes, of course, but until then?"

Ally pursed her lips in thought. "A briefcase?"

"We discourage you from taking any personal items into the home. Our caregivers have been victims of theft on occasion. So you want to keep everything in your sight at all times. If you have to use the bathroom at a client's home, take your case with you."

"Okay." Ally nodded, still not understanding what she was expected to do with the paperwork.

Then she watched as Linda lifted the top tray from the case. "Top tray, deep little pockets for your most of your supplies. Beneath it, your vital-signs bag."

Linda emptied the bag by turning it upside down on the table, and a blood pressure cuff, stethoscope, thermometer, and several other gadgets scattered across the shiny wooden surface.

"Perfect," Ally said.

"Yes, but there's more. Look here," she said, and Ally peered inside. Empty.

Linda smiled. Reaching to the bottom of the case, she pulled up on two plastic tabs on the ends and freed yet another tray.

"The secret paperwork compartment."

"That's neat," Ally said.

"Now, this isn't meant to smuggle drugs across the border. Anyone who emptied the case would find this hidden space, but why would they look? There's nothing in the case of value, so we figured it was a good bet that no one would take a closer glance. And so far, they haven't. No one has lost any paperwork since we started using the cosmetic bags a few years ago."

Ally put the tray back inside and examined it. If she looked for more than a second, she'd notice the tabs used to remove it. But if she was just rummaging through the bag, they wouldn't be evident. What it would be was a pain in the ass. Every time she needed to document, she had to take out both trays of the suitcase and everything inside it. She guessed it was a motivation to pack lightly.

She practiced wound care on mannequins designed for just that purpose, and Linda showed her pictures of different wounds so she could decide how to manage each one. The first choice was a simple bandage, the last resort was to send someone to the hospital, and in between was a variety of ointments and wraps Ally could deploy to encourage wound healing.

Just after three o'clock, Linda sat back in the comfy leather chair and studied her. "How do you feel?"

Ally looked at her for a moment and took another to assess how she was feeling. Breathing in, she felt the little flutter of her heart, but no anxiety. Peaceful. Happy. *You've got this.*

Finally, she smiled. "I feel really good." Nothing Linda had shown her was technically difficult, nothing beyond her abilities. And while she'd rather be pouncing on a trauma patient, for the moment, wound care would have to do.

"Seven a.m. meeting tomorrow, and then we're out on the road," Linda answered with a smile.

Ally felt the smile reach all the way to her heart. *You've definitely got this.*

CHAPTER FIVE

Freudian Slip

Ally sped through town, conscious of the time. Although she adored the counselor she'd worked with in rehab, the woman didn't see private patients. And the state required that she see someone they'd vetted. Her first meeting with the state-approved counselor was today, and she didn't want to be late.

Getting back her license involved working at a job in her general field and having her boss attest to things like punctuality and attendance, as well as job performance. She also had to participate in weekly counseling sessions with someone certified by the state to evaluate her capabilities to return safely to work. She had to be mentally fit, with her drug abuse well behind her.

It all sounded like a great idea, but Ally was nervous about meeting her counselor, a man named Herman Griver, PhD. Each time she'd had to move into a new group or work with a new professional, she had felt anxious at having to tell her story all over again. It wasn't just the stigma—she was always afraid of people's judgment. But she was also reopening painful wounds, because her tale of drug use had started with an awful accident and been escalated by totally avoidable factors.

Each time she opened up and talked about that night, and the days that followed, Ally felt angry. Though less and less as time went on, she was still angry. They should never have gone on that last run. They should never have flown her home before the surgery. They shouldn't have waited for Dr. Ball. Hell, they shouldn't have used Dr. Ball for her surgery in the first place.

Rolling her shoulders and thinking about meeting Dr. Griver, she tried to release the tension that had built up there. Then she was at his office, sitting in her car, and had no time left to worry, because her clock told her she had five minutes to get inside the building.

"You've got this, Ally," she said aloud as she locked the car.

The building was a strip mall, and his office was near the center. Ally strode to the door and rang the bell as instructed. She spoke her name into the intercom and was met at the door a minute later by the doctor himself, who faintly resembled Benjamin Franklin, although Dr. Griver was much thinner. He was older, though, and dressed in a button-down sweater vest that was the height of fashion in the 1970s. She suspected that was when his office was built, because she saw signs of decay everywhere, from peeling paint and wallpaper, to the intercom at the door, to the linoleum on the floor.

He turned and instructed her to follow him, and she did, down a hundred feet of hallway that opened into a tiny lobby area. She hung her coat on an empty rack and turned to find the doctor waiting for her. "Cash or credit?" he asked. "I don't take checks."

Ally was stunned. "You don't take insurance?"

He waved her off. "I don't have the energy to deal with that stuff. It's only me here, and I like to spend my time helping people instead of waiting on hold with insurance companies."

Fortunately, she had some reserve left on her credit card, because she didn't have the $125 in cash he required. But why would the state refer her to someone who didn't accept her insurance? Since she'd taken a leave from the ER, she was still covered on her work policy, but it was costing her nearly a thousand dollars a month. It was money she didn't have, but she'd worked out an arrangement with her parents. In addition to all the other bullshit she had to deal with, she was more than $10,000 in debt to them.

Ally handed over the card, then looked around. Like the exterior of the strip mall, the room was dated. The furniture was nicked and the fabric faded and dirty, the wall art covered with a layer of grime. A door to her right said *Restroom*, but Ally was afraid to even look in there.

He exchanged her credit card for a clipboard, which he asked her to fill out. "Just the first page. You can take the other pages home and bring them back next week."

Ally sat on the edge of the chair, afraid to sit all the way back, and filled out the basic demographics. She'd just finished when he told her to follow him.

They went through a door marked *Private*, and if Ally were dreaming, she would have thought she'd ventured back in time across the world to Sigmund Freud's office in Vienna. The room was painted a deep rust, the walls covered with tapestries and art, the corners filled with shelves of statues and pictures and glass and marble. An electric fireplace blazed along one wall, and beside it, a large velvet armchair sat flanked by a velvet-covered couch.

Ally had used her time in rehab to read, and Freud's office was the topic of actual research papers. The long hallway, the arrangement of the rooms, and the absence of windows all suggested a tomb, which was somehow intended to be comforting or inspirational to people undergoing psychoanalysis. Ally was neither comforted nor inspired. In fact, the whole place gave her the creeps.

With a sense of relief, she turned and noticed a desk in the midst of the clutter, with two straight-backed chairs sitting in front of it. Thank Goddess, because no way was she lying on that couch.

"Have a seat," he commanded, and made his way around the desk.

"Papers," he said when he'd positioned himself. Ally handed the clipboard over and watched as he placed his glasses on the tip of his nose and read about her.

"So, Ally Hamilton, how can I help you?" he asked as he leaned back in his chair and studied her over the top of his glasses.

Avoiding as much detail as possible, she told him she'd had an injury, needed surgery, and had become dependent on painkillers. That she'd given up her license and voluntarily gone to rehab. No details about the accident, or the two operations, or the intervention in the doctors' lounge at the hospital, or the past six months. She knew from experience that what she said didn't matter, that he'd poke and pry to find out what he wanted.

And he did. He asked about what drugs she'd used, and where she'd obtained them, and how much of her savings she'd blown on her use, and she told him all the dirty details. Then she mentioned her detox and the rehab program she'd been following for six months.

"What are you using now?" he asked with a piercing gaze.

"What?" Ally asked. She'd stopped using drugs, and she'd told him about the detox. Wasn't he listening?

"Are you using any drugs?"

Ally shook her head.

"None?" he asked.

"None."

"None of this so-called Medication Assisted Treatment?"

Ally had spent hours reading about MAT, the use of medications such as buprenorphine and naloxone to help people in recovery maintain sobriety. In the end, she'd decided against it. Before her accident, she'd been a healthy, well-adjusted, successful woman. She'd used opioids for only a little more than seven months when she'd gone into treatment, and she was confident she could live without medication. Some people, who'd used opioids for longer periods of time, or who had other issues like PTSD and bipolar disorder, had a much harder time in the traditional recovery plan. That's why the experts had come up with MAT, because the failure rate of sobriety was so high. Just because it wasn't for her, though, didn't mean it wasn't good for others. And the statistics showed MAT to be far superior than counseling alone at keeping people alive.

It didn't sound like Dr. Griver had read the same literature.

Ally shook her head.

"Good. It's just a crutch, you know. Exchanging one drug for another." He went on to explain how he'd been a high school chemistry teacher when he'd started drinking a little too much. After going through a rehab program, he'd decided to dedicate his life to others who had substance-abuse problems, and now he was a certified counselor. And he'd never had a drink since the day he quit and did it without medicine.

Ally had listened to all the debates during her time in recovery and didn't bother to argue with him. The patients in recovery from alcohol just didn't understand that opioids were a different drug. Because they could just quit, they expected heroin users to do the same. From personal experience, Ally knew that quitting opioids was hard. Really fucking hard.

She could drink wine for days without a problem. It relaxed her and made her social, and she could put down a full glass and walk away without thinking twice. She loved mixed drinks, too, martinis and margaritas, with all their fun, tasty combinations of alcohol and juice and flavorings. Chocolate and strawberry and everything good, all mixed in a shaker and served over ice. Mmm. And she could drink one and know it was enough. For whatever reason, alcohol wasn't a beast she had to battle.

Yet she didn't judge people in recovery from alcohol. Why did they judge people who used MAT?

Biting her lip, she listened to him, and she wanted to take out her camera and record the session when he pulled out his pipe and lit it. *He thinks he's Freud,* she thought. *What should I tell him if he asks me about my dreams? If he inquired about childhood scars, should she tell him about the time she and Jimmy climbed a tree, and he left her there?*

After blowing out a cloud of smoke, he inquired about her family.

"Any history of addiction in the family?" he asked after she gave him a detailed description of her mom's people as well as the Clan Hamilton.

Ally shook her head. "None."

"So how'd you end up here?" he asked as he looked at her sideways through the smoke.

It wasn't the first time she'd heard the question, so she had a prepared answer. "My injury."

Leaning forward, he squinted into her eyes. "That's just the excuse. Normal people don't end up here. We all have something we're hiding, some pain we're self-medicating with a needle or a bottle. Bottle of pills, bottle of booze—no difference."

Ally sighed. What *was* wrong with her? Why'd she keep using those pills, even though she knew she shouldn't? Was she weak? Or a coward? Or was she really just a junkie, looking for an escape when things were too hard? If it hadn't been the shoulder injury, would something else have pushed her over the edge?

This wasn't the first time for these questions either, yet she still didn't have an answer.

And she had no faith that the Freud impersonator would help her find it.

When she was quiet, he nodded. "That should be our goal, Ally. To figure out what makes someone like you—someone you might call a success—make such bad decisions." He sucked on his pipe and seemed to be staring at the end of it while he worked out his words. "If we can answer that question, we can save you from repeating your mistakes."

Ally stared at him. He was opinionated and full of himself, a relic from another era of medicine, but maybe he could help her after all.

CHAPTER SIX

Family Business

Feeling emotionally drained after her session with Dr. Griver, Ally headed across town again. After she followed a parade of big trucks heading to destinations in the industrial park, she arrived at the office of Hamilton Security Systems on Keyser Avenue a few minutes later. The office was smaller than most of the complexes in the area and reminded her of a miniature Walmart, with an entrance for the home-monitoring area on one side, management and sales in the middle, and service on the other end, distinctly separated by textured blocks and siding.

Driving around the lot, she found a spot close to the middle and parked between the thirty other cars scattered about. From there, it was a few short steps to the door, and she hurried inside and asked for her father.

The lobby was as unadorned as the exterior; few customers ever visited this place. They simply called or made inquiries online and set up sales calls at their home. Glancing around as she waited, Ally noted the numerous award plaques and certificates HSS had received, both locally and nationally. *Scranton Times* Home Security Sales and Service Provider of the year 2021, and a few other years as well. *Scranton Times* Home Security Monitoring Provider of the year, about a dozen times. Chamber of Commerce business of the year 2015, COC employer of the year several times. International Association of Security Systems Member of the Year 2018. American Home Security Network distinguished member every year since well before Ally was born.

If the company continued its success, her dad would need to build a bigger lobby to accommodate all the awards.

Ally felt a touch of something. Pride. She'd never been interested in her father's business. Like many young people, she'd wanted to go out on her own, find her own course. And she had. She loved medicine. But if her past prevented her returning to the ER, maybe this was the way for her now, the new path she should take. It might actually be nice to be part of something her father had created.

"Hi, honey," he said as he walked through the door and noticed her gaze directed at his accomplishments. "Almost as many awards as you have," he said modestly.

Ally thought of her own accolades—a few academic certificates, a public service award, some golf trophies—and she shook her head. "Yours are cooler," she said. "I mean, the *International* Association of Security Systems. That's saying something."

He waved a hand. "I think we bought that online. Besides, that lump of coal you got for winning the Anthracite League's Junior Ladies Golf Championship is something. If we ever lose heat, we can burn that for days."

Ally laughed. The trophy, actually a piece of engraved coal, was obnoxiously big.

"How was therapy?"

Ally whistled. "This guy is a character." She told him about the pipe and the velvet furniture, but also about the momentous idea he'd mentioned at the end of the session. "I think I'll stick with him."

He hugged her. "You've got this."

Ally looked up at him as he squeezed her and let go of a little more of her anger.

"Come with me," he said as he pulled back, and Ally detected some excitement in his voice. "I want to show you something."

She followed him back the way he'd come, appreciating his brisk pace. He worked hard and didn't waste his time, and she had to move it to keep up.

"You know he only takes cash?"

He turned and frowned. "I know. But he was the only place we could get you in on short notice, without going to a big corporate center. I figured he'd be better."

The conference room stood empty, and they walked quickly past that, and a dozen other offices, until she reached several secluded rooms. First came her dad's office, then her brother's, their secretaries, and another conference room, and then the secret passages to the other parts of the building that allowed her father and brother to come and go with ease. Ally remembered her childhood, on those occasional days when her mom needed a sitter and dropped her off at HSS. She'd wander the corridors and hide under desks and have a great adventure. She could see herself here now, working in the family business. Maybe it was an option worth exploring.

She followed him into the conference room, where she noted something resembling a large space heater sitting on the table. It was about three feet high and two feet wide, made of gray metal and plastic.

"I want you to meet my new baby," he said.

Ally walked closer, studying it. *Hamilton Security Systems* was printed across the top, and a handle was forged into the casing. *Stay-Safe*, it said in cursive script.

"What is it?"

"This is a battery capable of running every home security system we have." He paused to gather his thoughts before continuing. "You can think of it as an extra layer of protection."

Ally thought the phrasing resembled that of the adult-incontinence-product ads but didn't say so. "Why do you need that?"

"All systems have a vulnerability. Electrical power is a huge weakness. If power is lost, even for a second, it gives intruders opportunity. Our Stay-Safe eliminates that weakness. Power from the house is routed into the battery, keeping it charged, and then the battery runs the system. The only way to interrupt the power in this model is by compromising the battery or the connections. This is housed internally, so that's a very difficult challenge for a thief."

Ally nodded. It made sense. "So currently, home security systems are run by the house's electrical system?"

"Yes, with maybe a small battery to operate the control panels. But the moment the power is interrupted, a breach can occur. We're eliminating that risk."

"Great idea, Dad."

His smile filled the room. "It's the thing I love most about the job. Problem-solving. The numbers and the sales and the contracts are all a grind, but when I get to use that engineering degree, I feel like a little kid again."

His joy was infectious, and Ally felt the lift. "I'm proud of you," she said as she looked at him, seeking a connection.

He met her eyes and nodded. "Right back at you."

At that moment, she forgave him just a little more.

"So you want to see what we do here, huh?" he asked.

"I do."

"You're certainly capable of doing anything we need around here."

He nodded. "I like it. But are you really ready to give up medicine? Just because of a little bump in the road?"

Ally wasn't sure if she should scream at him for minimizing her ordeal or hug him.

"I'm not sure what I want, Dad." She paused and sighed, then looked deep into his eyes. "But my new job is going to be easy work, and that's not good for me. I need a challenge. I need to keep busy to stay out of trouble."

He said nothing but nodded, then looked around.

"Follow me."

A few steps away, he stopped, knocked on her brother's door, and entered without waiting for a replay. Jimmy quickly closed the Amazon window and looked from their father to her, confusion on his face.

"I'm going to show Ally around the place. She's thinking of becoming part of the family business. Do you want to join us?"

He forced a smile, but his eyes were dark as he looked at Ally. "No. That's okay. I have stuff to do before I head out."

Ally was relieved. Their relationship had never been a good one, and it had gone downhill since her battle with addiction became known to the family. Instead of support, it seemed Jimmy only antagonized her. Ally suspected he secretly wanted her to fail.

"Okay," her dad said pleasantly, unaware of the silent drama playing out between his children.

Ally didn't look back as the door closed.

They retraced their steps toward the front of the building and found an abandoned office. The pale-cream walls needed an overhaul, but the desk looked new. She sat in the chair and swiveled, then realized she was acting like the child she was trying to leave behind. "Comfy." The only other contents were an empty hutch and a plastic garbage can. "I can work with this."

"Okay. Now I just have to find you a job."

Ally chuckled, then leaned back in the chair. "I'd like to learn everything, Dad. How you order parts from China. How you build parts here. How you process payments. How they monitor the home systems. How you advertise. And maybe I'll find something I'm good at."

"I have no doubt you will."

Ally knew she was smart. She was capable. Hard work had never fazed her, either. She'd make good use of this opportunity. "Can I get a company car?"

Leaning against the wall, his suit draping elegantly over his lean frame, he crossed his arms and squinted at her. "Is that what this is about?"

The disappointment in his voice hit Ally like a punch in the gut. "No," she said softly. "No. But I don't like it when Jimmy gets ahead of me."

He let go a belly laugh. "Okay, then. If you stick it out for six months, you can get a car. Will your Jeep last that long?"

"It's great. Just outdated a little. Two hundred thousand miles, you know."

"It doesn't owe you anything. C'mon. We'll tour the place and see who you can pal around with when you're here."

"I can be here all morning on Saturday."

"Saturday is a busy day for maintenance. All the people with second homes come on the weekend, and that's when we do their service. That's perfect. A ton of sales calls on Saturday, too."

Her dad poked his head into an office, where a woman was on the phone. He waved and moved on. In the next office, a woman sat before her computer, typing.

"Lisa, do you have a moment?"

A big smile preceded her reply. "Of course. What's up?"

"This is my daughter, Allison. Ally. She's going to be working here. I want her to learn everything. Can you coordinate with her and take her on some sales calls?"

"Absolutely. Ally, do you have time now, or would you like to call me with your schedule?"

"Actually, we're doing a tour now. Can I stop in before I leave?" Lisa glanced at her watch. Ally knew it was closing in on five. "Or call you?"

Lisa laughed. "I'll probably be here for another hour. I'm finishing up a proposal." She handed Ally a card and told her to call if they didn't catch each other when Ally came back through.

After Lisa's office, they toured the warehouse, where the service trucks were housed and parts stored. "We have tens of thousands of dollars in supplies and equipment in each truck, so we don't want to leave them in the lot," he explained. "It's safer inside."

"Makes sense."

Ally met a few warehouse workers restocking bins filled with parts, technicians packing supplies for the next day's service calls, and a few others chatting as they ended the day. Against the far wall, someone was feeding cardboard boxes into a huge shredder that looked a little like a hamster wheel. On the other end, the machine spit out cardboard confetti directly into clear recycling bags.

While most of the spaces in the garage were filled, quite a few were empty. "They don't quit if they have only a few hours left on the job. Much more economical to pay them to finish than to have them travel back the next day, especially to some of those places out in the Poconos. Could take an hour just to get there."

It seemed like HSS was a well-planned, well-run operation, and he continued to explain little details as they walked back toward the monitoring area.

Inside were a dozen pods, each overseen by a technician wearing a headset, sitting in a high-backed rolling chair. A dozen computer monitors were located in each area, several phones, and other equipment that didn't look familiar to Ally. A few of the attendants were female, some were male, and they seemed to come in all shapes and sizes and colors. The one thing they had in common was their age. They were all young.

"It is a techie job, no doubt," her dad replied when she shared her observation. "Suits college kids well."

"Isn't this kind of boring for them? Talking on the phone to people?"

He laughed. "I wish. They wish. Just watch," he said, and they stood there silently as a young girl with dark skin and long hair typed into a computer as she spoke into the headset. She nodded, typed, talked, stopped, nodded, talked. Finally, she tapped the headset and leaned back.

"Hi, Nandita," her dad said. "This is my daughter, Ally."

Nandita turned and gave her a quick assessment, and Ally wasn't sure if she was being checked out. Hopefully not. She didn't want to get fired for fraternizing with a coworker the first day on the job. Still…it was nice to think someone was looking.

Before Ally could greet her, an alarm sounded, and the girl returned her attention to the screens in front of her. Ally and her father stepped closer and took a look.

Berger
404 Maple Road
Dalton, PA
Stone Contemporary
4,500 square feet

*Directions: From Route 6 travel east toward Waverly, the house is
one mile on the left side.*
Martin: code Darth Vader
Louise: code Princess Leia
Andrew: code R2D2
SAFE WORD: CHEWBACCA
REAR BREEZEWAY DOOR GLASS BROKEN
ACTION REQUIRED:
1.　Call LOUISE BERGER 570-555-5555
2.　Call MARTIN BERGER 570-555-5556

Nandita touched the computer screen over the speaker icon, and it
began flashing. *DIALING.*

A second computer screen showed what appeared to be the
breezeway of the Berger house. A woman entered the picture and began
punching numbers into the keypad, while a muted siren blared. Ally
could see the tension in her shoulders ease as the alarm stopped.

Nandita spoke to her through the monitor. "Hi. This is Nandita
from Hamilton Security Systems. Is everything okay?"

"I don't know. What tripped the alarm?"

"Can you tell me your name, please?" It was Louise, aka Princess
Leia. Nandita walked her through the process of checking the glass in
the rear breezeway door, which appeared intact, then instructed her to
search the area for something that might have fallen and triggered the
alarm.

Ally watched as the woman leaned down and picked up a large
bag of dog food from the floor. "This was on this table five minutes
ago. Damn dog!"

"I'm sure the vibration triggered the alarm. Is there anything else
I can help you with?"

Mrs. Berger shook her head.

"You have a nice evening, Mrs. Berger. Before you go, can you
give me your safe word?"

Laughing, she rubbed her eyes. "It's the dog. Chewbacca."

Nandita smiled. "Thank you," she said, then turned to them.
"That's it. Nothing to it."

Ally had no idea the surveillance capabilities were so sophisti-
cated, but it looked like Hamilton was offering a great service.

"Nandita, I'd like to come by and spend some time with you.
Learn about the job. Would that be okay?"

Grinning, she nodded. "Anytime. My schedule is posted on the board. And you can call me Nandi."

"See you soon, then," Ally said with a calm that contradicted the excitement of spending more time with her father's employee. But hey, if she had to learn from someone, wasn't a beautiful, exotic-looking woman a good option?

As they walked away, another of Nandi's alarms sounded, and she spun back toward the computer screens. Every other worker was equally busy.

"Is it always like this?"

"It's a little slower at night. Fewer accidental triggers. But yeah. It's a hopping place."

"Maybe I should just work here. I could be useful."

"HSS is hiring," he deadpanned.

They walked back to his office. "Will I see you for dinner?"

"I'm not sure Mom can top the coq au vin, but I'm going to give her the chance."

"See you there," he said, but before he walked away, he folded her into his arms and kissed the top of her head. "I'm glad you came by, even if you decide you don't want to do this."

Ally smiled against his chest, then looked up at him. "I'm glad, too."

Lisa was still at her desk when Ally poked her head in. "Are you by chance working Saturday?" she asked.

Lisa nodded. "I have two sales calls. Wanna ride along?"

They agreed to meet at the office at eight.

You've got this, Ally told herself as she practically skipped from the building.

It was too late for the meeting at the Recovery Hub if Ally wanted to make that dinner with her parents. And after spending time with her dad at the office, she thought that would be nice. She had a little different perspective on him after being there just that short while.

She'd trained to do one job and now was doing another, just as he was. He'd been so excited to tell her about the battery he'd developed, told her he missed the engineering he'd done before opening his company. Yet his company was tremendously successful and had given Ally and her siblings very privileged lives. Jimmy had gotten a degree in finance, which her parents had paid for. Her brother Kevin was a lawyer, also courtesy of her dad's success. And, of course, they'd covered all her expenses as well.

Ally had lived at home during college, but as soon as she and Gretchen, also a PA, had graduated, they'd moved into an apartment. It had two bedrooms, so Gretchen could continue lying to her parents, and was way too big for either of them when they split. Ally had moved right into the penthouse in her parents' building after the breakup, and they'd never taken a penny in rent.

Did her dad have any regrets? He'd been raised in a typical Scranton family. His father worked at the Topps factory, making bubble-gum and baseball cards, and he'd worked there, too, in the summers. But he was very bright and had the chance to go to college, getting his degree from Penn State. He'd gotten a good job but decided it wasn't what he wanted and had borrowed and risked it all to open the security business. His engineering degree was wasted, yet he was successful and seemed content.

Considering her own issues, she couldn't wait to talk to him further about all the curves in the path he'd taken.

It was funny, she thought as she drove toward her apartment. She'd always been somewhat serious, a little more mature than most kids her age, but she suddenly felt so stupid. It had never occurred to her to ask her dad if he liked his job or was happy with the choices he'd made. Ditto for her mom. She'd been a grade-school art teacher before Kevin was born, and by the time Ally was in school and Janine might have considered going back to work, the security company was doing well, and she didn't need to. They'd moved to the suburbs, and her mom painted.

They'd had these roles and lived in their house for as long as Ally could remember. Why should she question their choices? It just seemed to be how it was now. She thought more now, though, about everything. She guessed that was good.

In her apartment she changed into jeans and a sweater for dinner with her parents, then dialed the phone while she threw her laundry into the dryer.

Dr. Jessica Benson sounded breathless when she answered.

"Are you coming to Reese's place for the big party?"

"I wouldn't miss it. How about you?"

"I am. Any chance you want to meet for a coffee before?"

"Hmm. Mac's coming, too, but I suppose I could drop her off at Home Depot for a while. She could spend hours there, so I'm sure she won't mind."

"Perfect."

"Is everything okay?"

"Yes," Ally said. "It's okay. I just miss our talks." Ally had more time to connect when she was in rehab and could adjust to Jess's wacky ER schedule. They'd spoken practically every day for months while she was a patient, but only a few times since she'd been discharged.

"You can call me anytime. It's winter in Garden, PA, so I'm bored out of my mind."

"No skiing for you?"

"Yes, of course, and snowmobiling, and ice fishing, but I just do those things to pass the time. I'd much rather be in the sunshine."

Ally knew Mac, Jess's wife, was retired from the state police. "It must suck that Mac is retired and you aren't. Have you thought of moving someplace warmer?"

"My dad isn't well, and he'll never leave Garden. So I can't either." She laughed, and Ally sensed she was okay with that.

"How does Mac keep busy?"

"She's teaching self-defense classes, and now we're investing in real estate. Older houses that need upgrading. Mac and my dad do all the work."

Ally had learned a few home-repair tricks herself, a necessary skill when managing an apartment building. Maybe she'd get into real estate. Something else to talk to them about when she saw them Sunday. Jess asked about her job, and they conversed for another ten minutes about her recovery while Ally drove to her parents' place.

"Well, I look forward to seeing you."

"I'll text you about coffee."

"I can't wait."

Ally hung up the phone feeling something she hadn't experienced in a while—anticipation. Hope that something good was going to happen. It was a nice sensation.

CHAPTER SEVEN

Home Health

The next morning Ally was at Four H bright and early, and she shared some details about her past with the group. They were supportive but didn't seem to consider her a big deal. That was quite amazing, because to everyone outside the recovery community, she was the odd one, the one who'd gotten into trouble. Here, she was normal. And compared to some of her coworkers, she was downright angelic.

After the meeting, she climbed into the passenger seat beside Linda, and they headed toward the Pocono Mountains. The temperatures were still frigid, but the roads were dry, at least until they got to the smaller county roads so abundant in the area. They'd moved on from talking about work to discussing sports after Ally mentioned all the Philadelphia Eagles stickers on the car. When they arrived at their destination, a ranch-style home near Lake Ariel, they were still talking about the NFL.

"You'll like Tommy, our patient. He's a sports nut, too. Lung cancer. We check his blood after his chemo to make sure his white blood cells haven't dropped too low."

"And what if they do?"

"We'll come back and give him a shot of something to boost his bone marrow. Sometimes subcutaneous, sometimes intravenous. Exactly what and how depends on his insurance, and on what the doctor orders, but Greg would let you know that."

"Okay," Ally said, kind of hoping she'd get to administer the infusion. She'd never done it before, and she loved doing new procedures.

Ally followed Linda and her tackle box to the front door, and before they could ring the bell, it opened, and a woman of seventy smiled at them through a glass storm door.

"Good morning," she said cheerfully as she pushed it open for them.

They quickly entered, and she closed the door behind them, but Ally couldn't help but think the temperature in the house had dropped due to the frigid air. On cue, a gas fireplace hissed and came to life, and Ally noticed a frail-looking man lounging in a recliner on the far side of the room.

"Hi, Tommy," Linda called cheerfully, and the man struggled to lift his arm to wave. Ally followed Linda's lead and removed her shoes before they walked across the room toward him.

"This is Ally. She's the medical assistant who'll be helping you for the next few months."

Tommy shifted his gaze to Ally and smiled weakly. "Let's hope it's a few months," he gasped. "They're giving me only a fifty-fifty chance."

Ally remembered what an oncologist once told a patient facing a difficult surgery and chemotherapy regimen for pancreatic cancer. She repeated his words for Tommy's benefit. "Even if the odds are only one percent, you have a chance. One person out of a hundred will live. Why can't it be you?"

"That's looking at the bright side," he said with a wink and a smile.

"How's that blood of yours?" Linda asked as she whipped out a lab tube and supplies to access his catheter.

"I think there's still some left. Not much, after my last trip to the hospital, but I can spare one tube."

Linda held a purple-topped tube containing an anticoagulant and waved it. "It's very little," she said, then handed it to Ally.

You've got this, she told herself.

Ports were not something she worked with often, because most of the time nurses accessed them in the ER. She'd done this once or twice over the years, but she'd reviewed the procedure with Linda the day before, so she hoped she could draw the blood without looking like an idiot. After wiping the port, Ally unclamped it, withdrew the saline, then filled the lab tube with Tommy's blood. When she was done, she flushed the port and labeled the tube with a sticker Four H had printed with Tommy's demographics.

After she finished, relief fueled her smile. They had Tommy's wife sign the note for his care, then bid them farewell, and headed to the next patient's home.

"That was easy," Ally told Linda, and they spent the drive discussing lab draws.

Unlike Tommy's house, a well-maintained place on a paved road, the next client lived in a dilapidated trailer surrounded by abandoned cars and a partially collapsed barn. Linda handed Ally a small bottle of menthol rub. "A good investment," she said. "For the clients with an aversion to soap and water."

Ally chuckled as she rubbed the ointment into each nostril, then winced when she breathed the cool air. "Ow, wow," she said. "That burns."

"Trust me, it's better than the odor of a dozen pets and diabetic leg ulcer."

"The landscaping doesn't inspire hope," Ally said.

Linda rolled her eyes. "The inside's even worse. And it's not that I'm picking on an old woman," she said, lowering her voice to keep unseen ears from hearing what she said. "But she's got two grown sons living with her. It's disgraceful."

The barking of at least two dogs heralded their approach, and Ally heard a deep voice reprimanding them from the other side of a battered kitchen door. One of the aforementioned sons, desperately needing a bath and a change of clothes, answered their knock and ushered them into a cluttered kitchen. Every surface was covered, and Ally was saved from staring by the attention she paid to her legs, which several cats and one small dog assaulted.

When she looked up, the woman seated at the table smiled. She appeared as unkempt as her surroundings, and Ally was grateful for the menthol that overwhelmed her olfactory nerve yet couldn't help notice the happiness in the woman's eyes. This visit, the care they were providing, was important to her.

"How's that leg of yours?" Linda queried.

"Still attached."

"That's good news."

Linda and Ally both donned gloves before going to work. "Her X-ray shows the bone is okay. It's just the soft tissues that are involved," Linda explained. "But the wound is healing nicely."

Linda covered a footrest with a disposable pad, then propped the woman's swollen ankle in the middle. Her slippers were so worn the Velcro no longer functioned, and it easily fell from her foot. After peeling away a dressing, she leaned back to allow Ally access to the wound. The skin of the lower calf on the edges of the wound looked normal, and the wound tissue itself was bright red with no drainage. It wasn't deep and measured about an inch across.

"How long have you had this?" Ally asked as she cleaned the wound with salt water.

"About six months. When I went to the doctor after Christmas I showed it to her, and since then you people have been coming out to change the bandages, and it's getting better."

"It's about half the size, now," Linda said.

Ally applied ointment and a filmy dressing that resembled Saran Wrap, then slid the woman's slipper back onto her foot.

"We'll see you tomorrow," Ally said as she gave the woman the visit note to sign.

From the pocket of her hooded sweatshirt, the woman pulled two peppermint candies. "Thank you for being gentle," she said in a soft voice.

Ally's heart melted as she accepted the offering with a thank you of her own. *You've got this*, she told herself, for entirely different reasons than the usual ones.

"That's a sad case," Linda said, and all Ally could do was nod.

"But just to teach you that the great and the small are all equal in the eyes of the Lord," Linda said with a hint of sarcasm, "we're going to see another patient with a diabetic foot ulcer."

Ally wondered what she meant, but after she pulled out of the woman's driveway, Linda began telling her about their next patient. "Brodrik Rogan, multi-gazillionaire car dealer, has seen better days. He bought half of the Pocono Mountains and retired here with his fifth or sixth wife. I can't remember which. He drank like a fish, destroyed his liver, got a transplant, and then diabetes killed his kidneys. Now he's suffering from congestive heart failure and is basically circling the drain. But even with all that going on, he'll pinch my ass if I get close enough."

Ally laughed at the vision that came to mind, but it brought up a more serious issue. She remembered seeing something in the employee manual, but she was curious about specifics. "How do you handle someone who behaves inappropriately?"

"Zero tolerance."

"And yet…"

"Yes, well. I reported him, the first time, and Greg 'looked into it.' Rogan's wife says he's confused and blah blah blah. Greg said we'd give him another chance. That was like twenty chances ago. But it's nothing serious. He's a pain in the ass, but he's harmless. If I thought he was a threat, I'd fire him as a client, but really, he's just a sad, wasted little man. Actually, he's a big man. But he's fallen far, and I'm sure being so sick, so dependent, is hell for him."

Ally pulled him up on her phone as they drove. "He's a little famous. Brodrik Rogan, the Cadillac King, with dealerships in twelve locations in the northeastern United States," Ally said, and when she saw his face, she recalled seeing him on television. "I remember him. His commercials were on the New York cable channels."

"He's the one."

"It's true that we're all heading to the same place," Ally said as she looked out the window. They were on a county road, snow-covered in places, surrounded by mountains of pines holding armfuls of snow.

Linda chuckled. "But some of us are driving Kias, and some are the Cadillac King."

Ally laughed back at her. "Same destination, though."

"Yes, it is. Anyway, Rogan's place is a pain in the ass. The house has a gate, and a security guard lets us in. Another guard will let us in the house. Plus, he has a couple of sons and a daughter and a wife who come and go. He'll make us wait before he sees us, so Greg builds in extra time. The family will probably hover like flies at a picnic, so let's try to get in and out as quickly as we can before I strangle one of them."

"You seem to know the patients well, but I thought you were a manager at Four H."

"That's true. I am a manager, but I have to treat people when we're short-staffed. Plus, I go out for all the initial evaluations to write the plan of care."

Ally looked back at her phone, surprised to see the next article on Brodrik Rogan. *The Cadillac King Acquitted.*

"Holy shit, listen to this," Ally said as she began reading the article to Linda. "Brodrik Rogan, the Cadillac King, was acquitted on murder charges in the death of his third wife, actress Savannah Summers. Summers's body was discovered on Philbin Beach, on the island of Martha's Vineyard, two days after Rogan said she fell from a Jet Ski she launched from his yacht. One of Rogan's five homes is on Martha's Vineyard. Police became suspicious when toxicology results showed Summer's alcohol content was nearly five times the legal limit, a level they say would have rendered her too impaired to launch the Jet Ski on her own. Friends of Summers testified to a grand jury that she seldom drank alcohol because she was concerned about weight gain and instead used the prescription drug Xanax to help with stress, prompting Dukes County District Attorney Allison Dammer to bring murder charges. Even so, the jury didn't find the evidence compelling and decided in favor of the defense. 'I loved Savannah and miss her terribly,' said Rogan, who has since remarried. 'And I'm relieved the jury saw through the holes in the prosecution's case. Now, hopefully, she can rest peacefully.' When questioned about the verdict, Dammer simply replied, 'No comment.'"

"Holy shit is right," Linda said. "When was that?"

Ally looked at the date of the article. "Twenty-five years ago."

"He did it. I can tell. It's in his eyes."

"Well, thanks for adding him to my roster of clients," Ally deadpanned.

"What else does it say?"

Ally scrolled through her phone and found a dozen stories about Rogan. His fifth marriage was to a *Playboy* model, whom he divorced a few years later, and his sixth was his daughter's preschool teacher, Winnie Banks.

"That's her. Winnie is the current wife."

"This must be true love, then. They've been together fifteen years," Ally said as she scanned her phone. "How about this? He was involved with real-estate fraud, too." Ally read an article that described how Rogan had bailed on a development project just a week before the permits were pulled due to environmental concerns. He walked away with more than a hundred million dollars, which he then invested in land in the Pocono Mountains. A grand jury found insufficient evidence to bring the case to trial.

"He seems to have good luck with juries, eh?" Linda asked.

"I'll say. How about this one?" Ally asked as she read the next article. "The head of the parts department for his companies disappeared shortly before he was scheduled to testify about the use of counterfeit Cadillac parts in the service departments at his dealerships."

"Whoa," Linda replied. "When was that?"

"Ten years ago," Ally said. She googled the man's name and learned his wife had him declared dead just a few years ago.

"So they never found his body?"

"Doesn't sound like it," Ally said as she sat back and took stock. How did she feel about taking care of a man with Brodrik Rogan's history? How did she feel about even meeting the guy? If it was just one charge, Ally might have given him the benefit of the doubt, but she'd found three horrific incidents in just a few minutes.

"At least he hasn't been in the news lately," Linda said.

"Well, if I keep reading, do you think I'll find something else?"

Ally didn't have time to ponder the question as Linda pulled to a stop before a tall iron gate hanging from stone pillars. A guard stepped out from a small enclosure and peered at her for a moment before the gate swung open. He stood well over six feet tall and was broad, with legs that stretched the material of his ski pants. When he stepped into the car's path, Ally thought he might have dented the fender if they'd collided. Linda stopped and lowered the window as he approached.

"Who's your friend?" he asked.

"This is Ally. She's the new nurse, taking over for Macie," Linda explained.

"She didn't last long," he said with a shake of his head.

"Good help is hard to find," she retorted.

"Can I see your ID?" he asked Ally.

Ally pulled it from her wallet, and he looked from the picture to her and back. "Let me get security paperwork for her. She can give it to the guard at the house when it's finished, and they'll get started with her clearance."

A moment later he was back, holding an envelope. He handed it to Linda with a half salute.

"Is this for real?" Ally asked as Linda handed her the paperwork.

Linda shrugged. "They require everyone who goes through the gate to have a background check. It's pretty routine. If you passed Greg's screening, you'll pass Mr. Rogan's."

Ally nodded in relief. Why, she wasn't sure. She almost hoped she wouldn't pass, and Greg would need someone else to care for Brodrik Rogan's wounds.

The driveway was wide enough for two cars, and it was paved and plowed, though here and there drifting snow made interesting patterns on the surface. As Linda drove through a thick cluster of pines, the road curved, and then in a clearing she saw a huge mountain lodge appear in the distance. It had five different, steep roofs, held up by large logs, and a foundation of stone climbed halfway up the building. Linda followed the road to the left when it forked and pulled up to a portico on the edge of the property. They exited the car and were greeted at a tall double door by another guard, who asked the same question about Ally.

In response, Ally waved the envelope the first guard had given her. "I've already started filling out the paperwork."

"I'll escort you in. I need a copy of your driver's license."

Ally followed Linda into a great hall, where a chandelier hanging from a twenty-foot ceiling scattered light on the black-and-white marble checkerboard floor. She reached into her wallet and again retrieved her driver's license for the guard.

"Wait here," he instructed her. "I'll only be a moment."

"Sure thing," Linda said as Ally nodded and studied her surroundings. Antique chairs sat to the right, and behind them, in an ornately carved wooden frame, was a magnificent Impressionist landscape. It was at least three feet high and four feet wide. Ally stepped closer to study it and couldn't help reaching out to touch the finely chiseled piece. It moved ever so slightly beneath her hand, and she was surprised she didn't hear an alarm.

The painting was captivating. The canvas was crisscrossed with heavy brushstrokes in bright colors, showing a scene of a boy and his dog playing near a stream. The dog was a black-and-white sheepdog, and he jumped from the sea of green and blue surrounding him. The boy looked in wonder at his pet, and the artist had captured the adoration on his face. The signature read Brigette, and Ally thought for a moment, trying to place it. She couldn't.

Was this Brigette a minor period artist or a wannabe selling paintings on the boardwalk at the Jersey Shore? From what she'd read, and from the looks of his estate, Brodrik Rogan could probably afford the real deal, especially if he'd purchased it before art prices had exploded.

"If you like art, this is the place to be." The booming voice that interrupted her belonged to the guard, and she turned to see him smiling, his hand outstretched, holding her ID. Ally realized he was flirting with her, or at least trying to make an impression. And why not? She was an attractive, thirty-year-old woman with no ring on her finger. He was an attractive, thirty-something guy.

She didn't have the heart to ask if he had a sister, so she just nodded. "I love art."

"Mr. Rogan does, too. This is called *Shepherd's Boy and His Dog,* by Antoine Brigette, a nineteenth-century French artist who studied under Claude Monet. And that," he said as he nodded to the opposite wall, where a square, black frame held a painting of three musicians at work, "is a Vermeer."

"*The Concert,*" Ally said as she moved toward it, pulled by the magnet of her attraction to the masterpiece. The marble floor painted by

Johannes Vermeer matched the one beneath her feet, and Ally's breath caught at the sight of it.

"Yes. *The Concert.*"

"Over there," he said, pointing to the opposite wall just past the entrance to what appeared to be a dining room, where another piece with similar tones hung. Ally recognized *A Lady and Gentleman in Black,* the work of Rembrandt van Rijn.

"That's a Rembrandt," the beefy security guard confirmed, then nodded to the opposite wall, at the foot of a grand staircase. "And that's called *Landscape with an Obelisk,* by Govaert Flinck. He was a student of Rembrandt." The painting showed a massive, twisting tree in the foreground and a stone footbridge leading to the obelisk, all done in earth tones. She supposed the black-and-white storm clouds were the reason this piece was displayed in the foyer, since black and white seemed to be the commonality between the works.

"Are these real?" Linda asked, her eyes wide, as if seeing the paintings for the first time.

The guard shrugged and whispered conspiratorially. "Mr. Rogan acts like they are. Back in the day, he used to come out of his study just to stare at them, like he was visiting a museum or something. It was weird to watch him. And he'd show them off to his guests, talking about the artists and the kind of paint they used, and all that sort of stuff." He shook his head and wore a sad look. "Since he started to lose his vision, he doesn't look at them much anymore. Walks right past them, as if they aren't even hanging there. And other than his family, he hardly ever has any guests."

"Is that how you learned so much about art?" Ally asked.

"Oh, yes. Mr. Rogan has taught me a great deal."

Linda stared at the Flinck for a moment. "Well, this doesn't do anything for me. I kind of like the boy with the dog, though. How much would something like that set me back?"

When the guard didn't answer, Ally did. "You could get a nice, framed copy like this for a few hundred dollars."

"What?" she exclaimed. "I'd pay ten bucks for it at a yard sale, but not much more."

Ally chuckled. Her mother often did the very same thing.

The guard laughed, too. "I'd go as high as twenty. Anyway, ask Mr. Rogan for the tour sometime. He's got quite a collection. And it might do his spirit some good to show it off."

On cue, tall wooden doors opened, and a thin woman, the victim of a horrific face lift, stepped into the vestibule. She looked from Linda to Ally without smiling. "Mr. Rogan will see you now."

Instantly the light mood shifted. Ally's nerves were suddenly on edge, and the change had nothing to do with the job.

CHAPTER EIGHT

The Cadillac King

"Hiya, Mr. Rogan," Linda called cheerfully as she walked into a large study. This floor was made of wide wooden planks, as was the ceiling. To the left, before a set of tall windows, a massive antique desk sat unoccupied. Statuary filled every corner. Built-in shelves filled with books and objets d'art lined the walls, the spaces between peppered with more of the same. Paintings, reliefs, drawings, and abstract pieces of every shape and color brightened the darkly paneled room. The most eye-catching of all was a large oil on canvas. *Jesus in the Storm on the Sea of Galilee* was more than five feet tall, the great wave threatening to swallow the ship a wall of white in the darkness. Ally had to force her gaze away from the painting to the opposite side of the room, where a man sat on the floor beside a crackling fire.

He was much older but faintly resembled the pictures of the Cadillac King she'd viewed on her phone. He was much larger, too. The photos she'd seen on her phone had shown a tall, lean man. The man on the floor was twice the size of the young Brodrik Rogan. After hearing Linda's description of his medical issues, she expected to see a frail, gaunt old creature, not the robust one before her. Playing with him, stacking a pile of blocks, was an adorable boy of three or four, with a mop of curls on his head that reminded Ally of a younger Brodrik Rogan.

"Hello, Linda." He greeted her cheerfully. Then he pointed to the child beside him. "My grandson, Joseph," he said, then shook his head. His voice was a few decibels lower when he spoke again. "His mother's a junkie. We're sharing custody with the father's parents till she gets out of rehab, and I swear they give him IV sugar before they drop him off. He doesn't stop."

Ally winced at the word he used to describe his daughter. Apparently he didn't know that the caregivers from Four H were all in recovery, too. Ignoring the remark, she introduced herself. "Hi, Joseph. Hi, Mr. Rogan. I'm Ally."

Joseph jumped from his blocks and ran into Ally's arms, nearly knocking her over. His hug was ferocious, and just as quickly he jumped back and ran out of the room.

"His mom will get out of rehab next week. Not a moment too soon," he said as he closed his eyes and shook his head. "Ally, it's nice to meet you. But this can't be good news, seeing Linda here."

Ally kept one ear on the conversation as she discreetly took in the room. It was more a museum than a study, and she wanted to climb to the top of each shelf and touch everything, look at each piece up close. Even the desk and the couch appeared to be antiques. The only thing that didn't fit was a big, puffy recliner.

"Macie is no longer with us," Linda informed him.

"Shit. Whatever she said about me, it's a lie. I swear it. I've been on my best behavior." He held up his hands in surrender and wore a look of innocence.

Linda and Ally both laughed. "It wasn't you. This time, anyway."

He looked toward the open door and lowered his voice when he spoke. "Was it my wife? She can be a real bitch."

Ally saw Linda's face contort as she tried to suppress a smile. "No, no. Macie got a better job offer."

"Ah. I see. Good for her, then. Is Miss Ally here the replacement?"

"Yes. And she's even better than Macie. You're in good hands. How's that leg?"

"It's getting worse. It's hurting more than it did."

"Are you resting and elevating it?"

"I'm chasing a three-year-old around a 10,000-square-foot house. So, no."

Ally bit her lip to contain her laugh. In spite of what she'd read about Brodrik Rogan, she liked him.

"Well, climb up into your chair and let us have a look."

This was where his truth was revealed. Brodrik Rogan moved to his side and, with tremendous effort, pushed himself up to his knees. From there he struggled to the chair and rolled into it, gasping for breath as he landed with a thud.

Linda ignored the breathing, which caused Ally considerable concern, and went right to work on his leg. After opening her case, she pulled up a chair beside him, then hiked his pants up to the knee. His leg was grossly swollen and discolored, dappled with the scabs of small, healing wounds. A plastic bandage, four by six inches in length, was attached to the outside of his leg, covering a piece of gauze half that size.

"We've been using saline dressings and applying a wound cream to promote tissue growth. I haven't seen him in about a month, but Macie said it was improving."

"It's not improving," Brodrik barked.

Linda stood and stepped aside. "My type A takes over sometimes. Why don't you do it? You'll be in charge after today."

"If I approve, she's in charge," he said.

Ally looked into Brodrik's dark eyes. They were black, like coal, the same color his hair had been in the pictures from his younger days. Now it was shockingly white, but still thick and curly, and a bit untamed. Like him, Ally thought. If his face wasn't so puffy and mapped by broken capillaries, he might have still been handsome.

"May I?" Ally asked, challenging him.

He seemed surprised but nodded, and Ally took Linda's seat. *You've got this*, she told herself as she donned gloves, then in one swift motion removed the dressing on his leg.

"Fuck," he hissed, but he didn't move, and Ally didn't respond. Instead, she studied his leg. The wound was a one- by three-inch oval, with a pale-pink base covered with thick strands of pus. The surrounding tissue was red and looked irritated, and Ally wished Macie was beside her, to tell her what it had looked like before.

"Was this yellow stuff there yesterday?" she asked as she pointed to the wound.

"No," Linda answered. "At least not according to Macie's report."

"It was looking better. Now, this," Rogan told them.

"How'd you injure it?" Ally asked as she removed a tube from the tackle box and then swabbed the wound to send for a culture.

"In the garden." He sighed.

It was February. When had he been in the garden?

"Last summer." He answered the unspoken question.

It was a long time to have a wound, but his circulation was obviously impaired, and it might never heal. They might have to change bandages on his leg until the day he died. She didn't share that concern. "We should put a different dressing on, to pull the goo off the wound."

She was covertly telling Linda her treatment strategy, hoping she'd offer some advice. Without speaking, Linda handed her the supplies she needed, confirming support of Ally's plan. Ally carefully applied the dressing and a new bandage, then picked up the trash, putting it all into a small bag.

"Where can I throw this away?" she asked.

"The bathroom," he said. "Right behind me."

Ally looked behind him, where a collage of art made a diamond shape on the wall. She studied the works for a moment. All four paintings were masterpieces, and all the originals had been stolen. She stood and walked that way, her heart pounding as she silently counted the number of pieces hanging on the walls around her. Three in the lobby and five more on view in the study. And while she knew it wasn't unusual for art enthusiasts to collect copies of their favorite works, what gnawed at her now was the fact that every single painting she'd seen, except the Brigette, was stolen. Why would someone selectively display copies of them?

Behind Rogan's chair, Ally turned a doorknob and entered a large bathroom. Flipping on the light switch, she looked into the eyes of Raphael. His *Portrait of a Young Man* could have been a young Brodrik Rogan, with dark, curly hair and big brown eyes. She turned to the right, where a pedestal sink stood below a mirror. Across from it, Rembrandt's tiny self-portrait hung, and as she washed her hands, she gazed into his eyes.

"Holy crap," she whispered as she looked from one master to another. Rembrandt and Raphael. Raphael and Rembrandt. "Gentlemen, if you're real, you are worth a fortune. Are you real?" she softly asked Raphael as she stared into his eyes. The value of these paintings on the black market was mind-boggling. Could Rogan afford mind-boggling?

Of course, considering Brodrik Rogan's reputation, there was another possibility, and wow, that was even more mind-boggling. He might have stolen them himself or hired someone to do it. They just might be real. They. Might. Be. Real.

Ally turned and stared at Rembrandt as she dried her hands, feeling a little woozy. In the last ten minutes, she'd just had an up-close-and-personal view of some of the greatest works of art ever created. Not hanging in a museum, but in a house in the middle of the Pocono Mountains. Not in the possession of a legitimate collector, but in the hands of a criminal—a man accused of murder, of fraud on a huge scale. A man who had the connections to commit theft on the grandest scale, or the lack of scruples to buy the works someone else stole.

You have a right to be dizzy, she thought as she again calculated the odds that these were the original paintings. *Holy fuck.*

"Ally, you okay?"

She heard Linda's voice from behind the closed door and exhaled, a long, loud breath. *You've got this.* Ally swallowed and gave herself another moment before returning to the study, where Linda was talking with Brodrik Rogan.

"Have a seat," he commanded, and Ally sank into a stiff leather couch across from his chair. She was ten feet from him, yet it seemed too close. Her imagination had gotten the better of her, and she was all nerves as she sat on his couch, wondering if she was crazy.

He sat perfectly still, his arms folded and resting on his belly, his puffy ankles resting on the ottoman. "Tell me about yourself, Ally," he said as he stared her down.

Ally cleared her throat. "What would you like to know?"

"How old are you, are you married, where are you from? How'd you get into the home-health business?" He looked totally healthy, in total command of the conversation.

Ally thought for a moment. How much of her personal truth did she want to reveal to a man accused of two murders and who knew what else? She decided vague and not quite honest was best. She smiled. "Thirty, presently no, Scranton, and I've always wanted to help people."

He was quiet, then burst into a fit of laughter. The laughter caused him to cough, and the cough caused him to gasp. She watched him struggle to regain control, and he was visibly winded when he spoke again several seconds later.

"I believed you until you gave me that crap about helping people."

"Is that so unbelievable?"

"C'mon. I know what Hart charges for you to change my Band-Aid. You get paid big bucks for this."

Ally winced. If he only knew about her paltry salary and the circumstances that had brought her to Four H.

"Where are you from?" Ally didn't remember a New York accent when she heard him on television, but she detected something now.

"My feelings are crushed. You don't know who I am?"

Ally shrugged. "I saw your commercials on TV when I was a kid, but I wasn't really interested. If you'd been selling bicycles, maybe I would have paid more attention."

He laughed and shook his head, but this time he didn't lose his breath. "God, I really am old," he said, then paused to stare again. "Boston, originally. But I moved in my teens."

Boston, Ally thought. The former home of a fortune in stolen artwork.

Ally looked over Brodrik's shoulder again to the space on the wall where four framed pieces hung and back to him as he asked a question.

"What do you drive?"

"A Jeep."

"Good choice in the mountains. Although you know our SUVs are highly rated."

He said it as if he owned General Motors himself. Who knew, though? Maybe he did.

"I like it because it's sporty. I can load my kayak on top or take it into the woods without any worries."

"Oh, I see. You're an outdoorsy sort of girl. If you'd like, you can take advantage of my land. It's great for snowshoeing and cross-county skiing, and we have snowmobiles in the maintenance barn. If my grandchildren haven't crashed them! There's a small lake about a mile away, where you can skate. My older grandsons play hockey, just like I did when I was a boy."

A sweet smile spread across his face, and Ally wondered if he was remembering his own childhood activities or his grandchildren's.

Ally tried to show her appreciation without committing. "Thank you. That's a really generous offer."

He nodded. "Since you mentioned your marital status as *presently no,* I can have my bodyguard Rocco show you around. I think you met him on the way in. Tall, good-looking fellow."

"Yes, we met. And again, that's sweet of you, but…"

He didn't press it. "Well, think about it. The skiing and the date. Either one could be fun."

Linda interrupted the matchmaking. "Mr. Rogan, it's time for us to get along to our next patient. But if you agree, Ally will be back tomorrow."

His eyes met hers, and he nodded. "She'll do. What about Saturday?"

Linda told him the usual weekend nurse would be there.

"Then I'll see you tomorrow." He looked at Ally with a piercing gaze.

Once again, Ally didn't know if she should be relieved or worried.

CHAPTER NINE

After Hours

The rest of the day was rather benign compared to her time at the Rogan mansion, and Ally and Linda arrived back at Four H in the mid-afternoon. Linda told Ally she was ready to go on her own, and Ally didn't disagree. The medical care didn't concern her, but the situation at Brodrik Rogan's house caused her angst.

Ally filed all her paperwork and completed the electronic billing with no problems. Then she made sure her tackle box was ready for the next day before bidding the staff good-bye and heading to her other job.

The employee lot at Hamilton was still full, and this time Ally barely slowed her stride in the lobby as she headed toward her dad's office. He asked about her day, and she asked about his. They no longer talked about her shoulder, and it seemed he'd moved on from her recovery, as well. She didn't know if that was good or bad, but she supposed she had to own it and not worry about her dad's reaction. This was on her. She'd been angry at him for a long while after her injury, blaming him for much of what went wrong after she crashed on the mountain. He'd insisted she come back to Scranton for the surgery. He'd insisted his friend perform her shoulder repair, even though he was out of town and Ally had to wait almost a week for the procedure, and even though that same friend prescribed opioids by the truckload and didn't take her concerns seriously. It was only when his partner checked her that she learned something wasn't right, and even though a second surgery corrected the mistakes of the first, by that time, Ally was totally dependent on painkillers.

"I'm going to head back over to monitoring," she informed him, "and then maybe see what the installation guys do when they get back."

"Can you find the way?" he asked, and she nodded and headed out his door. "Catch you later."

Ally stepped out and walked not toward monitoring, but toward sales. Lisa wasn't in her office, but Ally stepped to her desk and wrote her a note before heading to the other section of the building.

Disappointed that Nandi wasn't there today, she instead sat beside Matt, another student working his way through college at her family business. He told her about the software and the checklist the monitors went through for each call. He was in the middle of this explanation when the words *PENDING ALARM* flashed on his screen. An icon below it read *ACCESS ACCOUNT*.

Matt clicked the icon, typed in a password, and the account holder's information was displayed on the screen.

"What's a pending alarm?" she asked.

"It's an alert that the alarm has been tripped, but the police haven't yet been notified. The delay gives the homeowner a chance to disarm the alarm before we send the police out. If that happens more than once, the homeowner could receive a citation."

That made sense, and Ally watched the screen as a new message flashed. *SYSTEM DISARMED. READY TO ARM.*

"So, it was a false alarm."

"It appears so. Almost everyone has a panic code they can enter that will disarm the system, if they were in a hostage situation, for instance. It would silence the alarm but still notify us to send the police."

Ally was familiar with that feature. They had it on their own home security system, as well as the one in her apartment.

Matt was informative, and Ally spent more than an hour with him, learning about the home monitoring, before she decided to visit the installation area to see if the vans were coming back in yet.

They were, and Ally introduced herself to a technician who was cleaning out his vehicle and restocking supplies for the next day. He showed her a printout of his work schedule and what pieces he needed to stock. It even told him which bin the parts were in, to save time. The tech was as informative as Matt had been, but after spending an hour with him and another installer, Ally couldn't help but wonder why Hamilton didn't have someone else restocking. It seemed simple enough.

She was about to leave when she turned a corner and nearly ran into her brother. "Hi, Jimmy," she said softly as she met his gaze. Her mouth grew instantly dry as she braced herself for whatever he might say. For reasons she had never quite understood, her brother despised her. There was an age gap of several years between them. Did he just resent all the attention paid to her when she was born, attention that had once been given to him? He'd tormented her as a child, and though everyone always said they'd be close when they got older, it had never happened. In fact, his animus had only gotten worse, to the point that Ally avoided him when she could.

"What the fuck are you doing here?" he asked with enough venom to paralyze an elephant.

Ally thought of the technicians under his supervision wasting time restocking trucks and unloading garbage and wondered the same thing.

"Checking things out," she said with as much calm as she could muster.

He stepped forward, so he was barely an inch from her when he spoke and looked down at her with fire in his eyes. "You are not wanted here. You are not needed here. Why don't you go back to giving little old men sponge baths and leave the real work to me?"

Ally wanted to back down. She was almost afraid of him. Would he actually hit her? In a boxing ring, she'd be no match for her brother. But she'd learned long ago how to spar with just words, and they didn't fail her now.

"I'm considering my options, bro. I mean, why should you have the cushy six-figure salary when I have to actually work for my money? If I come over to Hamilton Security, I can get an office, a secretary, and a car. Dad's already found me an office. I just have to figure out what color Lexus I'd like."

His expression was one of pure disbelief. "He gave you a fucking office? You haven't done a fucking thing to earn your keep, and just like that, you bat your fucking eyelashes, and boom—you're in. Well, I don't think so. You watch your step, Al. And if you make one little slipup, you're not going to be fired. I'll make sure you go to jail."

Now Ally was surprised. "For what?"

Her pursed his lips as he seemed to contemplate his answer. "Just watch your step, Ally. You're in my territory, and you may find it isn't very friendly."

He stormed away, and Ally fought to calm herself as she walked back to her dad's office. What exactly did the threat mean? She had no idea. She only knew he despised her, and she couldn't do much about it. He was a mean person, lazy and self-serving. If her parents didn't see the truth about him by now, they never would. But that didn't mean she was giving him control at the family business. If she decided she wanted to work here, and that was a big if, she'd fight him every step of the way to get where she wanted to go.

On the way out, she stopped in her dad's office. She'd thought about the protocol they were using, and it just didn't make sense. "How much do you pay the installers?" she asked when he told her to have a seat opposite his desk.

"It depends, but with overtime, some of them are bringing home six figures."

Ally bit her lip. "Dad, I just watched four different guys spend a half hour of their day throwing out trash and shopping for parts in the warehouse. Wouldn't it be more cost effective to have someone else do that? And considering these guys are on overtime while they're doing these things, it's really outrageous."

He leaned back in his chair and seemed to be thinking. "What do you have in mind?"

"Let them punch out when they pull into the garage. Then hire someone from four to midnight to clean out the trash and pull the parts for the next day. Since the work orders come with a parts list, it won't be difficult. And with all the service trucks you have, it would probably work out right. Maybe thirty minutes on each truck. Even if they finished early and sat around watching television for the last few hours of their shift, you'd hire them at half the price you're paying the installation guys, and you wouldn't be paying them OT."

Her dad chuckled. "You're a smart cookie, Ally." He blew out a big sigh. "And I know I shouldn't fuel the sibling rivalry, but your brother has been in charge of the installation division for ten years and never thought of that."

Ally's shoulders sank. She didn't want more trouble with her brother and wasn't trying to show off to her father. It was just a blatantly obvious misuse of personnel. She met her dad's gaze. "I didn't mean to cause a problem."

He nodded. "I know. You're a good girl, Ally. Jimmy is maybe a little too entitled. Takes things for granted."

At one time her father's praise had meant something, although not quite so much now. Still, it was nice to hear something positive, rather than the opposite. And it was good to know her father saw her brother for what he really was.

"I'll have my assistant crunch the numbers and see what it looks like on paper."

"Sure," she said, amazed that she'd had an idea that impressed him. She kissed him on the cheek and headed out. Her apartment was just a few minutes away from Hamilton, but she drove in and did the typical after-work search for a spot close to the building. After a moment she abandoned the hope of a short walk and parked in the last row. With her tackle box in tow, she headed inside, grabbed her mail, and hiked to her fifth-floor apartment. Once inside, she collapsed on the couch, used the remote to turn on the fireplace, and then stared into the flames, thinking of the art she'd seen at the Rogan mansion.

Could it be a mere coincidence that Brodrik Rogan, a Boston native, had the same paintings that were missing from the Gardner Museum? Rocco said he was very proud of the collection and had taken the time to teach him about the pieces. That gave Ally's speculation some credence. But then again, maybe Rogan just liked art and had purchased copies to display. After all, it didn't appear the paintings were connected to the alarm system. Would he keep the stolen paintings in his house with such scant protection?

Ally fired up her laptop and searched *Christ in the Storm on the Sea of Galilee*, the huge painting that sat across from Brodrik Rogan's recliner. The first hit was an ad, offering a framed print of the painting for only $32.95. That seemed rather inexpensive, so Ally read the fine print and laughed. While the painting on Rogan's wall was more than four by five feet, this one was eight by ten inches.

She zoomed in on the painting, stared in wonder at the light hitting the waves, the ship lurching precariously toward the darkness. Rembrandt was a master of using light and shadow, which was apparent in this painting. Christ looked calm in the chaos, while fear played on the faces of the disciples on the boat. Rembrandt, disguised as a fisherman, stared right back at Ally.

Scrolling farther, she found more options to purchase a print, then information about the piece itself. The work, an oil on canvas, was painted in 1633 by Rembrandt during the Dutch Golden Age. It had previously been located in Boston in the Isabella Stewart Gardner Museum, its current location unknown since 1990, when it was stolen.

Next Ally clicked on an article from *Multi Medium*, the international magazine focusing on all forms of art. The issue was Spring 1990, and the cover photo was of an empty frame hanging on a wall, presumably in the Garner Museum. She began to read.

While many Bostonians were still celebrating St. Patrick's Day, in the early morning hours of March 18, two armed men, disguised as police officers, robbed the city of some of its most valuable treasures. Experts estimate the value of the artwork stolen from the Elizabeth Stewart Gardner Museum at $200,000,000, making it the biggest art heist since the Nazi era and the most lucrative crime in United States history

According to the museum's guards, the men rang the doorbell and demanded entry to investigate a disturbance. Although no alarm had been sent out, the guards allowed the men to enter. They were quickly restrained, allowing the thieves full run of the museum, which held priceless works by hundreds of artists from around the globe. When they left an hour later, they took with them paintings and drawings by Rembrandt, Degas, Flinck, Manet, and Vermeer, as well as a vase and a finial from a Napoleonic flag.

The rest of the article talked about the pieces that were stolen, with pictures of each, and the offer of a reward for their safe return. She scrolled, studying them, one by one.

The Concert, oil on canvas, Johannes Vermeer, painted between 1663–1666. A similar painting was hanging in the foyer of the Rogan mansion, the black-and-white tiles on his floor a perfect match to the floor in Vermeer's painting.

Christ in the Storm on the Sea of Galilee, oil on canvas, Rembrandt, 1633. This must have been Rogan's favorite, because it was displayed prominently in the study.

A Lady and Gentleman in Black, oil on canvas, Rembrandt, 1633, was also in the foyer, fitting the black-and-white theme there.

Three Mounted Jockeys, ink, rose washes, and oil pigments on brown paper, Edgar Degas, 1885. Ally hadn't seen that one, but it was small, only twelve by ten inches, and might have been on one of the shelves.

Procession on a Road near Florence, pencil and sepia wash on paper, Edgar Degas, 1857. That was in a cluster of similar works, on the wall behind Rogan. He must not have been a fan of Degas.

Study for the Programme, chalk on paper, Edgar Degas, 1884. Ally looked at that and pictured the Rogan house in her mind and could see it behind his chair.

Study for the Programme II, chalk on paper, Edgar Degas, 1884. This was very similar to the other chalk on paper with the same name and hung beside it in his study. She compared them, looking for the differences. It was like playing one of those puzzles, but after a few seconds Ally saw quite a few changes from the first to the second drawing. Most had to do with shading, but also what appeared to be musical notes had been added.

Leaving the Paddock, watercolor and pencil on paper, Edgar Degas, nineteenth century. That was another in the grouping behind Rogan's chair.

Landscape with an Obelisk, oil on oak panel, Govaert Flinck, 1638. This one was in the foyer, at the bottom of the stairs.

Portrait of the Artist as a Young Man, etching, Rembrandt, 1633, was in the bathroom.

Chez Tortoni, oil on canvas, Edouard Manet, 1875. This small painting was on an ornamental easel on the sofa table in the study.

Eagle finial, gilded bronze, Pierre-Philippe Thomire, 1813. Ally hadn't seen the eagle, but there was so much clutter in the study, it certainly could have been there.

Gu, bronze, Chinese, twelfth century BC. Once again, she pictured the study in her mind, trying to remember this piece, but she wasn't sure. She'd have to look more closely the next time.

It wasn't a perfect match, but eleven of the thirteen pieces stolen from the Gardner Museum were on display in Brodrik Rogan's home. However, she was by no means an expert, had no idea how to authenticate a painting. She knew museums and collectors did all kinds of testing on the paint, X-rays of the canvas, comparisons of technique, and more to determine if a painting was authentic. Ally could do none of that. All she had to go on was her instincts, which were telling her Rogan's paintings were the originals, stolen from the museum in Boston before Ally was even born.

"So, what now, Ally?" she asked herself out loud.

Should she just walk away, finish her job with Four H, and pretend she'd never seen the treasures lining Rogan's walls? Even though the thought was revolting, she took comfort in knowing he'd cared for the collection over the years. But what would happen after he died? Did his wife understand the value of her husband's paintings? Maybe she did, and the pieces would be preserved, perhaps in the Rogan family, or sold to other unscrupulous people in the black market. That was better than the alternative, that Winnie Rogan didn't know and didn't care what became of these works. She might hold a yard sale, like so many people did, and someone like her mom could pick up the Vermeer and paint over it. Or, worse yet, keep the frame and toss the painting. Someone like Linda would pay ten dollars for it, but what would happen when she grew tired of watching a silent concert? Ally was certain landfills around the world were filled with valuable pieces of art, discarded by survivors after their loved ones passed away.

She sighed. Doing nothing was risky. Perhaps safest for her, but not for *Christ in the Storm on the Sea of Galilee*, and not for *The Concert* or *Chez Tortoni*.

Should she call the police? That was a thought. But would they even listen to the concerns of a disgraced PA with no formal art training? Ditto for an anonymous tipster calling about a wealthy citizen. And she had to consider another thing. Rocco had told her that few guests visited the Rogan estate, so wouldn't Brodrik assume she had ratted on him? Would he retaliate? They'd never found the body of the parts guy who was supposed to testify against him. Would she meet the same fate?

She took a big, deep breath and slowly exhaled.

She could take them. Repatriate the stolen works and collect the reward. She was in Rogan's house, she had access. But how? How could someone like her snatch all those paintings? Some were small enough to walk out with, hidden in her big winter coat, but the others were quite large. And she couldn't even imagine rolling a four-hundred-year-old canvas and stuffing it into a tube. She looked at the Flinck painting, *Landscape with an Obelisk*. It was done in oil on wood. How could she ever get that out of the house? Even if she took the risk and rolled the larger canvases, it was physically impossible to roll wood.

Wow, Ally, are you seriously considering this? Because if he murdered his wife and the parts guy, what would he do to you if you're caught?

Ally's growling stomach moved her to action, and she pushed aside her laptop and headed to the kitchen. She studied her near-empty fridge before deciding on a grilled cheese sandwich with tomato soup for dunking. While the food was heating, her mind was racing, and after she finished eating, she returned to the couch and her computer.

The Elizabeth Stewart Gardner Museum was located in a nice area of Boston, between Northeastern University and the children's hospital and Dana Farber Cancer Institute. A populated area. The thieves who'd robbed it had been brazen. Daring. They'd stolen *thirteen* pieces of art. Thirteen. An odd collection, according to the article she'd read before.

They'd left behind much more expensive pieces and took things that were not so valuable. Was it the thieves' preference? The police didn't seem to think the choices were random, but Ally didn't know why they'd reached that conclusion.

Did Brodrik Rogan organize the heist? Or was he just the lucky guy who purchased the collection from the thieves?

And then she thought of something Rocco had said, and she sat back against the couch, staring with unfocused eyes as she pondered it. "That could work," she said aloud. "Maybe."

With her fingers flying across her laptop keys, she searched the internet for a store that sold paintings, copies of famous works. When she found the right website, she began browsing, until she found a replica she liked. With a click she added it to her cart, then returned to shop a little more. After a few point-and-clicks, she had over a thousand dollars' worth of fake masterpieces in her virtual cart.

What are you doing? she asked herself. It was way more money than she could afford, and it would take months for her to pay off her credit card. Not only that, but this little plan of hers could land her in jail. Or the morgue.

Leaning back, she closed her eyes and took a deep breath. She'd lived such a boring life for so long, just getting up and going to work every day, never doing anything wrong. And look where she'd ended up. She was struggling just to get through each day, without much hope for what came next. At least this plan gave her something to think about besides her troubles. It gave her hope.

She went back to the internet and searched for the Gardner paintings again. What were they worth? How much was the reward?

"Holy Mother," Ally said when she read it. Ten million dollars for the return of all the pieces. In truth, the reward seemed a little light, considering the value of the paintings, but still, ten million was a lot of dollars.

Her job as a PA—her former job, actually—paid about $100,000 a year. She'd have to work a hundred years to earn ten million. She wasn't sure if she had one more year in her, and if she worked for Four H, she'd be employed until the age of four hundred to make that much.

The figure certainly made the prospect of robbing Brodrik Rogan a little more palatable.

It wasn't just the money, though, or even her concern over the fate of the paintings, considering Brodrik Rogan's state of poor health. Ally needed to redeem herself. She felt like such a failure, such a disappointment to her family. Her brothers were both successful. Jimmy, of course, worked at Hamilton Security, and Kevin was working toward partnership in his law firm. Sure, they'd been a little wild when they were young, but by the time they were Ally's age, they'd both settled down and started families. Ally's one serious relationship had been with someone so far in the corner of her closet she was marrying a man to maintain her cover. With a sigh, Ally turned back to her computer. Just for fun, she searched Raphael's *Portrait of a Young Man*, the other painting she'd discovered in the bathroom off Brodrik Rogan's study. The work, which had disappeared from Nazi hands during the war, was purchased—in absentia—by the National Museum in Krakow. They were offering a reward of $100,000,000 for its safe return.

Whoa, Ally thought. *This can't be real. These paintings can't be real.* But the stolen art had to be somewhere, right? Why not at Brodrik Rogan's estate?

Okay, Ally. Assume they're real. Now what are you going to do about it?

Her finger hovered over the purchase icon on the computer, when suddenly another thought flashed in her mind. If she purchased copies of Rogan's paintings, then stole his, the transaction could probably be traced back to her credit card. And her computer. The police would have her in cuffs about an hour after Rogan discovered the switch.

But if Rogan had the original paintings, he'd never call the police. He'd chop her fingers off one by one until she told him what she'd done with the pieces, and then he'd strangle her with his big bare hands.

No, she thought. He'd call Rocco, and his friend at the front gate. He'd do the strangling.

Ally looked at her computer screen, at the empty frames on the wall of the Gardner Museum. Then she clicked the *pay now* button, entered her credit card information, and put herself even further in debt.

"You've got this," she said aloud when she was done.

"No, you don't," a little voice whispered back.

CHAPTER TEN

The Lion's Den

One day didn't seem like nearly enough orientation for dealing with someone like Brodrik Rogan, Ally thought as she presented herself at the gate the next morning. No wonder Macie had quit and taken another position. Ally wiped her sweaty palms on her scrub pants and let out a deep sigh before ringing the intercom bell at the front gate late the next morning.

"Your clearance didn't come through yet," the guard said over the intercom. "You'll have to be escorted to the house."

"Okay," Ally said. "How long will this take? I'm on a schedule." She'd made a wrong turn after leaving Tommy's house and didn't realize it for ten minutes. Add that to the clumsiness inherent to doing a new job with new equipment, and she was running half an hour behind.

The guard didn't answer, and after waiting ten minutes, she phoned Greg to explain the situation.

"Let me see what I can do," he said, before telling her he'd reassign the rest of her patients to another provider.

Half an hour later, a snowmobile appeared at the gate, and Ally followed the driver, a short, stocky man, back to the house. He was dressed from head to toe in black, and his bulky snowsuit made him look huge. He pulled up beside the portico and then motioned for Ally to drive up toward the door, where Rocco was waiting for her. After a few words with Rocco, the guy on the snowmobile took off toward the back of the house.

Unlike the other man, who was prepared for the arctic, Rocco wore only a black sweater with his jeans, and a very large gun hung from his hip. A huge smile appeared on his face when his eyes met Ally's.

Fuck, she thought. *Just what I need.* She'd thought Mr. Rogan was joking when he'd mentioned a date with Rocco. Or maybe pushing her buttons. She hoped nothing would come of this, because she didn't need that complication. She'd be friendly but professional.

"Hi, Rocco," she said with a smile.

"Hey. How are you? I'm sorry for the delay at the gate. It seems one of the grandchildren was irresponsible with the gas cans for the snowmobile." He chuckled warmly and shrugged.

Ally had learned long ago not to judge, and people almost never fooled her, but Rocco surprised her. He was intelligent and well-spoken and seemed to have a soft side. Yet he looked like an Olympic bodybuilder and carried a handgun longer than Ally's legs.

Ally smiled and waved off his concerns. She didn't want to lead him on, but he was definitely someone she didn't want to piss off, either. It might even behoove her to have him in her good graces. "It's okay. I caught up on the news on my phone and read my email." She was surprised she'd had phone service, but grateful.

"Sometimes we have cell service outside, and sometimes we don't. Depends on the weather." He pointed to unsightly electrical lines connected to the house. "We still have a land line for that reason."

That made sense. "Good idea."

"Anyway, I'm sorry we delayed you. I hope this doesn't mean you have to work too late today."

Ally shook her head. "My boss canceled the rest of my schedule, so that works."

"Ah, off early on Friday. Any plans for the weekend? Or will I see you here?"

His look of interest was unmistakable, and Ally thought she should throw some water on the embers before they grew into a fire she'd have difficulty controlling. "I do work some weekends, but not this one. I have a date Saturday, so that should be fun."

Rocco's eyes squinted a fraction, but he smiled anyway. "Well, have a good time."

After escorting her into the house, he instructed her to wait. He proceeded to Mr. Rogan's study door, poked his head inside, and announced her arrival. She heard Rogan's reply from thirty feet away.

"Let her wait."

"Mr. Rogan says he'll be with you shortly," Rocco informed her, as he waved to one of the chairs beneath *The Concert*.

Ally took a seat, and then Rocco disappeared around the corner. When he was gone, she stood and pulled her phone from her jacket pocket, then casually began snapping pictures. She shot the entire room, then each of the paintings on the walls, before sitting back down and continuing to read her email.

A few minutes later Rocco reappeared. "Is there anything I can get you?" he asked sweetly.

"Normally, I don't need lunch on the job, but it appears things are a little different here…"

He shrugged. "Just yell if you need me," he said and disappeared the way he came. Ally listened and heard a door close and realized he must have an office nearby.

After a moment, she went back to her phone, and she checked her watch ten minutes later. Apparently, Greg knew Mr. Rogan well, and he'd been smart to reschedule her afternoon, because she sat there for another forty minutes. Finally, he appeared at his door, acting as if he'd been waiting for her. "Ally, you're here!" he said with delight. "Come in!"

He stood beside the open door until she entered, then closed it behind her before shuffling across the room. This was the first time Ally had seen him walk, and it was a frightening experience. He swayed and tottered, almost toppling over. Using the furniture for support, he made it to his chair and fell into it with a sigh of relief. He was quite winded when he spoke.

"How was your drive? Did you find the place okay?"

Ally's anxiety jacked up a notch as she found herself alone with him, and she worked to contain it. *Deep breath in, then out.* "I did make a wrong turn, but I figured it out pretty quickly and retraced my steps. I paid attention when Linda brought me yesterday."

"Yes, well, these country roads can be confusing. It's easy to miss a turn. Or you could drive off the road, and no one would find you until spring."

Ally knew he spoke the truth, but she wished he hadn't. Was it helpful advice or a veiled threat?

She'd be optimistic and take it as advice. "I've lived here my entire life, so I'm kind of used to it."

"You'd be lost in the city, though, huh?"

"Probably. How's that leg?"

"It doesn't seem any different," he said as he looked down at it.

"Let me take a look." She pulled the hassock next to him and went to work. When the wound was exposed, she sat back and examined it. It was essentially the same as the day before, and that was good news. It had been getting worse, so no change was actually better.

She told him her thoughts as she dressed the wound and felt much more relaxed than she had before she'd engrossed herself in her work.

"When will that Q-Tip test come back?"

"The wound culture? Probably Monday. Maybe sooner, but no worries. The treatment is working."

"Do I look like the kind of guy who worries?" he asked.

Ally sat up and found him staring at her again. "Well, actually, you do. You just hide it, I think."

He roared. "I like you, Ally."

She packaged her trash and took it to the restroom, along with her tackle box, and after washing her hands, she snapped pictures of the two portraits on the walls. When she went back to the study, he was sitting behind his desk chair.

"So, will I see you tomorrow?" he asked.

"No. And shouldn't you have that leg elevated?"

"In a minute. Who'll be here tomorrow?"

Ally didn't know. "Who normally comes on weekends?"

"Oh, that's Joanne."

"So it probably won't change. We have a regular weekend staff."

"Any plans?"

Ally looked at him. "As a matter of fact, I do. I have a date." She didn't tell him the date was with her mother.

"With who? Where is he taking you?"

"It's a she. We're going to the Schemel Forum, at the University of Scranton."

"And your date is a woman?"

Ally nodded.

He ran his tongue across his teeth, causing his upper lip to bulge out, but after a moment, he nodded, too. "Okay, then. What's this Smelly Forum?"

Ally laughed but didn't correct him. What was the point? "It's a lecture series. This one happens to be about African art."

"I like art," he commented.

"I noticed," Ally said.

"My mom used to drag us kids to the museum when we were little. Anytime it was free. We were poor, but she wanted us to have some culture."

"You're never too poor to appreciate art. Especially now, with so much on the internet."

"If you can afford the internet."

"Touché."

"I guess you like art, too."

Ally nodded. "I'm a fan. I dabble a little, too. Mostly in framing."

His eyebrows lifted an inch. "Really? That's an odd hobby."

"Just something I picked up. My mom's an artist, so I started out working with her. I like to pull apart old frames and refinish them, then put them back together."

"Is that a hard job?"

"It can be time consuming, especially if they need several coats of paint, because you have to let them dry. Skill wise, it's pretty easy."

"You like to work with your hands. It soothes you."

Ally blew out a breath. "Yes. It does."

"I work in the gardens. Just a little really. I have a landscaper who does the hard work, but I plant some seeds and grow them and put a few plants in the ground when it thaws."

"Did you ever think of moving to Florida?" The question was out of her mouth before she could filter it, but she didn't apologize.

"Isn't that where all wealthy New Yorkers end up?" He laughed. Ally shrugged.

"I wish I could. But I can't leave the Northeast."

"How come?" Ally wondered out loud. *Probation?*

"Let me tell you something, Ally. About kids. You don't have any, do you?"

Ally shook her head.

"Well, they're vultures. I have six of them, and each one of them would slit the others' throats to have control of my business. And my money. If I got any farther away than a coupla hours' drive, I'd have a funeral on my hands. Or two or three."

"It sounds dreadful."

"Don't get me started." He shook his head in disgust.

"How'd you end up here? In the Poconos?"

"My mother. She loves it here."

"I can understand that," Ally said, wondering how old his mother was. If he was eighty, she had to be close to a hundred. "Where is she now?"

"Oh, she hates Winnie. She goes to Florida for the winter. Can you imagine? She's ninety-seven years old and still going strong. When she comes back from Florida, Winnie goes to New York."

Ally wanted to laugh. He made her problems with women seem trivial. "Where's Joseph today?"

"He's napping, thank the Lord. C'mon with me. I want to show you my other children. The ones who don't misbehave."

Ally picked up her tackle box. Greg had emphasized how important it was to keep it safe, and she didn't intend to take any chances.

Brodrik Rogan pushed himself up from his chair, and they made a slow trek to the foyer. Ally watched again, worried as he walked.

"Mr. Rogan, have you thought of using a walker?"

"Oh, fuck that. You might as well cut my balls off if you force me to use that thing."

Ally bit her lip. "It would be a big problem if you fall. You're on a blood thinner, and if you hit your head, you'd be a goner."

"Why are all you medical people so negative?"

Ally thought about that question for a moment as she watched him work his way down the wall beside the staircase.

"Mr. Rogan, have you considered physical therapy? You could work on your strength and on walking, so you'll be able to play with Joseph."

He paused and turned, smiling. "See, was that so hard? Plant a good seed, not a bad one."

Ally had never heard that expression before, but she liked it. She could make it into a sign and hang it at Four H.

As they approached a door near the rear of the staircase, Rocco emerged, his right arm hovering over his gun. "Everything okay, sir?"

"Peachy. I'm taking the girl to see my greenhouse."

"Oh, that sounds nice. Mind if I tag along? I like to see how everything's coming along."

"Just don't get in my way. You'll trip me."

Rocco stepped aside, and they followed silently as Brodrik walked through a doorway, into another foyer. To the left was the kitchen, ahead was another small room, and to the right was a conservatory. Ally followed him in, instantly energized by the light from the floor-to-ceiling windows. The floor was composed of tile, but everywhere it was littered with dirt. A dozen tables were lined up in rows, and each held small plants in plastic trays, growing under greenhouse lights.

"Fetch me a box, Rocco," Brodrik commanded as he paused, holding onto the wall.

"What kind of box?"

"A cardboard box!" he boomed. Then in a softer voice he said, "I want to give Ally some plants."

Ally shook her head. "Oh, no, Mr. Rogan. I really can't use any plants."

"Why not? Don't you have a garden?"

"I don't. I live in an apartment."

He looked at her in disbelief. "Even when I was a kid, when we lived in an apartment, we always had a patch of garden. What's the world coming to?"

In truth, she loved to work in the gardens at her parents' house, but she was hesitant to reveal too much to this man. And any gift, no matter how small, changed the game a little.

"Do you have parents?"

Reluctantly, Ally nodded. "I do."

"Good. Give 'em to them. You've never tasted tomatoes like these. Friend of mine brought the seeds over from Italy. Just wait till you taste them. Mmm."

"That's very nice of you," Ally said, as she realized she'd get out of there sooner if she quit arguing.

"Do you suffer from melancholy?" He looked at her pointedly.

If he only knew the depth of her recent despair. "Not really," she said.

He ignored her. "I'm gonna give you some flowers. Nothing like flowers if you're in a sad mood. They'll cheer you right up."

He began walking again, between the rows of tables, holding on with one hand and pointing out each of the plants with the other. He had vegetables of all varieties in addition to his tomatoes, and dozens of annual flowers. He told her a little about each as they passed, how much sun and water they preferred, and where he planted them on his estate. Ally listened, not just out of courtesy, but because she too loved flowers in the garden.

She found herself asking questions as she followed him. Rocco returned with a cardboard box, and Brodrik pushed it along the table, filling it with plants as they walked and talked.

"Do you have a problem with deer?" Ally asked. "They love to eat the flowers at my parents'."

"No. We shoot the deer," he said, as if talking about swatting a fly. He continued talking, but Ally lost some of her enthusiasm after that remark. Ten minutes later, she thanked him for the tour and for the large box of plants he'd given her. "Buy a grow-light. They'll do great."

Ally had no idea what she was going to do with the box of plants, but she thanked him again for his generosity. "I'm going to take off now, Mr. Rogan. I'll see you Monday."

"Rocco will help you out. And make sure Joanne understands what you're doing. You know your stuff. I think it feels better already."

"In the last twenty minutes?"

"I'm a fast learner."

Rocco picked up the box of plants, and Ally hoisted her tackle box with one hand and waved with the other as she headed out the door.

CHAPTER ELEVEN

A Friendly Face

As she'd done on the previous days, Ally went from Four H after her shift and then headed to Hamilton Security, where she spent more time with the technicians coming in from their installation jobs. A few hours later, when the last truck was back for the night, she picked up a pizza and a bottle of wine and headed home. To her delight, she found a pile of boxes in the mailroom, all addressed to her. She grabbed the trolley and loaded the parcels, then took them up in the elevator before returning the trolley to the lobby.

As she ate her dinner and sipped her wine, Ally sat back and relaxed. The wine helped. Her counselor had cautioned her about drinking, in fact told her not to, but she'd talked to Jess about it, and she thought it was okay. Ally had never abused alcohol, had never used it as a crutch. She and Jess would monitor it and make sure it wasn't becoming another problem.

She thought about her week. The beginning had been a drag, just hanging around at the office doing her orientation work. The last two days, though, had been good ones. She'd learned a lot, and it felt good to be doing something again. It wasn't the ER, but that was okay. She could find meaning in this work—giving people who had pain or were dying some comfort and care, making them feel important for a few minutes during a difficult day. It wasn't what she wanted forever, but it would do for now.

Her parents, finally sensing she wasn't mere seconds away from a fatal overdose, were going to the club for dinner. Without her. And after being busy nonstop for the week and a half she'd been out of the halfway house, Ally was happy to have a drama-free night. Since most of the groceries her mother had purchased were gone, she planned to head to Wegmans in a little while, to restock her cupboards. Now, though, she was going to have a little Christmas.

She quickly washed her dishes, then went to work with her scissors, cutting open the long strips of tape that sealed the boxes holding her recent purchases.

Ally unrolled a small canvas and saw a gentleman in black staring back at her. "Chez Tortoni," she said aloud. "It's nice to see you again." It had been only a few hours, but Ally remembered their last meeting vividly, when she'd seen the painting on the table behind Brodrik Rogan's couch.

"Let's see your friends," Ally told the gentleman seated in the Cafe Tortoni as she reached for one of the large boxes. This canvas was a landscape, a copy of Manet's *Road Near Florence*.

Next to emerge from cardboard was *The Concert*. Even the copy was beautiful. Ally reached for her phone and scrolled through her photos until she found the painting in Rogan's grand hall. She zoomed in on the photo and then looked at the canvas, then back to the photo. "Okay," she said, nodding. "That won't be too hard."

Next came a canvas reprint of *Landscape with an Obelisk*. The original was painted on wood, but the canvas looked pretty good as well. She scrolled through the photos until she found the painting and zoomed in. "Yes," she said. "I can do this."

After she dispatched the rest of the boxes, she piled the canvases on the floor near her bedroom door and took the boxes to the chute. Back in her apartment, she stared at the pile. "Ally, you've gone mad," she said aloud.

Then she changed into jeans and a sweater, pulled on a warm pair of boots, and headed to the grocery store.

It was after nine when she grabbed her shopping cart and began filling it with groceries, enjoying the enormity of the fruits and vegetables department. She'd shopped during her time at the halfway house, but the grocery stores were not an *experience* like this one was. It was amazing. Wegmans had everything, and it all looked so bright and fresh and inviting.

Ally picked up bananas and studied the bunch as if seeing them for the first time. Then she tore off three and added them to her cart. Next, she grabbed a basket of strawberries the size of baseballs and blueberries the size of grapes, then headed to the cheese department. This was such a simple task, pushing the cart around, so mundane, but toward the end of her downward spiral, even grocery shopping had become too much for her. One day, just before she entered the rehab center, she'd visited McDonald's for breakfast, lunch, and dinner. Food hadn't been a priority then, but when she'd opened her refrigerator and found it completely empty—not a jar of pickles or a bottle of ketchup in sight—she knew she was in trouble.

Wandering the aisles, buying things she didn't need just because she wanted them—it felt so good. So normal.

In the frozen foods section, Ally studied the ice cream flavors, contemplating buying several. As she was about to choose the chocolate marshmallow, she heard someone call her name.

"Ally!"

Turning, she gazed into the big, brown eyes of Dr. Maria Alfano, and her knees went weak.

Shit! Fuck! In the time she'd been back, she'd been keeping out of sight, steering clear of public places, and she'd successfully avoided everyone she'd ever known from her prior life. Why hadn't she guessed she'd see someone at Wegmans? And not just any someone, but a very special someone.

Maria had just finished her residency and had started working in the ER a month before Ally went to Marworth. In that month, they'd had a dozen conversations, and despite the awful place she was in, Ally had felt happy with their blossoming friendship, excited about the prospect of something more.

Now, she felt mortified. Of all the people she could possibly run into in the frozen foods section at Wegmans, Maria was the last one Ally wanted to see.

But from the smile on her face, it didn't look like Maria felt the same way.

Rushing from behind her cart, she hugged Ally, then stepped back to study her. "You look great! How are you? How do you feel? Is everything okay?"

Ally couldn't help laughing as she nodded. "It's okay."

"I love your hair! It's gorgeous. I almost didn't recognize you!"

"I felt like I needed a change." Ally shrugged.

Maria met Ally's gaze. "That's understandable."

"So, how are you?"

"Okay. I'm okay. When did you…I don't know? Get out? Is that what you say?" She made a goofy face as she lowered her voice, and Ally bit her lip to keep from laughing.

"I was released from treatment last week."

Maria's face lit up. "I am so happy for you. I've thought about you all the time. I miss our chats over the X-ray screen." It seemed they were always in the vicinity of the X-ray computer system at work, and one would always share her cases with the other. Ally had to admit, she dragged her feet a little, always hoping Maria would come by, and more often than not, she did. They'd discuss a case, but there was more. There were *the looks*, the excuses to linger for a moment longer, the subtle suggestions that they should get something to eat after work. Maria was definitely interested. Back then, Ally didn't have the energy. Now, though? That was a thought to motivate her.

"Thank you. You're very sweet." Ally was embarrassed, but the sincerity of Maria's words eased her discomfort just a little. "Thank you."

"So what are you going to do now? When will you come to work again?"

Ally sighed. "I lost my license, you know. I gave it up. I'm in a program to get it back, but—we'll see." Ally didn't share her doubts about wanting it. It wasn't just the stigma of her past. It might be too much of a temptation, handling all the controlled substances. It had been a constant struggle before. Seeing all those opioids at work had nearly made her salivate, and she wasn't eager to repeat that experience.

"So are you just hanging out?"

Ally shook her head. "I started a job with a home-health agency."

Maria's face lit up again. "That's great! You're not wasting any time. Get back on the horse."

"This is more like a pony."

Maria cracked up, and Ally joined her, and then people in the frozen foods section began looking at them.

When they got themselves under control, Maria stared at her, tenderly. Sweetly. "What are you doing tonight? What's for dinner?" she asked as she nodded toward Ally's cart.

"I've already had a pizza. But I might have mozzarella sticks and wing bites when I get home. Just because, you know, I can."

"Ooh. That combination could be fatal. You can't do it." She paused, lowered her voice, and looked right into Ally's eyes. "Have something with me. I'll cook, and we can catch up."

If Ally hadn't gone away, she would have dreamed of this. But now she wasn't so sure. Was it smart, for either of them?

"It's just dinner," Maria said, seeming to sense her hesitation. "I don't expect sex."

Ally did her best to keep a straight face as she met Maria's gaze. "I'm not sure I can agree to those terms."

Maria's eyes smoldered. "We can negotiate."

Ally put the back of her hand to her forehead and leaned against the freezer dramatically. "Wow. This is not what I expected when I came to Wegmans."

Maria nodded. "Yeah. Me neither. Wanna follow me?"

Ally couldn't believe this, but she wasn't going to say no. "It's cold enough that my ice cream won't melt."

Maria eyed the container. "Maybe you could share."

Ally opened the freezer door and grabbed another quart. "I'll get you your own."

They headed to the register and paid for their respective purchases, then walked to their cars. They laughed when they discovered they were parked beside each other, and Ally followed Maria in her older-model Jeep to Interstate 81. They headed north, then took the Clarks Summit exit and made a few turns into a development Ally knew well. They drove past Gretchen's parents' house and pulled into a driveway a few doors down. After grabbing the ice cream, the wing bites, and the mozzarella sticks, she followed Maria into the garage.

"I know this house," Ally said. "Did you get the pool table with it?"

"Yes!" Maria said. "I swear I'm going to learn to play. How do you know the place?" she asked as they walked into the seventies-ish kitchen carrying their Wegmans bags.

"My best friend—former," Ally laughed, "former best friend, grew up a few doors down."

"I detect a story there," she said as she heaved her groceries onto the counter. Ally followed and did the same.

"I'm sure you've already heard it. High school crush, college romance—all secret, of course, because then she got engaged to a man, and we are no longer friends of any sort, best or otherwise."

Maria's voice grew soft as she leaned against the counter and stared at Ally sympathetically. "Yes. I have heard that one. Thankfully, I think it happens less and less."

"It's okay. By the time we broke up, I was sort of disillusioned. But I do miss my friend."

"That's the hardest part of a breakup, isn't it?"

Ally nodded. "You sound like you've been there."

"There are no new stories."

The words took Ally back to the halfway house, where one of the counselors had said that. There was nothing she hadn't heard.

"So when did you buy the place? I didn't know the Hummels moved."

"I moved in for Thanksgiving. They bought a townhouse, saved themselves a lot of work."

Ally looked around. She'd been in the house a number of times when she'd been visiting Gretchen, and it looked the same as it had fifteen years ago. It had been dated then. "At least you get to make it just how you want it. Your colors and style and all that."

Maria nodded. "I spend my free time going through these DIY books, getting ideas."

Ally's eyes shot up. "You're going to remodel it yourself?"

She chuckled. "Uh, no. But it's a great way to get ideas. I'm going to start with the master bath and put in a huge tub and a rain shower, then convert the bedroom next to the master into a closet. I have five bedrooms, so I won't miss that one."

"Unless you plan to have four kids, then maybe."

Maria looked at her sideways. "Only two. But not yet. First I have to work, and make some money, and pay for materials and all that stuff. Not to mention saving for retirement and getting a car that was born this millennium."

Ally realized how lucky she was to have the free rent at her apartment. However, if she didn't have so much disposable cash, she might not have been able to afford to buy so many pills. She pushed the thoughts to the back of her mind. It wasn't her parents' fault she'd made bad choices. They'd given her opportunities. She had just chosen to fuck them up.

"That will be fun, doing it a little at a time."

Maria'd been putting away the groceries while they talked, and finally she stopped moving. "Are you hungry? You said you had pizza, but…"

"Just one slice," she said as she reached into her bag. "But I have great stuff right here." Waving the box of wing bites, she grinned.

"I suppose that would be easier than cooking."

"It sure would. Not that I don't trust you…"

"Hey! I happen to be a decent cook."

"You're not selling it, Maria."

"You're right. Let's just open a bottle of wine and have a heart attack for dinner." Her smile quickly morphed into fear. "Wait. You can drink, right?"

Ally nodded and chuckled. "I can."

"Then let's do it."

Ally prepared the food to go into the oven while Maria opened the wine and poured two glasses. She lit a candle, and they sat at her kitchen table to wait for the oven to do its thing.

"How's work?" Ally asked as they looked at each other.

Maria shrugged. "It's a job."

"You don't love it? Because it always seemed like you did."

"I do. It's just…a lot of people die."

That was hard for Ally, too. "I get that."

"I think I'm going to study for the board exam in addiction medicine."

Ally was surprised, but she wasn't. They'd never talked about the subject, yet here she was, a recovering opioid addict, sitting in Maria's kitchen. "Can you do that?"

She nodded. "I just passed my emergency med boards, so that's out of the way. Now I can do a sub-specialty. And I like addiction."

Ally laughed and took a sip of her wine. "That's an interesting way to put it."

"You know what I mean," she said, then sipped her own wine. "My sister is in recovery."

"Oh," Ally said. That explained a lot. Maybe this little candlelight dinner wasn't about anything Maria felt for Ally as a woman, but as a patient. "What did she use?"

The oven timer began beeping, and Maria jumped up to check the food. "Everything, just about. She's been doing well, though. Sober for three years, dating a nice guy. Back at work. It's all good."

"That's great to hear."

They were quiet while Maria readied the food. Then she came back with the wings and blue cheese dressing, and plates for them.

"What were you using?" Maria asked as she slid some food onto her plate.

Ally wasn't sure if this was professional curiosity or Maria's attempt at being friendly, but she needed to know. "Is this Dr. Maria or friend Maria asking?"

Maria grew still at the question. "I'm so sorry, Ally. I didn't mean to pry. I just want you to know I'm not judging your mistakes. This happened to my sister, and it can happen to anyone. I was attracted to you before this happened, and when I saw you tonight in Wegmans, I just felt like I had a second chance."

The look on Maria's face was so sweet, it melted Ally's heart.

"Oxycodone," she said softly.

"And how are you without them?"

"I have some pain in my shoulder, but it's really not too bad. I liked the way the drugs made me feel. Not high, but happy. They gave me a sense of well-being. But I don't feel unwell without them." She paused. "I feel scared, but not because I don't have drugs. I'm just not certain where to go from here. Professionally, personally. I pissed off a lot of my friends, and I'm not sure I want to go back to the ER."

"Why not?"

Ally told her.

"That's understandable. I guess it's all the bad shit we deal with, but people in the ER can be heartless."

"Yeah, they can."

"I'm not sure if this helps, but I haven't heard anyone talking about you. I didn't even know you'd been released."

"I'm sure they'll have plenty to say when they find out."

Maria shrugged. "Fuck them."

Ally laughed. If only it were that easy. "I appreciate you telling me about your sister."

"I'll introduce you. She's amazing." Maria's face glowed as she spoke of her sister, who'd been a studious, shy young lady and made some bad choices in college, resulting in a spiral that ended in an overdose. "It was the scariest moment of my life. And as a doctor, I felt so helpless. I could save people having heart attacks, but I couldn't help my baby sister with her drug problem."

Ally nodded patiently as she listened. It was so obvious that Maria loved her sister and shared her pain, and Ally wished she could climb across the table and hug her. Instead, she reached across and squeezed her hand. Maria squeezed back and didn't let go as their eyes met. This is nice, Ally thought, as she sensed Maria's pain ease a little.

Maria's voice was softer when she continued. "But fortunately, there were great people who could help her. She's worked hard, and it hasn't been easy, but she's going to beat this disease."

Ally looked from the place their hands met to Maria's eyes. "What's her name?"

"Brianna."

"Thank you for sharing your story with me."

"I'm happy I had the chance. I was afraid I'd never see you again."

Though they'd flirted during the month they'd worked together, they'd never exchanged phone numbers.

"If you give me your number, I promise to call," Ally said.

"Oh, I'm not letting you out of here without getting digits."

They cleared the dishes, and Ally leaned back against the counter watching Maria. Her brown hair was cut to just below her ears and had a wave that didn't come from a bottle. It looked thick and rich, and Ally would have liked to run her fingers through it. She'd kiss her neck, at the place where she might feel her heartbeat, and nibble her earlobes, right around the snowflakes hanging there. Her brown eyes would close, and she'd kiss the lids and, finally, that full, beautiful mouth.

"Hello?"

Ally heard Maria speaking and had to force herself back from fantasy island.

"You were far away," Maria said softly. "Okay?"

Ally smiled. "Okay. But I think it's time for me to head home. I have work in the morning."

Maria rolled her eyes. "Me too."

They exchanged phone numbers and made tentative plans to see each other Sunday evening.

They walked out through the garage, and before she knew what was happening, Maria wrapped Ally in a hug. It was gentle this time. Ally hadn't bothered to zip her coat, and Maria nestled into it. Warmth infused her. They were almost exactly the same size, and the softness of Maria's breasts was the next thing Ally noticed as they settled into each other. Then Maria pulled back slightly and found Ally's eyes. A small smile appeared on her lips, and then she leaned forward again, focused on Ally's mouth.

The kiss was just a peck, a soft meeting of lips that started and ended before Ally could do anything to alter its course. Yet it had the impact of a bomb, as her heart rate exploded and her senses dimmed, and when Maria pulled back, Ally couldn't think of anything but more.

"Wow," Ally murmured.

"You've been wowing me since the day we met."

"Same."

"I'm so happy I decided to drag my butt to Wegmans tonight. Drive carefully," she said.

Ally nodded. *You've got this.*

CHAPTER TWELVE

Work and Play

Ally had been warned to dress for the weather, so she wore her stadium coat over her warmest boots that morning and arrived at Hamilton just after seven. She'd thought about the kiss on the drive home, and then again as she brushed her teeth, and of course as she stared into the darkness from beneath the blankets on her bed. It had made her tingle, but more importantly, it had given her hope.

Maybe she wasn't as broken as she thought. If someone like Maria still found her attractive, maybe there was a reason.

Maybe. Or maybe she was a project for a budding addiction specialist. Ally hoped that wasn't the case. It couldn't be that, right? Maria had confessed that her attraction had been instantaneous. Well, before she knew about Ally's problems. *It was real*, Ally told herself. *It is real. The kiss was real.*

She'd fallen asleep thinking of it, and she'd been up before the alarm, made waffles for breakfast, and topped them with all those juicy berries. She was one of the first to arrive at the office, and she was off on her sales call just a little while later.

The house they were visiting was in the foothills of the Poconos, not far from the Rogan estate. It wasn't quite a house, though, Ally realized as they drove along a snow-covered drive. It was a humongous two-story structure, framed, but with only parts of a roof and some walls in place. It wasn't quite ready for human habitation.

The owner, Ted, met them in the driveway and explained there had been a lot of theft and property damage due to the price of building materials, and he wanted to deter would-be thieves by arming the place.

They walked the perimeter of the two-acre property, with Lisa stopping to take notes every so often. She spoke aloud, for both their benefit, saying things like "fifteen feet of trees between the right edge of the property and the property line" and "a hundred feet of clearing behind the house before a forty-foot stand of dense trees." Next, they circled the house, taking note of the location of windows and doors, on both floors.

They stepped through what would be a grand front door, and Ted gave them the tour. Lisa asked questions about his ideas. Outdoor cameras? Indoor cameras? Both? Motion-activated or continuous? How many control panels? They discussed the best place for motion detectors and smoke and water detectors, and two hours later, they headed back the way they'd come.

"I had no idea this process was so detailed," Ally said.

"There are certainly many options. My job is to explain them."

"He seems to want it all."

"He'll regret getting notifications on a motion-activated camera in the woods. Animals, you know."

"It's nice to watch animals on the security system." Ally did it all the time at her parents' house.

"Not at three in the morning."

Ally snorted. "Good point."

They were back at the office by noon, and Ally thanked Lisa before saying good-bye and turning her car toward the Waverly house. She had plans with her mom that night, but she had work to do before then. She found her parents in the kitchen, rearranging the contents of the kitchen cabinets—the picture of domestic bliss.

"I'm going to head out to the studio," she informed them.

"Would you like lunch?" her mom asked.

"That would be great," Ally replied as she set an alarm on her phone.

Her mom motioned to the canvas Ally had brought with her. "What's in the box?"

"A painting I want to frame."

"Anything good?"

"A copy I bought," Ally said as she escaped from the room, giving no details. What she was planning was illegal, and potentially dangerous, and the less her parents knew about it, the better. She changed clothes, then headed to the studio and immediately went to work. She found a piece of oak panel, three millimeters thick, and cut it to the perfect size. Next, she cleaned it to remove the sawdust, then painted on canvas glue. Using an old ruler, she smoothed the glue across the entire front of the wood. When she had an even surface, she removed the canvas from the tube and carefully placed it on the oak, then smoothed out all the wrinkles and air bubbles with her hands. After working it for a few minutes, she felt the glue starting to set, but that was fine. She'd done a good job matching the edges, so she wouldn't need to cut the canvas at all. The frame would hide them.

She was cleaning her tools when the timer on her phone began beeping. Before heading in for lunch, she put the oak aside to dry and pulled out the pieces of Sid Sandon's frame. She'd work on that after lunch.

"How's your project?" her mom asked while they ate.

"Good. I'm ready to paint Sid's frame."

They talked about another project her mom had picked up and their plans for the evening, and then Ally went back out to the studio, where her mom joined her. Janine immediately went to *Landscape with an Obelisk* and studied Ally's work. If she was curious about why her daughter had glued a canvas to an oak panel, she didn't ask. Instead, she busied herself with her own work, and Ally did, too.

After she painted the pieces of the Sandon frame, Ally pulled another length of wood and cut it to match the oak panel she'd cut and glued. After cleaning the wood, she painted it a silvery green. It was an interesting color for a frame, but Ally had to admit that it worked.

Hours later, her mother announced it was time to get ready for dinner. They were meeting her mom's friend, a college professor, before the lecture. After a quick shower and another change of clothes, Ally was back in the kitchen half an hour later.

She had decided to spend the night with her parents, so she could finish working on her frame in the morning, and they climbed into her mother's Lexus and headed into Clarks Summit for dinner at one of their favorite restaurants.

In the vestibule, Ally stopped short. Maria was standing there, talking with her mom's friend, Sister Bernadette, and an elderly woman with salt-and-pepper hair and an older version of Maria's face.

Seeming to sense her, Maria stopped mid-sentence and turned. A smile appeared on her face, and she seemed to glow when she recognized Ally. Stepping forward, she once again enclosed Ally in her arms, but this time for just a second.

"Hey, friend. Nice to see you."

Janine Hamilton closed the space to her daughter in a heartbeat and put a protective arm around Ally's waist. Ally looked to her and smiled and introduced them. "This is Dr. Alfano. I worked with her in the ER for a little while."

She felt her mom stiffen, ever so slightly, but Maria's warm smile defused any tension she might have felt.

"It's lovely to meet you, Doctor."

Maria bowed her head just a notch. "You as well. And please, call me Maria."

"Janine, hello!" The booming voice of Sister Bernadette echoed through the small waiting area. Then she smiled at Ally and Maria. "Wait. Do you know each other?"

Ally nodded and explained the connection.

"I should have put that together. Maria, your mom has told me so much about you," Sister said and explained how she'd taught Philomena Alfano when she had just begun her career at Marywood University. Later, they reconnected and served on the board for the food bank.

When the introductions were complete, the hostess returned to seat the Alfanos. "Hold on," Sister said. "Would you like to make this one big party? We're all going to the forum when we're done, so why not make a night of it?"

Ally nodded, excitement coursing through her. Dinner with her mom and Sister Bern would have been a hoot, but adding Maria to the mix made it a whole new level of interesting. The hostess smiled, and Ally could tell she was annoyed, yet who denies a nun a simple request like combining tables during rush hour on a Saturday night?

The three older women talked about their college experience, and Maria inched closer to Ally. "How was your day?" she asked.

"It wasn't as nice as last night, but it's getting better."

Maria blushed, and before she could respond, Ally asked about her shift in the ER.

Maria smiled. "I worked with Reese. I hope you don't mind, but I told her I ran into you and that we plan to get together for dinner tomorrow."

"I'm sure Reese is still processing that info."

"She kept a straight face and didn't ask anything other than how you're doing, but I could see the wheels turning."

"She'll be discreet."

Maria reached out and gently grabbed Ally's hand. "I'm not concerned if people know we're having dinner."

"What if it becomes more than dinner?"

Maria swallowed. "I, um. I could only hope."

Ally squeezed back, and the hostess led them to a large round table in the middle of the restaurant, where Ally and Maria sat beside each other. The talk was of Marywood. Four out of five of them were alumnae, except for Maria, who'd chosen the University of Scranton for its stellar pre-med program. They took a moment to order food and then talked about the lecture they were about to attend.

"African art could be an entire college course," Sister exclaimed. "I'll be interested to see how they've narrowed it down to an hour."

"I suppose it will be the *CliffsNotes* version," Maria responded. "But that's okay, because I know nothing about art, African or otherwise, and it will be an eye-opener for me."

"What made you decide to attend the lecture?" Janine asked.

"My mom and I are doing something fun together once a week, whether we want to or not. Someone at work suggested this lecture, so here we are."

"I'm sure you won't be disappointed," Janine said kindly. "And maybe we can make this a monthly gathering."

"Oh, yes!" Sister said. "That's a marvelous idea!"

Ally knew about Maria's work schedule. Sometimes the ER job demanded a Saturday-evening shift, but she was sure it could be worked out.

After dinner, Ally volunteered to drive, and she and Maria dropped the others off at the doors of DeNaples Center, then parked the car. "That nun's a piece of work," Maria observed.

"I have been dealing with that my entire life."

"Really?"

"They were best friends in college. That didn't stop when Bern took her vows. She spends more time at my house than she does at the convent. But she's harmless. Sweet, somewhere down deep inside. Did you enjoy your dinner?"

Maria had ordered chicken stuffed with brie and pears, and Ally pasta. "It was incredible. How was the pasta?"

"Really good," Ally said.

"I don't usually order Italian food unless I'm at an Italian restaurant because I'm so spoiled. My mom and my nonna are amazing cooks."

Ally remembered Maria's offer from the night before. "Were you planning to cook me a family recipe last night?"

"It's all I know."

"Tomorrow?" Ally asked. "Or is that too much after your day in the ER?"

"It's easy. But I might want to push it back an hour. I have to stop at Reese's for her daughter's birthday party."

Ally laughed. "Maybe we should skip dinner and just eat at the party."

Maria's eyes flew open wide. "You're going?"

Ally nodded. "I've been one of the go-to babysitters since Stephanie was born."

Maria looked shocked.

"What? Do I look like I can't change a diaper or something?"

Maria shook her head. "Nooooo," she said. "It's just an odd moonlighting job for a PA. How'd that happen?"

"One of my neighbors is a plastic surgeon, and I watched her kids when they were small. She was in the ER one day, and Reese saw us talking, and when I told her about my amazing skills with kids, she hired me."

Maria just stared.

"How do you say no to the boss?" Ally asked. "Besides, it allows me to have a nice friendship with Reese outside work. And I like her."

"Well, I do, too, but she's not going to steal you for dinner. That's at my house."

Ally liked the idea. "What can I bring? Bread? Wine?"

"Both. I already have dessert."

"Oh, we forgot the ice cream." Ally slapped her hand to her forehead.

"Maybe you did. I scooped myself a bowl before you were out of the driveway."

Ally laughed. "I had some as soon as I got home."

They entered the DeNaples Center and followed the signs for the Schemel Forum, then mingled in the lobby with the others. Ally was having a lovely evening—out of the house, relaxing, spending time with her mom and Maria, getting to know Maria's mom. It all felt so normal. Then Dr. Benjamin Ball caught her eye. He saw her before she could turn and headed their way.

Ally felt her heart sink, literally. Dread. She never wanted to see that man again, didn't want to have to speak to him. But he opened his arms to her mother and spoke so cheerfully Ally thought he must be demented. Could he have forgotten? After he was done slobbering on her mom's cheek, he closed in on her. She felt the kiss and the pressure of his body against her, but the lights were blurry, and so was the sound of his voice. Janine seemed to sense Ally's panic and signaled Maria, and they each took an elbow and guided Ally to a bench. Her mom pushed her down and asked Maria to find her a drink.

"You're okay, sweetheart. He's gone. You're safe." The words were muffled, but Ally understood, was comforted by her mom's touch and the cola Maria put to her lips. She sipped reflexively, like an infant suckling, and her head cleared.

"What happened?" Maria asked, her voice soft.

Ally cleared her throat. "He was my surgeon," she said.

Maria rubbed a soothing hand on Ally's thigh, and her mom squeezed her hand. Ally felt at once comforted and mortified. She was thirty years old and acting like a toddler. *C'mon, Ally. You've got this.*

"I'm so sorry," she said to both of them.

"Shh," her mom said. "It's fine. Do you want to leave?"

"No, Mom. I want to punch the fucker."

Maria laughed, and after a pause, her mom did, too. And a few seconds later, Ally joined them.

"I would expect we'd be asked to leave if you do. How much do you want to see a slide show on African art?"

Feeling herself again, Ally stood. Dr. Ball had certainly done his share to add to Ally's problems, but she'd put that behind her. She was in recovery, and she was doing well. "Are you kidding me? I live for this."

With them beside her, Ally walked into the auditorium. *You've got this.*

CHAPTER THIRTEEN

Family and Friends

Sleep had become elusive without drugs, and Ally still found herself awake each morning before the alarm. It was Sunday, and she could have slept as late as she wanted, but instead she emerged from her cocoon with a sense of purpose at just after six.

Dressed in work clothes, she made coffee and poured it into her Yeti, then walked to the studio. It was cold, but within a few minutes of turning on the heat, she started thawing. Her first priority was Sid Sandon's frame, and she put a second coat on that and set it aside to dry before resuming work on her oak panel and another frame.

The silvery-green paint had dried, and she didn't think it needed a second coat, so she applied a sealer to make it shine, then went to work on another one. She used a long board she'd purchased a while back and cut it to the specs she'd put into her phone. After she finished, she cleaned, primed, and painted it. By that time, the green pieces were dried, and she started framing the panel.

Her phone rang before she'd done more than arrange her tools, the classical ring tone telling her it was her mom.

"Good morning," Ally said. "What are you cooking?"

"French toast for six."

"'Kay," Ally said, with dread. Of course it was six. Jimmy and his family often joined them for breakfast before mass on Sundays. Jimmy would be wearing a suit, his wife would look like a model, and their daughter would resemble a mini-model, and then they'd go make nice with the priest and pretend to be good people. Which they weren't.

Worse, Ally had no warning. If her mom had told her, she would have come in from the studio and changed. As it stood, she had to walk past her uppity brother and his obnoxious wife dressed like a homeless person.

She didn't like them, and her recent interaction with her brother at Hamilton Security hadn't done anything to improve her opinion of him. He seemed to resent her place as the baby of the family. He'd told her once that, because of her, he had to split his inheritance. Ally had been just a teenager, and she was alarmed that perhaps her parents were on their way out, but he'd just laughed and called her an idiot. More than once he'd told her he hated her. And when she'd been injured, needing a shoulder replacement at the age of twenty-nine, in a hospital bed thousands of miles from home, he'd told her to suck it up, so they could all go back to Scranton and not have to reschedule their flight.

His wife, a successful photographer, was just as bad. She was gorgeous, but unfortunately, her beauty was all on the outside, and Ally had as much difficulty talking to her as she did to Jimmy.

"Fuck," Ally said out loud. Did she really want to change for the family breakfast, then change again to come back out to the studio? It didn't make sense. And she certainly didn't want to spend time with her brother and his family.

It would make her mom happy, though, so Ally pulled on her coat and walked the path back to the house. She heard laughter as she entered the mudroom and said a polite hello to everyone. "Just let me change, and I'll be down in a minute."

Everyone smiled, but judgment clouded her sister-in-law's eyes. Her brother's, too. Even her niece, who was only seven, seemed to look at her with disdain.

After quickly shedding her clothes on the bathroom floor, she scrubbed her arms and pulled on the pants and sweater she'd worn the night before. She ran a brush through her hair, slipped her feet into a comfy pair of boots, and headed back to face her family.

"You've got this," Ally said aloud as she scampered down the stairs and found them in the same place, in the kitchen. The only thing different was the pitcher of Bloody Marys her father had mixed and the set of rocks glasses on the tray on the island in front of him.

He'd just finished pouring the mix into a glass when he caught Ally's eye. "Bloody Mary?" he asked.

Ally would have consumed a bottle of mouthwash with breakfast to numb the pain of seeing Jimmy and Colette. "Absolutely," she replied, immediately noticing Colette's eyes open wide. She must have kicked Jimmy, or nudged him, because suddenly he looked at her, and then their parents, then back to her.

He cleared his throat. "Is it wise for you to drink?" he asked in a condescending tone.

Ally wanted to take the glass from her father and throw the contents right in his face. Instead, she took a sip and smiled sweetly. "Thanks for your concern, Jimmy, but I don't have a problem with alcohol. I think that would be you and Colette." She laughed to soften the remark, but she could literally see her sister-in-law's nostrils flare as she shot Ally a look of hatred.

"Ally's doing really well," her dad said. "We're not worried."

"Yes, that's right," her mom added. Ally knew her mom wasn't fond of Jimmy's wife, but she made peace for Jimmy's sake and so she could see their daughter, Madison. "Ally is on her way back. She started work this week." Janine took her drink and headed to the stove, where a griddle was heating, all the food ready to cook.

"Oh, yes," Colette said. "Tell me about it—you're a home-health aide now, I hear." If a voice could drip with nasty, Colette had mastered it.

Ally didn't want to reply, didn't want to take the bait, but she couldn't help it. She smiled sweetly. "Unlike my brother here, I've always been an overachiever. So in addition to my home-health-aide job, I'm working at Hamilton Security now. Learning all the ropes, so I'll be in a position to take over one day."

Colette's eyes widened, Jimmy grew still as his shoulders dropped, and her dad choked on his olive. After he cleared his throat, he leveled his gaze at Ally, as if telling her he'd heard enough. Her mother called over her shoulder to them. "It's a good thing you've made such a big, successful company, Russ. There's room for everyone. Even Madison can work there when she grows up."

Her mom was the peacekeeper, but Ally knew nothing she said now would calm Colette. Sure, they'd have to split the value of the company one day, but Jimmy planned to run the entire operation, with the hefty salary that went along with it. Ally's presence could derail his plans.

There was a victory in that, but she was trying not to think that way. She was working at her recovery, forgiving, not harboring negative thoughts. And her brother and his wife were a negative thought under the best circumstances. Under these—this was bad.

"I'm going to help Mom," Ally said and did her best saunter

toward the stove, where she kissed her mom on the cheek. "God, I hate her," she whispered, and her mother shot her a look.

Oh, well, she thought. *I might as well piss everyone off all at once.* That wasn't her intention, though. She wanted nothing more than peace and happiness. Didn't everyone? she thought as she pulled dishes from the cabinet. How to get it was the greatest mystery of the universe.

"Maddy, do you want to help me?" she asked her niece sweetly.

Maddy looked up from her phone. "No, thanks," she said, and Ally laughed. In her day, the request for help wasn't a question. But like her sister-in-law, her niece was spoiled.

So Ally set the table, not minding playing the role of servant, because it allowed her to avoid her brother and his wife. After the plates and water glasses, Ally put out utensils and large serving spoons, then took a large platter to her mom beside the stove.

"Linen or paper?"

Her mom screwed up her mouth. "Oh, paper, I guess."

Ha! Ally thought. Her mom wasn't trying too hard to impress Colette if she was willing to use paper napkins.

Her mom brought the food to the table, and they made small talk. Ally tried engaging Maddy, but like her mom, the child just seemed to be difficult. School was so-so. She met every question with a yes or no answer, until Ally asked how she'd enjoyed her Christmas gifts. None of the clothes fit her, or they were the wrong color for her eyes, or she already had that toy, and she hoped that next year everyone would just give her gift cards, because it was such a *pain* to have to return *everything*. Ally nearly choked to hear the words come out of a seven-year-old's mouth, but what was more concerning was the parents' response: silence. Clearly, Maddy was out of control, but Jimmy and Colette didn't seem to mind. Ally recalled another reason why she didn't like her brother. Like Maddy, Jimmy had been an entitled little brat, too.

When her mom stood to begin clearing the table, Ally jumped up as well. It beat staring at them. "I can do this, Mom. If you need to get to mass."

"I need to get away from the table," she whispered with a wink.

So Ally helped clean up, and half an hour later they all left for their family church.

"You're sure you don't want to join us?" Colette asked sweetly. "Isn't God a part of recovery?"

Ally nodded. "In some programs She is. But I'm not a fan of our church. Too many mean, nasty people are there, pretending to be good Christians. But you have fun."

She left to change before they were out the door, and when she came back down the stairs, they'd left. "Here's my religion for the day," she said aloud. "Thank you, Lord, for taking them away."

Back in the studio she finished assembling the frames for the two pieces she was working on, then cleaned up. By the time she'd showered and gotten ready, it was time to go to Reese's house. She left a note on the island and, twenty minutes later, headed to town. While the attendant at the store inflated three pink balloons, Ally picked out an educational toy for Stephanie, then a fresh loaf of bread and a bottle of wine for Maria. From there, it was a twenty-minute ride to Lake Winola, where a dozen cars were wedged into snowbanks around Reese's house.

"Oh, fuck." For some reason, she'd thought this would be a small, intimate affair, not a big shindig. Glancing at the clock, which read one thirty, she decided she'd give it an hour. She could do it. Just sixty minutes of socializing. *You've got this.*

As she hiked along the snowy road, Ally was grateful for her boots, and she laughed when she saw a huge pile of footwear on the front porch. The door opened, and Jess Benson beckoned her inside, then threw her boots back out the door before shutting it.

"You look great," Jess said as she pulled Ally in for a hug. "And it's so nice to see you."

Ally smiled. Jess had become a friend and was a strong support person for her. She'd made such a great decision in becoming a sort of spokesperson for addiction awareness, and Ally knew from listening to Jess's podcasts that she'd helped many other people, too. Did Jess and Maria know each other? Considering the path Maria was contemplating, they'd probably had a lot to discuss. "You too."

"Sorry about the coffee. My dad had a rough night, and we decided to bring him with us rather than leave him alone."

"What's going on?"

"He's been having difficulty for a few years, but now he's rather forgetful. In the middle of the night, he showed up at our house to help Mac with the water heater. But they replaced it last summer, so…"

Ally rubbed Jess's shoulder. "I'm sorry."

"Yeah. Me too," she said, and her sadness was so blatantly evident that Ally wanted to hug her again, but before she could, Ella Townes-Ryan, Reese's wife, ran over.

She wrapped Ally in her arms and squeezed. "It's so good to see you! When can you babysit?"

Ally laughed. "It's good to be needed."

"You certainly are," she said as she pulled back and looked Ally in the eye. "I'm so happy you came. Stephanie will be glad to see you."

"Do you think she'll remember me?"

Ella held her gaze. "I do. When we say our prayers at night, she always mentions Owey. And she has a picture of you on her wall, the one of you from last Christmas when you watched her during my office party."

Ally smiled. She remembered that shot. She'd taken Steph to her parents' house as a diversion, because how much can you do with an almost-two-year-old on a Saturday night? But they'd made cookies, and her mom pulled out a box of toys that had been Ally's, and Steph had a great time.

Talking to Ella made Ally realize she'd missed Steph, too. She'd originally agreed to the babysitting job because she'd just split from Gretchen and wanted something to fill her time. She didn't want to date then. She just wanted her life to be simple and uncomplicated. Unlike Maddy, Steph was a sweet little girl, who loved to color and play with art supplies, so Ally had fun with that. Ally had taken her to the studio once and let her create a masterpiece, and they'd done her handprints in rainbow paint and other fun projects like that. Mostly, though, being around such a happy child filled her with joy and made Ally think she might want to have kids of her own one day. "Just let me know when you need a sitter," she said.

"I will. Now join the party, friend. I think you know everyone."

Ally glanced at the group and realized it wasn't the work crowd she'd been expecting, but instead a bunch of friends. Other than Reese's sister Cass, an elderly gentleman, who she guessed was Jess's father, and the neighbor, Mrs. Gates, they were all people who Ally knew socially. Some happened to work at the hospital, but most were just from golf and softball, friends that Reese and Ella had collected over the years.

Somehow, that made Ally feel much better.

Everyone waved and smiled when they saw her, and some got up to come over and hug her. The only one who made her feel even the slightest bit nervous was Natasha Peterson, the CEO of the hospital. But she, too, was friendly, politely avoiding the topic of Ally's recovery while making it perfectly clear that she was welcome to come back to work whenever her license was reinstated.

Wow.

Paige Waterford, an ER doctor, was talking to her about her new partner, Carly Becker, when the birthday girl pranced into the room, dressed as Ariel, the Little Mermaid. Reese was close behind, carrying a stuffed fish and crab and looking in wonder at her daughter.

The crowd cheered for her, Stephanie bowed, and Reese came over to hug her. "How's it going?" Ally asked.

Reese pursed her lips. "I should be asking you the same thing."

"What?" Ally asked, confused.

Reese began to sing softly. "Maria! I just met a girl named Maria!"

Ally laughed, then got serious. "I can't believe it. She was stalking me in the frozen foods section."

"You could do worse."

Ally wasn't sure she should be doing anything, not with her future so uncertain. Not when she was contemplating heisting Brodrik Rogan's art collection. Yet Maria was there, on her mind while she painted and glued, while she drove her car, while she washed her hair in the shower. Suddenly, Maria was everywhere.

"I could."

Suddenly Stephanie turned and ran toward Reese, but at the last second, she noticed Ally standing beside her mom. "Owey!" she said and reached her arms up to Ally.

Ally bent down and scooped her up, careful of her right shoulder.

"You came back!" Steph said as she hugged Ally ferociously.

"I did. I couldn't wait a minute longer to see you."

"It's my birthday," she said proudly.

"Is it really?"

Steph nodded.

"Well, then, I want some cake."

Stephanie pointed toward the kitchen. "Take me."

Ally walked into the kitchen with Stephanie in her arms, and she pointed at the island. "Look, it's there."

At the island, Stephanie wiggled free and bent down next to a teal-and-orange frosted cake with all the characters from *The Little Mermaid* printed on the surface.

"It's beautiful," Ally said, thinking it looked too nice to eat.

"I'm Princess Ariel," she said. "But I'm not a mermaid."

The look on her face was so serious, and she sounded so disappointed, that Ally had to bite her lip.

She picked up the bottom of Stephanie's dress and inspected her feet. "Nope. No tail. Just legs."

Shaking her head, she responded, "I know. I keep wishing for a tail, but I never get one."

Ella and Reese walked in to search for them and cracked up at Steph's comment, and Reese scooped her up and twirled her around. "No tail. You're a girl, not a fish," she said as her daughter laughed delightedly.

Just then people began coming into the kitchen for food, and Ally took a small plate and talked more than she ate. She did have a dinner date and wanted to save some room for whatever Maria had in store.

After everyone finished their food, Stephanie opened her presents, and then they cut the cake. And before she knew it, she felt a soft hand on her back and turned her head to stare into Maria's dark eyes.

"Hey," Ally said.

"Hey, yourself. You look like you're having a great time."

Ally took a moment to do a self-assessment. "I am." Happiness. This was happiness. "How was work?"

"Easy day," she said.

Jess and her wife, Mac, walked over, and Ally introduced them and mentioned their mutual interest in addiction medicine. Even Mac, a retired state-police officer, had an interest in the topic of addiction. "These two could become great friends," Mac whispered to Ally.

"I think so," Ally said.

Ally hoped she'd have a chance to talk to Jess about her panic attack the night before, but it just didn't seem like the right time. It was the third one she'd had since she'd started her recovery journey, and while that wasn't a lot over a six-month period, each one was paralyzing. She needed to figure out a strategy for neutralizing them. Hopefully, they'd talk soon.

An hour later, as people began grabbing coats to leave, Ally hugged her hosts and the birthday girl and headed out the door, Maria beside her. "I have wine and bread in the car," she said.

"I'll follow you. I love a woman with wine."

When they reached Maria's place, Ally pulled to the side of the road and allowed her to pass, then pulled into the driveway behind her. With her bread in one hand and the wine in the other, she followed Maria into the garage and into the house.

Without warning, Maria turned and kissed her.

"Oh, Ally," she murmured into Ally's mouth. "I've been wanting to kiss you for twenty-four hours. It's been torture."

Ally pulled her close but kept the kiss soft, and after a minute they pulled away.

"I like your way of welcoming me."

"I like you. Can you open the wine, and I'll get the food started?"

"Of course," Ally said.

Maria pointed out the right cabinets, and Ally made quick work of the cork and poured two glasses for them. "What else can I do?"

"Can you grate the cheese? I made stuffed shells, so we'll sprinkle that on top."

Ally did as requested, and Maria put the food into the oven a moment later, then pulled her back in for another kiss. "They need forty-five minutes. Wanna sit by the fire?"

"Sure," Ally said, and followed Maria into her living room, where she pushed a button and brought her fireplace to life before joining Ally on the couch.

"So, hi," Maria said, and Ally found her so adorable, she leaned forward to kiss her.

"Hi."

"You seemed to have a fun time at the party," Maria observed.

Ally told her about how nervous she'd been, and so relieved to discover a group of friends rather than colleagues, and how nice they all were.

"Even Tashy, huh?"

"She seems like a bad-ass, but she's sweet," Ally said. "Although I was a little nervous when I first saw her."

Maria nodded. "Unfortunately, she knows my name."

Ally laughed. "Do tell."

Maria shook her head and waved Ally off. "Typical bullshit with a specialty consult."

Ally remembered all too well how hard it could be to get a doctor out of bed to see a sick patient at three in the morning. It was like they had brain fog and couldn't remember that lives were on the line, because they were different people at three in the afternoon.

"Jess should be a good contact for you," Ally said, and Maria's dark eyes opened wide.

"She's amazing. I can't wait to listen to her podcasts."

"You'll enjoy them. And learn a lot, too."

Sitting quietly, they held hands, sipped wine, and looked at the fire and each other. The glances at each other inevitably morphed into kisses, which were becoming as hot as the fire.

Ally needed to slow this down. It wasn't that she wasn't attracted—it was just the opposite. If last summer had been a bad time for a relationship, this wasn't much better.

Maria seemed to sense her hesitancy and changed the subject, talking about her house.

"I like this room," Ally said. It was a long room, with the fireplace on one end, a couch in front of it, and a big TV above the mantel. On the other end, a chaise lounge and chair sat opposite a bookshelf crammed with books. The flooring was hardwood, with throw rugs woven from thick yarn strategically placed beneath the sofas and chair.

"I repainted before I moved in, but that's all I really did in here. I thought it was perfect how it is. Do you want to see the rest of the house?"

Ally wasn't so sure it was a good idea to visit Maria's bedroom, but she figured she could handle herself. She was spared, though, when the oven timer began beeping.

Ally followed Maria to the kitchen and sat while she brought over the food. It looked amazing and tasted great, too.

"You seemed comfortable today at the party."

Ally swallowed. She'd felt comfortable. "It was a nice group of people," she said, then thought about breakfast at her parents. "They say friends are the family we choose. Sometimes I'd like to trade in my birth family."

"Really? Why?"

She told Maria about her brother and his wife, and even their daughter.

"They sound like jerks. Is it just the two of you?"

Ally shook her head. "Jimmy is the middle child. Our older brother, Kevin, lives in Philly. He's married to a nice woman, and they have two great kids."

"At least you have one sibling you like," Maria said as she sipped her wine and looked at Ally.

"He's just so far away."

"How often do you see him?"

"We vacation together twice a year. It's always been skiing in the winter and a beach house in the summer." Ally didn't mention they'd been all together when she'd had her accident, and she hoped Maria didn't ask. "I go down to Philly about once a month. They come here occasionally, but it's hard with kids. They have soccer and dance and all that stuff happening on weekends. There's no free time. How about you? Is it just you and your sister?"

"Yes. My parents are divorced, and Bri lives with my mom. That's why I was so motivated to find a house—it's hard to get in the middle of that dynamic."

Ally nodded. "I hear you. My parents wanted me to move back in with them after I was released, but I just needed my space."

"Understandable."

"What does Bri do?"

"She's done quite a few things, but at the moment she's working in an office. She's an administrative assistant for the boss."

"Sounds like she's doing okay."

Maria nodded. "Yeah."

They'd finished their food, and Ally sat back in her chair and studied Maria. Her round eyes were nearly black, framed by thick lashes. She had a cute little nose and a full mouth that looked so soft and kissable. And Ally liked kissing it.

"What are you thinking?" Maria asked.

"That I like kissing you."

Maria puckered up. "Wanna watch a movie? We can kiss all you want."

"Only if I get to pick."

"Okay. Since you're my guest. But I have veto power."

Ally liked the dynamic they had going. Working together. Compromising. "Sounds fair."

They cleaned up and sat before the fire as they watched a rom-com on television. After a few minutes, Maria slid down the couch and rested her head on a pillow she placed in Ally's lap.

It seemed so comfortable to be there with Maria. Normal, just like at the forum the night before. And at Steph's birthday party. Ally hadn't felt normal in a long time. She looked at Maria's head there as she ran her fingers through the thick curls of hair.

Maria rolled onto her back and looked up at Ally. "I feel your mind going at warp speed. What's up?"

Ally felt tears form in her eyes and sniffled and swallowed to prevent the spill. Gretchen had hurt her, and even though Ally had been prepared when they split, she'd still been left feeling inadequate. What was wrong with Ally that kept Gretchen hiding the secret of their love? What was wrong with her that her own brother despised her so much? Why didn't her father love her enough to put her needs—critical medical needs—above his own?

So here she was with this lovely woman, a brilliant, kind, fun person who genuinely liked her, who made her laugh, who she connected with, fearing Maria would eventually crush her. Ally shouldn't be here. She wasn't ready to be hurt again. She needed to work on herself, focus on recovery and rebuilding her life.

But like oxycodone, Maria was too hard to resist.

"I was thinking next week is Valentine's Day, and I don't have a date."

Maria smiled up at her, a big, bright, wide smile that seemed to reach out and hold Ally's heart. "Oh, yes, you do."

CHAPTER FOURTEEN

Fake It Till You Make It

Ally felt a little nervous as she approached Brodrik Rogan's gate on Monday morning. Nothing like the panic attack she'd experienced when she saw Dr. Ball, but she was jittery. And she should be, considering the two fake masterpieces in the back of her Jeep. She was about to cross a very distinct line and do something that could never be undone.

"You've got this," she whispered.

Pressing the buzzer, Ally looked through the railing to the guard house, relieved when the man on duty raised a hand and the gate opened. He waved her through with just a glance in the car, and she once again found Rocco awaiting her arrival. He opened her door before she could reach for the handle and then walked the ten feet to the back of the Jeep where she'd left her tackle box. The tackle box, and a huge plastic bag containing copies of two masterpieces.

"What's this?" he asked as Ally pulled out the paintings.

"I mentioned to Mr. Rogan that I do some art restoration, and I brought this to show him my work."

"Oh, that's really nice," he said, without glancing further at the paintings hidden behind two layers of semi-transparent plastic.

In the foyer, it went much the same as on the last visit. Rocco knocked, and Rogan told her to wait. Then he waved at the chairs and told her to have a seat. Thankfully, he wasn't in the mood to talk.

As she watched him disappear around the staircase, her mouth went dry. On the prior two visits she'd observed the lobby for signs of a camera and didn't see any. And even when she'd touched the *Brigette*, no one had come running. These paintings had absolutely no security, she was sure of it. Yet if someone walked in on her…

Swallowing, she placed the paintings upside down on the floor and easily slid off the outer bag. She folded it carefully and tucked it next to her tackle box. Then she pulled the Flinck copy from its own plastic sheath. Carefully folding the bag, she casually looked around and then slowly made her way to the foot of the stairs where *Landscape with an Obelisk* was hanging. She held her painting up, as if comparing them. She stood that way for at least a minute, and when no army of armed guards burst into the hallway, she put her painting on the floor, directly beneath Brodrik's. In a move she'd practiced a hundred times the day before at her mom's studio, she lifted his from the wall, pivoted to the right, placed it at the foot of the stairs, pivoted left, lifted her painting, and hung it on the bracket nailed into the paneled wall.

The entire exchange took six seconds. She knew, because she'd counted them, one Mississippi at a time.

Twelve *Mississippis* later, she was back on the other side of the foyer, and clutching the Flinck tightly in both hands, she eased herself into the chair beside her tackle box. In another swift, practiced move, Ally covered the masterpiece with the plastic, propped it against the chair beside her, and let out a thunderous sigh.

Leaning her head back, Ally closed her eyes and willed her heartbeat to slow. *Holy fuck*, she thought. *What did you just do? Put it back, you idiot. Put it back. Yes, that's the rational thing to do. The smart thing. Because what will you actually do with it anyway? You can't just waltz into the Gardner Museum and hand them the painting, right? And even if you were an evil shit who would sell this kind of masterpiece, you don't exactly know the sort of people who would buy a stolen painting.*

"Okay," she said to herself. "I'm going to put it back."

No, you're not. Keep going, Ally. You've got this.

On a deep inhale, she removed her copy of *A Lady and Gentleman in Black* from its plastic and walked to the wall opposite the Flinck. Once again she pretended to study it and then quickly exchanged the paintings. Back in her seat, she eased the Rembrandt into the plastic, then slipped the larger bag over both paintings just as the door to Brodrik Rogan's study opened, and he waved her in.

Ally picked up her tackle box with one hand and the bulky plastic bag with the other and walked into the study.

"Ally, how are you? How was the Smelly Exhibit?" He seemed to be moving a little more slowly, seemed more winded when he spoke.

"I'm a little stressed today," she said, "but the forum was really enjoyable."

"And your date? Who's the lucky woman?" He made it to his chair and sat down with his typical thud, and Ally noticed Winnie Rogan sitting at her husband's desk. She waved, but Winnie didn't seem to notice, so Ally concentrated on her husband.

"Women, actually. My mom and some friends. But more important, how are you? How's the leg?" Ally pulled up the hassock and opened the tackle box.

"I heard the Q-Tip test came back awful. But it doesn't hurt as much. What's that?" he asked as he nodded toward the paintings beside her.

"Oh. I brought this to show you. It's an example of my work." Ally carefully pushed the open tackle box aside and pulled the smaller painting, the Flinck, out of the bag, moving slowly and deliberately to still her shaking hands.

"It's a, a copy, the same one you, you have, but I, I did the frame." Ally wasn't sure if she choked on the lie or her fear, but either way, it was telling. Brodrik Rogan didn't seem to notice.

"Hand it over," he demanded.

Ally stood and removed the second plastic and carefully placed the landscape in his hands. She watched in silence as he studied it. "It's not bad," he said. "You have some talent," he said as he handed it back to her, and she covered it with the plastic.

"Thank you, Mr. Rogan. That's kind of you. I brought you this so you can see my work. In case you're interested in me repairing your frames."

"What the hell's wrong with my frames?" he demanded.

"Well, sir, um, they're old," she said with a shrug as she met his eyes.

"I'm old," he barked.

Ally stared at him for a moment. "Exactly."

His gaze was piercing, and Ally felt true fear. Her mouth dried, her heart rose to her throat, and she was about to apologize when he burst out laughing. The laugh quickly turned into a gasping, choking cough, and Ally stood and went beside him as he turned purple, then blue. She thought he was going to code right there, but the coughing began to ease, and he began taking in air once again.

Ally pulled the stethoscope from her bag and applied it to his chest. His heart was pounding just as fast as hers, but she was pretty sure her lungs didn't have the same rattle.

"You sound awful," she informed him.

"What kind of awful?" he gasped. "Heart or lungs?"

"It's hard to tell. Maybe a little of both. We should call the ambulance."

"Absolutely not," he gasped.

Winnie suddenly appeared at her husband's side. "Brody, you okay?"

Rogan nodded at his wife, even though he was still struggling.

"Where's your inhaler?" Ally asked, and when he told her, she walked to his desk. On the top, two small, framed pieces from the Gardner heist flanked a large scheduling calendar. The word *nurse* was written in a shaky scrawl in each of the little boxes. Occasionally, other things were written, such as Winnie's car service and dinner with Fr. Finnerty. Opening the top drawer, she shuffled some papers, pens, and candy before pulling out the wrong inhaler. Finding the correct one entailed a search by Winnie, who brought a Gucci leather cosmetic case filled with her husband's medication.

Ally quickly sorted through the water pills and the pressure pills and the sugar pills and found a fast-acting inhaler. "Use this," she said and handed it to him.

She watched in horror as he put the wrong end of the inhaler in his mouth. Ally stared for a moment, unsure if he was joking, but he seemed genuinely confused. She turned the inhaler around and helped administer two puffs, then clipped the pulse oximeter onto his finger. It read eighty-seven percent, which was way too low for the human brain to function normally.

"Do you have an oxygen tank?" Ally asked Winnie.

"Why? What's wrong? Rocco!" she screamed as she ran from the room.

Fuck, Ally thought, but her tension eased as she saw the number on his monitor going up. Eight-nine, ninety, and then Rocco burst into the room and whipped open a closet door. He ran to his boss and placed an oxygen mask over his face, while Ally dialed the flow on the regulator up as high as it would go.

"Slow, deep breaths," she told him, and she did the same. To keep herself busy, she listened to his lungs again and thought the wheezing had diminished slightly. His color was improving, too, from blue to red.

Winnie reappeared. "Should I call the ambulance?"

Brodrik waved to her, shaking his head, and murmured through the hissing of the oxygen mask. "No, no, no!" he said.

"Do you want to fucking die?" She was sobbing, pacing back and forth across the room.

"I'm...not...dying!" he managed to say.

"Shh." Ally scolded him. "No talking, just breathing." Turning, she stared down Winnie. "Mrs. Rogan, please try to get it together. Yelling at your husband is not going to help him."

Ally watched as Winnie stormed from the room.

Turning back to Brodrik, she looked at his fingertip. Ninety-three. His brain should be doing better at ninety-three. His heart rate started to slow as well, and his breathing seemed calmer.

Ally rubbed his back. "You're doing great, Mr. Rogan. Your oxygen is coming up. You're going to be fine."

It was obvious the spell had sapped his energy, and when he was breathing easy enough to sit back, she evaluated his wound. It was no better, but no worse either. What troubled Ally, though, was the swelling in his legs. They were significantly larger than they'd been the day before. Fluid in his legs could mean fluid in his lungs, and that could have triggered the coughing spell and the low number she saw on his pulse ox.

Ally had had a relatively brief orientation, and she wasn't sure if she could direct Mr. Rogan to take an extra dose of his water pill. It wasn't like the inhaler—that he could take as needed. The water pill was a fixed dose, to be used as prescribed by a physician. Or a physician's assistant, which she no longer was.

"I need to call my boss," she explained as she walked a few feet away, toward *Christ in the Storm on the Sea of Galilee.* She punched in the numbers on her phone and called Greg. Thankfully, she had service. While the phone connected, she looked in awe at the painting, for a moment transported back in time to the biblical scene before her. How terrified Christ's disciples must have been as the storm tossed their boat.

Greg's voice on the phone jarred her to the present again, and after Ally quickly explained the situation, Greg gave her some guidance. "Ally, if you think it's necessary, do it. It's his medicine. You're just advising him to take an extra dose, which he is free to do, if he wants to keep breathing."

Ally disconnected the phone and asked Winnie for a glass of water and, after explaining to Brodrik what was going on, handed him two tablets. He sat forward and promptly swallowed them before easing back in the chair.

"Can you talk?" Ally asked.

Pulling the mask away from his face, he smiled at her. "What do you want to talk about?"

Ally smiled at the full sentence he spoke and his flirtatious tone. His brain was back.

"Mr. Rogan, when was the last time you had a chest X-ray?"

He looked heavenward, then back at her. "Christmas?"

"We're going to schedule one. They can come out to the house. Does this happen often? Where you can't breathe or start coughing like that?" It had happened the day before, but the episode had been brief and resolved on its own. This one had been alarming.

"Oh, once or twice a day."

"Seriously?"

"Okay, maybe three. I think it's worse the past couple of days."

"Mr. Rogan, this is a problem." Leaning forward, Ally looked into his eyes.

He shrugged and offered a sad smile. "As you so eloquently stated a few moments ago, I'm old."

Ally started to speak but stopped. That remark had been totally insensitive. "I'm sorry," she said after a moment. "That was rude."

He waved her off. "It's true! I've worked hard my whole life. Since I was a kid, really. Cleaning used cars on a lot for a few bucks a day. Worked my way up to sales, then started buying my own cars to sell. Before I knew it, I was the Cadillac King. But I played hard, too. And now I'm paying for it."

Ally swallowed. What could she say?

"Hey, it's okay. It's been a sweet ride. And I know I'm running out of gas. I'm tired of doctors and nurses and hospitals. I'm tired of feeling like shit. I just want to be comfortable, not suffer too much. Can you help with that?"

Ally looked at him. What was he asking of her?

"Can you, or not?" he asked again, impatience evident in his voice.

"Are you asking if we can start hospice care? Shift from trying to cure you to making you rest a little easier?"

"Exactly!" he said.

Ally's head was spinning. This was not what she'd expected today, but one of the Hs in Four H stood for hospice. They could do that, if he wanted to stop aggressive treatments. She nodded. "We can make you comfortable. But perhaps you should discuss this decision with your family. It's sort of sudden."

Shaking his head, he looked at her. "It's not sudden for me. I've been thinking about this for months. Do I have to sign something? So no one starts beatin' on my chest and shoving pipes down my throat?"

Ally nodded. "I do have those papers, but, again, maybe it would be best if you talk to your lawyer and your family, maybe your primary-care doc."

"My doctor won't call me back. And my lawyer will just send me a bill for five grand to do something you'll do for free. And my family—that will be a war, and I don't have the energy to fight. This is what I want. So be kind to a dying man, would you, honey?" He reached out his fingers and wiggled them, as if he were caressing her, but he was several feet from the mark.

Ally laughed and sorted through her paperwork to find the appropriate form. "I'll be back tomorrow, Mr. Rogan. Read this through before you make your decision. Talk to your wife and family."

He reached out his hand. "Give me your pen."

Ally handed him a pen, and he scribbled his name onto the *Do No Resuscitate* form. "Rocco, be my witness," he demanded, and handed him the pen and paper.

"Mr. Rogan, sir…"

"Shut up, and sign."

Rocco looked at Ally, then back to Rogan, then signed the paper.

"Can you still take care of my leg?"

Ally nodded. "Yes, of course."

"Then I'll see you tomorrow."

Ally gave Rocco instructions about weaning down the oxygen, and he was kind enough to carry *Landscape with an Obelisk* and *A Lady and Gentleman in Black* to her car. She followed, barely able to move her legs.

Fuck, she thought. *I didn't have days this stressful in the ER. You definitely haven't got this.*

CHAPTER FIFTEEN

Group Therapy

Ally's head was spinning as she left the Rogan estate. He was a sick man, and he'd just decided to put the brakes on aggressive treatments that could prolong his life. Wow. That was a game changer, and it had Ally's emotions on overdrive. First, the visit had been adrenaline-filled, and for a few minutes, Ally had been really worried her patient would code. Her training had kicked in and instincts took over, and she'd done her job well. She'd felt a little rush at the end, when she'd watched the oxygen level climb, only to crash when he'd told her he didn't want further medical care. And that was just her emotions as a provider— when she thought of the artwork that might disappear after Brodrik Rogan's death, she felt an entirely different type of angst.

On the drive home, Ally took great care to obey the speed limit and come to a complete stop at every intersection. She didn't cut corners or tailgate. The last thing she needed was a run-in with the police while transporting stolen art in the back of her Jeep.

Wow. She'd just stolen two paintings. Not just any paintings, though. Very expensive, famous paintings. Go big or go home, right?

Brodrik's decision to forgo advanced medical care certainly complicated her plans. How long would it take to get all those paintings out of the house? Two more weeks, at least. When she'd first seen him, playing on the floor with Joseph, she'd never imagined he'd be so close to death less than a week later. But none of us have any guarantees, and certainly not for an eighty-year-old man with an encyclopedia of medical issues.

What if his condition deteriorated further, and he decided to discontinue wound care? Or, even worse, what if he died? A patient who had such a sudden episode like that could probably have another one. And what if this time, he didn't come out of it? What if the stress of that coughing and choking caused him to code?

He'd be a goner, and so would his artwork.

That sounded harsh. Even if she'd removed all the pieces from Rogan's house, she still wouldn't want him to die. For some strange reason, she liked him.

Okay, Ally. Think. No. What I need is a drink. A bottle of wine and a bubble bath, and I'll call Greg in the morning and tell him I'll taking a sick day. Or a sick week.

Fuuuccccckkk! She turned the word into five syllables, and the act calmed her just a bit.

Think. First, she had to take care of the paintings she had. She couldn't do anything about a fire, but she lived in an apartment building owned by a subsidiary of a security company. The artwork wouldn't be stolen from her apartment. It would be safe at her place, until she ultimately decided what to do with it.

Okay. See, Ally? You've got this. Just stay calm and figure out your next move.

She found a parking spot at the front of the lot and hurried into the building, carrying the bulky plastic bag with the two paintings. She moved as quickly as she could, hoping she wouldn't run into any tenants. She preferred there be no witnesses who saw her with the paintings. Luck was on her side, and a minute later, she was safely in her apartment. Flicking on the light, she looked around, half expecting to see Rocco or another of Brodrik Rogan's people waiting for her.

The place was empty, though, and cold. After a few more breaths, she adjusted the thermostat, hung up her coat, and removed *Landscape with an Obelisk* and *A Lady and Gentleman in Black* from the plastic. After pulling down two Georgia O'Keeffe prints, she hung the Flinck and the Rembrandt. Then she simply sat back, forgot her worries, and stared at the paintings.

Ally preferred light, colorful works like the O'Keeffes, and the Flinck was a dark piece. But it was still magnificent, with attention to details like light playing on the stream and two men talking beneath the giant tree. It had once been credited to Rembrandt himself but was later determined to have been crafted by his student, Govaert Flinck, who finished the work in 1638. He'd painted on wood, and Ally had chosen it first for that reason. She couldn't roll this up and sneak off with it. She'd had to be brazen and walk out carrying it. The best way to do that, she'd rationalized, was on day one.

Ally smiled. She had been bold. Not fearless, but brave. She had crafted a plan and executed it perfectly. And she'd gotten away with it. No silent alarm, no hidden security camera, no death and dismemberment. She retraced her steps in her mind, wondering if she might have done something wrong, left some clue behind, but she couldn't think of anything. Unless the original pieces contained secret markings, she didn't think Brodrik Rogan would know they'd been switched.

Smiling, Ally studied *A Lady and Gentleman in Black*. This work was practically colorless. The entire right half of the painting was a black shadow, and the lady and gentleman were, of course, wearing black. Other than the huge, white collars adorning both their outfits, nothing was bright about the enormous painting. Yet the brushwork was exquisite, the details of their faces and hands and even the floorboards as realistic as a photograph.

It was an amazing sight to behold, and Ally did that, for half an hour, wondering if she had the guts to keep going. She'd been able to switch these two paintings with little effort. All the work had been in making the copies that would pass for the pieces hanging in the Rogan mansion. She could probably get away with it again, but then what would she do next? The other works were not as accessible. She couldn't very well swap out the paintings in the study with Brodrik Rogan watching. And as far as Ally knew, he never left that room. She'd never be alone, with a chance to even inspect the art, let alone steal it.

With her stomach in knots and no appetite, she skipped dinner and changed into jeans and a Marywood University sweatshirt and headed downtown to the Recovery Hub, where she talked to some of the volunteers and sat in on a group meeting. Halfway through, a gorgeous young woman with dark eyes and long dark hair began to speak. Ally had been discreetly checking her out, thinking she knew her, but couldn't quite place her. Then she introduced herself, and Ally knew. This was Maria's sister, Brianna.

After the meeting, Ally approached her and introduced herself. She was as warm and animated as Maria, hugging her and talking with her hands as she offered Ally invitations to breakfast, lunch, and dinner, coffee, and Sunday brunch at her mom's house.

"But how are you doing?" she asked. "Maria said you just left the halfway house."

"I'm spending a lot of time with my parents. And working. Staying busy, you know—avoiding the people, places, and things."

Brianna nodded and smiled sweetly. "You have to create a new normal."

Ally sighed. "Yes. And I'm really afraid of that."

"How so?"

Ally looked into the distance as she tried to organize her thoughts. Avoiding the people, places, and things that reminded her of drugs gave her fewer opportunities to use—that was easy. She'd never done drugs socially, with friends. She'd used them for pain and then to prevent withdrawal symptoms. Her real worry was work and being in an environment where opioids were around all the time. Would it be a constant temptation, like walking into the mall and smelling Cinnabon? Most of the time, Ally could walk right past, but every once in a while she stopped and bought a big, gooey cinnamon roll and ate it on the spot. How could she fight that temptation forty hours a week? She'd go mad. "I guess I just don't know what I want to do with the rest of my life."

Brianna nodded. "I hear you. I finished my degree in accounting and realized I hate that sort of work. I'm good with numbers, but not so much the tedious, isolated work it entails. So, I'm working as an administrative assistant."

Bri smiled widely, and Ally nodded, thinking of something she'd once heard. "I think the FBI hires accountants. Financial crimes, you know?"

Brianna roared. "OMG. Could you imagine that? I'm going to tell my parents I'm joining the FBI, just to see the look on their faces."

Ally thought of how her own parents worried and figured Bri's must be the same. Plus, she had Maria as well. Ally asked about them.

"It's good support," she said. "But it's hard sometimes, living up to their expectations."

Ally didn't have that worry. Her parents supported their children's interests and nudged a little when needed, but they weren't overbearing. They never judged or criticized. They said things like "if this is your goal, you may need to work a little harder to achieve it." Their expectations were based on things learned in kindergarten: share, be kind, help each other.

Her addiction didn't disappoint them; it worried them. "I just feel bad that I've caused them so much grief."

"That's what love is, though. Caring about someone even more than you care for yourself. It leaves you open to pain."

True of all love, Ally thought, not just the parental kind. But she only hoped her parents would eventually relax. From the sound of things, even after three years, the Alfanos weren't there yet. Then she thought of some people she'd met in rehab and was reminded how lucky she and Brianna both were.

"I know a woman from rehab who started doing heroin when she was eleven. Her mom gave it to her, so she could relax when the mom's boyfriend raped her."

She looked at Bri, saw her pupils dilate. "I've heard those kinds of stories, too. Incest, rape, neglect, abuse. Give me my overprotective parents any time."

People started to move toward the front door, and as much as Ally would have liked to keep talking, she had a long night ahead of her.

"I suppose I should head out."

"We could get that coffee."

Half an hour, Ally told herself. She was enjoying her time with Bri, and she needed someone to talk to. "I'd love to," Ally said.

Before they reached the door, one of the recovery specialists approached her and handed her a flyer. "Ally, here's the information about the art classes. I know you said you were interested. The next session is tomorrow. You should come and bring your mom."

Ally was excited about the prospect of taking her mom to the recovery center. She smiled at the young man. "Thank you."

"I love the art classes," Bri said. "It's a fun time. You should come."

Ally nodded. "I think I will."

They met for coffee at a place in Clarks Summit, and on the way, Ally called her mom. Although she could have taught the art class, she decided to go with Ally just to see the Recovery Hub, and they made plans to meet for dinner before they went. At the coffeehouse, Ally bought a pastry to complement her decaf, and they sat in cozy chairs by the fire and talked about their stories.

After they'd both shared, Brianna pulled her legs up under her and leaned a little closer. "You're going to be fine."

Ally thought so, too. It was a difficult task, a little like taking a test. It wasn't just that she wanted to pass. She wanted an A. She couldn't cram the night before. She had to do a little work each day and keep reinforcing what she'd already learned. Surviving wasn't enough. She wanted to live the life she'd dreamed of before her accident—meeting a great girl, settling down and getting married, maybe having a child like Reese and Ella. Traveling. Working at an exciting job. Just a year ago, all of that was a forgone conclusion. It had just been a matter of time. Now, though, Ally wasn't certain of anything.

She blew out a breath.

"Okay. Let's change the subject. What's up with my big sister?" Bri asked as she comically pursed her lips and squinted.

"Whatever do you mean?" Ally said playfully, buying time. She didn't quite know how to answer that question.

"My mom said you two were practically inseparable at the Schemel Forum."

"True. But we were the only ones there under a hundred years old."

Brianna laughed.

"We met last summer, when Maria started working at the hospital. I was a PA in the ER. But then my colleagues had an intervention for me, and that was the end of that."

"So, that was then. What's going on now?"

While Maria had talked lovingly of her sister, Ally wasn't sure how much she talked *to* her sister. Was this Ally's tale to tell, or should Brianna be talking to Maria?

Wagging her finger, she tried a fierce glare. "You are not getting anything out of me."

Brianna held up her hands. "What?"

"I'm sure Maria will tell you everything she'd like you to know about our relationship if you ask her."

Brianna nodded. "I see how you are. You two are perfect for each other."

Ally bit her lip. She did think she and Maria were a good fit. She just hadn't decided if she should even be looking. How could she worry about someone else when she couldn't even take care of herself? Yet she couldn't stop thinking of Maria, wanting to be with her, anticipating their next time together.

Brianna read her perfectly. "My sister is really a wonderful person, Ally. And I think she's ready for a relationship. If you're not—which is understandable—you should probably let her know."

Ally nodded. Was Bri someone she could talk to? She'd been there. Yet Maria was her sister, so Ally wasn't sure how objective her opinions would be.

"How long were you in recovery before you started dating?"

Bri covered both eyes with her hands, then dragged them down to her mouth, where she folded them as if in prayer. Her sigh was enormous.

"The guy I was dating was a big part of my problem. Not that it was his fault—I was already in trouble when I met him. But I thought I was in love, so not only did I have to come off pills, but I had to get him out of my system, too."

Ally could only imagine how difficult that was. When she and Gretchen had started having problems, Ally couldn't find solace anywhere. Her parents were great but happily conjoined, just like so many of her friends who were in relationships. It was as if she was all alone holding a piece of her heart in each hand, not sure what to do with it. So she did what she thought would help—she kept busy. Picking up additional shifts in the ER gave her some extra cash and killed time. Working in the studio, making frames was another way to while away the hours. She went out more, too, for dinner with the guys from her building and old friends, and she played a ton of golf. And she'd done okay. She'd known for a long time that she and Gretchen were drifting apart, yet she'd still had to go through that mourning period, and it still hurt. How had Bri done that while detoxing?

"I can't imagine."

"To answer your question, I met a nice guy in the halfway house, and we started hanging out." She lowered her voice and rolled her eyes. "Sleeping together. It lasted a few months."

Ally always wondered about couples in recovery, and she asked Bri about it.

"In some ways it's good. He understood what I was going through, right? We could support each other. On the other hand, there's a constant comparison. Who's doing better? What's the best way to skin the cat? And of course—if one person in a relationship relapses, what happens to the other?"

Ally asked the question she'd been asking herself since meeting Maria in Wegmans. "Why do you think your sister wants to get involved with someone in recovery?"

Bri looked at her. "I could give you a few answers to that question. But I'm going to turn it right back on you and tell you to ask her."

Ally chuckled. "I suppose I should." Just not yet. "She's just agreed to be my valentine."

"That sounds nice. Just level with her, Ally. I'm sure she'll be patient and give you time to figure things out. There's nothing wrong with going slow."

Ally had met a lot of wise people in recovery, and she could add Bri to the list. "Thank you, Bri. I will."

Chapter Sixteen

Long Live the King

After coffee, Ally realized she had to hurry if she was going to accomplish everything on her agenda. Instead of heading home, she went straight to her parents' and raided the refrigerator. While eating the leftovers of their roast-beef dinner, Ally talked with her mom, told her about meeting Brianna at the Recovery Hub.

"She sounds like she could be a good mentor for you," her mom said.

"Yes. I think so, too."

"Is she as attractive as Maria?"

"She's gorgeous, but I get straight vibes."

"I don't get straight vibes from Maria." Her mom raised her eyebrows. "As a matter of fact, she hardly noticed anyone in the room except you."

"It's odd, isn't it?" Ally asked. She really couldn't figure out the attraction Maria had for her. Maria was successful and had such enormous potential. What would she want with someone whose future was as uncertain as Ally's?

Her mom's jaw dropped. "Have you looked in the mirror? You're beautiful. And smart. And funny. Not to mention kind and sweet."

Ally heard the words. Once, she'd believed them. Not so much now, but she loved that her mom tried.

She hugged her tightly. "I love you. Thank you for not giving up on me."

Janine appeared shocked. "How could I ever?"

"I'm not sure I can work on a relationship right now. I'm working on me. Yet with Maria there's a connection, and it's magnetic. I'm drawn to her, from before, from the moment we met. If I hadn't been so screwed up, something might have happened last summer."

"She's waited six months, Ally. I'm sure she can wait a few more."

"Bri told me I should tell her I need to go slowly."

Janine smiled. "That sounds like great advice."

"I have some work in the studio."

"More framing?"

Ally nodded. "Yeah. It's for this guy. My home-health patient." She didn't want to say too much, to involve her mother in anything unscrupulous or mention something that might raise her suspicions.

"Have fun."

"Is it okay if I stay over?" Ally had lost an hour with Bri, and staying at her parents' house would help make it up. Yet her mind shot to the paintings in her apartment, and she hoped they'd be safe without her.

"It would be okay if you move back in."

"Let's just settle for the night, okay?" Ally laughed. "And there's no need to wait up. I'll see you in the morning."

"Breakfast at six?"

"See you then," Ally said and headed out the door. She pulled one of the cardboard boxes from the car and carried it into the studio. Removing the tube, she unrolled two canvases and went to work. Three hours later she finished, and though it wasn't her best work, under the circumstances, she was pleased. And she didn't need perfection. Brodrik Rogan could hardly see.

She was in bed half an hour later and up early. After breakfast, she headed to Four H for the morning meeting, where Carlene, the head of billing, confronted her in the lobby.

"You didn't turn in your paperwork last night! May I remind you that is confidential patient information? It needs to be returned."

Fuck, Ally thought. How could she have forgotten? Then she spoke without thinking and realized it was probably the truth. "I was really stressed, and I needed to go to a meeting."

Carlene's face softened, and she grabbed Ally's hand. "Are you okay?"

Briefly, Ally explained Brodrik Rogan's health crisis, and after she finished her tale, Carlene beamed.

"Ally, I'm so proud of you. It sounds like you saved his life, giving him that inhaler and the oxygen. He could have died. But your training kicked in, and you did what needed to be done. Good job!"

Ally felt her shoulders collapse. She really had been stressed the day before, but not only for the reasons Carlene thought. Still, she had totally forgotten about the paperwork.

"It won't happen again," she said, dug all her paperwork out of the tackle box, and handed it in. Some went to Carlene, but the DNR she placed in Greg's box.

At the meeting she told everyone about her experience the day before, mostly because everyone shared work issues. It was a way to learn. But it also felt good to talk shop again. For twenty minutes the day before, once again she'd been Ally Hamilton, PA-C, doing critical care, even if she was wearing a different uniform. And it had felt great.

She left the meeting with energy, and it carried over to her patient care. Tommy, her cancer patient, was now suffering from diarrhea, and Millie, the cat lady, was actually looking better. At the Rogan estate she was admitted without delay, and she arrived at the portico to find Rocco in his usual spot.

"Another painting?" he said as he pulled it from the back of the Jeep.

Ally nodded. "I'm hoping he'll hire me."

"Well, good luck," he said as he escorted her to the foyer, then knocked on Rogan's study door. After he announced her arrival he waved and disappeared down the hallway.

Ally wasn't sure how long he'd be gone, or how many minutes would pass before Brodrik Rogan saw fit to admit her to his study, but she knew how long it would take to make the switch. With one swift movement, she removed the painting from the plastic and set it down. She had *The Concert* off the wall and replaced with her reproduction five seconds later. And that was when she heard the door to the study open.

A younger, much thinner version of Brodrik Rogan stepped out. "What are you doing?" he barked.

Ally stepped back and stammered when she spoke. "I…I brought this to show Mr. Rogan…"

From where he stood, Ally was sure it seemed like she was comparing the two paintings. She didn't have a chance to explain.

"You're not here to peddle paintings. You're here to take care of him. What's this about a DNR? I want that paper. My father is not giving up. Not yet."

"Pete, shut up and bring her in here." Brodrik Rogan's voice was loud and strong, with no hint of shortness of breath.

He smiled when she entered the room. "Ally, this is my oldest boy, Peter. Ignore him. I'm happy to report you fixed me right up, young lady. I'm ready to run the Boston Marathon."

Relieved, Ally felt the sense of accomplishment that came with a job well done. A smile exploded on her face.

"Do you by any chance weigh yourself?"

He pointed to his stomach. "They don't have a scale that will hold all this."

Ally sucked in a breath. "It's a good way to tell your fluid status. Your weight fluctuates way faster than your breathing, so we can monitor it."

"Dad, this is serious. I'm getting you a scale." He looked at his phone and then at Ally. "What are you doing for him? Did you get an X-ray? How about blood? Does he need antibiotics?"

"The X-ray and blood work are good ideas, if he revokes the DNR, but not the antibiotic. He doesn't have an infection."

"What about the leg? Isn't that infected?"

"Yessss," Ally explained patiently, "but because of his poor circulation, pills won't work very well on the leg. We're putting antibiotics right on the wound, on the dressing."

"Okay, well, I want an X-ray done, and I want blood." He looked fierce, and Ally wanted only to get out of there as quickly as possible.

After taking Rogan's vital signs, she listened to his lungs. "All clear," she said, and she leaned back and smiled at him.

"Let me see the leg." The wound was no better, but the swelling had lessened remarkably. "You need an adjustment in your water pill," she said. "I'll call your doctor. In the meantime, I'm going to draw some blood."

"And how about that DNR?" Peter demanded.

She looked at Brodrik. "Up to you."

"Maybe I was a little hasty. Let's table that for now. Can you just give the paper back to me?"

"I actually turned it in at the office. But you can sign another paper to revoke it."

"How do I know you're going to turn that in? What if they don't get it, and they refuse him care?" Peter demanded.

Ally stood tall and looked at him. "It's a matter of honesty. Professional integrity."

"Yeah, well, I don't believe in that crap. I want reassurance."

Ally was at a loss. "I don't know what else I can say, sir."

"I'm calling my lawyer," he said, and he stormed out of the room.

Ally pulled another form from her folder, this one revoking the DNR, and Brodrik and Ally both signed. "Congrats," she said. "You'll live to fight another day."

He roared. "I've been fighting for eighty years. I'm good at it." His stare was challenging, but Ally didn't let it bother her. After seeing him yesterday, she understood how frail he really was. The bravado was a facade.

She pushed another paper in front of him, for the wound care, and he scribbled his signature with no more than a glance at what he was signing.

"Let me tell you the plan," Ally said as she tied a tourniquet on his upper arm. "Lab work—I'm getting that now. A chest X-ray—Mr. Hart will arrange that ASAP. Anytime in the next few days is fine, because your lungs sound good. I'm going to submit this form and update your status to Full Code. We'll do everything in our power to keep you alive and well. And finally, I'm going to reach out to your doctor and ask him to increase the dose of your water pill. Until I hear from him, just take your regular dose. But I think much of your cough and shortness of breath is because of your heart, and the water pill will help that."

"So I can keep smoking?"

"Absolutely. *Not.*" Ally gave him the same look he'd given her earlier.

She packed up his blood tubes and collected the trash. "Let me take care of this," she said as she picked up her tackle box and carried it into the bathroom. She quickly washed her hands but left the water running. She opened the box, removed her equipment, and then lifted the bottom drawer. With one hand she took Rembrandt's self-portrait from the wall and with the other she pulled the copy from the tackle box and replaced it. Working quickly, she returned everything to her tackle box, and only a few seconds later she turned off the water and opened the door.

Brodrik Rogan was standing just in front of her.

"What's going on?" he asked, that look of controlled anger once again evident in his eyes.

With as much cheer as she could cram into her voice, Ally waved her free hand and answered. "I was washing my hands."

He nodded toward the tackle box. "Why'd you need your medical bag to wash your hands?"

Ally's mouth went dry, but she remembered her training with

Linda. "I'm not supposed to leave it out of my sight. There's a lot of stuff in there—needles, syringes, drugs."

"Mind if I take a look?"

Ally breathed out as she nodded. Really, what could she say? She couldn't stop him. And she certainly couldn't ask for someone to intervene. Oh, well. There was nothing she could do but pray. Handing it to him, she stepped back and watched as he placed it on the nearby sofa table and opened it. He scanned the contents of the top shelf, then removed it. Beneath, her equipment mingled with a padded bag of blood she'd drawn from him and another patient, as well as a bag containing a cup of light brown liquid stool from her cancer patient.

"Holy Christ," he said as he held it at arm's length and looked away. "Is that what I think it is?"

Ally nodded. "Cancer patient with diarrhea. We have to make sure he doesn't have an infection in his bowels."

He stepped back and pushed the case toward her. "I could never do your job."

Ally quickly and quietly restored her gear to good order, then picked up the Vermeer from the other side of the couch. "I guess you don't want to see this?"

"No. I looked already. It's a nice frame. Listen, write up a proposal—what you wanna do, how much it's gonna cost me—and bring it tomorrow. I'll look it over and let you know."

Ally's knees were still wobbling as Rocco escorted her to her Jeep. *You don't have this. Not at all.*

Chapter Seventeen

Family Fun

This time Ally remembered to stop at Four H on the way home.

"How's our patient?" Greg asked when she poked her head in his door. She approached his desk and chuckled as she handed him the form that canceled his DNR.

"Planning to outlive us all." If all the drama continued, he might outlive Ally, anyway. She wasn't cut out for this kind of stress.

"What made him change his mind?" Greg asked.

"The son was there today, but I don't think it's just that. Maybe he's depressed. He doesn't seem to have a good relationship with his children, his wife needs a sedative, and he doesn't feel well. So it may have been an impulsive decision, or maybe he was just testing the waters, trying to see what his options are."

"And maybe it was for attention."

Ally had considered that possibility. "For sure." She told Greg her treatment plan, and he promised to schedule the X-ray for the near future. "I'm waiting on a call from the primary-care doc, but maybe an increase in the diuretic would be helpful."

"Is he calling Four H? You'll need to do a triage so whoever takes the call is up to date on the case."

Ally remembered discussing the protocol with Linda during orientation, but she'd thought it would be easier if she just handled it herself. "I actually gave his office my cell-phone number."

"You did?" Greg studied her.

Ally nodded but suddenly felt a little nervous. Had she crossed some line? "I did. Is that okay?"

Greg's smile eased her tension. "It's going above and beyond, which is exactly what makes for good health care. Thank you. Make sure you document the call in the notes for legal purposes, then fax any order changes to the doc for a signature. We need that on file."

"Of course."

"And how's the leg wound? The actual reason we're visiting this guy?" he asked with a laugh.

Ally shrugged. "About the same. Nowhere near healed."

Greg folded his hands and rested them on his belly as he leaned back in the chair, studying the light fixture. "Give it the week. If it's not improving, we'll get our wound doc out there again to see him. Maybe a fresh set of eyes will help." He looked back to Ally. "And I just want to say, good work. Yesterday, today, all of it. You're a great clinician, Ally. I'm afraid Four H is going to be just a memory to you soon."

A well of emotion sprang from nowhere. Ally had felt like a failure for so long, well before she'd gone to rehab, that it was hard to start thinking positively again. She sniffled, then laughed as Greg handed her a tissue. "Thank you. It feels good to be useful again."

"I bet."

"There's more though. It's…" Ally thought about her next words. "It's just normal. So much of medical training is about developing reflexes—springing to action when a code comes through the door, putting pressure on a bleeding wound. And then there's the thinking through a differential, figuring out what symptoms are important to make the diagnosis and which are the red herrings. Then deciding on the treatment. All that takes so much brain activity that I don't have time to be an addict."

Greg's eyes literally twinkled. "Precisely. As long as the stressful situations don't stress you too much."

"This one actually inspired me," Ally said, thinking of the high she'd felt when she was taking care of her patient.

"You're meant for critical care, aren't you?"

"I don't know," she confessed. "I wish I did. I'm still figuring it all out."

"Well, keep doing what you're doing."

If you only knew, Ally thought as she handed him her paperwork.

In the parking lot, she opened the hatch of the Jeep just to make sure *The Concert* was still there, and then in the front seat, she pulled the tiny Rembrandt from her glove box. Her sigh was audible. The masterpieces were still with her. Half an hour later, from the safety of her couch, she studied her little collection.

The Concert was, in her opinion, the most important piece in

Rogan's collection. Johannes Vermeer, the Dutch master, had only a few dozen paintings to his credit. A Vermeer was truly a rare gem as compared to something from the guy looking back at her from beside *The Concert.* Rembrandt had produced thousands of drawings, etchings, and paintings in his lifetime. And though both were priceless, because neither artist was putting out any new work, the Vermeer was special.

Ally looked at both pieces, trying to imagine the artists at work almost five hundred years ago, utilizing natural light because oil lanterns and candles cast crazy shadows on their subjects. Mixing paints with urine and blood and animal fat to find new and vibrant colors, striving for consistency in an unpredictable world. Making their own brushes with animal hair and quills. Those guys had been really invested in their work.

The size of the Rembrandt made it look almost cute, but Ally wasn't deceived. The skill it took to create a recognizable image using only pencil was immense, and doing it in that size was even harder. Vermeer had created his work using colorful pigments and precise brushstrokes, and just as much talent. The artists were contemporaries, but because of the sheer volume of Rembrandt's work, he was much more famous.

Ally still couldn't believe what she'd done. She had smuggled four priceless pieces of art from a guarded mansion. But she wasn't looking at herself as a thief. If these works were just copies, then all she did was switch them for other copies, with newer, better frames. If they were the originals, well, then, she had no guilt at all. It wasn't a matter of choice. She had to rescue those paintings before Brodrik Rogan's heart gave out, and they disappeared again.

How to get the rest of them, though?

Her first two acquisitions had been easy. The paintings in the foyer and the bathroom were the low-hanging fruit, out of his sight in places where Ally found herself alone. How would she get that Rembrandt gem, *The Storm*, out of his study? It was nearly as tall as Ally herself, and his chair was positioned so he could stare at it constantly.

She needed a better plan, that was certain. Unfortunately, she didn't have one.

Half an hour later, she was in the gym on the first floor of her building, pumping her arms and legs on the newest piece of equipment designed to give her the greatest cardio workout in history. It did. After fifteen minutes, with her heart rate in the low thousands and her body dripping sweat, Ally was relieved to hear her phone ring.

Until she saw the caller ID.

She hadn't spoken to Gretchen for almost a year. Gretch had reached out to wish Ally well after her injury, but then they went back to avoiding each other. For a second, she thought of ignoring the call, but then she realized it might be important. Gretchen was not calling for something trivial.

"Hi," Ally said, trying to keep the surprise from her voice.

"Back at you. I'm actually returning a call about Brodrik Rogan. I'm working with his family doc now, and you're doing home health, huh? How's that going?"

Gretchen didn't sound all judgy or stuck up, and Ally was relieved. "It's great. After months packed in bubble wrap, I'm using some of my skills again. How about you? You made quite the career change." The last time they'd spoken, Gretchen was working in the OR. And the last time they'd spoken, Gretch hadn't been engaged to a man. Ally decided she didn't want to discuss that topic. First off, it was none of her business, but more importantly, she didn't want to open old wounds. They were nearly healed, and she had worked hard on that recovery, too. She saw no point in bringing that up.

After clearing her throat, Gretch continued. "Yeah. I need a change, and for some crazy reason I thought primary care would be easier than surgery."

"Well, I'm sorry to complicate your night," she said as she walked out of the gym and hit the elevator button. She could not do the stairs, and she wasn't even going to try. The last thing her parents needed was for her body to be found on the third-floor landing with stolen artwork in her fifth-floor apartment. "But I think this could be an easy fix. Just a little bump in the water pill. He's already ordered a scale, and I'll monitor his weight."

"I'll fax you the order for the dosage change and arrange a chest X-ray," Gretchen volunteered, and Ally had an epiphany. If she could be there during the X-ray, she might be able to take advantage of that situation to pilfer more art.

"Can I be there when they shoot the film?" Ally asked. "Then I can get a look at it."

Gretchen laughed. "You always did like the fun things like blood and guts and imaging studies."

Ally smiled at the thought. "That's the best part of medicine."

Gretchen was quiet for a moment. "You sound happy, Al."

Ally didn't hesitate. "No. Not even close. But I have happy moments, like the one you just picked up on. So that's a start."

She sighed. "I've been worried about you, but I didn't want to upset your parents by reaching out. I was afraid they'd think I was just looking for gossip."

"Yeah. That was probably wise." Gretchen and Ally had hardly spoken for a year before her injury. "But now you know I'm fine. Can I be there for the X-ray?"

Gretchen chuckled. "I'll put in the order, and I'll text you the tech's number. You can coordinate with her."

"It was nice talking to you."

"This isn't over, Al. You have to call me to let me know what the X-ray shows."

"You can't push me around anymore, Gretch."

Gretchen laughed, and the sound was amazing. It reminded Ally of what they'd had for fifteen years before their relationship fell apart.

"I'll talk to you then," Gretchen said, and as Ally disconnected the call, Maria's face was on her mind as she turned on the shower and climbed in.

Half an hour later, her wet hair pulled back in a headband, Ally pulled into the parking lot of a local Italian restaurant and walked through the door. She found her mother chatting with the hostess and gave her a big hug. They didn't have much time for dinner, but they could walk to the Recovery Hub from the restaurant, so Ally wasn't worried.

"Did you bring your own easel?" Ally asked as she nibbled on buttery garlic knots.

Janine delicately dabbed at her mouth with the corner of her napkin. "I have to admit, I'm a bit confused about the etiquette of taking an art class as a student."

"How so?" Ally asked.

"Do I introduce myself? Would that make me look snobbish? Or even intimidate the instructor? Who is the instructor, by the way?"

Ally reached into her purse and pulled out the brochure for the art class. "It just says they have weekly classes taught by local artists."

"Okay, then. I'm going in like every other participant. I'll use their paints and brushes and a paper smock, if they have one."

"You should probably paint with your right hand, too. To make it challenging."

Janine's eyes shot open wide. "Let's both."

Ally laughed. "No way. I can barely function with my right hand."

An hour later they walked into the Recovery Hub and were directed toward the large room where a group had gathered. They paused, and Ally immediately noticed Maria mixed in with fifteen other people, even though she wasn't looking for her. And Maria found her, turning as if she felt Ally's eyes caressing her cheek.

A smile came slowly to her face, as if the idea of Ally had just occurred to her, and she turned back to her acquaintances and nodded, then headed over to Ally and her mom. "Bri said you might come," Maria said as she opened her arms first to Ally and then her mom.

"I thought you didn't like art?" Ally said with a smile.

"I'm trying to open my mind to new possibilities." Her gaze held Ally's, and Ally felt it pierce her. What possibilities there were.

"Shall we set up next to each other?" Janine asked.

Maria looked frightened. "Please, yes. I am the only person who almost didn't get out of grade school because of art class."

Janine nodded. "I'm going to use my right hand tonight, even though I'm a lefty. So you probably won't be the worst artist in the room."

"Seriously?" Maria asked.

"She doesn't want to show up the instructor," Ally whispered.

"That's very polite," Maria whispered back.

Ally felt a buzz of positive energy in the group as they headed toward the back of the room, where supplies in plastic bins had been organized on tables. From the easels and canvases, it appeared the class would be Painting 101, and before they could further discuss the situation, the instructor introduced herself and directed them to pick up their supplies.

When they had all they needed, they positioned their easels in a semicircle, two deep in places, and the instructor set up in front of the room. After pulling up a famous Monet print, she gave them a step-by-step tutorial on how to paint it. The class wasn't so much about technique as it was fun, and Ally found after the end of an hour she'd created a rather nice little painting. Biting her lip, she imagined it in her living room next to *The Concert*.

"What's that smile about?" Maria asked.

Ally met her gaze. "I was thinking I don't have to buy you a gift for Valentine's Day."

Maria opened her eyes wide. "OMG. That's what I was thinking."

They laughed. "Let's check out the professional job." Ally nodded toward her mom, who refused to show her work before it was done.

Janine's copy was stunning, even with her non-dominant hand. "It's all in the mind," she said with a wink.

"Imagine what it'll look like once it's framed," Ally said, thinking she'd frame Maria's as a gift.

The teacher came over and gave appropriate positive remarks about their work, and they talked over cookies and water while the paint dried.

"This was so much fun," Maria said between nibbles.

"If you enjoyed yourself, you're welcome to come to my studio and play around."

"Really?" Maria asked with such excitement that Ally couldn't help being excited, too. Then she had another idea for a date night, and she smiled. Yes, that would be perfect. She'd help Maria make her own frame.

"Anytime," her mom said, bringing Ally back to the present.

"Yeah," Ally said. "It would be great if you could come by."

"I'd love to." Maria looked at her longingly, and Ally felt herself blush.

"I'll make arrangements," Ally said with a wink. "But now, we need to exit the building, so this nice art instructor can go home." Plus, Ally needed to finish a few frames, and with Brodrik Rogan's unpredictable health, sooner rather than later.

"I'll see you soon," Ally said as she hugged Maria, and she realized that once again, she felt happy. She knew it wouldn't last, but that was okay, because each time, the good feelings stayed with her a little longer than before. And even after they left, and she felt sad or angry or scared, she could look to these moments and know they were possible. She had hope.

CHAPTER EIGHTEEN

Imaging Studies

Ally was working on her laptop when her alarm sounded the next morning, and she smiled with satisfaction as she got up to shut it off. She'd needed to complete some paperwork, and she was able to get it all done with a few seconds to spare. Removing everything except the essentials from the secret compartment of her tackle box, she placed two small, framed pieces inside and closed it with satisfaction. "You've got this, Ally," she told herself as she hopped in the shower.

Ally spoke with the X-ray technician from the car on her way to the office, and the conversation went exactly as she hoped. For a client as important as the Cadillac King, the woman was happy to arrange her schedule so she could be at the Rogan estate at the same time Ally was there doing his wound care.

"Perfect," Ally said as she hung up and immediately placed another call.

"It's ready and waiting for you," her friend Ryan from the ambulance said. "And don't forget the doughnuts."

Ally turned into Dunkin' and ran in for a box of doughnuts and coffee, then headed to the ambulance station near the office. The door was open, and she walked in to find the crew of the unit hanging out watching the news.

"Hey, Ally!" they said in near harmony. She'd worked with all of them in the ER over the years, but she knew Ryan better than the other two, because he was in PA school and working his way through. They often talked about patients, and Ally did her best to teach him little things here or there when they shared a case. She hadn't seen him since she'd been out of treatment, and they hadn't spoken, but he hadn't hesitated when she told him she needed a favor.

You've got this.

"How's life on the streets of Scranton?" she asked.

They collectively moaned and groaned and made her laugh.

Then, inevitably, Ryan asked when she'd be back in the ER. "One day at a time," she told him, and while they all seemed attentive to her response, no one said anything. They simply nodded and smiled in a way that suggested she might already be old news. To them, she was just another member of the team, on her way back from a little misadventure. Nothing could have made Ally happier.

"How's school?" she asked, and Ryan ran his fingers through his short, graying hair. He was a non-traditional student, with a wife and two kids, and a full-time job. The administration at Marywood had spread out the five-year program for a master's degree to eight, but Ally knew it was still hard to find the time for all those classes along with his other responsibilities. Yet they seemed to sense something in him that typical students lacked—a fire, a passion and compassion that would make him a phenomenal PA, no matter how long it took him to earn that degree. Ally sensed it, too, and it was why she and Ryan clicked.

"I just need about four more hours every day, and I'd be fine."

She knew he used the downtime on the overnight shift to study, which helped, but he still carried a lot of weight. Since his clinical rotations had started, he'd essentially been working two full-time jobs. "How much longer do you have?"

The smile on his face was radiant. "One hundred and thirty-three days."

Ally nodded. She understood the counting. "And then what?"

"Oh, the ER, of course."

He'd be great there, and Ally told him so.

"And speaking of work, I need to get going. Do you have what I need?" she asked, and when Ryan nodded, she offered up the Dunkin'.

He walked her to the door, carrying a thirty- by twenty-four-inch cardboard box under one arm. "So, Macie is working out great," Ryan said.

Damn. Ally had so much on her mind, she'd forgotten about Macie, but she shouldn't have. Small details were likely to cause her demise. Ally forced a smile. "That's good to know. I hear she's really amazing."

Ryan nodded. "She is. When you recommended her, it sounded like you knew her personally. Yet she says she's never met you. She says she was working for Hart, and this offer came out of the blue."

Ally's brain had been spinning since Ryan mentioned Macie's

name, and she was ready. She dropped her head a few degrees and shrugged, lowering her voice when she spoke. "You know I can't talk about this."

Ryan's eyes flew open. "Oh, yeah. I get it. But it's no secret that people who work at Hart are in recovery."

Ally shrugged again.

"I know, you can't say anything. But I just don't understand one thing. Why didn't you take the management job on the ambulance instead of recommending her? You're more qualified than she is."

Now Ally could be honest. "I need to get my license back, and Four H is the proven path. Macie's a nurse, so it's a little different for her. Plus, she's only a month or so away from getting her nursing license, and she might stay on as the ambulance company manager forever. That's a great position."

"But not for you?"

She winked. "You know I love blood and guts."

Ryan nodded. "Yes, you do. Now promise to stay in touch," he said. "I miss you."

Ally hugged him. "See you soon," she said, and he handed her the box, which was much heavier than she would have thought. After nodding toward Ryan again, she placed it in the back of the Jeep and tried to rearrange everything there. When Ryan finally headed in, Ally emptied the box he'd given her and quickly put her own things inside, arranged perfectly to fit in the small space. After she finished, she lifted the box again to test the weight and then sighed with relief. It was perfect.

She ran the plan for Brodrik Rogan by Greg when she talked to him a few minutes later. "If I wait around for the X-ray, it may mean I'm there a few minutes longer."

Nodding, he rolled his eyes. "What else is new? Just keep me informed, okay? If I have to rearrange any clients, it's better to do it early, rather than late."

After reassuring him that she'd do just that, Ally headed out and began her day. Her clients were doing well, but she had a nervous energy about seeing Brodrik Rogan that morning, and her palms were sweating as she drove up to his gate. She needed to be there before the X-ray people, and when she inquired with the guard, he told her they hadn't yet arrived.

"Perfect," she said aloud as she was ushered through. If she could get his wound cared for before they got to the house, she might just get away with her plan.

"Good morning, Ally." Rocco greeted her under the portico.

"Hi," she said. "The portable-X-ray people are coming. I'd like to take care of Mr. Rogan first, so he's all ready to go when they arrive."

"We'll have to do the normal clearances," he said sternly.

Ally had been counting on it. "Of course," she said. "I brought an X-ray box with me, so I can look at the film right away. It's important. Can you carry it in for me? It's heavy."

He flexed his muscles and winked, and when Ally pointed out the box she'd gotten from Ryan, he easily lifted it and followed her into the house. "Where would you like this?" he asked when they reached the hall.

"The study, I think. That way I can show Mr. Rogan the X-ray."

"That's a pretty good idea. I'll see if he's ready for you," he said, but before they could move, the study door opened. Peter Rogan came out, followed by the most beautiful woman Ally had ever seen. She was tall, with blond hair cascading down her back, and big blue eyes that seemed to take in the entire room at once. Ally remembered the picture of Savannah Summers from the internet, and this woman was a carbon copy. This was the daughter the article mentioned, the child that the actor had with Brodrik Rogan.

"Oh, it's you," Peter said. "What's the plan with my dad?"

The siblings approached, narrowing the space between them to a few feet, and Ally introduced herself.

"I'm Grace Rogan. Your patient is my dad."

Peter waved his hand impatiently after the introductions ended. "My father. An X-ray?" he asked.

Ally nodded and summarized all the things she'd done and what she'd set in motion. "Any chance that scale arrived?"

He looked angry at the question. "I can't control the mail!"

Ally took a breath and spoke soothingly. Clearly, Peter Rogan was a hothead. "No. Of course not. I was just inquiring because it's one of the things we can follow to prevent your dad from having those episodes."

"How so?" Grace Rogan asked as she looked at Ally.

Aware that the clock was ticking, that the narrow window she needed could close, she patiently explained about fluid overload causing weight gain.

"What about this X-ray?" Peter asked.

"It'll give us an idea of how much fluid is in the lungs. Or it could even pick up something else." Ally regretted the words the second they were out of her mouth, and Peter Rogan jumped on them.

"What else? Cancer? You think my dad has lung cancer?" He shook his head and continued before Ally could speak. "All the fucking smoking all those years. I told him. Everyone told him. Shit fuck."

"Um, Mr. Rogan, I was actually thinking more of an infection, or maybe inflammation." The specifics didn't matter, and the less Ally told him, the better. To her relief, he nodded and didn't ask what kind of infection or inflammation the X-ray might show.

"Shall we?" Ally asked. "I'd like to finish with his wound before the X-ray people arrive." She was hoping the family would be uninterested in seeing their father's ulcer, but to her dismay, they nodded and led her back into the room. Ally swallowed. This situation was a disaster. She'd counted on Rogan being alone, on having time to herself in his study while the technicians wheeled him out to their X-ray van. She'd have to come up with another way to get the remaining paintings. And she had to hope no one tried to open that box from Top Notch Radiology.

In his study, Brodrik Rogan was seated at his desk, and he pushed away a paper and smiled when he saw Ally.

"Here's my hero. She saved my life," he said to no one in particular, but Ally was happy to hear the words anyway.

"Good morning, Mr. Rogan," Ally said as he stood and made his way slowly across the room. She walked in that direction too and sat on the couch, opening her tackle box to take up as much space as possible. Maybe if they couldn't sit, they'd leave.

"Where should I put this?" Rocco asked of the box from Top Notch Radiology.

Ally indicated the floor next to the couch, and Rocco gently set the box down before excusing himself.

Wasting no time, Ally went to work on the leg, noticing the swelling as soon as she raised his pant leg to expose his wound. The elastic of the pants bit into this flesh, and his entire foot was tattooed with the pattern of his sock. "Did you take the extra water pill yesterday?" she asked, and to her dismay, Brodrik Rogan looked to his children for the answer.

"Yes," Peter said. "The doctor called and increased it to three times a day. He started yesterday."

Ally nodded and peeled back the dressing from his leg ulcer, happy to see the results of her work. It seemed to be improving, with less gooey drainage, but it wasn't changing in size at all. Perhaps this was a good time to mention Greg's idea of a consult. Then the children would know what was happening and wouldn't freak out about it. But Ally also knew she wasn't the one in charge of this case. She wasn't a PA anymore, just an unlicensed home-health aide who didn't have the authority to order consults with wound specialists.

Peter and Grace sat across from their father, on the end of the couch and on a large chair, but when Ally exposed the wound, they both came closer to see it.

"Does it hurt, Dad?" Grace asked.

He snapped. "Of course it hurts! How would you feel if half your leg looked like you'd been attacked by a shark?"

Grace nodded, accepting his criticism, and stepped back. So did Peter. "I'll be in the family room. Call me when they do the X-ray."

One down, one to go, but Grace Rogan showed no sign of going anywhere. Instead, she sat to talk with Ally and her father. Her father, though, didn't even seem to notice her, as he directed his comments to Ally.

"My favorite painting," he said as he nodded to the large seascape behind Grace's head. "The power of God on full display. God the Father creating the storm, and then God the Son calming it." Although he sat tall and spoke loudly, Ally noticed the big gasp of air he sucked in at the end of the sentence.

"I like the face of Rembrandt looking out at us."

He smiled. "You noticed that, huh? I like that, too. A little humor in art."

"Yes! And speaking of your painting," she nodded toward the Rembrandt, "can I come by Saturday to repair the frame? It's the only free time I have, since I work during the week."

He looked at her as he might a small child who was begging for a new toy at the store but then slowly nodded. "Of course. Grace, would you mark that on my calendar? I have another appointment on Saturday, so I'll get everything out of the way at the same time."

"Sure," Grace said as she stood and began walking toward the desk, leaving their view of *Christ in the Storm on the Sea of Galilee* unobstructed.

"I'm a very religious person, Ally. Most people don't know that. I give the church a small fortune."

Ally was familiar with people trying to buy their way into heaven, so Rogan's statement didn't surprise her. "It's a worthy charity, I'm sure."

"Oh, yes. They do so much, with helping the poor and such. It's the least I can do."

How could she argue with helping the poor? "It's very kind of you, Mr. Rogan."

"How are those plants I gave you?" he asked, seeming very comfortable to have Ally to talk with. And although Ally didn't dislike talking with him, she'd witnessed his anger the day before when he'd asked to examine the tackle box. She couldn't forget his violent past, and it made her suddenly determined to not say anything more than was necessary in their interactions.

Ally told them she'd kept them alive, on a sunny spot on her kitchen counter where she couldn't ignore them. "Best tomatoes you'll ever eat," he said, then looked at Grace. "I gave her the secret tomatoes."

Grace smiled at her father, then turned to Ally. "You'll love them."

"What's the secret?" Ally asked as she slowly began to take everything from her tackle box, making a show of organizing it while she waited.

Brodrik Rogan leaned forward. "A friend of mine smuggled the seeds out of Italy. You can't get anything like this anywhere else in the world. Just Italy and my garden."

Ally nodded as she processed the information. Probably, someone else had those seeds too, but Rogan liked to think he was exclusive. Just like his art, Ally thought. No one should have it but him. "Can I get arrested for having smuggled tomatoes, or am I okay?" she asked.

Rogan shrugged and didn't answer the question. "We're expecting some more snow tonight. Good time to come over and have a little fun. Take the snowmobiles out. My grandchildren are coming this weekend. Now that I'm sick, everyone wants to pay me a visit."

Ally smiled. "They'll probably bring you presents."

"What do I need?"

Ally nodded in understanding, but suddenly Brodrik Rogan began to sob. Unsure what to do, Ally called to him, and Grace rushed to his side. Waving her off, he reached for a tissue from a table beside his chair. "My health, Ally. That's what I need now, and all my money can't buy it."

He leaned back in his chair and looked at his daughter. "I need to call my lawyer. About my will."

"I'll tell Peter," Grace said as a loud knock sounded on the study door. It opened, and Rocco came in.

"Mr. Rogan, the people are here to do your X-ray."

"Bring them in," he said, and Ally quickly finished fussing with her equipment.

Two young men dressed in scrubs entered the study and approached Brodrik Rogan. "How you doing?" one asked, and after ascertaining he could walk, they explained they were going to escort him to their truck for an X-ray of his chest. The entire process would take only five minutes.

Five minutes was pushing it, even if Ally was alone and had the freedom to operate in the study. But with Grace sitting just a few feet away, it was impossible. No way could she make the switch today.

Then, to her amazement, as the two men stood on either side of Brodrik Rogan and began walking him toward the door, Grace rose from her chair and announced she was going to talk to her brother.

This was the opportunity Ally needed!

She sat, trying not to follow the agonizingly slow procession, but watched from the corner of her eye until Rocco disappeared from view. Knowing she could be caught if anyone—Rocco, Grace, Peter, or even Winnie—walked by the study, Ally used the couch to shield her actions from view. Pushing the X-ray box onto the cushion, she pulled the tape that held it closed and quickly dumped the contents.

Framed pieces—drawings, washings, and even a painting—were neatly stacked within the largest frame, like a series of nesting dolls. Ally grabbed the big one, a panel, and rushed to the bathroom. Raphael looked back at her with a curious expression as she took him from the wall and replaced him with her copy. A few seconds later, with one eye on the door, she placed him on a sheet of bubble wrap and picked up three more pieces.

The Degas works, two pieces entitled *Study for the Programme,* were hanging behind the chair where Rogan most often sat. Beside it, another Degas, *Three Mounted Jockeys*, was on display. Careful not to mix the order of the works, she pulled them from the wall one by one and replaced them with her copies. A few steps across the room, she stacked the pieces onto bubble wrap and then on top of the Raphael.

Ally sighed but didn't stop moving. Pulling the tray from her tackle box, she lifted two small pieces and picked up the final painting from the couch and headed across the room. At Brodrik Rogan's desk, she switched out the small prints *Procession on a Road Near Florence* and *Leaving the Paddock.* At the couch, Ally placed *Chez Tortoni* down and picked up the original from the sofa table, then circled around as she glanced at the door, then the clock. There was no activity in the hallway, but three minutes had passed since Rocco had left the room.

The two small pieces easily fit into her tackle box, and she carefully placed her other items over them. Satisfied that it looked as it should, Ally tucked *Chez Tortoni* onto the stack on the Raphael and went to work sliding the large panel into the box. It was heavy and awkward, but the wrap was slippery, and once she cleared the edges of the cardboard, the task was easy. Pushing the box to the floor, Ally taped the edges and was just closing her bag when she heard voices in the hall.

"This girl wants to look at the X-ray," Rocco told the technician. "She brought an X-ray machine with her."

They'd paused at the doorway, and the technician and Rocco looked in Ally's direction.

Ally pointed to the box. "I thought I could show Mr. Rogan his film," she said.

The tech looked apologetic. "We don't actually have films anymore. But if you would like to come out to the truck, we can show you the digital image."

It was just as Ally planned. No one had used X-ray film for years, and just like photographs in a camera, everything was stored on a disc and viewed on a computer. "Okay, sure."

The tech nodded, and Ally smiled at Mr. Rogan. "I'll look at your X-ray and be back in a jiffy."

The two men settled Rogan in the chair, and then Ally hoisted her tackle box. "Would you mind helping me carry the X-ray box?" she asked the tech. "My Jeep is just outside the door."

He smiled and nodded, and Ally moved aside as he easily lifted the cardboard.

"Thanks for coming out," Ally said as she walked beside the man toward the front door.

"Oh, it was no trouble. All in a day's work, you know? I can't believe you still have a view box," he said.

"We use it for teaching. A lot of great X-rays are still floating around. Back in the day, you could just cut the patient's name off the corner of the film to preserve confidentiality. These days..." Ally shrugged.

"So true," he said pleasantly.

At the front door, Ally turned left, with him following her, and she locked the Jeep after he placed his package in the hatch. When they turned, Rocco was behind them, with Peter just a few feet beyond.

"Oh!" Ally said as she put her hand to her heart. "You startled me."

Rocco looked as if he was noticing them for the first time, as if it just occurred to him that Ally might be up to no good. For a moment her mouth went dry as she breathed in the cold mountain air, but then he smiled.

"I was wondering if we could see the X-ray, too?"

Ally looked at the tech. "It's all right by me," she said.

"I don't have a problem with that," he replied.

Ally followed the tech into the truck, where two images were displayed side by side on a computer screen. It was a chest X-ray, but instead of the heart sitting in its normal position slightly to the left of center, this one filled most of the chest cavity. Two lungs, normally black with air, were filled with fluffy white patches, suggesting fluid.

"What's it look like?" Peter asked.

Ally pointed out the enlarged heart and the pulmonary edema, the lines that told her fluid was trapped in the gravity-dependent spaces.

"So, it's not good?" he asked.

Tilting her head, Ally sighed. "I hoped it would be better."

"So what are you going to do about it?" Peter stood tall, striking an intimidating pose.

But what could Ally do? Brodrik Rogan was failing, and as he'd stated earlier, his money couldn't buy him a new heart. Then a chill went down Ally's spine as she thought that, perhaps, in some parts of the world, it could. And considering what she knew of him, he had connections in those places.

Punt, she told herself. "When was the last time he actually saw his doctor? In person, not a telemedicine visit. Not a nurse, but the doctor?"

He threw up his hands. "I don't know. Until recently, he was doing great. Then the leg. Now the breathing. He's falling apart all of a sudden."

Ally wondered if that was true, or if Peter had just not been around to witness the slow decline. "I think a checkup with the cardiologist is in order."

"Can't you just admit him to the hospital? Get everything taken care of at once."

Ally nodded. It was possible to admit him. And considering Mr. Rogan's mobility issues, and the shortness of breath he suffered with even the smallest amount of exertion, perhaps it was the best option. "Let's talk to him," Ally suggested.

"No way!" Brodrik Rogan replied when Ally told him her thoughts about the hospital.

"I think you need more than a little tune-up. All the adjustments of medications, some tests you should have—it's easiest if you're in the hospital."

He sat forward, and Ally glimpsed the man he must have been when he ruled an empire. "I'm not going, and that's that. Give me an extra water pill, and get me in to see my doctors. Tell Hart. He has connections."

Indeed, Greg Hart did have some influence with Rogan's doctors. Ally wasn't sure it mattered, though. He was clearly failing, and no matter what sort of magic they worked with medications, no matter what new information they gleaned from testing, one fact wouldn't change. Brodrik Rogan was a sick man.

"I'll speak with him today," she said.

"Good. Now go water your plants and give me a rest."

Ally called Greg just as soon as she turned on the Jeep. "I'll see what I can do," he responded to her request. She disconnected her phone, and it immediately pinged, telling her she had a message. Scanning her phone screen, she smiled. She had a text from Maria.

Dinner Friday?

The question made Ally forget for a moment that she was carrying seven of Brodrik Rogan's paintings in the back of her Jeep. The presence of a security guard on a snowmobile reminded her, and Ally delayed answering Maria. The most important thing at the moment was to get off the Rogan property. Later, when she was home, with the artwork safely deposited in her living room, she'd breathe easy. Until then, she was going to smile politely, drive slowly and carefully, and not do anything to attract attention.

At the gate, the guard stepped out of his hut, and Ally held her breath as she approached, fearful he'd stop her. Perhaps someone had seen her or suspected something. Perhaps one of the pieces of art she'd left was hanging crooked or had left a smear of dust where it shouldn't be.

Then he waved, and the gate opened, and Ally sucked in a breath she didn't exhale until she saw the gate in the mirror closing behind her.

"You did it," she whispered. "You did it!" she screamed as she slapped the wheel. Then she reminded herself to be cautious and held the wheel tightly with both hands. Yet she couldn't help smiling. *You've got this.*

CHAPTER NINETEEN

Another Step Forward

Instead of heading to the office, Ally decided to drive directly to her apartment after her last patient. It was nerve-racking, the acts of drawing blood and changing bandages and acting as if everything was perfectly normal when a fortune in stolen art was sitting in the back of her Jeep, just waiting for some wayward teenagers to steal it. So as soon as she finished that last patient duty, she sighed, checked to make sure the art was still where she'd put it, and drove home.

After parking, she picked up the luggage trolley from the mail room and easily maneuvered it outside. Then, with the X-ray box and her tackle box in place, she pushed it across the lot and up the ramp to the wide double doors of the building. When she reached the lobby, she met Carlos and Steve, two tenants who spent hours each day in the gym. Their bulging muscles were proof of their commitment, and both wore cutaway shirts to show them off.

"Need a hand?" Steve asked sweetly.

Ally shook her head. "It's not heavy, but thanks."

"Doing some work at home?" Carlos nodded toward the box from the X-ray company.

Ally shook her head. "I review X-rays with the paramedics once in a while. Just the cool cases."

"Do you like the new job?" Steve asked.

Ally appreciated their concern. They were thirty-something, a couple, and had been friends since she'd moved in after her breakup with Gretchen. They'd even looked after the building while she was in rehab. She nodded. "It's really great. I like working with patients. I feel useful." And then she thought for a second of something that had been at the back of her mind since she started working at Four H. "And I like the people. They appreciate the good care they're given."

"Unlike the ER," Steve said.

Ally nodded. "Yep."

"When are we going out?" Carlos asked.

She pursed her lips. "Normally, I might put you two at the top of my list for Valentine's Day. But I happen to have a date this year."

Carlos crossed his massive arms across his chest and squinted at Ally, putting on a pouty face that made her smile. "Who is she?" he demanded.

Ally told them about reconnecting with Maria, and they were excited to hear the news. They'd been pushing her to ask Maria out when she first started in the ER, but Ally's mind hadn't been in the right place then. Hell, she didn't know if it was in the right place now, either. Yet thoughts of Maria kept coming into her head, and with them a happiness that she welcomed.

"Well, I'm glad you're home. The snow is going to start soon, and you shouldn't be driving."

With all the things Ally had been doing, she'd neglected to watch television or check the weather. "When does it start?" Ally asked.

"Any minute," Steve said.

Great. She had to drop her paperwork back at the office, and then she had an appointment with Dr. Griver. After saying good-bye, Ally pushed the trolley to the elevator and rode it to her floor. Once inside her apartment, she unloaded the box of artwork, breathing a sigh of relief that she hadn't damaged anything when she so hastily packed it. Her walls were now filled, so she set the new additions on the floor, and on a shelf, and sat back to take stock.

It was unbelievable. The new things she'd brought were not the most valuable of the Gardner collection, but they were still created by the hands of Degas and Manet. The Raphael, on the other hand, was one of the most valuable missing pieces of art in the world. And here they sat, in a tiny apartment in Scranton, Pennsylvania, in possession of a young PA who'd stolen them from a client's house.

Ally remembered reading a story of a discovery of great art in an apartment in Germany. The works had been stolen during World War II, and the man who held them had "inherited" them from a family member who'd been involved in the Nazi art looting. If something happened to her today, if she died in a car crash on the way home from her psychiatrist's office, or if she was killed in a holdup at the gas station, she'd probably make the international headlines as well.

Not what she wanted to be famous for, that was for sure. Maybe she should write a note, explaining it all, just in case. The idea sent a chill down her spine, but she shook it off. She didn't have time for second-guessing now.

Ten of the thirteen pieces stolen from the Gardner were now in her apartment. The vase and the finial were still unaccounted for, and Ally just had to forget them. She'd looked at purchasing similar items on the internet, just in case she found the originals at the Rogan mansion, but she couldn't be sure they'd fool anyone. Even if they looked similar, how about their weight? Would the finish rub off when the housekeeper sprayed a little industrial-strength cleaner on the surface? Ally didn't feel confident about dealing with them, and an attempt could be the thing that exposed her. Best to stick to the paintings and drawings and hope she could fool an old man's eyes.

That left just one painting, arguably the most valuable from the Gardner, and most certainly the most valuable to Brodrik Rogan. He sat and stared at it all day long. And that was exactly what made stealing the last of the collection such a challenge. Ally needed full access to *Christ in the Storm on the Sea of Galilee*, and she needed to be alone with it. She hoped she'd have her chance in a couple of days.

You've got this.

Smiling, she looked from Raphael to Rembrandt, then stood and went into her bedroom. There, she changed into jeans and a sweater for her trip back across town. Then she picked up the long tube containing the full-size replica of *Christ in the Storm on the Sea of Galilee*. Swapping out this sixty-three- by fifty-one-inch work of fake art for the Rembrandt masterpiece would be the biggest challenge Ally had faced yet.

Grabbing her coat, she hoisted the print and headed out. A few minutes later she'd returned the trolley and was in her car and soon at the office of Four H.

Hoping to slip in and out, Ally kept her head down as she walked toward the billing office. Unfortunately, she was on Greg's radar, and he called her in.

"Thanks for taking care of Rogan," he said.

Ally smiled. "That's my job. Any luck with his doctor?"

"Yes. We've scheduled him for tomorrow. Two appointments, actually. Family doctor first, followed by the cardiologist, if he's able to make it out. This is going to be some storm tonight."

"So I'm told. What's our policy with visiting clients in the snow?"

He blew out a breath. "That's a tough call. I don't want my

providers getting in an accident, right? But people still need care. So I look at the clients and try to figure out who can wait a day, or push them back until the evening."

"This snow stops in the morning, right?"

"Yes. I'm leaning toward a two-to-eight shift tomorrow."

Ally could do that. It meant having a morning off, sleeping late. What better way to spend a snowy morning?

"Everything else okay?" he asked.

A warm flush began in her chest, and Ally fought hard to suppress it. Could he possibly know? Did someone from the Rogan circle call him and relay suspicions about Ally stealing artwork?

"Yes. Great."

"You've been making our meetings. That's good. Are you seeing your psychiatrist?"

Ally nodded. "In about ten minutes."

Greg laughed. "Then you should head out. Thanks for your hard work," he said, and Ally felt a little guilty for the crimes she was committing under his watch. Certainly his name would be mentioned if she were caught.

Yet no matter how many times she considered what she was doing, and reconsidered the consequences, the fact remained that she was doing something good. Once she'd become convinced that the artwork might be real, she knew she had to repatriate it. She couldn't sit by and watch Brodrik Rogan die and see those treasures destroyed by unsuspecting family members or sold on the black market, never to be seen again. So she swallowed that bit of doubt and smiled. "I'll see you tomorrow."

It was a short ride across town to Dr. Griver's office, and he answered the door just a moment after Ally rang the bell. He turned and immediately began walking down the long hallway, leaving Ally to follow.

"Here we are, right on time. Punctuality is very important in recovery, Ally. It's a sign you're taking things seriously. Respecting authority."

Ally might have rolled her eyes at his pomposity, but she feared he'd see her on one of the security cameras scattered around the office. A necessary precaution given his line of work, but an invasion, nonetheless. If Ally wanted to pick her nose in the waiting room, that was her business, not his.

She didn't stop there, though. With her paperwork completed on the last visit, he ushered her straight through the small lobby and into his private office, sat in his chair, and motioned for her to do the same. Then he looked at her and smiled.

"Tell me about your week," he said.

Ally talked about working at Four H and her budding relationship with Maria. "I'm not sure I'm ready to be with someone," she said.

"What are you afraid of?" he asked.

Ally knew the answer because she'd been asking herself the same question. "Many things. I'm afraid if I'm working on an 'us' there won't be much time for working on 'me.' I'm afraid of disappointing her, because she'll find out I'm really nothing special. I'm afraid she'll disappoint me, because she'll ditch me when she figures it all out."

"Tell me five good things about yourself."

After six months of recovery, none of the questions surprised Ally, yet this one did. She pursed her lips as she reviewed her best qualities. "I'm intelligent. I have a sense of humor. I'm kind. I work hard. I'm artistic."

"All wonderful attributes. Tell me five nice things about Maria."

"All the same things, except she says she's not artistic. I'd substitute artistic skills for culinary abilities."

"So she cooks?"

Ally nodded. "Very well."

"A form of art, itself. But let's set that aside and look at the other attributes you mentioned. You have four of the same very important good things. Why do you think she'll figure you out? What's to figure?"

"The bad things."

"Oh," he said dramatically. "The bad things. Let's hear them."

Of course the first thing that came to mind was art theft, but she pushed it aside. This wasn't the time to share that little tidbit about herself. What else, though? What was really bad about her?

"C'mon, Ally. You must do something bad. Leave your dirty laundry on the floor? Dishes in the sink."

Ally nodded. "I'm pretty neat."

"Any violent tendencies?"

"No." Ally thought of her brother Jimmy. "I don't like my brother."

Dr. Griver looked surprised. "Really? Why is that?"

Ally shared some of her history, early memories of her brother's nasty nature and meanness.

"It sounds as though he's not very likable. How's your other brother?"

"Kevin?" Ally smiled. "He's great."

"Can you really expect yourself to like someone who's not very nice to you?"

"My parents expect it! And they don't see him how he is."

"He's their child, so they want to see the good in him. But I'm sure they see the bad, too. They just overlook it. That's love, isn't it? Overlooking someone's flaws."

Ally saw where he was heading. "But a child is different. He's yours, and you love him no matter what. It's different with a lover."

"I'm not so sure it is."

Ally thought of Gretchen and all she'd excused because she cared for her and wanted their relationship to work. Still, they weren't able to overcome their differences. Ally told him that.

"Okay, but you're saying that you didn't accept her with her flaws and couldn't agree on a strategy to move your relationship forward."

Ally laughed, then thought about what he'd said. It wasn't that Ally was too laid back or too neat, or that Gretchen was the opposite that caused them to break up. Gretchen was interested in a man. Breaking up wasn't about Ally. It was about Gretchen.

"I think you're right."

"So tell me your flaws," he said.

"I like alone time. Sometimes, I just like it quiet, and I'm not open to hearing everyone else's opinion."

"Everyone needs alone time."

"Me more than most, and it's hard to find it when you're in a relationship." She looked him in the eye. "I loved that about rehab. I could just go off on my own, and it was okay."

"How long ago did you and Gretchen break up?"

"Two years."

"How have you been spending your time?"

Ally told him about the year prior to her injury, the things she'd done with her family and friends.

"It's all healthy stuff, Ally. Do you think you could talk to Maria about your needs?"

Ally thought she could talk to Maria about anything.

"So what's the real issue, then?" he asked.

This was the hard thing, the only thing that mattered, and it was so defeating, because no matter what she did, she couldn't change it. "I'm a drug addict," she said softly. "And she's not."

She met his gaze, and she saw it darken.

"What if she was? What if there was someone else, another woman, in recovery? Would you feel differently about a relationship?"

Ally thought of someone, a beautiful and intelligent woman she'd met in rehab. They'd hit it off, and she let Ally know she was interested, yet Ally wasn't. Part of it was that she felt off-kilter, still figuring out how to think and function without opioids in her system. Another part was simpler, though. She'd been thinking of Maria, quite a bit. One of the thoughts and goals she'd kept in mind, a motivation of sorts, was the hope that when she was sober and out of rehab, she might have a chance at a relationship with her.

"So this woman is very special to you."

Ally breathed in, and the air seemed to be filled with the scent of Maria, just from thinking of her. "Yes."

"Ally, I can't tell you you're a good person. I can't tell you you're worthy. Well, actually I can. But it won't matter. What matters is you have to tell yourself that. You have to believe it. Write down all the good things, not just five of them. And write down the bad. If you total them up, the good far outweighs the bad. You have a lot to offer. And from my perspective, you're ready."

"You don't think it's too soon?"

"Absolutely not. I like to see my patients in healthy relationships, because they provide support for you. And a partner makes you accountable, because it's hard to hide from one."

"I'm seeing her on Valentine's Day."

"Excellent."

She looked around his crazy office and still thought he was a little off, but it didn't matter. He was smart, and Ally needed that. She liked that he was older, too. It somehow made him seem wiser, and that was good for Ally. In her rehab, she never liked being older or more educated than the people who were telling her what to do.

"Have you been thinking about the Golden Question?"

Ally knew just what he was talking about. How she'd gotten here.

"It all goes back to my childhood." She held his gaze for a moment before smiling, and he laughed.

"I like you, Ally."

"Same."

"Answer the question."

Sighing, she looked at the ceiling. It was just a plain white plaster ceiling, nothing fancy, and seemed so out of place in his busy office. Yet she found it calming. Compared to all the color and contrast, it was a relief to stare at nothing. After a moment, she told him her thoughts. Even though she knew the risks, she'd thought she was too good, too perfect to become addicted. So she'd taken more and more pills, without fear that it would happen to her. And when she felt herself stumbling and knew she was heading for a fall, she didn't want to disappoint the people who thought those good things about her. She'd tried on her own to stop using opioids but couldn't do it.

"What was different at rehab?"

"Everything. First of all, the game was over. Everyone knew, so I didn't have to pretend anymore. That was the most wonderful feeling—after hiding for months, I could finally be honest. And I was ready to accept help, too. I'd tried to manage my drug use and tried to control it, and I couldn't. You've heard this story before—it was just bigger and stronger than I could handle. In many ways, it was a relief to share the burden."

He seemed to understand, and they were quiet for a moment.

"I can't promise you'll never get hurt. But you've earned the right to date someone. You're worthy."

Ally so wished she could believe him.

CHAPTER TWENTY

Finishing Touches

The snow had started falling, big puffy flakes that were beautiful to look at but treacherous on the ground and roadways. Ally let her Jeep warm up while she swept the windows, then headed to her local appliance store in town. Lackawanna Appliance, one of the last local family-owned stores of its kind, had been in the Tomassoni family for generations, and Ally's parents had been buying from them for as long as she could remember, both for their home and their rental units. Ally knew the salespeople by name.

"Hi, Gerri," she greeted the woman at the counter when she walked in.

No one else was in the store, and Ally commented on the weather.

"I live a block away, so I figured I'd stay. Some crazy person always needs a new stove during a blizzard. And here you are."

Laughing, Ally held up her hands. "It's just a box I'm interested in. Something from a big TV."

Ally looked at the dozen televisions on display, then back to Gerri.

"We usually keep them, because we sell the floor models. But you can have one as long as you don't tell anyone where you got it. Follow me."

Ally walked into the side room and then into a storage area, where dozens of boxes of all sizes were folded and piled. The largest were on the bottom, and the largest was just what she wanted.

"How's your business?" Gerri asked as they moved the pile, one box at a time.

"Excellent. No vacancies at the moment, so that's good."

"I always say, if you have a good landlord, you'll stay put."

Ally agreed, and she'd tried to be attentive to her tenants' needs. They kept the lot clear, so people could park their cars without a hassle.

She continuously upgraded the gym equipment and hired yoga and Pilates instructors for classes every day. The mail room provided ample space for all the Amazon packages that allowed people to shop on their phones. And when an appliance broke, Ally came to see Gerri and had a replacement delivered the next day.

When they reached the bottom box, Ally picked it up and leaned it against the wall. It was taller than she was, and wide, but she wasn't sure if it was wide enough. "Do you have a tape measure?" she asked Gerri.

"What on earth do you need with a box this big?" Gerri asked as she walked to a work area and came back with the tool in hand.

"It's for an art project," Ally replied immediately.

"Oh." Gerry pulled the end of the measure and handed it to Ally. "Seventy-five wide," she said. "And fifty-four tall."

Wow, Ally thought. It's going to be close. But she couldn't come up with anything else, so she'd have to make it work. "Perfect," she said.

Gerri picked up one end of the box, and Ally was surprised by how heavy it was. She worried, too, that it wouldn't fit into the Jeep. She could bend it, though, if she had to.

After thanking Gerri, Ally carried the box and managed to stuff it into her hatch, and then she joined the trail of cars inching their way along Interstate 81. The weather was really awful, and she was happy Greg had given her the morning off. She'd spend the night with her parents and maybe sneak out in the morning to snowshoe in the woods.

At their exit she turned off the highway, and a few minutes later she pulled into the spare garage. First, she carried the box to the studio, and after she deposited it there, she went into the house to talk to her parents.

Something savory filled her nostrils as she opened the door, and Ally realized she was starving.

"Ally," her mom said in greeting when she walked into the kitchen. "What a lovely surprise."

Ally hugged her mom and then peeked into the Crock-Pot. A roast was swimming in a sea of potatoes and carrots, and it smelled wonderful. "Mind if I join you guys for dinner?"

"Honey, you're always welcome. Dad just went up to change, so we're eating in a minute. Would you like wine? I bought a Beaujolais."

"That sounds wonderful," Ally said as she pulled glasses from the cupboard and poured.

"How are you doing?" her mom asked, and Ally filled her in on work.

"And how's the doctor?" she asked as she eyed Ally over the top of her wineglass.

"We have a date," Ally said, and told her about their upcoming plans.

"I like her," her mom said.

"Me too. I talked to my shrink about her today."

"Is that the guy from the state board?"

"The one and only. He's a trip," Ally said and told her about his office decor in the style of Sigmund Freud. "But I like him."

Janine smiled at her. "You seem happy."

Ally sipped her wine. "I'm getting there."

She'd be much happier after Saturday, after she had the chance to work on *Christ in the Storm on the Sea of Galilee.* Until then, she'd be nervous and couldn't do anything about it. She'd work tonight on the copy and then count the ticks on the clock until she made it to Rogan's house.

Her father joined them, and after dinner Ally helped clean up, then trudged through the snow to the studio. She'd turned on the heat, so it was already toasty, and went right to work.

Using a marker and a tape measure, she drew a line on the box she'd gotten from the appliance store. Then, using a straightedge and a razor, she cut the box to her specifications. When it was done, she repeated the process with the back side of the box and created an identical copy of the first piece of cardboard.

Next, Ally took out an industrial-strength glue gun and plugged it in. While it was heating, she opened the tube, unrolled her copy of *Christ in the Storm on the Sea of Galilee,* and placed it atop the first piece of cardboard.

It fit perfectly, with an inch margin on all four sides, and Ally let out a sigh of relief. Taking the glue gun, she squeezed a quarter-size dot on the corner of the cardboard, and before the glue could dry, she placed the second piece of cardboard over the first, sealing her copy of the painting between the two pieces. Working slowly and carefully, she made her way around the cardboard, depositing gobs of glue between the pieces every few feet, until she'd completed the circle.

After she finished, she inspected the edges. She saw no telltale glue but worried it wouldn't hold with the small amount she'd used. With too little, the panel would fail. But too much could seal the painting inside so well that she might not be able to remove it when she needed to.

"You've got this," she said as she picked up the sealed painting.

The glue held.

"Yes!" she squealed.

If everything went according to plan, it didn't have to hold for long, just enough to get the painting into Brodrik Rogan's dining room, where she planned to work on his frame. Once she made the switch, she'd use a gallon of glue to seal the real painting inside these two pieces of cardboard.

It took only a few minutes to clean up, and Ally had almost finished when her phone rang. She pulled it from her pocket and smiled at the screen. Maria.

"Hi," she said.

"What are you up to?" Maria asked.

"A little work in the studio. How about you?"

"Missing you. Wanna play in the snow with me?"

Ally loved playing in the snow. And she definitely loved spending time with Maria. "What do you have in mind?"

"How about snowshoeing in the park?"

Ally had been thinking of trekking around her parents' property, but she liked Maria's idea so much better. "I'll bring the hot chocolate," Ally replied.

"Really? You'll come?"

"Of course!"

"This confirms you're a little bit nuts. In a good way."

"Sanity is overrated. What time would you like to meet?"

They agreed that Ally would pick Maria up at her place, since it was on the way to the park, and they would leave as soon as possible, because the roads would be slippery when the snow got heavier.

"Change of plans," Ally announced to her parents when she went in the house. "I'm going to Maria's to snowshoe."

Her mom sat up and stared at her. "Ally, is it wise to drive in this weather?"

"Mom, it's only a few miles. And I'll take an overnight bag. If the roads aren't plowed, I'll just camp out with Maria."

Her mom puckered her lips. "Ah. Now I understand. Just be careful."

A few minutes later, with her bag and a thermos of cocoa and Baileys Irish Cream, Ally was out the door and on her way to Maria's house. Even though it was only nine o'clock, she didn't see a single car until she got close to the grocery store, and that turned out to be a plow cleaning up the parking lot. The road crews had done a decent job, though, and she found if she went slowly, the Jeep held traction. Even on the hill near Maria's house, she had no trouble but was relieved when she pulled into the driveway and honked.

A second later, the garage door opened, and Maria appeared dressed in ski clothing. Ally pressed the button that released the hatch, and Maria deposited her bag of gear there before hopping into the passenger seat.

"You got here pretty quickly," Maria said.

Ally laughed. "I had the roads to myself."

Maria reached over and rubbed Ally's right leg. "This is an adventure. I'm so excited."

"So a snowy night by the fire didn't appeal to you."

"Not by myself. But if you tell me you want to go back into the house, I'm game."

Ally shook her head. "I feel I'm being tested here. If I fail the *sense of adventure* component, I might find myself alone on Valentine's Day."

Maria laughed. "I thought I was being discreet, but you see right through me."

"So this is late. No work tomorrow?"

Maria told her she had the next two evening shifts, so she didn't have to worry about waking early.

"I don't have to work until the afternoon, so I don't either!" The idea of spending a few hours with Maria, or maybe even the night, was exciting. Not that she wanted to jump into bed. Even though Dr. Griver thought she was worthy, Ally wasn't in a hurry.

Once again hers was the only car, and the roads were plowed, so she had no trouble until they reached the lot at South Abington Park. She hit her brakes, and they skidded. "I hope they don't decide to plow. They could block us in."

As Ally drove toward the trailheads, she realized Maria was right about the park. It was deserted, the snow undisturbed and pristine as it landed on the fluffy cushion of flakes that had come before. Lampposts all along the walking trails were visible in the night, and their light seemed to set the snow around them on fire, creating big halos of dancing snowflakes every ten feet.

"Wow," Ally said as she looked out the window.

"It's so beautiful."

They sat for a moment, and Maria grabbed Ally's hand. "Thanks for doing this."

"My pleasure," Ally whispered into Maria's mouth as she leaned in for a kiss. It was a soft one, meant to last a second or two, but neither of them pulled away, and it slowly grew deeper. Ally gently slid her tongue across Maria's lower lip and then into her mouth. Maria's tongue found Ally's, and they circled each other for a second before Ally pulled back, breathless.

"Wow. Should we just stay here?" Ally asked as she nibbled Maria's neck.

Maria moaned. "We were at my house five minutes ago," she said breathlessly. "And now we're acting like two teenagers out in their parents' car."

Ally smiled. "It's kind of fun. Exciting."

Maria nodded. "So noted. Now let's go play in the snow."

Ally's gear was also in the back, so once again she popped the hatch and met Maria behind the Jeep. They sat side by side as they fastened the straps on their snowshoes, and then Ally donned a ski hat and goggles, and finally, she wrapped a warm scarf around her neck and face. When Maria jumped down from the Jeep, Ally closed the hatch and locked it, deposited the key in her chest pocket, and pulled on her thickest gloves. They were off.

By unspoken agreement, they headed across the park, toward a trail that followed a stream. The snow seemed to be heavier, but no obstacles impeded their progress, so it was easy going. They paused before a covered bridge and then picked their way across, stopping in the middle to look out. The edges were frozen, but a ribbon of water still flowed briskly in the middle, in spite of the cold. Ally watched the snowflakes land on the surface and dissolve into the inky blackness.

Maria nudged her, and they continued, climbing a little hill on the other side of the bridge, farther away from civilization. The trail followed the stream, and they walked for a quarter of a mile in silence before Maria stopped.

"You okay?"

Ally looked around at the beauty that surrounded her. Here there was no light from the street or the parking lot, just the lampposts, and it was darker, but the brightness of the snow created an artificial light. With the wind stirring it, under a canopy of trees, and the complete silence of the trail, Ally felt as if she were inside a snow globe.

"Perfect," Ally replied, and they continued farther down the trail.

"This could be a Robert Frost poem," Maria said as she stopped at the top of the hill and looked around. Ally did as well and appreciated Maria's sentiment. The branches of pines were draped with blankets of white, and everywhere the layer of fluffy snow blunted the sharp edges of nature. The stream roared below them, but even that sound was dampened by the flakes still falling.

Ally finally settled her gaze on Maria. Like everything else, she was covered with snow, from the fuzzy ball on top of her hat to the tops of her shoulders and the tops of her boots.

"If I wrote poetry, it would be about this," Ally said. "But maybe it's time to head back." The wind seemed to be growing stronger, and the snow was heavier than it had been forty-five minutes earlier when they started out. When Ally turned, she could barely discern the tracks they'd made on the trail.

Maria nodded and did an about-face. "Let's write a poem together," she said as she began walking again.

"Hmm," Ally said, wondering what Maria had in mind.

"I'll start. Give me a sec." They walked silently, the wind and the stream and the sound of her own breath breaking the stillness before Maria spoke again. "A girl wearing snowshoes took me out to play. Now it's your turn."

Ally thought for a moment. What rhymes with *play*? *Bay*, *cay*, *day*. *Day* would work. "It was the end of a snowy winter's day."

Maria repeated the first two stanzas, huffing with the effort of walking uphill, and added a third. "The air was cold as the wind whipped by."

Ally repeated what they'd come up with so far, all the while trying to think of a word that rhymed with *by* and would make sense in the next line of verse. "And big snowflakes were drifting down from the sky."

Maria laughed. "Ha! It sounds great!"

"Should we write it down, so we don't forget it?"

Maria quickly repeated all four lines and added another. "Through the virgin snow they walked side by side."

Ally went through the list of words she could rhyme with side. *Cried* probably wasn't great. It beat *died*, but not by much. *Fried*? *Lied*? *Spied*? She'd hit a mental block. This was getting harder. Then she came to the letter *r*. *Got it!* "Wishing she had a sleigh to ride."

Maria laughed as they continued to trudge through the snow. "They had no sleigh, just their sturdy snowshoes."

Ally repeated her rhyming process. *Bruise, cruise, dues, glues.* Nothing seemed to work, so she started again with the letter *B.* Then she smiled and stopped, pulled off her backpack, and slipped out the thermos. After opening the lid, she sipped it and handed it to Maria. "And a bit of hot cocoa, laced with booze."

Laughing, Maria took a sip of the proffered hot cocoa, then nodded in approval. "The end."

Ally laughed, too, and stepped into Maria's space and kissed her, relishing the warmth of her mouth and the taste of chocolate. "Mmm. You taste yummy. And warm."

"It's getting cold."

Ally took another sip of the cocoa and then stored it in her bag before they started off again. The snow was now falling so heavily their tracks were completely buried, and the wind was blowing it, so they had to wipe their goggles to see. Beneath her layers, she was wet with sweat, and her leg muscles were beginning to burn. She was actually relieved when she saw the bridge, but they stopped under the light to take a selfie.

Back at the Jeep, Maria stepped into Ally's space for another searing kiss, then tilted her head back and caught a snowflake on her tongue. Ally felt warm all over. Maria was just so genuine. So real. Unafraid to be herself, even if herself was a four-year old acting in the moment. Ally needed to read a few pages from Maria's playbook.

"Thanks for doing this," Maria said as they threw their gear into the back of the Jeep.

"I had a great time," Ally said she leaned nearer for another kiss.

Maria pulled her in, deepened the kiss. "You don't have to go home, you know. You can stay with me."

Ally pulled back. Wow. That would be nice. Maria felt warm, and inviting, and comforting. And the kiss was such a tease.

Ally leaned in again and found Maria's mouth.

"We don't have to have sex," Maria said around the kiss.

"Why not?" Ally whispered, caught up in the moment.

Laughing, Maria pulled back. "Let's get out of here, before we're buried alive."

Ally smiled. "I can think of fun ways to stay warm."

"You can show me back at my place."

They quickly swept the snow from the car, then headed out. The drive was short, and Ally's Jeep had no trouble on the salted roads. In just a few minutes she pulled safely into Maria's driveway. "You can park in the garage," Maria said, and she hopped out to open the door.

It felt a little strange to pull her Jeep in beside Maria's car, but it fit perfectly. Maria had parked as if she was expecting this visit and had made room for Ally's car beside hers. Was that crazy thinking on Ally's part, or had Maria really had this in mind when she'd pulled into the garage after work?

"It looks like you planned this," Ally said through pursed lips.

"Huh?" Maria asked, and when Ally pointed to their cars, Maria grinned.

"Would it freak you out if I did?"

Ally thought for a moment. Her attraction to Maria was undeniable, and Maria was just the kind of woman Ally could see herself with. The problem she'd wrestled with in the past week—if she was honest, it was the last seven months—was her self-worth. It was why she hadn't jumped at the casual references Maria made about getting together back when they first met. It was why she'd never gotten Maria's phone number, why she never once tried to contact her when she was in rehab or at the halfway house. Ally just didn't think she was worthy.

Yet here Maria was, offering herself—whatever Ally wanted of her, friendship or more—yet again. And Ally was finally ready to take the chance that Maria might just be real. Ally supposed before they went any further, they should talk about it.

She popped the hatch so they could get their gear out. "You've freaked me out since we met."

Ally handed Maria her snowshoes and grabbed their gloves and hats before closing the hatch. When she turned, Maria was staring at her.

"What freaked you out?"

Ally didn't hesitate. "I didn't want to hurt you. I knew I was heading off a cliff, and I didn't want to take you with me."

They laid out their wet clothing on a table before heading into the house, and Maria didn't respond until they were sitting beside each other on the couch, a fire dancing behind them. Maria sat cross-legged and sideways, facing Ally, who leaned against the armrest with her knees bent to make room.

"I suppose you had bigger priorities back then," Maria said. "And it makes sense now. I knew we had a connection, and I knew you were into girls, so I couldn't figure out why you kept blowing me off. So, yeah. Question answered."

"I wasn't blowing you off," Ally said as she shook her head. What was she doing, though? Just keeping out of reach, but wasn't the result the same? "Although I can understand why you felt that way."

"I sense you still have some reservations."

Ally met Maria's gaze and sighed, then explained just what she'd talked about with Dr. Griver. Ally watched Maria's eyes fill with tears and saw her quietly wipe them away. Ally, too, began to cry, not because she was sad, but because she felt so cared for. Maria was a great doctor, and a great person, and she had real affection for her. The idea was amazing. And yes, she had some reservations about whether she was worthy of Maria, but they were growing less credible by the second. She told her that.

"We have time. I mean, where can you go in a blizzard?"

"True."

"Would you like to watch a movie?" Maria asked. "I think a rom-com is in order. Laughter is healing."

"I'd like that," Ally replied softly.

So they chose a movie, and Ally snuggled behind Maria as they shared a pillow. She felt Maria's warmth along the length of her and smelled her with every breath. She didn't really follow the action onscreen but was lost in her thoughts. When was the last time she'd felt this close to someone? Even though it had been two years since she split with Gretchen, their intimacy had died long before that. Ally didn't want to compare them, but she couldn't help it. From the first she'd been drawn to Maria, for all the same reasons she'd been drawn to Gretchen so many years ago. Yet Maria was different, and this attraction seemed so much deeper. The fact that Ally hadn't been looking for something, that she practically had to be hit over the head, seemed to make it so much more powerful.

And Ally had no question about Maria's sexuality.

At that moment, Maria shifted and leaned a little closer to Ally, and she groaned. Then, effortlessly, Maria rolled so she was facing Ally.

"Are you enjoying the movie?" she whispered.

"I'm loving it."

Maria kissed her softly, and their tongues met for a moment. "You're not watching, are you?"

"Not really."

"It's almost midnight. Maybe we should go to bed."

"I brought my jammies," Ally said.

"Oh. Now who's planning ahead?"

Maria sat up, then stood, and reached for Ally's hand and pulled her up. Ally retrieved her bag from the Jeep and found Maria waiting in the kitchen. Once again, she took Ally's hand and didn't let go until they reached her bedroom, where she flipped a switch, and the light of a single lamp cast a soft glow across the room.

"You can use the bathroom first," she said and motioned to a door hidden in the shadows.

With the door closed behind her, Ally let out a deep breath. "You've got this," she said as she changed and then brushed her teeth, her thoughts all over the place. Hoping Maria was asleep on the other side of the door, and at the same time praying she wasn't. Then she decided to let it go, She trusted Maria, and knew she wasn't going to push Ally to move too fast, no matter how much Ally flirted with her. When she finally emerged, she found Maria loitering, her soft smile suggesting she knew just how nervous Ally was. "My turn," she said, and she gently rubbed Ally's shoulder as she passed by.

Now what? Ally wondered as she looked around.

Maria's room was painted a bright pink, with floral curtains. A thick, white comforter covered the bed, and half a dozen brightly colored pillows were propped against the headboard. The walls were covered with pictures and art, a relief, and a metal panel fashioned into the shape of a flower bouquet, as well as a few paintings, all Impressionist. It was a romantic room, and it made Ally feel warm and welcome.

Maria interrupted her musings. "It's the only room that's really finished," Maria said. "What do you think?"

"It's very you," Ally said, and Maria seemed pleased by the comment as she smiled.

"It's really so much fun to shop for the house and decorate." Maria walked around to the far side of the bed and climbed in, but Ally just stood and watched until Maria beckoned her. "C'mon. Don't play hard to get." Her wink softened her remark and had the desired effect of relaxing Ally.

She lifted the blankets and climbed in on her side, then rolled over to face Maria. Maria inched closer until they were nearly nose to nose, then slid her arm over Ally's side. It felt nice, and Ally scooched closer again and draped her arm over Maria's hip.

"Hi," Maria said.

Ally smiled. "Hi."

"Do you mind the light? I usually fall asleep reading and just leave it on."

The light was soft, the wattage low, and Ally wondered how Maria could possibly see to read. Yet it was enough that Ally could see the dark brown of her eyes, and the fullness of her lips, and the smile turning up the corners of her mouth. "It's perfect."

"Good."

"So the bedroom's all done? What's next?"

"I think a security system. Can you help me with that?"

"Absolutely. I've been on a sales call, so I know just what you need. I can show you in the morning."

Maria's eyes opened wide. "Thank you. That would be great."

"Then what? After the security system?"

Maria told Ally about her plans for the house. Of course the kitchen and the master bath were her priorities, and then maybe an exterior makeover. Ally loved watching her as she spoke, because she was so expressive. She practically talked with her eyes as they opened, then shuttered and squinted, and Ally wanted to touch them, to kiss her, but she held back and instead just enjoyed the sound of Maria's voice. It seemed to grow slower, and she yawned, and Ally felt her own lids growing heavy.

How nice this is, she thought as she forced them open and saw Maria sleeping beside her. *How normal, and sweet, and wonderful.* She could do this. She could let herself go and have something amazing with this woman.

You've got this, she thought as she gave in to her fatigue and closed her eyes again.

CHAPTER TWENTY-ONE

Intermezzo

When Ally awakened, Maria was asleep beside her, her dark hair a wild halo on the pillow. Outside, the sky was bright, suggesting the storm had passed. Grabbing her phone, she checked the time. Almost nine. When was the last time she'd slept this late? She felt wonderful. Rested, peaceful. Happy.

Slowly and carefully she eased from the bed and made her way to the window. Maria's bedroom faced the pool, and Ally wasn't sure how much snow had been there before, but now the backyard was just one blanket of white. She had to stare at the neighbor's yard, where a car was parked, to see that a foot of snow had fallen.

"How's it look?" Maria called.

Ally turned around and saw her propped up on both elbows. "Beautiful," she said, and she wasn't talking about the snow.

"What time is it?" she asked as she glanced at her clock. "Wow. What a great sleep. Did you just get up?"

"Yeah. I slept in, too."

Maria smiled. "Good morning, Ally. Welcome to my bedroom. Do I have amazing bedhead?"

Ally studied the rumpled mane and nodded. "Pretty much."

Maria shook her head and finger-combed her hair. "You're supposed to lie and tell me I'm beautiful."

"If I told you you're beautiful, I wouldn't be lying."

Maria stopped what she was doing and gazed at Ally. "You're pretty gorgeous yourself. Are you hungry? I'm thinking chocolate-chip pancakes."

"I'm thinking that sounds great."

They brushed their teeth and headed downstairs, where Ally made coffee, and Maria worked on the pancakes. They ate across from each other, then ventured to the garage to check out the snow. When Maria pressed the control to open the wide double door, the snow had made a foot-high wall.

"We have some shoveling to do," Ally said.

Maria pointed to the corner of the garage. "Snowblower," she said. Ally walked over and saw a small machine. How would it possibly move everything the blizzard had deposited on the driveway? But Maria seemed unfazed. "Wanna have a snowball fight?" she asked.

"I'm excellent at snowball wars. Neighborhood champ, in fact."

"Game on," Maria said, and they quickly donned their ski clothing. After throwing snow at each other for a few minutes, they went to work. While Maria started the snowblower, Ally began with the shovel, creating a path out of the garage for her to follow. And much to her surprise, the little machine did a great job, throwing the snow nearly the width of the driveway. In no time, they'd cleared the entire surface, and just as they were finishing, the family across the street came out to their yard and began building a snowman.

"Oh, we can't let that poor snowman be all alone out here," Ally said.

"No, we can't," Maria said, and they began rolling a ball, patting more and more snow until they had a big, lumpy base. They made another small ball and added it to what they had, then built on it until they had a middle. The combination was as tall as Ally, and they struggled with the top section, standing on tiptoes to finish it. Then Maria ran into the house and came out with a carrot and a hat, and a pair of sunglasses for the face, and a scarf that Ally wrapped around the middle.

"She's gorgeous!" Ally said. "What shall we name her?"

"Oh, you pick," Maria said.

"Beatrix," Ally said.

Maria laughed. "Okay, then. Does she need anything else?"

Ally assessed their snowlady. They could certainly do lots more, but she was adorable just as she was. "I don't think so."

She pulled out her phone, and they were taking a selfie when Ally heard someone call her name. She looked up and saw Gretchen walking her parents' dog, and she was filled with dread. Talking to Gretch on the phone had been hard. Seeing her, here, at Maria's—this was much worse.

"Hi," Gretchen said, as she looked from Ally to Maria.

"Hi," Ally said, feeling awkward. "Do you know Dr. Alfano?" she asked Gretchen. "She's a colleague from the ER."

"Nice to meet you," Gretchen said. "I'm sure I'll see you eventually. I work with one of the family docs in town."

"I'm sure you're right," Maria said as she followed Gretchen's gaze toward the garage, where Ally's Jeep was parked. Gretchen's eyes flew open wide, and she seemed suddenly rather uncomfortable.

"I should get going. Enjoy the snow," she said as she began walking again, pulling the dog.

"That wasn't too weird," Maria whispered as Gretchen practically ran down the road.

Ally shook her head. "Not at all."

"The ex?" Maria asked.

"Yep."

"This looks pretty bad," Maria said as she waved her finger between the snowlady and Ally's Jeep.

Ally sucked in a big breath of the clean, fresh air. "No, Maria. It actually looks really good." It felt good, too. She was definitely ready to move on.

Maria grinned. "Yeah?"

"Absolutely."

They walked into the house together, and Ally was disappointed when she saw the clock. She wasn't quite ready for their date to end. Yet it was nearly eleven, and she'd worked up a sweat shoveling the driveway, so she wanted to shower before work. She told Maria she needed to head out.

"What about the alarm proposal?"

Ally had forgotten. "Of course. I can't really assess the perimeter with this snow, but let's assume basic things like a few cameras outside, and we can walk through the house and get your exact needs inside." They started in the kitchen, near the garage door, and decided that would be the place for a control panel, so Maria could arm the system as she entered and left the house. Then they discussed strategic positions for motion detectors and cameras. All the first-floor windows would be alarmed, as well as the rear-facing ones on the second floor. Ally recommended a second control panel at the top of the stairs or in the master bedroom.

"So what now?" Maria asked.

"I'll write up the proposal and bring you a brochure, as well as a few pieces to look at so you can see the options and decide which you like best."

Maria smiled in response. "Thank you."

"My pleasure. Hamilton Security appreciates your business." While they were on the second floor, Ally gathered her things, and then Maria walked her to her car.

"I had a great time," she said as she leaned on her hip against her car in an extremely sexy pose.

Ally couldn't resist and stepped into Maria's space and kissed her hungrily on the mouth. "It was a perfect night," she said when she pulled back. "The park, the cuddling, the talking. All of it."

The corners of Maria's mouth turned up as she gently touched Ally's face. "Have a great day."

They kissed again, and then Maria watched as Ally backed out of the garage and onto the street, blowing her another as she pulled away. A moment later her phone rang, and Ally was eager to talk to Maria again. Even though she'd just left, she had more to say, and she wanted to hear the excitement in Maria's voice as she talked about anything and everything. When she reached for her phone, though, she saw Gretchen's face, not Maria's.

For a second, Ally debated answering. Her mood was high, and she didn't want a conversation with Gretchen to bring her down. Yet she had to talk to her at some point, so she might as well get it over with.

"Hi," Ally said. "Long time no see."

"That's sadly true. Ally, you used to be my best friend. Long before anything else happened between us. I miss you. I miss being friends."

Whoa. Not what Ally was expecting to hear. She and Gretchen had met in middle school and had been inseparable through college. In high school, they'd chosen their career paths so they could work together for the rest of their lives. And even though Ally had understood the crush she'd had on Gretchen as they went off to Marywood University to become PAs, it wasn't until a drunken kiss at a college party that Gretchen seemed to realize what was happening between them. So she was right. They had been friends first, and Ally had to admit, sometimes she missed Gretchen, too.

"Your new girlfriend is beautiful, Ally."

"Yeah, she is."

"Is she gay, because the bi situation didn't really work out too well."

It would have worked out a lot better if Gretchen had admitted she was bi at the beginning of our sexual relationship, rather than the end. Ally swallowed hard but said nothing.

"But seeing you today sort of made me sad, because we were great friends. We should get together for dinner and get back to being friends."

The last time they'd done that, Ally hadn't quite understood Gretchen's feelings, and she'd seduced her, and they'd had amazing sex. But then Gretchen had left again, to date men. Ally hadn't been willing to live with that situation, and that was the last time they'd really said more than a few words to each other.

Ally wasn't sure they had much more to say now. But she'd been opening her mind to new possibilities, and perhaps a friendship with Gretchen was one of them.

"It wasn't you, Ally. You're a great person. This is about me. I'll never regret the eight years we had together, but I'm not gay. I want to be with a man. But I want to be able to see you, too."

What? "Gretch, what do you mean by *see*?"

Gretchen let out a nervous laugh. "Oh, no worries, Ally. I've gotten girls out of my system."

Ally had been to bed with Gretchen, and she wasn't convinced. But it wasn't her problem anymore.

"You can call me, Gretchen. And hey, if Maria is working or I don't have anything going on, maybe we can get together for dinner."

Gretchen sighed. "I'd like that."

Ally thought she might, too.

"Thanks for calling," Ally said.

"Wait! That's not why I phoned. When I saw you making your snowlady, I realized you weren't working today, and you might not know."

"Know what?"

"The Cadillac guy was admitted last night. Heart failure."

"What?" Ally asked, shocked. She shouldn't be. He was very sick, after all, and just days before he'd signed the DNR. Still, she hadn't expected it.

"Everyone thinks you did a great job. I went in to the hospital last night to see him, and he and his wife couldn't say enough good things about you."

Ally wished she could have done more and told Gretchen so. "But thanks for letting me know."

"Ally, you're a great PA. Don't forget it. And don't forget to call me for dinner."

"I won't," Ally said, thinking she just might call.

After they disconnected, Ally felt a little down. She certainly didn't want Brodrik Rogan to die, but she also didn't want his demise to foil her plans for *Christ in the Storm on the Sea of Galilee*, either. It was a lose-lose situation.

"Fuck," she said softly and with a big sigh. Oh, well, there was no use worrying about it. She had a busy day ahead of her. She called her mom to check in, ran home to shower, then stopped at Hamilton to talk to Lisa about Maria's security system.

Lisa walked her through it, and Ally was able to write up the estimate for a few different options. After eliminating her sales commission, Ally had the cost down forty percent. Then she talked to her dad.

"What's the best price I can give her on this?" she asked.

"Family discount is cost, so thirty percent of retail price," he informed her.

"Wow!" she said. That made it really affordable. She would have liked to do it for free, but if all the employees did that, the business would go bankrupt.

When she finished with her father, she checked with installation. "How far out are we scheduling?" she asked. She'd like to give Maria an approximate date when she furnished her the estimate and the brochures, so she could make a decision.

"It's pretty quick. Three days, if it's a standard order, meaning nothing customized, because we have all the parts in stock."

After thanking the man in scheduling, she asked if she could see the job list for Saturday. "I went out last week with Lisa, and I'm thinking I might go this weekend as well."

With a few strokes of the computer keys, he pulled up the information Ally requested, and she glanced at it. It was organized alphabetically, with the client name, an order number, a brief description of the job, and then the last name of the technician assigned. Twenty names were on the list, which seemed like a lot for a Saturday.

"Weekenders," he said with a shrug. "Any of the techs in particular you want to go out with?" he asked.

Ally shook her head. "No, not really. Thanks," she said before walking back toward the office she'd claimed. Once there, she picked up her things, said good-bye to her father, and headed to work.

Despite the foot of snow that had covered the streets of Lackawanna County overnight, the combination of plowing and salt and sun had left just a bit of slush to contend with. Ally had no trouble making it to Four H and went in to check her client list a few minutes later.

"Hi, Greg," she said as she knocked on the door to his office. He waved her in, and Ally sat. "Good call on going out later today. The roads are fine."

"You may find some snow in the Poconos," he warned her.

"Speaking of that, I heard Mr. Rogan is in the hospital."

Greg sat back in his chair and frowned. "It's not looking good for him, Ally. His heart is shot, and his breathing is quite labored. They were debating a ventilator this morning, but I'm not sure what way he decided."

Ally exhaled sharply. "That's really too bad," she said, wondering if he'd ever come out of the hospital. If she couldn't get back into the house, if she couldn't switch the last painting, it wasn't the end of the world. She'd still return the bulk of the stolen artwork. She knew the reward was for the complete collection, but even if she never collected, that was okay, right? Her goal wasn't money, it was redemption, and she'd just have to settle for what she'd been able to accomplish.

Although the money would be nice, too.

Without the excitement of visiting the Rogan estate, Ally had to admit her job seemed rather boring. She bandaged wounds and drew blood, all routine encounters, and though her patients were appreciative, Ally had to remind herself to stay present for them. Each of her clients was a human being, and each was suffering in some way. They all deserved her full attention. Reminding herself of that fact helped, and Ally found herself smiling as she left her last client's house at seven o'clock that night.

Back at home later, she ordered a pizza, changed into sweats, and waited for the delivery while walking on the treadmill. It wasn't a meeting, but the running was a different kind of therapy, and Ally's nervous energy responded to it. With each step, she felt calmer.

After her pizza arrived, she went back to her apartment and sat and stared at the stolen artwork, wondering how Brodrik Rogan was doing. Ally had known he was sick, but she hadn't expected this when she'd left his house the day before. Even though she sensed he was not a good man, and capable of horrific crimes, she felt compassion for him. He was lonely, and she suspected that, in spite of his tremendous wealth, he hadn't lived a happy life.

If these paintings were real, what had motivated him to steal them? He obviously loved art, *Christ in the Storm on the Sea of Galilee* in particular. Why take it, though? Why hide it in the Poconos, where it was subject to changes in heat and humidity that could damage it? Why keep it from the public, from millions of people who could be inspired by seeing this masterful display of God's power?

Ally supposed this was the question at the heart of all art theft. What made one individual think he had the right to buy a stolen masterpiece and keep it for himself?

With her feet up, she leaned into the cushions and stared at Raphael. He looked so young and innocent, staring back at her. Ally could imagine him whispering to her. *Send me home.* She hoped with all her heart that he was the real deal, and he'd be back in Poland soon. Then she looked at *Chez Tortoni*. The man in the hat staring up from the canvas looked dangerous. He could have been the thief who'd stolen all the other artwork and was watching Ally, plotting a counter move.

"I hope you're real, whoever you are," she said to him. "And I'm sending you back to Boston, where you belong."

If everything went as planned, in less than forty-eight hours, these paintings would be on their way home. Ally went to work to get them ready.

She'd ordered packing materials on the internet, and they sat in large boxes just inside her door. One by one, she began wrapping the Rogan pieces in bubble wrap, starting with the smaller ones. After cutting a piece, she set the first painting, *Chez Tortoni*, on the edge and flipped it over a few times before securing it with plastic outer wrap. Using a Sharpie, she wrote the letters *CT* in large print and set the package aside.

Ally repeated the process with all the other works, then carefully packed everything she could into her suitcases. After she finished, everything except *A Lady and Gentleman in Black* was stowed securely. That one, nearly five feet wide, was just too large, so she'd taken extra care with the wrapping to give it protection for its next journey.

By the time she finished, it was after ten, and she decided to turn in. She doubted she'd sleep, but she had to try. Tomorrow she had work, and the day after that—well, she was putting on a magic show of sorts. A sleight of hand, with the prize a hundred-million-dollar masterpiece.

CHAPTER TWENTY-TWO

The Canvas Snake

Ally held her breath as she approached the gate at the Rogan estate on Saturday morning. It was only eight o'clock, but another storm was inching toward the Poconos, and by afternoon they'd have blizzard conditions. She wanted to get in and out of the house in two hours. Instead of medical gear, today her Jeep was packed with all the tools and supplies she'd need to pull apart a frame and put it together again.

"Mr. Rogan isn't in," the guard said when he recognized Ally.

"Yes," Ally said. "I know. I'm here to fix his painting," she said, crossing her fingers that this plan worked. She'd had his daughter, Grace, write the appointment on the calendar and only hoped someone was in the house to confirm it.

His eyes opened wide. "Oh. You're wearing another hat today. Yes, you're on the list. It just says 'frame repair,' no company, so I didn't realize it was you."

"I'm not actually with a company. I'm just doing it for Mr. Rogan. It's a hobby of mine, collecting and restoring old frames."

He looked bored as he nodded. Collecting and repairing old guns might have interested him, but not so much the art. It didn't matter, though, and Ally thought perhaps it was better that he didn't show an interest. Too much attention to what she was doing couldn't be good.

She slowly made her way up the winding driveway. Even though it had been plowed and salted, there were still patches of snow and ice, and the last thing she needed was to end up stuck in a snowbank. She pulled under the portico, wondering if Rocco was at the estate or with Mr. Rogan at the hospital.

"Good morning." Ally was greeted with a wave and a smile by a man she'd never seen before, but he had the same general look of all the Rogan guards—big. They were all friendly, too, which didn't seem to fit the image. They were probably bored guarding an old man who never left the house and didn't have many callers, and Ally was one of the few distractions in their monotonous day.

Ally introduced herself, and he nodded. "Mrs. Rogan said to let you into the dining room. She said you'd make provisions to protect the table."

Ally nodded. "Yes. Can you help me? I brought a piece of heavy cardboard to lay everything on, as well as a tarp, so I shouldn't damage the furniture."

Ally popped the hatch, and with a swift tug, the bulky security man removed the cardboard holding the copy of the Rembrandt. Ally watched him carefully, hoping her glue held. He needed two hands, so Ally grabbed the rest of her supplies. Her tools were in one bag and a canvas tarp in another, and she picked them up and followed him into the house.

"Right this way," he said as Ally followed him past the door to Brodrik Rogan's study, across the hallway and into a formal dining room that ran half the length of the house.

"I'd like to put the tarp down first, and the cardboard on top," Ally told him.

He nodded and waited while Ally unzipped her bag and removed the tarp, then placed it across one end of the dining-room table. "Right on top," Ally told him, and he positioned the cardboard over the tarp. Even though it was enormous, there was still six inches of tabletop to spare on both sides.

"Thank you so much," Ally said. "Now all I need is the painting."

"Do you know which one it is?" he asked with a look of confusion. "He has about a hundred paintings in this place."

Ally smiled. "I do. It's in the study," she said. "I'll show you."

They walked to the study and opened the door, and the guard stopped abruptly. "Oh, Mr. Rogan. Excuse me, sir."

Ally looked around him and saw Peter Rogan seated at his father's desk.

"What is it?" he asked impatiently.

"This girl is here to repair a painting," he said.

"What? I don't know anything about that," he said dismissively.

"It's on Dad's calendar," a feminine voice said from inside the study.

"Dad's in the fucking hospital, with a breathing tube shoved down his throat. What do I care about a painting?"

Shit, Ally thought. Brodrik Rogan was in bad shape. She might not get a chance to switch the paintings after all. Not today, and not ever.

"Pete, if Dad pulls through this, you're going to have to explain why you sent this girl away. I was here with him the other day, and he wants that frame repaired, so I don't think you should interfere."

Grace, Ally thought. She'd put the appointment on Brodrik Rogan's calendar. Thank Goddess.

Peter's sigh was audible, even in the hallway. "Fine. Just make sure she stays out of my way," he said.

The guard walked into the room, with Ally behind him, and they turned right. Grace Rogan lay sprawled out on the couch, her phone in one hand and her son asleep in the other. Pulling her eyes away, she glanced at Ally and the guard, then quickly returned to whatever she'd been looking at.

"It's this one," Ally said, pointing to the Rembrandt.

Grabbing it from the bottom, he lifted the wooden frame, and it slipped from the hook that held it. He turned to carry it from the room.

"Just a minute," Peter Rogan said, and they both stopped.

"Stay with her," he said. "I don't want any strangers wandering around the house."

"You got it," he said.

Fuck, Ally thought. She left the room with the guard trailing close behind. A minute later, the Rembrandt was laid out on the cardboard panel on the dining-room table, and Ally was wondering what the hell she was going to do next.

"Thank you so much," Ally said.

"My pleasure," he said as he sat in a straight-backed chair beside the double door.

Ally turned and opened her bag of tools. How was she going to make this work? All she could do was be ready, and when she had a few minutes alone, she could make the swap.

First, she walked to the opposite side of the table, looking around the room for cameras. While he took his security seriously, Brodrik Rogan apparently didn't want his privacy violated. She saw no cameras anywhere in the house.

Okay, she thought. *You've got this.*

Using a putty knife, Ally found the space between the pieces of cardboard and sliced the glue free. It was easier than she hoped, which told her she needed to do a better job with the glue when the real Rembrandt was hidden between the panels of cardboard. *If,* she realized. *If* she could make the switch.

With one eye on the guard, she made her way around the edge, rotating the cardboard so she could continue operating on the side opposite him. When all the glue seals were broken, she went to work on the frame.

Whoa, she thought as she reached out and gently touched the gilded wood encasing *Christ in the Storm on the Sea of Galilee.* It was a little overwhelming to realize she was staring at the face of Rembrandt himself, at the brushstrokes his hand had painted. She moved her fingers, mimicking the master's own movements as he applied paint to canvas. She didn't touch the work, but the energy she felt made it seem as if she did. She focused on the massive white wave threatening the ship and the sun breaking through the clouds above it, the frightened expressions of the disciples as they looked to Jesus for help. It was simply magnificent. Ally wasn't particularly religious, yet the power of this painting moved her.

Pulling on a pair of white cotton gloves, she went to work, turning the frame over so she could begin. She gasped when she saw the jagged edges of canvas peeking out from the wood of the stretcher, a reminder that the masterpiece had been brutally cut from its original frame. Whatever doubts Ally had about the provenance of Brodrik Rogan's paintings were resolved in that moment. This was the original.

With a sigh, she snipped the picture wire from one side of the frame.

This is fucking real.

Staples, all loosely applied, held the wood at the corners. She grabbed her pliers and quickly removed them. After that, she wiggled the pieces of the frame, and the glue holding the corners together gave way. In seconds, she held four pieces of mahogany.

She glanced at the guard sitting twenty feet away and smiled. He was watching her, but did he have any idea what she was doing? Probably not. She decided to keep going.

Once again using her pliers, she began pulling the staples holding the canvas to the stretcher. This work wasn't necessary to repair the frame, had nothing to do with the frame in fact. But it was necessary to switch the canvases, and she was going to pray her opportunity came.

Movement in the corner of her eye caused Ally to look up, and she saw the guard staring at her.

"How's it going?" he asked.

"No problems so far," she said.

"Good," he said as he approached. He looked down at the table, at the pieces of frame and canvas, then continued to the window. Then Ally heard his phone ring.

"Hello," he said, pausing while the other party spoke. "Okay. I'll let them in."

Ally was careful to keep her eyes on her work, but her heart raced as she listened.

"I have to step out for a moment," he said. "Don't go anywhere. Don't leave this room."

Ally looked up and met his eyes. "Okay," she said, then followed him with her gaze as he disappeared through the doorway.

As soon as he was out of sight, she was in motion, pushing the pieces of wood to the edge of the tarp and freeing the canvas from the stretcher. Next, she lifted the top piece of cardboard from the bottom and set it next to the table. When the reproduction was before her, she began at one end and rolled it, then moved it to the edge of the tarp. Finally, she placed the Rembrandt on the cardboard. The cut canvas was easily two inches smaller than the original, so it fit nicely. She covered it with the top piece of cardboard and let out a huge sigh.

Glancing at the doorway, she moved the fake painting to the cardboard and unrolled it, then placed the stretcher over it. She stapled one side, pulled the canvas tight, and stapled the opposite. Working quickly, she grabbed her razor and ran it along the stretcher, trimming an inch of painting on each side. She made a jagged cut, similar to the one the thief had made when he'd removed the original painting from its frame at the Gardner. The snake of canvas left over was huge, probably eighteen feet long. What the hell was she going to do with it? Slip it between the pieces of cardboard? Or maybe just put it in the bag with her tools? It was probably too big to fit in either place.

Think! Ally bit her lip and looked around the room for a place she could stash it. She couldn't see a trash can, just a long table and a huge china cabinet, and a serving buffet opposite. The corners of the room were filled with extra chairs and plants, and a large statue. No place to discard an eighteen-foot-long, one-inch-wide strip of canvas. Could she staple it to the underside of the table? No one would ever find it there, but what if they caught her in the act?

Maybe she could just pretend it was always there, a piece of the canvas that had been trimmed at the time it was framed. She quickly grabbed the snake and stapled it to the inside of the stretcher, then added another staple, then another. In less than a minute, she'd secured the extra canvas inside the wood, and then she went back to the task of securing the painting to the outside and back of the stretcher. When all four sides were tacked down, she began working on the corners. She'd finished the first when the security guard came back in.

He walked over and glanced down at her progress, then sat back in his chair, just as Ally heard voices in the hallway. She looked down when she saw the Hamilton security technicians talking to Peter Rogan.

They were a little late, but that was okay. Ally had scheduled them to arrive at the same time she did, to do routine service on the system and talk to Brodrik Rogan about the new back-up battery. They'd arrived just in time to allow her to switch the paintings. Now, all she had to do was get the authentic painting out of Rogan's house.

After making sure the canvas was attached to the stretcher, she pulled out her glue gun. While it was heating, she cleaned the frame, then quickly deposited a zigzagging trail of glue along the edge of the cardboard. Since this painting was smaller, she was more liberal with the glue. She needed it to hold. She spun the cardboard and finished sealing in the original painting before moving on to the frame. The rest of the work was easy. A few drops of glue on the corners of the frame brought them together, and then a dozen staples anchored it. Finally, Ally secured the stretcher to the frame and reattached the wire.

When she finished, Ally checked her work, then turned the painting over again so it was facing her. Everything looked great, and she took some deep breaths as she stowed her tools back in the bag. When her nerves were settled, she slid the painting to the floor, then slipped the tarp out from under the cardboard holding the Rembrandt. After folding that, she placed it neatly in the bag, and she was ready to make her escape.

"All done," she called out to the guard. "Should I hang this, or would you like the honor?"

"I should probably do it," he said. "But you can make sure it's straight," he said with a smile.

The man lifted the painting by the sides and carried it before him, pausing at the door to the study to knock.

"Come in," Peter Rogan said loudly.

"All finished, sir," the guard said as he turned toward the empty wall where the painting would go and, with surprising gentleness, met hook to wire and rehung it.

"Good. We need to get these people out of the house. I don't like having people here when my father's not around."

"Okay, Mr. Rogan. I'll check on the others. Will you be going to the hospital, sir?"

He scowled at the guard. "I was there all night. I need to take care of the business. You, Ally." He nodded toward her.

Ally looked from the painting to Peter Rogan.

"C'mere."

She turned and slowly approached him. "How much do I owe you for the frame?" he asked with a scowl.

"A hundred dollars," Ally said without hesitation. It was the price she'd negotiated with his father.

"Can I have a receipt?" he asked.

Ally nodded. "Sure. Can I mail it to you?"

He stared at her, studying her, as if wondering who she was to ask something of him. "Let me see this masterpiece," he said as he rose from his chair and walked to the far side of the room, near his father's chair. He stopped and cupped his chin in his hand as he stared at the painting, then walked closer. When it was in reach, he took a finger and rubbed it across the wood, checking for dust. "Very clean," he pronounced with a scowl. "What's that smell?"

"Vinegar," she replied.

He turned abruptly and walked back toward his desk. "How about ninety in cash, no receipt necessary."

Ally nodded. "Sure." Anything to get out of this house.

Peter Rogan pulled out his wallet and counted the money. "Thank you. I'm sure my father will love it. He likes old junk."

"I hope he's home soon to enjoy it," she replied, certain the moment his father passed, that painting would be in a landfill.

The guard interrupted them. "I have your things, miss," he said.

Ally looked down and saw two bags in his hands, one holding the tarp, the other her tools. Noticeably absent was the huge cardboard holding *Christ in the Storm on the Sea of Galilee*.

"Bring those here," he instructed the guard, and Ally watched silently as he obeyed his boss's command. Then Rogan looked at Ally.

"What's in the bags?" he asked with an eerily soft voice.

"Tools. A tarp."

"Let's see," he said. The guard closed the space between them and set Ally's bags on the desk.

Rogan looked up and smiled as he dumped the tarp onto the

desk, then shook the bag. He unfolded it and threw it to the side before picking up the other bag. He spilled the entire collection of framing tools onto the blotter. When it was empty, he dramatically looked inside and then reached in, feeling for something that might still be trapped. Satisfied that it was empty, he examined the tools, one by one. Holding up pliers, he looked at her.

"What do you use these for?"

"Pulling out staples and nails from the frame and canvas."

He held up the vinegar, enclosed in a plastic bag, along with dirty microfiber cloth and some cotton swabs, and studied it before unzipping and sniffing. His expression told her he got a good whiff of the acid.

Next he turned to the hot-glue gun. "It's pretty big," he said when Ally told him what she used it for.

"It gets the job done."

"Show me," he softly commanded, and Ally sensed he loved his power. Like his father, she wouldn't want to cross him.

"Can you please pull the painting down again?" Ally asked the guard.

When he held the massive frame in his hands, she spoke again. "Step out here, so I can show Mr. Rogan."

Then Ally beckoned Rogan and pointed to the tight corners. "There was space here, and it moved too much." She asked the guard to turn, so they were facing the back of the painting, where she knelt and pointed to the freshly stapled and glued corners. She pulled, and the corner held. "These were loose before, the staples missing, and the glue dried and cracked. If the frame is lax, the stretcher can warp. If that happens, it will damage the canvas."

Nodding, he pointed to the ribbon of canvas.

"What the hell is that?"

Trying to keep the same, even demeanor, Ally answered. "I'm not sure. I think the painting was trimmed because it was too big, and the framer just left the extra."

"Why would he do that? It's just garbage, right?"

Ally shrugged. "I don't know why, but yes. It appears to be trash."

"Then trash it. No, wait. Give it to me. I'm showing this to my father. Let him have a look at the shoddy work. Whoever framed this is going to get an earful from him."

Ally walked across to the desk and grabbed her pliers. What was she going to do now? Maybe if she distracted him, he'd forget about the canvas strip. She knew one thing for sure—if Rogan saw the snake of canvas, he'd know his painting had been switched. Ally had no idea who else had touched it over the years, how many people would be on the list of suspects. But she knew for sure her name would be at the top.

Using the pliers, she carefully removed one of the staples from the canvas snake. After the first, she just used a gentle tug to pop the others, and in a few seconds, she had a giant mass of canvas in her hands.

Walking back to his desk, he turned and looked over his shoulder. "A man in my position can't be too careful, Ally. People are always trying to get something from me." Then he meticulously placed each of her tools back in the bag. She wanted to take the tarp from him and begin folding it, but she sensed this man had a temper, and she didn't want to invoke it.

So, she stood silent and breathless, thankful she hadn't tried to smuggle out the strand of canvas she'd removed from the painting. Thankful she was about to escape the Rogan estate.

Rogan looked at the guard as his phone rang. "You can show her out."

Where's the cardboard holding the Rembrandt? Ally asked herself as she turned to follow him. She couldn't leave without it. At least before it was safe, hanging on the wall across the study. Now, it might be thrown out with the garbage or burned on a trash pile. Ally would never forgive herself if that happened. She'd thought she'd be a hero and repatriate the paintings. What if, instead, she was a villain?

"What?" Rogan screamed, and she and the guard both stopped and turned.

He looked visibly shaken as he sat forward in his chair, clutching the phone next to his dark-red face. "What?"

Ally didn't speak, but the bodyguard stepped forward. "Is everything—"

"When?" he asked softly, and Ally knew in her heart why Peter Rogan was so upset. She closed her eyes for a moment and said a silent prayer.

"I'll let everyone know," he said. He hung up the phone and stood. "My father is dead. We need to get this place cleaned up."

His tone was so dispassionate he might have been talking about the weather. "I'm really sorry," Ally said, but he cut her off.

"Thank you again," he said and rushed past her from the room.

So, the crisis with the canvas snake was averted, but where was *Christ in the Storm on the Sea of Galilee*?

"Where's the cardboard panel?" she asked the guard as the entered the foyer. "I wanted to save it, because, uh, it's so big. It's hard to find one that big."

He stopped and scowled at her. "Just get a box from a flat-screen TV."

Ally nodded. "What a good idea. But can I just take that one with me? Then I don't have to worry about getting a new one."

"Too late," he said. "It's gone."

Ally's mouth went dry. "What do you mean?"

"I threw it in the trash, and the guys took it."

If it was possible that one's heart could stop, at that moment, Ally's did. If that painting was lost, for as long as she lived, she'd never forgive herself.

"They had some boxes from the alarm equipment, so I asked if they could take it, too. They said they had room in their van."

And then her heart beat so fast Ally thought it would burst through her chest.

"Well, it's no problem," she finally said. "Like you said, I can pick up a TV box."

Ally had no idea how big a head start the Hamilton techs had, but she'd been in the study for about ten minutes. That might be just enough time for a disaster. She had to beat them back to the office. If they cleaned out the truck and put that piece through the cardboard shredder, the Rembrandt would be destroyed beyond repair. Ally knew the service techs started early on Saturday so they had the rest of the day to enjoy themselves. Was this their last call, or their first? Were they on the way to another job or just heading into the office?

Would it help if she called the Hamilton Security office? Could they reach the techs and tell them to put that piece aside for her? Ally didn't recognize the techs who'd been at the Rogan house, but she knew at least one of their names. Petrucci. She'd seen it when she checked the schedule the other day. Could she somehow get his cell-phone number and call him? Explain she needed that piece of garbage for her frame-repair business?

Ally was desperate enough to try anything. She reached the gate, and it seemed to take an hour for it to open, but she dialed the office while she waited. No service available. Shit! What was going on? She'd called from here before. Perhaps the coming storm was affecting the cell-phone signals.

A mile down the road, she pressed the button on her steering wheel that automatically redialed the last call, and this time it connected. After one ring, the phone beeped twice, and she lost the call. It took almost fifteen minutes, until she reached the interstate, before she could finally get through.

"Yes!" she exclaimed when the phone finally rang. Instead of a human, though, a recorded message played, telling her to call back on Monday, unless it was an emergency. This qualified, she thought. *This is an emergency.*

Ally put her foot to the floor, listening to elevator music while she was on hold, searching the road ahead of her for the Hamilton service van. All she saw were tractor trailers and a few cars, but no white van. She was still half an hour out from the office, so she hoped she could catch them. They couldn't have more than a ten-minute head start on her. Maybe less. She hadn't been in Rogan's office that long.

After a minute and nine seconds on hold, Ally got to speak to a human. She gave the woman her name, and the woman promised to have someone in the service department track down Petrucci's number.

This is crazy. Ally drove as fast as she dared, her speedometer topping eighty miles per hour at times, but the trucks dominated the lanes, forcing her to slow to a crawl as they struggled uphill. Five minutes later, her phone rang. It was Hamilton Security.

"Hello," she said anxiously.

"I have Paul Petrucci's phone number for you," the person from service told her.

Driving like a madwoman on Interstate 84, Ally wasn't about to take her hands off the wheel to write. "I'm driving. Can you phone him and ask him to call me? It's urgent."

If her last name had been anything other than Hamilton, Ally was sure he would have told her no, but it was, and so he said "Of course," and Ally went back to driving and waiting. Then she came around a bend and saw a line of trucks that stretched for miles, crawling along the interstate ahead of her. In the lead, a state police cruiser drove with its lights flashing, leading two Penn DOT trucks that were spreading salt ahead of the coming storm.

She could do nothing but fall in line and hope that somewhere ahead of her, the Hamilton Security van was suffering the same fate.

She followed the line until the highway ended and then turned toward Scranton. She was nearly back in the city forty minutes later when her phone finally rang.

"Hi, this is Paul Petrucci. I was asked to call this number."

After introducing herself and thanking him for calling, she explained the situation. "Oh, wow. I wish I'd talked to you half an hour ago. I'm all finished and on my way to my son's hockey game."

Ally wasn't sure she'd ever had such a day of emotional highs and lows. She swallowed, hoping against the odds he'd left the cardboard somewhere in the warehouse instead of destroying it. "What did you to with the cardboard?" she asked.

"Oh, uh, nothing. The new guy was there, the one they hired to clean and stock the trucks. I imagine he'll shred it."

"When did you drop the truck off?" Ally asked excitedly.

"Twenty minutes ago," he said.

"Thank you!" Ally said as she hung up and called the security company again. Of course, she was put on hold. What to do? she asked herself.

Then she pulled out her phone and pulled up the app for her home security system. With one eye on the road, she hit the panic button that called the alarm company directly. If this worked correctly, they'd call her immediately.

Sure enough, Ally's phone rang seconds later. "Hi. This is Hamilton Security. We got an emergency alert from your alarm. Is everything okay?"

"Nandi," Ally asked excitedly, "is that you?"

"Uh, yes, this is Nandi. Is this Miss Hamilton?"

"Yes, it's Ally!" Ally explained her situation and asked if Nandi would check on the most valuable piece of cardboard in Scranton, and Nandi said she could. Ally was still fifteen minutes out, but those minutes could be vital to saving the Rembrandt.

Sure enough, fifteen minutes later, Ally pulled into the back of Hamilton Security, to the garage bays where the vans were parked at night, and ran to the door. It opened, and she walked in to see row after row of Hamilton vans and little else. She heard voices, though, and followed them.

Along the side wall, Nandi stood talking to someone she didn't recognize, who appeared to be explaining how the large shredder worked.

Ally wasn't sure her heart could take much more as she slowly walked toward them. She was still twenty feet away when Nandi spotted her and smiled. "This is George," she said. "He's in charge of cleaning the trucks."

Ally tried hard to smile at him. "Hi, George. It's nice to meet you."

"Miss Nandi told me about your cardboard box, and I was just explaining to her about the shredding. Nothing but ribbons left after it goes through that machine."

Fuck. "So you shredded it?"

He chuckled. "Heck no. That's what I was saying—it's a good thing I didn't, because you'd have nothing left if I did."

"That's a relief," Ally said. Understatement of the year. "Do you have it?"

"Me? No. I guess it's still in the truck."

"Let's find out."

George looked at the log and found the number of the truck Paul Petrucci drove, and they found it in the bunch, the very last one that had come into the garage, parked just beside the shredder. If he was working in sequence, George wouldn't have gotten to it for hours, and Ally wanted to laugh at the trouble she'd gone through to get here in minutes.

George made a big deal of opening the back of the van, and Ally strained her neck to see around him. There, on the floor beneath all the other trash, was the piece of cardboard she'd carefully cut and glued to protect a masterpiece.

"Can we just slide it out?" Ally asked as George was about to climb in the truck. The idea of him walking across *the Sea of Galilee* was not quite as nauseating as the shredder, but awful just the same.

"Sure," he said, and with Ally pulling one side and him the other, they easily freed the box from the van. The trash came with it, and Ally helped George carry it to the shredder before carrying the box to her car.

Nandi walked beside her. "What's in there?" she asked.

Shocked, Ally tried not to blush. "What do you mean?"

"You didn't go through all that trouble for a piece of cardboard."

Ally burst out laughing. She had gotten through Peter Rogan and his security team only to have a college student moonlighting as a home security monitor find her out.

Ally smiled and winked at her. "I wrote a cute girl's phone number on it. Without this, I may never see her again."

"Lucky girl," Nandi said through a half-smile.

"For sure. Thank you so much for your help," Ally said, anxious to get away from Nandi.

"Happy to be of assistance. Please give me a good review on Google."

"I'll see you soon," she said as she placed the Rembrandt in her Jeep and headed for home.

CHAPTER TWENTY-THREE

Brotherly Love

"Hi, bro," Ally said when Kevin answered the phone five minutes later.

"Hi, baby sister. How are you?"

"I'm great. How about you?"

"Finishing up some work. Then I'm going to enjoy my weekend."

"It's Saturday."

"Really? My wife didn't tell me."

Ally laughed. She could picture him, seated at the desk in the office she'd visited in Philadelphia, looking out over the city as he talked to her. She could sense him listening to her. And since Ally didn't often call him, she could feel his concern.

"I have something going on," she said. "And I need your help."

"Okay. Details."

She tried to sound reassuring. "Nothing bad. Well, maybe a little bad, depending on how you look at it." Letting out a huge sigh, she rambled on. "Can you be my lawyer?"

"Uh, why do you need a lawyer?"

"I'll tell you when I see you."

"When will that be?"

"How's tomorrow at lunchtime?" Ally figured she'd take the rest of the day to catch her breath before loading the Jeep and heading south.

"I'm sure I have carpooling or soccer or something, but I suppose I can squeeze you in. Will you be staying over, or is this a drive-by?"

"I think I'll stay. If you'll have me."

"Of course," he said.

"You may change your mind, Kev. I won't hold you to it."

"Ally, fuck. What's going on?"

"I'll tell you tomorrow. Do you have a safe?"

"Of course. In the bedroom closet."

"No, no. Not at your house. At your office."

"Yes…"

"Is it like a home safe, a small one, or more like a blast-open-with-sticks-of-dynamite, big-ass bank safe?"

Kevin laughed. "Are you planning to rob my office?"

"Kevin!"

"Ally!"

She supposed the question was a fair one. "No, Kevin. I'm not robbing your office."

"Are you robbing someone else's office?"

All the robbing was done. Now, she just had to figure out how to get those paintings back to the museum and collect the reward. "No."

"It's a big safe, Ally. Why do you ask?"

"Do you have access to it on Sunday?"

"Ally, I'm a junior associate. I don't ever have access to it."

"Kevin, if you get access to that safe, you could be on track to become a partner."

"What…"

"I'll explain it all when I see you."

"Tomorrow?"

"Yes. Tomorrow."

After disconnecting the call, she breathed a sigh of relief. Almost home, literally and figuratively. The sooner she had this artwork out of her apartment and in a safe, in a lawyer's office, the better she'd feel.

Pulling into her parking lot, she was thrilled to find a spot up close. She popped the hatch and stared at the cardboard holding *Christ in the Storm on the Sea of Galilee.* It was the largest of the works, but she still had to fit two suitcases and *A Lady and Gentleman in Black.* If she could simply stack everything, it would be okay, but she'd piled the pieces into suitcases, which had nowhere to fit in the back of her car.

Shit, she thought. *This isn't going to work.* Sighing, she knew what she had to do. She'd hoped to not involve anyone else in this drama, but maybe she had to. She dialed the phone again.

"Can I borrow your car tomorrow?"

"Okay. May I ask why?" her mother replied.

"I'm going to a show. In Philly." Ally quickly scrolled through her phone and found what she needed. "I found a piece of art, something I want to give to Kevin. It won't fit in my car."

"What is it?"

"What is what?"

"This art. That won't fit in your car."

"Oh, um, it's a statue."

"A statue. Hmm. I'm sure they'll find room for that somewhere in their tiny house."

"Not to worry. It's for his office."

"Oh, that's better. What is it?"

"It's a statue."

"Ally, are you being deliberately evasive? Because it seems like you are."

"It's Justice. You know, the scales of justice and all that."

"Okay. I see. You randomly bought your brother a statue of Justice, and you need my car to transport it."

Fuck, Ally thought. *It's never wise to lie to my mother.* She pulled up her Amazon account and found a statue of Justice. It was perfect, and it cost $4,000. She could barely afford gas. She could not tell her mom she'd bought a $4,000 statue.

"It's okay, Mom. I'll figure it out."

"Ally, stop. I think you're lying to me. Should I be worried?"

Ally knew the next, unspoken sentence was a question about relapse, and she deserved it, but it was crushing just the same.

"Nothing to be concerned about."

"When are you leaving? We're expecting a storm."

Fuck. Fuck, fuck, fuck.

"It's going to start soon. Can you postpone?"

Ally really didn't want to do that. Even though the paintings had been sitting in her apartment, she suddenly felt anxious about getting them out.

"Maybe I should go today," she said.

"Maybe you should go *now*."

Ally slammed the hatch.

"I'm packing as we speak. I don't need your car. I'll make the statue fit."

"Ally, whatever you're up to, please be careful."

"I love you," she said for no particular reason. "And I will."

Ally was hesitant to leave the Rembrandt in the Jeep, so she carried it into the lobby and picked up the luggage trolley from the mail room. Then, after a quick elevator ride, she was at her apartment door and inside. She wished she hadn't already wrapped everything, that she could look at it once more. Even if she went to Boston to visit these paintings, she suspected they'd be back on display as Isabella Stewart Gardner had intended, with some in the Dutch Room, and some in Short Gallery, and *Chez Tortoni* in the Blue Room. And the Gardner works would surely never sit beside the Raphael again, because if Ally had her way, he was heading to Europe.

First, she loaded *A Lady and Gentleman in Black* beside the other Rembrandt, then stacked the suitcases beside them so they wouldn't fall. Then she threw a few things into her overnight bag and headed back out the door. After lowering the passenger seat as far as it could go, and then reclining the seat back, Ally squeezed the suitcases onto the front seat. Then she put the large paintings in the back, buckled her seat belt, and turned on the Jeep. Before she left the lot, she called Kevin.

"We're getting a storm. Can I come now?"

Kevin laughed. "Too late. It's already snowing here."

"Fuck!"

"Listen...whatever this is—can it wait?"

Ally looked to the passenger seat and her heart pounded. "No. Can you stay at your office?"

"Ally, it's Saturday."

"Kev, I promise, it's important."

He finally answered after a few seconds of silence. "I suppose I could find a few more hours of work to do before I head home."

"Perfect," she said.

She picked up the turnpike in Taylor and, with a cautious glance at the gray sky, headed south. The traffic was sparse, and she pushed her speed, hoping to get ahead of the storm. She was successful until she reached Allentown, where the first few dry flakes made windshield wipers necessary. By Quakertown, the snow was really falling, and the wipers could barely keep up. But she was one of few idiots on the road, so she didn't have to contend with traffic. When she reached the Schuylkill Expressway, she called Kevin.

"I'm about ten miles out," she said. "So I should be there in about two hours," she said with a laugh.

"Perfect! I should be wrapping it up by then."

"Seriously?"

"No, no. I'm waiting on you."

"I have some packages. Where do I park?"

"Underground garage. No snow to worry about."

Ally thought about the packages. She could carry one painting, and Kevin could get the other, and they could each pull a suitcase. "There's an elevator, right?"

"Not on Saturdays."

"Ha, ha."

He gave her directions and promised to meet her at the entrance, where his security card would be needed to gain access to the garage. "Is it a far walk to the elevator? Because there's no room in my car."

"Ally, am I going to need a drink?"

"Probably two."

A few minutes later, Ally weaved through the streets of Center City and found her brother's building. He was huddled against the wall, with snow blowing all around him, when she beeped the horn. He smiled and waved, then passed a card across a sensor, and the gate opened. She drove through and stopped.

"Where to?" she asked, and he pointed toward the centrally located elevators. She parked, hopped out of the car, and waited as Kevin walked over. Breathing a deep sigh of relief, she hugged him.

"I'm so happy to be here," she said.

"I'm sure it was an awful drive."

"That, too. But it's mostly this," she said as waved toward the front seat, where the suitcases took up the entire space.

"Staying a while?" he asked, and she laughed.

"Oh, brother. Help me out here," she said as she popped the trunk and tugged on the top painting. *A Lady and Gentleman in Black* slid out, and she handed it to Kevin.

"What do we have here?" he asked as he looked at it.

"Five more minutes, Kev, and I promise it will all make sense."

After pulling free *Christ in the Storm on the Sea of Galilee,* she closed the hatch and tugged both suitcases from the car.

"To your office?" Ally asked.

"Of course," he said, and they headed toward the elevator.

Once inside, Ally leaned against the wall and began laughing. "You are not going to believe this," she said.

"I'm thinking this is going to be a doozy," he said. "Involving stolen art."

Ally felt her eyes open wide. "How'd you know?"

He frowned and looked down. Even wrapped in the thick layers of plastic, the object beside Kevin on the elevator floor was obviously a painting.

"How much trouble are you in?"

"Is it safe to talk in here?"

Kevin looked around. "Maybe not."

A moment later, they were in his twelve-by-twelve-foot office, and Ally sank into one of the club chairs sitting in front of his large desk. Kevin pulled the other chair a few feet away, spread his long legs, and leaned forward with folded hands. "Talk to me."

Instead of speaking, Ally stood and pulled a ten-dollar bill from her pocket. "I saw that on television. Now you're my lawyer."

He laughed. "Okay."

She walked a few steps, knelt, and opened the smaller suitcase. The postage-size Rembrandt self-portrait was on top. Setting it on the edge of Kevin's desk, she peeled back the plastic and rolled it into itself. The bubble wrap sprang open when the plastic was removed, and the etching sat before her. Kevin leaned closer, but Ally spared him the effort, picking it up by the corners of the frame and handing it to him.

"It's Rembrandt," he said.

"Yes. Not just any tiny little Rembrandt. This one was painted by RVR himself, in 1640. In 1991, it was stolen from the Isabella Stewart Gardner Museum in Boston. And last week, it was stolen again, by me. Now I need you, oh wise legal eagle, to repatriate it and obtain the reward. The ten-million-dollar reward."

Kevin looked from the face of Rembrandt to Ally. "Where did you get this?"

"Do you really want to know?"

"Duh. Yeah."

So she started with the first day on the job, and her suspicions, and went on to her planning to switch the paintings, making frames for the copies, and pulling off the heist, one piece at a time.

"You could have been caught. Killed."

Ally shrugged.

"You don't care."

"I'm starting to care again."

He looked into her eyes. "Good."

"Do you want to see a Raphael? Or how about a freakin' Vermeer?"

"Hell, yeah."

They worked carefully, unwrapping each piece so they could preserve the plastic wrap, and a little while later they sat on the floor, surrounded by twelve incredible works of art. "Oh, my God, Ally," Kevin said. "I could cry right now."

He looked at her, and she didn't stop her own tears.

"My baby sister is a hero," he said as he pulled her close. "This was so stupid. But I am so proud of you."

"Thank you."

"I need to call my boss. Okay?"

She nodded, and they decided to start rewrapping some of the lesser pieces while they waited. Twenty minutes later, a man of sixty knocked on Kevin's door and walked in.

"Hi, Ally. Nice to see you on such a lovely day." Dave Lane's white hair was wet, and he told them he'd walked from his apartment and said this mysterious call was the most exciting thing that had happened to him all day.

"I'd bet it's going to get even better." Ally told him the short version of her story.

"How certain are you they're authentic?"

Ally sighed. "Who knows? But let me show you something." She removed the top piece of cardboard from *Christ in the Storm on the Sea of Galilee.*

"O ye of little faith," Dave said softly.

"What?"

"That's what Jesus said to his disciples that day. See how afraid they are? They didn't have faith that the Lord would save them."

"Is that where that expression comes from? I didn't know."

"Interesting," Kevin said.

"What's really interesting is the edges of the painting. It's just a little smaller than it should be, and the jagged cuts probably match what was left in the frame at the Gardner," Ally said.

Dave nodded. "How much is the reward?"

Ally told him, and he didn't even flinch.

"But that's not all," she said excitedly. "There's a separate reward for the Raphael."

"How much is that?" Kevin asked.

"One hundred million."

Both men's jaws dropped as they stared at her.

"One. Hundred. Million?" Kevin asked.

"That's what the internet says. You might have to negotiate. That's why I'm hiring you. And also to keep my identity confidential."

"Sounds like you've given this a good deal of thought, Ally. Our firm will do our best to get this artwork authenticated and returned to the rightful owners without exposing you to any risk."

He held out his hand for Ally to shake.

"I'd also like my brother to be named partner in your firm, if you can manage that."

Dave laughed. "Let's see how this goes. For now, let's get these masterpieces into the safe."

A little while later, after they were stored, Ally named all twelve works for the receipt he gave her.

"It was a pleasure to see you again, Ally," Dave said.

She hugged him. "Thank you for doing this."

"It's the right thing," he said, and when Ally looked at Kevin, she saw him beaming at her.

You totally got this.

CHAPTER TWENTY-FOUR

Repatriate

It had been three weeks since Brodrik Rogan's death, and Ally was just starting to feel like her life was returning to normal. This version of normal, anyway.

Greg had assigned her two new clients in his place, relatively normal, stress-free patients who didn't require security clearance or armed guards at their doors. They didn't keep her waiting and were grateful for the care she provided.

If only her brother would call, everything would be perfect.

"Hi, Dotty." Ally greeted her last client of the day, a woman being seen for lab draws. "How are you feeling?"

Dotty smiled. "I'm okay, Ally. I think I'm going to beat this. Hopefully the blood test proves me right."

"I hope it does."

Ally made quick work of drawing two tubes of blood, then showed herself out. Her phone rang before she made it back to the Jeep. It was an unfamiliar number, not on her contact list, but since working for Greg, she'd begun answering those calls. Patients, doctors, therapists—they all called her cell when they needed her. Expecting one of them, she answered the phone.

"Ally Hamilton," she said.

"Hello, Ms. Hamilton." A female voice greeted her. "This is Attorney Austin Rose's office. Do you have a moment to speak with Mr. Rose?"

Whose heart doesn't pound a little faster when a lawyer calls? "What's this about?" Ally asked as her heart found its way to her throat.

"Mr. Rose will explain. Is this a good time?"

"Sure." Ally closed the door and turned on the Jeep, cold air blasting her face. "When is this winter going to end?" she wondered aloud as she pulled out of Dotty's driveway and headed from the Poconos back toward Scranton. Hopefully by the time she reached Four H, she'd be thawed.

"Hello, Miss Hamilton?" a friendly voice asked.

"Yes. This is Ally."

"Hi, Ally. My name is Austin Rose, and I'm an attorney here in the Poconos. I represented Brodrik Rogan in some of his estate planning. I'm calling you today to inform you that he's remembered you in his will."

Somehow Brodrik Rogan always managed to throw Ally off, even after death. What the fuck? "He left me something in his will?"

"Yes. That's correct. I'm wondering if you can stop by my office to pick it up?"

"Pick it up? Can you tell me what it is?"

"He left you some artwork. A few things, in fact. It's all been appraised, for tax purposes, and I'll give you a copy of that document for your accountant when I see you. You'll be taxed on your gift, of course, unless you decide to donate it yourself. All totaled, it comes to about $10,000."

Ally was stunned. "I'm confused, sir. Why would he leave something to me?"

"He wrote you a letter, explaining it all, and I'd be happy to open it and read it to you, if you'd like. I can say that he included you just a few days before he died, and I did ask why. He told me his family would probably just throw his collection to the curb, and he didn't want that to happen. And I think the family is probably happy to see you haul it all away. It's old stuff, obviously nothing too valuable."

Hmm, Ally thought. Why would Rogan leave this stuff to her, if it was real? He had to know it would be appraised, that he would be found out if he was holding the Gardner art. Right? It didn't make sense. Unless, of course, his collection was all fake, and she'd endured all that stress for nothing. The framing, the stealing, the transporting to Philadelphia in a blizzard. Bringing Kevin into it. She'd been hoping to get him a partnership, and he might end up unemployed.

Fuck.

"Can you come by tomorrow?"

"Mr. Rose, I have work. And unless you tell me Mr. Rogan left me ten *million* dollars, I can't miss it. Can I come in afterward?"

He chuckled. "Of course. How's six o'clock?"

"I'm usually done by three or four. Unless you like working late."

"Why don't you come by when you finish for the day, and I'll squeeze you in."

Ally hung up with her head spinning and could think of nothing but the phone call for the duration of the trip to Scranton. Should she call Kevin? She didn't want to bug him, again, but maybe she should. If those paintings were fake, it would affect him more than anyone.

"Hey, baby-sister-turned spy," he greeted her jovially. In the weeks since she'd given him the paintings, his normally sweet disposition had turned almost unbearably cheerful. He was counting his share of that money, counting on the partnership. How could Ally take it away from him? Yet how could she keep this information from him?

"I have news. Possibly awful, devastating news."

"Okay. You have my attention." The happy tone was gone, replaced with one of fear.

Ally told him about the phone call from Austin Rose. "It makes no sense, Kev. Why would he leave me those paintings if they're authentic? I could throw them out. I could turn them in, expose him. Or the appraiser would have figured it out before I ever got them."

"I agree with you. It doesn't look good."

"Any word from Boston?" she asked.

"Ally, you know this takes time. And it's not one painting we're talking about here. It's twelve."

"It was good that they agreed to examine the Raphael, too."

"I'm sure they'll display it for a month or two before it goes back to Poland."

"You're talking as if you think they're real."

"You think they are."

"I did. But, Kev—what if I'm wrong? What if I stole those paintings and risked jail for $10,000 worth of reproductions?"

"You'd have quite a tale to tell, if you weren't confessing to a crime."

Ally groaned.

"Do you want me to come with you when you meet with him?"

"Maybe just to carry me."

"Listen, Ally. No matter what, this will be fine. Maybe you have some junk art you can sell. And maybe you've recovered some of the world's greatest treasures."

"I guess we'll soon know."

Ally hung up with her brother as she pulled into the Four H parking lot and found Linda practically skipping to her car.

"The Cadillac King left me something in his will!" she said in greeting.

"Get out! Me too."

"What did he leave you?"

"Art," Ally said.

"Me too! The painting with the dog. The lawyer called and said that picture is worth $25,000. Some guy in France painted it, a hundred years ago, and Mr. Rogan knew I admired it, so he left it to me."

Ally was so genuinely happy for Linda she forgot her own worries. "That's such great news, Linda. Congrats."

"I'm going first thing to meet the lawyer. Greg's giving me the morning off. How about you? How much is yours worth?"

"The lawyer said $10, 000."

"Well, he did pinch my ass," she said with a shrug. "That's about a grand per pinch, if you add them all up."

Ally laughed. "You have a great outlook."

Inside, Ally found Greg and told him her news. "I'm aware," he said. "Congrats."

"It's really unexpected. I only knew the guy for a couple of weeks."

"Why do you think he'd leave you his art collection?"

"Is that what it is? The entire collection? The statues and all?"

Greg blew out a breath. "No, not everything. From what I understand, though, it's about twenty pieces. But why would he leave you anything at all?"

Ally shook her head, then grew still when she saw him studying her. "Greg, what are you thinking?"

He shrugged. "Don't know what to think."

"Greg, I swear, there was nothing inappropriate about my relationship with Mr. Rogan."

He laughed. "I know. It's just…there's something I never told you. Brodrik Rogan was my uncle. My mom's brother. So my family is a little curious. Not that they need the money, but…"

Ally studied him, noticing for the first time the resemblance between the two men.

"You resemble him," she said.

"He wasn't a bad-looking man, before he let himself go."

"No, he wasn't."

"I thought he looked a little like Raphael. The painter. He had that self-portrait in his bathroom."

"That must have been it, Ally. He loved to talk about those

paintings, like they were real. In fact, a few people in the family thought they were real, until they saw the appraisal. But other than his bodyguard, no one had any interest. Until you came along."

Ally suddenly felt very uncomfortable. She needed this job, needed a letter from Greg when it was time to reapply for her license. "Greg, I'd be happy to give up the gift. I don't really need it. Or want it. His stuff is dark. I'm more of a bright-and-cheery art fan."

He shook his head and waved her off. "Nonsense. My uncle had a fortune, Ally, and this means nothing to his children. They won't miss it. In fact, between old friends and family, he named more than a hundred, uh, what's the word? Entities in his will."

"I hope he remembered you. You arranged for a lot of cute nurses to take care of him."

Greg sighed. "He was harmless," he said sweetly.

Ally remembered the things she'd read on the internet. "What about the drowned wife? And the missing parts guy?"

"Ancient history."

That's what Brodrik Rogan was to her, and Ally was glad for it. She'd be even happier tomorrow, when this was all over.

"I'm going to the Recovery Hub tonight, so I won't see you in the morning," she said as she was leaving.

"Everything okay?" he asked.

Ally smiled. "Oh, yeah. They have an art class there. Art therapy. I enjoy it."

Ally wasn't sure what to think of Greg as she walked out of his office. It was creepy that he hadn't told her that Rogan was his uncle. Worse, that he had subjected his staff to Rogan's harassment.

Nothing is ever easy, she thought.

Ally couldn't wait to get home, couldn't wait to get to art therapy. It had become a date night for the four of them, and Ally was enjoying getting to know Maria in the company of the other two women. It made it more of a friendship and took some of the pressure off them. It wasn't a mating dance, just some fun with friends, and Ally liked that.

She was healing, beginning to see the good in herself again. Even if the art she'd turned over to the museum was fake, her effort had been real. She'd been brave, and creative, and gutsy, and she'd done something she thought was right. Something that would make the world a better place. That did a lot for her morale.

Maria did a lot for her, too, and Ally was trying hard to be worthy of her. She was an amazing woman, and Ally wanted nothing more than to be with her. The things she was doing, the things *they* were doing—the art classes, cooking together, hanging out, yoga—all of it was taking her down the first part of that pathway.

This new love interest felt good, but she wasn't focusing on the destination. One of the things she'd learned in her recovery was to enjoy the journey. Maria was going to be an amazing one, and where they ended up didn't matter. It wasn't the point. For now, it was about the two of them, learning and discovering and exploring. Minds, hearts, bodies.

And, wow, what a body she had.

They'd gotten into the habit of having dinner before the class, and all of them drove together to Ally's, to save on parking. For the same reason, they always chose a restaurant close to the Recovery Hub, so they could walk there after they finished their food.

Maria gave her a five-minute notice when they were approaching her place, and she was waiting in the lobby when her mom's car pulled up to the door.

"You will not believe my day," she said as she fastened her seat belt.

They were still talking about the Rogan artwork when they finished dinner. Maria was so excited she pulled pictures of the artwork up on her phone, and they all speculated on the same questions Ally had been thinking about all day.

At the art class, Ally was barely able to focus on her landscape, and in bed that night, she couldn't sleep. The next day, she was a jittery mess and said a prayer of thanks that she'd arrived safely when she pulled up to the door of Austin Rose's law office after work.

It was an old building in East Stroudsburg, a grand two-story colonial with tall pillars supporting the low-pitched roof, and patriotic bunting draped below each of the many windows facing the street. Wow.

Ally announced herself to the receptionist and was ushered directly into Mr. Rose's office. He was a small man, younger than she'd expected, probably only a few years older than she was. Most striking was his vivacious personality.

After introductions, he pointed to a large collection of packages and boxes taped in bubble wrap.

"You have here a collection of paintings, drawings, etchings, carvings, castings, and other art. The complete list is here," he said as he handed it to her. "I cited the value from the appraisal, that Mr. Rogan had done many years ago. His family didn't want to pay for a new one, so—good for you. Chances are, it may have gone up in value. Probably didn't go down." He handed her a large, rather stuffed envelope. "Each piece has been individually evaluated, and that's what you have here. For taxes, as I mentioned, or if you want to auction things on eBay. Whatever. The stuff is yours now. You can do what you want."

Ally looked at the list. The items were listed in alphabetical order. *A Lady and Gentleman in Black* was first, followed by *Chez Tortoni*, and then by Chinese Gu.

Ally stopped. A Gu had been stolen from the Gardner, but she'd never seen one at Brodrik Rogan's house. And why had Rogan possessed yet another stolen item from the Gardner? Either he had the Gardner collection in his possession, or he was obsessed with it.

She read the list, counting as she did. All thirteen pieces from Boston were there, as was the Raphael and a few pieces of art that came from the same charity Greg Hart supported. When she finished the list, she opened the envelope of appraisals and pulled the contents. Like the first paper, it was organized alphabetically.

"Oil Painting On Canvas Stamped *A Lady and Gentleman in Black,* Village Collectors, New York, New York. Value, $1100."

Ally stopped and stared at the attorney, stared right through him, actually. She'd taken that painting on the first day and had worried about some tell-tale marking that might have identified the piece and let Rogan know it wasn't genuine. She'd carefully examined it, front and back and found no stamp from the Village Collectors in New York, New York. In fact, there was no mark at all on that painting. The one she'd taken and given to her brother clearly wasn't the same painting that was appraised. The painting she'd substituted wasn't stamped either, and no one seemed to notice, which was even more confusing.

What the fuck was going on?

Flipping to the next page, she continued reading. "Oil Painting On Canvas stamped *Chez Tortoni*. Alfred's Fine Arts, Nantucket, Mass. Value: $400." She flipped to the next page. "Vase stamped 'Faux Bronze Statue Marked China.' Value $50." Next came "Oil Painting On Canvas stamped *Christ in the Storm on the Sea of Galilee*, Alfred's Fine Arts, Nantucket, Mass." This one was valued at $1500. Well, it really was a huge painting, so Ally could see it. "Okay," she said when she finished reading. Next came "Oil Painting on Canvas, stamped '*Landscape with an Obelisk*, Fine Arts of Manhasset.' Value $500."

Ally continued reading, twenty-four appraisals, before finally looking up to find Mr. Rose staring at her.

"Everything okay?"

She swallowed. "Yes, perfect. I accept." Except nothing was perfect at all. Something was very, very wrong.

"If you'll sign here, you acknowledge the appraisal and agree to work with your accountant to pay any applicable taxes, and we'll be almost done."

Ally read, then quickly scribbled her signature, anxious to get out of there.

"Next, this is the receipt, that you've actually taken possession of the twenty-four items today. I'll help you carry them to your car. I hope it's a large car. Two of them are pretty big."

Ally remembered from her trip to Philly. "I have an SUV, but it'll be tight."

"Do you want me to unwrap everything, so you can inspect it all?"

She shook her head. All she wanted to do was to be somewhere else.

Austin Rose stood and led her toward the corner of his office. "No, not that stuff," he said. "That's for the bodyguard."

Good for him, Ally thought. She hoped he'd find another job quickly.

While the attorney carried the largest piece, Ally hoisted a box, and they made their way to the Jeep. She placed the box on the front seat, while he fixed the seats and squeezed the painting in. Ally waited with the car while he made two more trips, and then she headed home, pondering the whole experience.

The more she thought of it, the more it nagged at her. She couldn't pinpoint what it was, but something was wrong.

At the traffic light before Interstate 80, she dialed Kevin's number. "Well?" he asked, the stress evident in his voice.

"Kev, the appraisals say these are worthless copies. But something strange is going on here." She told him about the stamps.

"Maybe it wasn't an ink stamp, but an actual paper stamp, like a sticker, and it fell off."

Ally's mood lightened. "Maybe," she said, trying to inject some enthusiasm into her voice, for her own benefit as much as Kevin's.

"So the appraisal says they're worthless, but I really believed they were authentic. *Christ in the Storm on the Sea of Galilee* was cut from its frame, just like the real Rembrandt Oh, Kev, what is going on?"

"Is the appraisal legit? Who did it? Maybe I should check them out, to be certain."

"I'm on the highway, so I can't be sure, but it looked real…it was typed, on an old carbon copy. My copy is pink, the customer copy. I can tell you the name of the company when I get home."

"Carbon?" He said it in three syllables and sounded calmer. Ally wished she felt that way. "You don't see that much anymore. Computers just print two pages on plain paper. It must be an old appraisal. Hell, the company might not even be in business anymore. Call me with the name, and I'll investigate."

"Okay. But, Kev, something else doesn't seem right." She breathed deeply, trying her best to relax. How could she have made a mistake like this, thinking the art was real?

"What do you mean?" Now he sounded agitated again.

Taking more deep breaths, she told him about the paperwork, what she could remember of the descriptions of the art, stamped with the dealer names and the values.

"That sounds right. Did they describe the frames?"

"Yes. They even described the mediums. Pencil on paper, oil on canvas."

"Oil on oak panel," he added.

Ally paused. That was it! Or rather, that wasn't it. She'd read the descriptions of twenty-four pieces of art, but none of them described anything painted on wood. Yet two of the works of art she'd switched at the Rogan mansion—the Flinck and the Raphael—were painted on wood. She knew, because she'd made the copies and switched them, then smuggled them off the property. "Kev! There was no oil-on-oak panel described on my paperwork."

"Are you sure?" he asked.

Ally was confused about a good many things, but this wasn't one of them.

"Yes! Absolutely! Could they have made a mistake like that? Because, you saw them, right? They were definitely on wood."

"Yes. They were. So either this company is profoundly incompetent, or they examined a different group of paintings," he said.

"You're right."

"Ally, think about it. There's no stamp on the paintings you swapped. And no oak panel on the paintings you got today. Someone made another switch. There must be a third set of paintings!" Kevin said.

Ally paused. It made sense. "The question is who made the most recent switch."

"Yes. And the other question goes back to Rogan. So, why appraise fake art?"

Ally's brain was still in overdrive, but she didn't have any idea of Rogan's motives. "I'm not sure, Kev."

"Ally, listen to me. Hear me out. Suppose the paintings you stole were real. Are real. Rogan knows that one day, they're going to be doing this. Dividing his estate. If his family called in appraisers now, it's out of the old man's hands. They'd know the paintings were real, and he'd be exposed as a thief. His kids get nothing."

"They get nothing now, since he gave the art to me."

"Maybe they did know. What if they were in on it? Maybe *they* took the art from his study and replaced it with the fakes you got in the will."

"They took my fakes and replaced them with his fakes?"

"Yes."

"If that's the case, Kev, we could be in real trouble when the family finds out their art is worthless."

She heard a soft whistle. "Fuck."

"Fuck is about right." Noticing the exit for Mount Pocono, Ally flipped her turn signal and pulled onto the ramp, then eased to the side of the road and hit her flashers. Leaning into her headrest, she sighed.

Kevin was silent, then began laughing hysterically. After a moment, Ally joined him, and she laughed so hard she couldn't speak for a few moments. Finally, she found her voice. "So, after all this, all we know is that the paintings the Gardner is evaluating right this very minute, the ones I repatriated, are not the paintings in his will."

Kevin agreed. "Yes. We don't know the origin of the paintings you got from Austin Rose. Are these the ones you bought online?"

"They're all wrapped. I can't tell. But I just pulled off the highway, so let me check." Pulling her emergency knife from the pocket of her door, she popped the hatch and walked to the back of the Jeep, switching the phone to speaker.

The two largest paintings were angled at the top of the pile, so she pulled a smaller one from beneath. After carefully cutting the tape, she unwrapped it, explaining to Kevin as she progressed. "It's *Landscape with an Obelisk.*" She tapped on the center, and it gave. "And it's definitely a canvas."

"Finish opening it. See if it's stamped."

Ally did as commanded, and when she flipped the painting, a canvas, she immediately saw a bright-blue stamp in the right upper corner. "*Landscape with an Obelisk*, Fine Arts of Manhasset."

"So this is the painting from the appraisal!" Kevin said as Ally ran her fingers along the frame and inspected the canvas. She'd used a utility knife to cut the canvas, then glued it to an oak panel. She'd made a frame—not this frame—and attached it. Then she'd hung it in the vestibule of Brodrik Rogan's mansion, near the bottom of the stairs. It was the first painting she'd switched. If she lived to be a hundred, she'd never forget it.

"Yes. So where is the painting I substituted? And who switched this one?"

"That's actually two questions, but both are equally relevant."

Both are equally problematic, Ally thought. "What do we do now?"

Kevin sighed. "I don't know. Wait? What else can we do?"

Ally sighed. "I don't know either. What about the Gardner? It's been three weeks."

"Be patient," he said as Ally heard his office phone ring. "Hold on," he instructed her.

"Kevin Hamilton?" she heard him answer.

"Hi, Dave. Yes, I'm sitting…What? Oh, wow…Holy…crap. I…Oh, wow…Thank you. Thank you so much…I'll let her know."

Ally could hear the conversation, and it could have been about anything. Phillies season tickets. A new client. A bonus check. Anything at all. Yet somehow, Ally knew the call from Kevin's boss was about her. And she knew what her brother would tell her before he even spoke.

"Ally?" he said when he came back to the call.

She could hardly speak. "They're real, Kev. They're real, aren't they?" she whispered.

"Yes," he said. Then he shouted it. "Yes!"

Fear suppressed Ally's joy. "This just got so much more complicated," she said. "We found the real paintings, and it's just a matter of time until someone figures out we switched them."

"They don't know it was us. The paintings could have been switched at any time. Rogan himself could have done it, twenty-five years ago, when the appraisals were first done. It could have been when he had his carpets cleaned." She quickly rewrapped the painting and placed it back in the car.

"And it could have been last week, when Hamilton came in to install the backup battery."

"Ally, we can't stop this train. It's left the station. All we can do now is hold on and see where it stops."

That could be true. "What are the details about the reward?"

The Gardner had agreed to pay the ten million dollars posted for the return of their art, even though Ally hadn't included the finial and the vase. The Polish government agreed to the published reward for the Raphael, no questions asked. After the legal fees Ally had agreed to, her share came to ninety million dollars.

Ally suddenly wanted to run around the car. Do back flips from the roof, perhaps even a little dance on the hood. In spite of her anxiety over the unknown players who'd switched the paintings, she was overjoyed. "When will we get the money?" she asked. "How will they handle it? They won't put it in the newspaper, will they?"

"Are you kidding? This will be front page, around the globe."

"Kev, I thought this would be anonymous. That's why I did it this way."

He sighed. "Everyone in the world will want to know your name. And your story. But it will go through the firm. No one will ever know it was you."

"Unless you make partner, and your name goes on the building."

"That's why you did this, isn't it?"

"Well…you are my most awesome brother."

"I've already talked to Dave about it. We'll share our fee with the firm in Boston. They'll get the credit, and we'll remain anonymous. No one, including the Rogan family, will ever know anyone named Hamilton was involved."

Ally's relief was so profound she started to cry.

"Hey. No tears. This is the best day of your life. Mine too. Hell, those kids have been a pain in the ass since they were born. The wedding was only so-so. There was the 2008 World Series—that was good. But this, this is fucking amazing."

As intended, Ally laughed. "Thanks for your help. So when are you going to cough up the money?"

"Don't quit your day job just yet. A few more weeks, I'd say."

"And you know what we need to do about the reward?"

"I sure do."

"Call me later, bro. So I know I'm not dreaming."

"I will. Ally, thanks for picking me. This is…this is a game changer for me. For my career."

"I love you, Kev."

"Same."

CHAPTER TWENTY-FIVE

A Steal

When Ally arrived at home, she sat on her couch and turned on the fire, looking at the O'Keeffe prints. Light and bright, just the kind of art she preferred. Still, thinking of *The Concert* and the other works from the Gardner that had been in this room just a few weeks ago, she smiled. For a few hours, she had beheld a collection no one else in the world had ever seen. Works so magnificent, powerful men had stolen them, and someone was going to pay her millions of dollars for their safe return.

Her smile lingered as she leaned back into the couch, thinking now of the money. At her current salary, she'd never earn as much as she'd be given for the return of the stolen artwork. From now on, or from whenever she cashed that anticipated check, she'd work because she enjoyed it, not because she needed to. She'd find that house and the girl—her thoughts immediately jumped to Maria—and work at something she enjoyed. It probably wouldn't be at Hamilton, or at Four H. Maybe back in the ER?

She wasn't sure, but for the first time in months, she wasn't worried about her future.

Something else entirely was on her mind. Where were the paintings she'd placed in Brodrik Rogan's house, and who'd switched them?

"The envelope!" she thought suddenly, as she reached for her purse and removed the letter from Brodrik Rogan that his attorney had given her.

Not bothering with an opener, she tore it with her fingers and pulled out two handwritten pages, spreading them on the table before her. Even though she'd seen only his signature, the large, shaky scrawl appeared to be Rogan's.

Dearest Ally:

I must face the reality that you so courageously brought to the forefront of my mind: I'm old. As I'm thinking what comes next, I can't help but consider what I leave behind— worthless, bitter children. Maybe the grandchildren will be better, but I'm not hopeful.

As I'm sure you are aware, I've done some things in my life that I regret. Selfish things. I can't undo them, but perhaps I can unshoulder some of my burden by making things right, and I'll die with a little less worry.

For years I've entertained people in my home—my family, my friends, business associates. I've attempted to excite them about the artwork I've so carefully collected, but until you walked in, I've never found anyone with that interest. You've come into my life late, but I argue it was just in time! The last days with you as my nurse have been most enjoyable. You've put a smile on an old man's face, and that's a nice thing.

As a fellow connoisseur, I'm leaving you a select portion of my art collection. You can do with it as you wish—scatter the works around your personal space, taking exquisite pleasure in the simple act of sitting and looking at them. Or you can sell them and ensure some measure of personal financial security. Or you can be noble and send them back to the masses.

I would suggest that, before selling them, or sending them to your attic for storage, have the Gardner look at them first. Their appraisal will be more accurate than the one my attorney has given you.

It's not my worry anymore. My soul feels lighter already.

Whatever you choose, do it, and have no regrets. And please, don't ever mention my name.

With my fondest regards, Brodrik Rogan

Ally sat back again, thinking about the note. It was cryptic, for sure. He alluded to the theft of the art but said nothing that would arouse suspicion, unless you were specifically thinking the art was stolen in the first place. Yet, the suggestion she might have financial security was telling. How much security would she get from $10,000? It wasn't nothing, but it wasn't an early retirement, either. And he mentioned the

Gardner—that was telling, wasn't it? Finally, he suggested she could send them back to the masses. That could only mean the museum, right?

Grabbing the letter, she reread it. It was eloquent, showing the side of Rogan she'd glimpsed from time to time—the side he'd cultivated, or perhaps the real Brodrik, the one hiding in the gangster suit. He wasn't admitting to a crime, but it seemed he was confirming her suspicions, counting on her to study this letter, to question, to investigate the paintings.

It was a question, for sure, and didn't answer the other ones. Who'd switched the paintings? After talking with Kevin, she'd thought it was all part of a master plan for Rogan's kids to get the stolen art and be able to avoid taxes or closer scrutiny. After all, the way their father had shown off the collection, they were bound to have questions about it. Yet after reading the letter, it didn't seem his kids were in on it after all.

The question remained: Who knew? Or who suspected enough to exchange the paintings? Who had access?

Maybe she should look at the paintings.

Ally grabbed her car keys, then found the luggage trolley in the mail room and pushed it toward the front door. Carlos was just entering the gym, and he removed his AirPod to say hello, yet Ally was too distracted to linger. As she walked out the door toward her Jeep, her mind raced about everything that had happened since she'd first walked through the door of the Rogan estate. Aware only of her thoughts, she pressed the button on her remote and watched the hatch rise. She was just about to pull the top painting from the pile when a voice behind her startled her.

"Hello, Ally."

Ally looked up. "Rocco!" she exclaimed, as she reflexively stepped back from him. Even though he wasn't guarding Brodrik Rogan today, he was dressed in his normal uniform—turtleneck sweater and jeans, Timberland boots. The only thing missing was the gun, although it was probably on him somewhere, out of sight.

"What, what are you doing here?" she stammered.

"The paintings are fake."

"What? I, I know they're fake. I just got them from the lawyer, and he gave me the appraisal. They're worth about $10,000."

He laughed dryly. "Not these paintings. These paintings have been in storage ever since Mr. Rogan used them for that phony appraisal. I'm talking about the paintings he had in the house. The ones you were so interested in. *They're* fake. I just had my own little consultation, with an art expert. They were probably bought on the internet for a few bucks, although they had custom frames. Very expensive, well-made frames. Something like the frames you make."

He stopped talking, spread his legs about two feet apart, and puffed out his bulky chest as he clenched his fists at his sides while he stared at her.

"What, what are you asking me?" Ally stammered.

"I'm not asking you anything. I'm telling you. You took the original paintings. First I noticed *Landscape with an Obelisk* was a little crooked. And then I noticed how clean it was. All of them, as if someone had dusted every single frame, although no one did, because Mr. Rogan wouldn't let any of the staff touch his artwork. Then, when the expert told me they were fakes, I knew it was you. You have the real stuff, and I want it back."

Ally's brain raced. Think. "It wasn't all paintings." She pointed to the cargo area. "There are drawings, too. Ink and pencil."

"Tomato, tomato."

Her mouth grew dry, and she swallowed. "Rocco, I don't know what you're talking about."

He stepped forward, pointing a finger at her, anger painting his features an ugly red. "Oh, I think you do. You somehow faked your way into Mr. Rogan's house, pretending to be a nurse. And you switched his paintings with these internet fakes. And now you have a very valuable collection on your hands."

"I, I don't."

"Why don't I help you with these?" He nodded toward the hatch. "We'll take them inside, up to your apartment, and we can talk more."

Shaking her head, she stepped back again, so her leg was now touching the Jeep's bumper. "That's not a good idea. We can talk here."

Rocco glanced at the line of cars backed up at the light. "No. It's a little noisy out here. A bad place to…talk."

"I…"

He scowled at her. "You do remember I have a gun, don't you?"

Ally nodded. "How could I forget?"

"I could use it, you know."

Ally sucked in a breath. "The chances of you using it are a lot better inside than out here."

"It's not a request, Ally. We're going to put these paintings on the cart and take them into your apartment, and then I'll bring the real ones back out. After that I'm going to drive away, and you're going to forget you ever met me."

"Why are you doing this?"

He laughed and looked toward the bright-blue sky. "Why? Are you serious? Money, Ally. Just like you. I can sell those paintings for a fortune."

"I, I'll split it with you. Fifty-fifty."

He chuckled. "Why would I want to share, when I can have the whole pie to myself?"

Ally felt bold, mostly because she now knew the truth, and she could work with that. "Without me, you have nothing."

"When I get you inside, I will."

"What makes you think I'd leave a fortune in stolen artwork here?" She pointed at her building.

Rocco nodded. "So, you do have it."

She turned her head slightly and squinted at him. "Let's just say I do. Why would I keep it here?"

She looked around, wishing someone would notice them and call the police. But why would they? It just looked like a normal conversation. Maybe she could fall to the ground, and a passerby would call 9-1-1. Or she could run, right out into the traffic. He might shoot her in the back, and she might get squished by a speeding car, but she liked the odds better than going inside with him.

Seeming to read her thoughts, Rocco stepped forward and grabbed her arm. "Don't get any ideas, or I *will* shoot you. I'll take my chances on finding the real art. Even if I don't find it, I haven't lost a thing." His voice was steadily rising, as the color in his face darkened. "So what do I have to lose by shooting you? Nothing!"

"Rocco, please, calm down."

Ally took a breath. "Let's unload the artwork. We'll take it inside," she said softly, thinking she'd reach the front of the Jeep and then take her chances with the cars on Keyser Avenue. She reached out and tugged at the corner of *Christ in the Storm on the Sea of Galilee.* "Help me with this," she said as she stepped aside.

Seeming to regain his composure, Rocco pulled the painting from the hatch in one swift motion and placed in on the trolley. He reached for the next one, and then next, and in a matter of a minute, the trolley was stacked.

"There's a box on the front seat," Ally said as she began walking that way. She hadn't started her second step when she felt his arm on her, pulling her back.

"Not so fast," he said, and then he was beside her, opening the door, cutting off her escape route. She stepped aside for him to take the box, but he just smiled. "I need to keep my hands free."

So Ally lifted the box and placed it on the trolley and looked at him again.

"You're a strong girl. You've got this."

You most certainly do not have this, she thought.

She pushed the cart, and under her full weight, it moved slowly. It was a large, sturdy cart, but it was carrying a heavy burden of canvas and wood.

"C'mon, shove," Rocco demanded. "Put your weight into it."

Ally struggled with it, but she forced it up the slight incline from the parking lot to the sidewalk, and then onto the handicap ramp beside the building. At the base, she paused. "There's no way," she said as she turned to him.

"How'd you get the real ones in?" he asked.

"Two at a time," she answered honestly.

Just then Ally heard the beeping of the front-door alarm, and she turned to see Carlos step out. He looked from Ally to Rocco.

"Everything okay?" he asked.

"Why wouldn't it be?" Rocco replied.

Rocco stood tall again, and Ally noticed his right hand inching backward.

Carlos laughed. "You look like you need some help with the trolley."

Rocco shook his head. "Ally wanted to show me how strong she is, but it looks like she does need a little assistance. I've got it, though. Thanks."

"I'm Carlos, by the way," he said, then pointed his thumb over his shoulder. "I live here."

Rocco nodded.

"And you are?"

"What fucking business is it of yours?"

Carlos cleared his throat. "No business at all. Maybe I can get the door for you, though."

"That's okay. Ally can handle the door."

"Cold day to go without a coat," Carlos said to Rocco.

"Cold day to be outside practically naked," Rocco shot back.

Carlos looked down at his cutaway T-shirt and spandex shorts. "Especially when you're covered in sweat. I do a little fighting, though, so I'm pretty tough."

"I've done some fighting myself. I'm pretty tough, too."

Ally was torn as she watched the exchange, wanting to chase Carlos away, yet hoping he'd use his fighting skills to clobber Rocco.

"That's good. You can protect Ally. She's tough herself, but, you know...the world is brutal."

Judging from the color of his cheeks, Rocco seemed to be growing impatient with the exchange. Carlos pulled the door open and pointed inside, and on cue, Rocco leaned his weight into the cart and started it crawling up the ramp.

Just then Steve poked his head out the door. "Carlos, close the fucking door. It's fucking freezing out here."

Steve looked at Ally and Rocco, then to Carlos, and back to Ally. "Everything okay here?"

Sensing her chance, Ally stopped walking, causing the luggage cart to run into her, halting its progress. "Actually, it's not. I'd like this man to leave. He's making me nervous. Steve, can you call the police?"

Carlos pointed to a Scranton police car pulling up at the curb in front of the building. "Already done."

Rocco looked at the police car and seemed to debate his options, then leaped over the railing and took off toward the parking lot. Ally turned to watch and saw another police car pull into the lot, its lights flashing. Rocco stopped, then turned and ran between the cars, toward the back of the building and the mountain behind it.

Steve and Carlos began chasing him. "Guys, stop. He has a gun. Let the police handle it."

Two officers were already out of their cars, and yet another pulled into the lot behind them. Ally noticed the first car pull out from in front of the building and head toward the next drive, one that led to the apartment complex next to Ally's. They could probably head him off there. "Guys, stop," Ally shouted.

They looked at each other, then at her, then slowly began walking back toward her. The trolley had stopped against the rail, and Ally picked her way around it, greeting them at the bottom of the ramp with a hug.

"My heroes," she said.

"Ally, what the fuck?"

Ally wanted to tell them, but she couldn't. Not without implicating herself. "He's upset. He worked for one of my patients, and the patient left me something in the will, and he's angry."

"Talk about 'roid rage," Carlos said.

"Let's just hope they catch him," Steve said.

Suddenly, a shot rang out. Then another, and another, and another, and then it was quiet, except for the traffic on Keyser Avenue.

Ally freed herself and began running toward the shots.

"Ally, stop. He could still be shooting."

"Or a police officer could be down. I'm an ER PA, guys. I have to help."

They were right behind her as she sprinted into the woods, up an embankment, and into the parking lot of the apartment behind hers. She saw the police car several hundred feet in front of her, surrounded by officers. Four of them were standing, one talking into a radio, and two were on their knees, aiding the man on the ground.

Ally ran all the way to the group. "I'm a PA, in the ER. Can I help?"

She looked down at the scene. One of the officers was doing chest compressions on Rocco, who was floating in a puddle of his own blood. So much blood, all over his chest, and on the ground beneath him.

Ally jumped in, pulling on a pair of gloves from one of the officer's hands. "Hold CPR," she said, and when the officer complied, she applied pressure to Rocco's carotid, feeling for a pulse. One Mississippi, two Mississippi, three Mississippi, four Mississippi, five Mississippi. Nothing. "Continue compressions. Do you need a break?"

Shaking his head, he began another cycle. "We'll switch out at the next cycle."

Ally sat back on her heels and assessed the situation. From the pattern of the blood, it appeared all three bullets had struck Rocco's chest. Each compression only added to the volume seeping from his body, draining him of any chance of surviving his wounds. Yet to do nothing would deprive his brain of any blood at all, any chance of having a meaningful existence if by some miracle he did pull through.

An ambulance siren was suddenly audible in the distance, growing louder as Ally moved into place and took her turn on Rocco's chest. Looking up, she avoided his lifeless eyes and pushed harder, feeling tears fill her own. This was her fault. She'd wanted to do something good, but it had been selfish, too. She'd be rewarded for her efforts, a reward that was most assuredly going to cost Rocco his life. By her count, he'd been down for a few minutes since he was shot, and every one that ticked took some hope with it.

She sighed with relief when an ambulance pulled up next to the scene, and she gave a brief report to the medics as they took over Rocco's care and loaded him into their rig. "All I know is his name is Rocco, and he was Brodrik Rogan's bodyguard."

The police pulled his wallet and got his information. "We'll lead you," one of the officers told the ambulance driver. Ally imagined they were as eager as she was for Rocco to live.

"Is it okay if I come to the hospital?"

"I'll drive you, Ally," Steve volunteered.

The downhill jog to his car was much easier than the uphill trek, and Ally climbed into the front seat beside Steve while Carlos got in back.

"I thought your switch to home health was supposed to be less stressful," Carlos said.

"Me too."

The ambulance and police were out of sight, so there was no chance of catching their draft, yet Steve made good time to the hospital, and they arrived at the ER door five minutes later. Three police cars and the ambulance blocked the entrance, and Ally hopped out before the guys had a chance to speak. "Wait for me in the car."

Rushing through the doors, Ally headed to the trauma bay. In the back of her mind, she thought of the last time she'd walked these halls but quickly pushed the notion aside as she followed the commotion and rushed past the staff and officers and pushed open the swinging door to the trauma unit.

A group of doctors and nurses and technicians crowded the stretcher in the middle of the room, all of them doing something. Securing the ventilator, inserting a bladder catheter and an extra IV, readying a warming blanket. Two IV poles were positioned at the head of the bed, with bags of blood hanging, the red fluid snaking down the tubing to Rocco's arms. Maria, dressed in an impervious gown, wearing goggles and a face mask, was just stepping back from the X-ray box.

"Ally," she said. "What are you doing here?"

"I know him. How is he?"

Maria looked down and saw the blood Ally had collected during the CPR. "Are you hurt?"

Ally shook her head. "It's all his. Is he going to make it?"

Maria nodded toward the X-ray. "Blood in both lungs, left lung collapsed. At least one bullet is in the right spot to have hit the heart. He has no pressure, and the bedside hemoglobin is four. So I'm going to guess no."

"Fuck," Ally murmured.

"Ally, what's going on? How do you know this guy?"

"He was my client's bodyguard. Um, he attacked me."

"What? Why?" Both her voice and expression showed her concern and she took Ally by the elbow and steered her out of the trauma room and into the ER. "What's going on?"

Ally took a breath and realized she needed to share this with someone. "It's a long story. Would you like to come over after your shift?"

"At midnight?"

Ally chuckled. "I probably won't be sleeping. Or going to work tomorrow."

Maria nodded. "Sure. This is some extreme way to get me to your place, though."

Ally smiled. "I've cleaned it up."

"Good to know."

"Will you call me, let me know what happens?"

Maria looked at her gently. "Ally, you know what's going to happen."

Ally knew. It was just a matter of time and how aggressive the trauma fellows wanted to be. They could call off the efforts in the ER, and they could all go back to work helping people who might survive, or practice their surgical techniques on Rocco, perhaps keep him alive for a day or two, until all his organs failed from the insult of the shock his body had suffered. Either way, Rocco was dead. The only difference was the date they wrote on the death certificate.

"Still…"

"I'll call you."

Ally headed back the way she came and found the guys double-parked near the ambulance entrance. They were both sitting in the front seat, so Ally opened the back door and climbed in.

"Well?" Steve asked as he turned.

Ally filled them in.

"Holy fuck," Carlos said.

"You've got that right. This has to be even more exciting than boxing," Steve commented as he started driving. "Good thing you called the cops, Carlos."

"Yeah. Sure is."

That explained that, Ally thought. "Why did you call? I mean, how did you know I was in danger?"

"I saw the whole thing through the window, Al. His expression—he was facing me, you know? But your body language was screaming, girl. You kept backing up until you were practically in the driver's seat. I watched that for a minute and said, 'Oh, no. Girlfriend's in trouble.'"

"Thank Goddess you did, Carlos."

"I was hoping for a chance to practice my fighting skills, but you know these cans of steel are no match for lead."

Ally knew that and was so grateful none of them had gotten hurt, that the police officers who were called out to help her were going home to their families after their shift.

"We should eat. Food is an excellent therapy for shock," Carlos said.

"I actually think it's the alcohol you consume with the food," Steve countered.

"I have blood on me," Ally said. But the thought of going back to her empty apartment, where she might have been murdered if Rocco had his way, terrified her. "Can you give me a minute to clean up?"

"Sure," Steve said.

"Absolutely."

Ally sat in silence during the drive, thinking. She needed to call off from work. It was something she'd done only once, when her flu vaccine failed and she was confined to her bed for days in a near coma. And she couldn't stay at her place. She'd invite Maria to her parents' home to talk, if she still wanted to, but she wasn't staying in her apartment. That was two more calls. She had to change her bloody clothes and pack a few things to take to her parents', and she'd be ready.

Steve parked, and they made their way toward the apartment building, where they found the trolley, still laden with Brodrik Rogan's art, just where they'd abandoned it.

"What should we do with this?" Steve asked.

Ally had no idea, but she couldn't leave it on the sidewalk. "Can you help me bring it all up to my apartment?" She dreaded the idea, because she'd only have to haul it all back down at some point, but she was too tired to think, and even if she could, she doubted she'd come up with a better plan.

In her apartment, the guys unloaded the art while she slipped into her bedroom and pulled off her clothing. Holding the work clothes at arm's length, she debated for a moment, then tossed them in the trash. Without even informing the two men in her living room, she turned on the shower and quickly scrubbed off the events of the day.

Then she threw a few things into her bag and dressed while she called Greg. He answered quickly, and without any preamble or detail, she told him she had an emergency and couldn't make it in the next day. Without questions, he told her to call him when she could talk. Her next call was to her mom, and she told her she'd be spending the night. "I'll explain when I get there," Ally said, though how much she wanted to explain, she didn't know.

Second-guessing her decision to go to dinner, she took a fortifying breath and opened her bedroom door. Carlos and Steve both stared her down for a moment, then rushed her, enveloping her.

"You sure you want to go out? I mean, maybe we were a little hasty in our impromptu dinner plans."

Ally sighed. It was probably just what she needed.

She locked the door behind her, then followed them to the elevator and back to the parking lot, where two police officers stood waiting for her. Fuck, she thought. She'd hoped to be able to organize a story in her mind before she spoke with the police. But a man lay dying in the ER—could already be dead, in fact—and he'd been at her building, about to accost her, when he was shot. It only seemed reasonable that they'd want to speak with her.

The officers smiled, and the first one spoke. "Sorry to bother you guys. One of you is Mr. Rodriguez, I'm guessing? And you're Ms. Hamilton?"

When they nodded, the second one chimed in. "And who are you?" He directed his question, and his gaze, at Steve, who relayed his role in the recent events.

"We need to talk to all three of you. Where? Your apartments, perhaps? Or would you prefer the gym?"

"No, my apartment," Ally said, not wanting to create a scene in the lobby.

"We'll start with you, Ms. Hamilton. Would you gentlemen mind waiting in your quarters?"

He jotted down their apartment number and instructed them to wait for him. Then the officers rode with Ally to the top floor. The guys walked, and Ally suddenly felt nervous to be alone with the two policemen who she'd been so happy to see pull up to the curb an hour or so earlier.

After taking her demographics for their record, they asked her to explain everything in her own words.

She told them how she'd been working for Four H for about six weeks, and that she'd met Rocco when he was on duty at Brodrik Rogan's house. Deciding for truth, if not complete truth, she told them that she shared a love of art with Mr. Rogan, and that his attorney had called her the day before, requesting an audience at his office. She'd just arrived at home with her inheritance when Rocco appeared. She told them Carlos had seen their encounter from the gym window and had summoned the police, and she described how Rocco had confronted her about the art she'd inherited and wanted to go into her apartment to talk. She explained how she'd stalled, hoping someone would notice her, but that he'd become physical and threatened to shoot her, although she never actually saw his gun. Carlos and Steve stopped the would-be attack at her front door.

"And that's when you guys showed up."

"Sounds like a pretty awful day, Ms. Hamilton. Would you mind if I ask a few more questions, just to clear up any confusion?"

A few questions was more like a few hundred, but Ally supposed it was necessary. She was as honest and vague as could be, but they certainly knew how to probe. They asked about her employment with Four H, considering she'd told them she was an ER PA when she jumped in on the CPR.

"Unrelated and irrelevant," she responded.

"Well, if you lied to the police, it's relevant, Ms. Hamilton," one of them said.

"Let me clarify my statement, then. For the past few years, I've worked as a PA in the ER. For the past few weeks, I've been working in the home-health field. The whys of that switch are not something I wish to get into."

"Okay. We'll save that for later, then." He wasn't unfriendly, and something told her he had knowledge of and empathy for the kind of employees Greg Hart hired.

"What about Rocco? Did he raise any concerns when you met him? And contact you outside of work?"

"No, and no. He told me he copied my address from my driver's license, which I gave him for a background check when I went to Mr. Rogan's house."

They nodded, and officer one wrote that in his notebook.

"Why would Rocco be upset about this art?"

Ally shrugged.

"Was it jealousy?"

Less is better. "Apparently. Listen, I only talked to the man for five minutes in the parking lot. He didn't go into too much detail. He wanted to talk inside, and most of our conversation was me trying to stall him."

"Is that the artwork?" officer two asked, nodding toward the pile leaning against her wall.

Ally nodded. "Twenty-four pieces."

"We probably should take it into evidence."

"It's worth about ten grand, so can you give me a receipt?"

They puckered simultaneously. "Ten grand, and you only just met the Cadillac King? That's pretty generous, wouldn't you say?"

Shaking her head, she replied, "I was just as surprised as you are."

"No wonder Rocco was pissed."

Ally shrugged but maintained silence and decided she definitely wouldn't tell them about the note from Brodrik Rogan. In fact, as soon as they left, she planned to burn it, and she'd take the ashes and scatter them along the Scranton Expressway as she screamed madly from the window.

"Do you know how he's doing?" Ally asked.

"Rocco?" number two asked.

Ally nodded.

"He's dead."

Sucking in her breath, Ally nodded. "I figured."

"We'll be in touch," number one said, and Ally directed them to the luggage trolley, still in the elevator, so they could load the art. She just watched. If she never saw it again, that was fine by her. Screw the $10,000, although she did suspect the Chinese Gu was real, and somewhere in the collection she expected she'd find an authentic Napoleonic finial.

When they left, Ally sent a warning text to the guys, asked for a rain check on dinner, and in fact she did burn the letter from Brodrik Rogan, envelope and all. She took the ashes and placed them in a bag, then stopped at the McDonald's near her apartment and flushed them down the toilet. There, she ate a Big Mac and a large fry, washing it down with a cola. And then, she went home.

She still had to face her parents, and Maria, but she'd figure that out a little later. It was already after eight, and she was exhausted.

CHAPTER TWENTY-SIX

Confession

"Honey, is everything okay?" her mom asked as she clicked off the television when Ally walked into the family room.

"You will not even believe the day I've had."

Her dad swiveled in his chair, and her mom sat and faced her. Ally sat on the couch, between them.

"What happened?"

Ally sighed and started her story with the phone call from Austin Rose, ending it with the police interview. She was deliberately vague regarding the art switch. Was that something she wanted to share with them? But then her mom asked, and she knew she couldn't lie.

"You know, I've always been sort of a perfect child, right?"

Her dad scoffed, but her mom agreed.

"So this fall from grace—it was a hard one. Not a little trip where I skinned my knee. It bruised my ego, really affected everything I always thought about myself. My intelligence, my abilities, my self-control, my will, my dignity. My addiction shattered it all."

Both her parents sat still, staring at her, and she understood their fear. She wasn't going to try to assuage it, though. She'd been doing that for months, and it hadn't helped her one bit. It was time to face it, and own it, and move on.

"Going back to work helped. Being useful and caring for people—that's a great feeling. Earning money, also great. But something else happened when I went back to work, and I saw an opportunity to do something amazing. It was a little risky, but I thought it was worth it. And I was right."

"Ally, you're making me nervous," her dad said as he looked down his nose at her.

"I probably always will," she said with a sad smile.

"Please tell us what's going on."

"What I say is in confidence. Other than Kevin and a couple of his lawyer friends, no one knows what I'm about to tell you."

"Okay. You have lawyers involved. That's scary," her mom said.

"Don't be scared. Here goes," she said with a dramatic wave of her hand. "When I first walked into Brodrik Rogan's house, I noticed an unusual pattern to his art collection. He has all kinds of art, all mediums. But it seemed odd that Rogan had almost all the pieces of the stolen art from the Isabella Stewart Gardner Museum in Boston."

Janine's hand went to her heart. "What an awful tragedy, that theft."

Ally nodded. "He told me about himself, that he was from Boston. That he'd visited the museum. But his bodyguard—the same one who wanted to kill me tonight—told me so much more. How Rogan, this fabulously wealthy car guru, who'd been married to a movie star and dined with important people—he showed off these pieces to his guests. He made the security guard learn about the pieces. Don't you find that kind of odd?"

Her father looked at her mom, and she could tell what he was thinking. Ally was acting kind of odd.

"I mean, the guy is wealthy beyond belief. Why would he showcase thousand-dollar prints in the grand foyer of his mansion? Just inside the door is an original oil on canvas by a French painter named Brigette that he paid $25,000 for. He could afford that. Why display it next to a fake?"

"Why indeed?" her mom asked.

"So I thought maybe the art was real. The actual real collection from the Gardner Museum. And I decided to steal it back."

"You what?" Her mom sat forward, her voice just shy of a scream.

Ally put both hands in the stop position, and her mother did.

"It all goes back to my fall, to redeeming myself. I love art. I love that we've traveled all over the world to see masterpieces and attend the Schemel Forum to learn about art, and that we work together on little pieces for our neighbors. The idea that someone was keeping those pieces for himself, depriving the world of these treasures—it annoyed me beyond belief. So, I decided to do something about it."

"You stole his art?" her mom asked.

Ally explained her thoughts about the switches, and even though she knew it was probably illegal, she figured she was canceling her crime by substituting better-quality frames on the prints she left at Rogan's.

"Ally, I can't believe you would do this," her dad said. "I thought you made some bad decisions when it came to drugs, but this just…this is perhaps worse. Because for this, there's no excuse."

"Let me go on, because there's more."

"I'm not sure I want to hear it," he said.

"Please?" she asked, and after a loud sigh and a nod from her father, she continued. "I was able to switch out all the paintings and drawings from the Gardner heist, and I took them to Kevin's office, and his firm contacted people in Boston, and they verified that the paintings are authentic."

"Wait a sec. You mean you were right? You found the actual pieces stolen from the Gardner?" her mom asked.

Ally nodded. "Unbelievable, right?"

"It sounds like a prank teenagers would pull on their friends' parents. Not something an adult would try. Have you been talking to Reese? Or Jessica? Because it sounds like you need some guidance," her father said as he shook his head.

Ally nodded. "Every day, but not about this."

"So this Rocco knew the art was real?" her mom queried.

"Rocco suspected Rogan had the real art." Ally explained about the appraisals done on the pieces she'd been given and surmised Rogan had done that for inheritance purposes. For some reason, he'd kept the reproductions he'd used for the appraisal, and after his death, Rocco had switched them, only to find the pieces he'd stolen were fakes, too.

Her mom sighed before speaking. "And he suspected you had the real stuff."

"Yes."

"What if he shared that information with someone else. Like someone named Rogan?" her father demanded.

"I'm assuming he wouldn't want them to know he was stealing from their dad. But it makes sense that the kids didn't know about the art, because he wouldn't have been able to steal it if they did. They'd want to sell it themselves. And besides that, Mr. Rogan willed it to me. If the Rogan clan thought the art was real, they wouldn't have allowed it to leave that house."

They both were silent for a moment.

Her dad leaned back into the couch and met her gaze. "So what now?"

"Rocco is dead, and as awful as that is, it means he's not going to kill me, so I'm not unhappy."

"Why would he shoot at a policeman? That's suicide," Janine asked as she shook her head.

"I suspect when they dig into Rocco, they're going to find some bad things. It would explain why he was hiding out in the Poconos guarding Mr. Rogan. He had to be bored out of his mind, so he must have had a reason for staying."

Ally hoped they'd find bad things. It might dull the sharp edges of her guilt, if only a little.

"And you're going to get the reward?" her dad asked.

"Kevin says in about three weeks, I'll be getting a very large check from the museums."

"Museums?" he said as he cocked his head.

Ally had forgotten to tell them about the Raphael, so she briefed them.

"Oh, my goodness," Janine said. That's been missing since World War Two."

Ally sighed. The Gardner collection turning up in Brodrik Rogan's house was not all that far a reach. But how had a painting missing since 1940s Poland end up in a mansion in the Pocono Mountains of Pennsylvania? She'd wondered about that ever since she'd stolen it, and she had no answer. Except someone knew someone who knew Brodrik Rogan collected stolen art, and that was all it took.

"It's going home now. What a triumph for the people of Poland."

"Because of you," her mom said, with a look of pride.

"It was a stupid thing to do. Dangerous, obviously. Yet it's given me one of the greatest feelings I've ever had. And I don't regret it."

As he shook his head, the corners of her father's mouth tilted up, and she thought he might be forgiving her a little. "You won't regret the reward. How much is it?"

Ally's lawyers had negotiated with the Poles on the Raphael, and they'd agreed to keep the number confidential. Ally assumed the information would leak, but it didn't matter. No one would ever be sure, and that was what she really wanted.

"I'll be set for life."

"Ten million?" he asked.

"Russ, those paintings are worth hundreds of millions. It has to be more."

Ally bit her lip to contain her smile, then told them the number. "But I have to give a big chunk to Kevin's firm, and another bit to the people in Boston who are making sure my name is never mentioned."

"That's worth the money."

"I thought so."

"Good to know you're capable of good decisions once in a while," her dad said with a wink.

"Ouch," she said.

"Kidding, but not really."

"I know. I know. I want to use this money to support myself, so I can work doing something meaningful. I don't know what yet. I'll stay at Hart until my probation is over and I get my license back. Then I'm going to work on me, on being less of a 'yes person' and worry more about my own needs. This decision to steal the Rogan artwork was a very bad one, based on my need to prove myself. I shouldn't have to prove myself, yet I feel I do."

"Are you working on this issue with your counselor?"

Ally thought of Fake-Freud. "Yes. He told me this was the goal, to figure out why someone with so much to lose would make such bad choices. And I think this is part of the answer. I want to please people—especially you two—and I sacrifice myself to do it."

"And that's why you became addicted to drugs?" her father asked, his voice rising to match the color of his ears.

Ally held up both hands to calm him. "I thought I was too good to be an addict, so it shocked the shit out of me. And then I was too good to admit it. The quest for perfection takes its toll."

They digested her words silently, and Ally was happy they were listening. Really listening.

"How do we help?" her mom asked.

"Listen, just like tonight, and love me, even if I do something crazy stupid because I'm human, and I will. And I don't want to be afraid of screwing up. Being perfect is too much pressure."

Her mom rose from her seat and closed the space between them, then pulled Ally to her, cradling her tightly. A second later, she felt her dad's strong arms around her.

"Honey, we never expected you to be perfect," her mom whispered. "You just are."

Ally didn't bother wiping her tears. She simply let them fall. This conversation had been a long time coming, and it took the art caper to make it happen, but it had happened, and that was all that mattered.

Two hours later, after a nap that left her with just enough energy for the ten-minute drive to Maria's, Ally found herself sitting next to Maria on the couch. The fire was crackling, and the room was cozy, but still, she welcomed Maria's heat as she snuggled close to her.

"I'm so sorry about what happened to you. I wanted nothing more than to leave work and go home with you, so you weren't alone."

Ally told her about Carlos and Steve, and then the visit from the police, then the trip to see her parents. "I've been well protected," she said as she rested her head on Maria's shoulder.

"You don't have to talk about it. We can just cuddle."

Ally pulled back and looked into Maria's eyes. "Would you rather not know?"

The smile started in Maria's eyes, with just a little squint, and ended at the corners of her mouth. "I love you, Ally. I want to know everything."

Tears formed in Ally's eyes, and her throat tightened. That's what this was, wasn't it? Love? The constant thinking about someone, the desire to be with them, the need to confess your darkest secret, just so there are no boundaries between you.

"I love you, too. But..."

"There's no need to explain. We'll take it slowly, have some fun, get to know each other better."

"I knew I loved you the day I met you," Ally said softly. "It was your first day in the ER, and you pushed the surgeon out of the way to get to the bedside of a trauma patient. You were fierce."

"So you like that I'm rebellious?"

Ally sighed. She loved so much about Maria. "You're kind. And extremely well mannered."

Maria bit her lip, obviously to keep from laughing.

"You're silly sometimes, and serious when you should be." Ally punctuated her remark with a soft kiss.

"Your IQ is off the charts," she whispered into Maria's mouth. "And..." she sighed, "you're so, so sexy."

Maria nibbled back, and Ally was suddenly swept up in her, all other thoughts absent as she simply felt the passion building between them.

A passion that couldn't be fulfilled. Not yet anyway.

"I need to share something with you."

Maria met her gaze. "Is this about today?"

Ally nodded. She wished she didn't have to tell this truth, but if she wanted to have a future with Maria, she had to. Ally couldn't move forward with all this between them—not the stupid, criminal thing she'd done with the Rogan art, not the death of the bodyguard Maria had tried to save, and not the money that was coming her way. That money would change her life in ways that would bring with it big, difficult questions if she wasn't honest now.

So she began her tale, much as she had with her parents, in talking about her failings, her need for redemption. And she ended with the police in her apartment, taking her statement.

Maria's eyes were the size of softballs as she listened, asking a question here and there, but mostly she just sat quietly as Ally spoke.

"Did you tell the police about the real paintings, and the reward?"

Ally shook her head. "No, and I'm hoping I can remain anonymous. Who knows? It depends on how much they dig into Rocco's history, I suppose. If they're searching for a motive for his actions today, they might suspect he was looking for something when he came to my house."

"Something more than $10,000 worth of art."

Ally nodded. "Yes, but who knows? People have killed for less. And maybe they won't try to explain it at all, just pick the case up at my front door, when they responded to the call Carlos made. He fled, he pulled a gun, they shot him, he died."

"Maybe he took the secret with him."

It was a horrible way to look at it, but it was true. This might all be over because Rocco was acting on his own and hadn't shared his theory with anyone else. "I hope so," Ally said with a sigh. "I really do."

"You did a stupid thing, Ally," Maria said with a not-too-gentle punch to the arm. Then her eyes softened, and her voice did, too. "I'm sorry we pushed you to that."

"Who's we?"

"The world! I mean, if you had contracted diabetes, would you have felt a shame that made you feel you had to do something so desperate to make amends?" Maria didn't wait for a response. "No! You would feel a little sorry for yourself, then get a plan to manage your disease and move on with your life. Instead, your head is filled with these horrible ideas, and you're out trying to get yourself dead just to prove you're worthy of living."

Stigma. There it was again. Yet Ally had to get beyond that. It was just as Maria had said about diabetes, needing to manage it. Getting over the stigma was part of managing recovery.

"You really are very understanding." Ally chuckled. "Because I'm pretty sure I'd be kicking me out the door right about now."

Maria sighed. "I'm expecting you to wise up."

Ally nodded.

"Plus, you're going to be super-rich, and I like that in a girl."

Ally's smile exploded. "It's unbelievable, right?"

Maria shook her head. "It is. But not just the money. The whole thing. I mean, what are the odds that you'd notice his paintings were the exact same ones stolen from the Stevens Garner?"

Ally chuckled. "You need to keep up with your art classes. It's Stewart Gardner."

"Tomato, tomato."

"OMG. That's what Rocco said to me today. He was talking about paintings, and I was trying to stall him, and I said some were actually drawings. And he said, 'Tomato, tomato.' "

Her observation seemed to divert Maria's attention from the coincidence she'd been mentioning, and Ally was relieved. The less she spoke of it, the better.

"I'm sure there's more to the Rocco story, Ally. If he was just there trying to rob you, why shoot a cop? That's insane. He was in some sort of trouble, and he was desperate."

"I hope so," she said as she told Maria how guilty she felt about his death.

"It's not your fault." Maria yawned.

"I should let you get to bed."

Maria reached out and softly caressed Ally's cheek. "You could come with me."

Ally was as relieved by the invitation as she was excited. "You know all my secrets, and you still want me?"

"I'm going to have to draw a line somewhere, but since you're a hero and savior of priceless art, not to mention soon-to-be-wealthy, I'm going to let you push it a little."

Ally let out a huge breath. She so wanted to be done pushing it. It had been such a long and difficult journey from that mountain in Utah that she wanted nothing but months, perhaps years, of boring. Working and tinkering with frames, exercising and hanging out with the people she loved, which she knew included the woman beside her.

Maria laughed when she revealed her thoughts.

"I can't imagine you boring, Ally. You're too alive, too full of thoughts and ideas. Maybe you just have to work on channeling your energy constructively. But anyway—up for a sleepover?"

"I have nothing to wear," she said as she puckered her lips.

Maria smiled devilishly. "Oh, I could have so much fun right now. But I won't. Let's just say I'll find you something." She stood and pulled Ally up beside her.

"So does this mean you don't sleep nude? 'Cause I've been imagining that."

"Only in the summer," Maria said as they walked hand in hand up the stairs.

"This is a terrible conversation as a prelude to taking it slow."

They reached the landing, and Maria stopped and turned to face her. "The attraction between us is insane, Ally. The naked part is inevitable."

Maria was right, she knew. Every kiss seemed to turn deeper and hotter; every time their eyes met, the connection between them grew. And every time, Ally pulled back. Why? What would going slowly do for her?

This attraction wasn't weeks old. It had been more than eight months since they'd met on the Fourth of July weekend, on that first shift Maria worked in the ER. Since then, Ally had hit an all-time low, with Maria there to witness it, and she hadn't balked. In fact, she had turned out to be an incredibly positive force. So why did Ally keep holding back?

"What are you thinking?" Maria asked. "You have a look."

Ally puckered. "I'm thinking slow is a bad plan."

"Try these," Maria said as she handed Ally a soft cotton shirt with long sleeves and matching fleece pants.

"We're the same size," Ally said. "It should be perfect."

Maria nodded toward the bathroom, and when Ally came out, the room was bathed in the light of a dozen twinkling candles.

"How nice," she said as she looked around. "But how did you light them all so fast?"

Maria held out her hand and clicked a button on a tiny remote, and the candles shut off. Another click, and they came back to life.

Ally chuckled. "That's fantastic!"

"I know, right? Bri bought them as a housewarming gift," Maria said as she hurried into the bathroom. "They sing me to sleep, then turn off in six hours."

Ally stood, studying the generic art and posters on the wall, the pictures Maria chose to display—each of her parents, in separate photos, and a few of Bri, plus some with other people who seemed to be friends.

She was studying one when she felt Maria behind her, felt two hands on her shoulders and soft lips on her neck. The touch might have been all above the waist, but Ally felt it below, in her wobbling knees and throbbing center.

How did this woman affect her like this?

Ally turned slowly so they were face-to-face, and their lips met again. The desire in Ally exploded with the kiss, and she didn't want to wait a moment longer to feel Maria naked beside her. *You've got this,* she thought as she reached below Maria's top and inched her hands up the softness of her skin.

CHAPTER TWENTY-SEVEN

Silent Partner

It was a bright, cloudless Saturday morning three weeks later when Ally walked down the street toward the Recovery Hub. March was crawling off the calendar, defeated by the powerful force of spring, and Ally was dressed in jeans and a T-shirt in celebration of the good weather.

In the lobby, she nodded toward some familiar faces and placed a container of cookies on a small table as she sat in the adjacent chair.

It had been three weeks since the artwork had been authenticated by the Gardner, three weeks of anticipating her reward check. Three weeks since Rocco had died, of wondering if the police were going to come around with more questions.

They hadn't. In fact, she'd learned most of the information about him from the news, which had talked for days about the death of Brodrik Rogan's former bodyguard. Rocco, it turned out, had been questioned about the disappearance of the parts guy from the Cadillac dealership and was the prime suspect. Hearing that chilling news clip had caused a considerable lump in her throat. Carlos's observation and quick action had saved her life.

And while the police hadn't reached out to her, she knew from a friend of her dad that they weren't looking into her. They didn't seem to concern themselves about why Rocco paid her that visit on the day he died, only what he did once he got there. That he'd run from them, and pulled his gun, and fired a shot at a Scranton cop.

Even though she'd had no official news from the police, Ally had heard from Kevin. Both museums had issued checks to the Boston firm handling the artwork's return, and they in turn had paid Kevin's group. He'd appeared at her parents' home the night before, handing her one of those big checks like they give the lottery winners on TV.

It was just the four of them, Kevin and her parents, but they'd had champagne to go with their favorite pizza and had spent a nice few hours together. Although she realized how dangerous her task had been, with a killer just around the corner at the Rogan mansion, she knew her family was proud of her. She'd done something brave and honorable.

More important, though, she was proud of herself. She'd not only repatriated stolen art, but she'd repatriated herself, moving back into the world as someone who could hold her head up high. Even if no one ever knew Ally Hamilton had returned the stolen works of art to the Gardner, she did. She was a good and righteous person. A year of drug abuse had twisted her self-image, and this one brazen act had done wonders to bring things back into focus.

Now, the ordeal was almost over. She'd stopped at her bank a few minutes ago and made the largest deposit she'd probably ever make, then rushed to the Recovery Hub to put this all to rest.

"Hey, Ally."

Ally looked up to see a smiling Grace Rogan looking down at her.

Ally stood and hugged her. "It's great to see you. Have a seat," she said with a wave.

"How are you?" Ally asked when they were sitting kitty-corner beside the table.

"Eh." She shrugged. "There's been a lot of arguing. Lot of drama. It seems I'm not the only one who was cut out of the will, but I'm the only one who saw it coming."

"So you were disinherited?" Ally asked.

Grace nodded. "He left me a small amount of money, to finish my education. If I don't use it in five years, it'll be donated to charity."

"Wow. You called that one."

Grace blew out a breath. "When I met you in rehab, Ally, I told you I was clean. I know my own brother drugged me, then arranged that surprise visit from my probation officer. It wasn't hard to guess why. Peter knew my dad was failing, knew he didn't have long to arrange all the pawns on the board so he could get what he wanted."

"And he got it, huh?"

"I don't think he'll get more than me," she said with a huge smile. "My dad had six kids, so a lot of hands are out right now. Winnie's two are still teenagers, so my dad had to take care of them. And Winnie has a lot of skin in the game—he was with her twice as long as any of his other wives, so she's getting a nice chunk. And, of course, he provided for all the grandchildren as well. Joseph has a generous trust fund set up. Not enough to corrupt him, but to support him until he's out of school."

Ally smiled. "That's good news."

"It is. Not that I couldn't have taken care of him with my share of the reward money."

"Forty-five million buys a lot of ice cream."

"Ice cream?"

"That's what my niece and nephew eat."

"Joe likes hot dogs."

"Even better."

Suddenly, Grace started laughing. "I can't believe we pulled this off. You pulled it off."

Ally leaned back and looked at the ceiling. "When you told me your dad was half-blind and would never notice we switched the paintings, I wasn't too worried. Who knew he'd given his bodyguard such an education in art?"

Grace leaned forward and touched Ally's knee. "I didn't know about Rocco, Ally. Please believe me. He always seemed like such a nice guy. Even when everyone else treated me with such disdain, he was always a gentleman."

"How could we guess he'd turn out to be a murderer?"

"Well, birds of a feather, and all that." She looked into Ally's eyes. "My father wasn't a good man. He murdered my mom, you know?" Grace smiled softly. "My mom was a sweet woman, just a farm girl from South Jersey who happened to be gorgeous. Her career was starting to take a good turn when she met him. He was older, and charming, and very, very rich. She fell for him, and it destroyed her."

Ally felt Grace's pain, still so sharp after all the years, and her eyes began to tear. She'd had to deal with death in the ER, and she'd learned much from the social workers on the trauma team. "She's not really gone, you know? As long as you're still talking about her. To me, today, but mostly to Joseph. He needs to know who his grandmother was. And then, you see, she'll live on in him. He'll probably name his daughter Savannah one day."

"Her name was really Susan."

"Even better," Ally said.

"Do you believe in fate?" Grace said as she leaned back in her chair.

"Absolutely."

"It was fate that brought us together."

Ally thought about it for a moment and supposed it was true. She'd been at Marworth for a week when Grace was admitted, looking broken. Ally was standing by herself in one of the group rooms, staring past an uninspiring painting to the sunshine beyond, wondering if she'd ever enjoy another beautiful day.

"When I saw you standing there, I felt like we were destined to click. That you were going to be my recovery buddy."

"How astute."

"Maybe hopeful. It wasn't my first rodeo, you know, and one thing I can tell you for sure is that a pretty girl in rehab makes a lot of friends. Mostly with horny guys. I needed you to protect me."

"Do I look that fierce?" Ally asked.

Grace shook her head. "No, but I got gay vibes, and I figured if I could get close to you, it would keep the vultures away."

"What if I was a vulture?"

Grace smiled, just a little turn of her mouth. "I was willing to chance it."

A blush heated Ally's face, and she looked down. "You are a beautiful woman, Grace. Inside and out."

"Just not the one for you?"

"I told you when we met there was someone in my heart. It's official now. She waited for me, and we've been seeing each other again."

Grace nodded. "Good for you."

"You do have a nice consolation prize," Ally said as she nodded toward the plastic container filled with cookies, and a forty-five-million-dollar check. It was half of Ally's take, just as they'd discussed when they formulated the plan at rehab. And what a plan it was—from using Ally's contacts in the ER to arrange another job for Macie, Brodrik Rogan's prior nurse, to Grace talking her father into upgrading his security system, they'd discussed every detail on walks around the grounds and over lunch and late at night in their room.

"It'll do."

"Do you have a plan for your money? Someone to invest with or give you financial advice?" Ally worried about Grace. Unlike Ally, who was surrounded by supportive people, Grace was really alone. Joseph's father was in jail, and her surviving family was completely dysfunctional.

As if reading her mind, Grace nodded. "I have a few good friends.

I haven't touched a drug since my son was born. Before that, actually, when I found out I was pregnant. I'm friends with his friends' moms, and my bestie and I are pretty tight. In spite of what my dad thought, I'm not a failure."

Ally didn't even try to deny the allegations against her dad. "Will you go back to school?"

Grace's face lit up. "I'm three years into my degree in business, so maybe. I'd really like to become a travel agent. Maybe just something online, but who knows? My dad knew a lot of people with money, and maybe I can start arranging travel for them, for the Rogan businesses."

Ally thought it sounded like a great idea. She was just happy to see Grace smile. When they'd met in rehab, Grace had been so despondent about her life, and even though many addicts lied, Ally sensed that Grace really was telling the truth about being drugged by her brother. That sibling animosity was an entirely different burden to carry, one that Ally had to bear as well. It was just another bond between them. "I'll use you. And I'll let my parents know about you. You'll do great."

"Thanks. I'll let you know when I'm ready. I'm going to take Joe to Disney for my first trip."

"Count me in."

They were quiet for a moment, and Grace reached over and opened the plastic container. Her jaw dropped when she looked inside. "You made cookies."

Ally nodded. "I thought it would look suspicious if I just handed you an envelope."

Grace pulled out two chocolate-chip cookies and handed one to Ally, and they sat back chewing.

"Delicious. Maybe you should open a bakery."

Ally still wasn't sure what she was going to do, but it was nice to have options. She shared that thought with Grace.

Grace nodded. "It sure is."

"Can I ask you a question?"

"That is a question," Grace said as she reached for another cookie.

"Okay, another question."

"If I get the rest of the cookies."

Ally pursed her lips in thought. "Deal."

"Shoot."

"Whatever made you think those paintings were real?"

Grace shook her head. "It's crazy, isn't it? My entire life, those paintings decorated the walls of my dad's house. They were like the wallpaper, you know? I had no idea about real or fake or stolen or what. Then, one day, I was reading on the couch in his office. It was during one of those times when the market was down, and he was all worried about money. No one buys luxury cars when the economy is on the skids. He came in to take a call and didn't notice me there. Anyway, he put the phone on speaker, and the guy he was talking said he'd found a buyer for *The Concert*, but only if he could get *Storm on the Sea of Galilee*, too."

"And?"

"The guy offered my dad twenty million dollars for those two paintings."

Ally couldn't even imagine overhearing a conversation like that.

"My dad turned him down, just like that. Said they were worth fifty million, and he wasn't selling them for a penny less."

Ally nodded. "They're probably worth much more."

Grace nodded. "Yeah. You're right. I started reading about the paintings, and the heist, and I realized my father probably orchestrated the entire thing. And then I filed that information away, wondering how I could use it."

"And along came Ally."

"Along came Ally, and art therapy at rehab, and talk about painting and framing and all that stuff that made my mind whirl. I thought the Fates had brought us together so we could make it through rehab, but then I realized it was all about the art. It was our destiny to return it."

Ally nodded and leaned forward. "We did a good thing, Grace."

Grace nodded toward a sign on the wall behind Ally. Another inspirational message, like the ones on the walls of rehab hospitals and recovery centers everywhere.

Do your little bit of good where you are;
it's those little bits of good put together that overwhelm the world.
Desmond Tutu

"That's a great one," Ally said after she read the message. Then she smiled at Grace. "We've got this recovery thing down. Wanna go do some good?"

Grace nodded, and Ally reached out and pulled her to her feet. Grace secured her container of cookies before taking Ally's hand. "Let's go, friend."

"We've got this," Ally told her.

About the Author

Jaime Maddox is the author of seven novels with Bold Strokes Books and was awarded the Alice B. Lavender Certificate for her debut novel, *Agnes*. She has co-authored a book on bullying with her son, Jamison, and written an unpublished children's book about her kids' uncanny ability to knock out their teeth. A native of Northeastern Pennsylvania, she still lives there with her partner and twin sons. Her best times are spent with them, hanging out, baking cookies, and rebounding baskets in the driveway. When her back allows it, she hits golf balls, and when it doesn't, she does yoga. On her best days, she writes fiction.

Books Available From Bold Strokes Books

Catch by Kris Bryant. Convincing the wife of the star quarterback to walk away from her family was never in offensive coordinator Sutton McCoy's game plan. But standing on the sidelines when a second chance at true love comes her way proves all but impossible. (978-1-63679-276-7)

Hearts in the Wind by MJ Williamz. Beth and Evelyn seem destined to remain mortal enemies but are about to discover that in matters of the heart, sometimes you must cast your fortunes to the wind. (978-1-63679-288-0)

Hero Complex by Jesse J. Thoma. Bronte, Athena, and their unlikely friends must work together to defeat Bronte's archnemesis. The fate of love, humanity, and the world might depend on it. No pressure. (978-1-63679-280-4)

Hotel Fantasy by Piper Jordan. Molly Taylor has a fantasy in mind that only Lexi can fulfill. However, convincing her to participate could prove challenging. (978-1-63679-207-1)

Last New Beginning by Krystina Rivers. Can commercial broker Skye Kohl and contractor Bailey Kaczmarek overcome their pride and work together while the tension between them boils over into a love that could soothe both of their hearts? (978-1-63679-261-3)

Love and Lattes by Karis Walsh. Cat café owner Bonnie and wedding planner Taryn join forces to get rescue cats into forever homes—discovering their own forever along the way. (978-1-63679-290-3)

Repatriate by Jaime Maddox. Ally Hamilton's new job as a home health aide takes an unexpected twist when she discovers a fortune in stolen artwork and must repatriate the masterpieces and avoid the wrath of the violent man who stole them. (978-1-63679-303-0)

The Hues of Me and You by Morgan Lee Miller. Arlette Adair and Brooke Dawson almost fell in love in college. Years later, they unexpectedly run into each other and come face-to-face with their unresolved past. (978-1-63679-229-3)

A Haven for the Wanderer by Jenny Frame. When Griffin Harris comes to Rosebrook village, the love she finds with Bronte de Lacey creates a safe haven and she finally finds her place in the world. But will she run again when their love is tested? (978-1-63679-291-0)

A Spark in the Air by Dena Blake. Internet executive Crystal Tucker is sure Wi-Fi could really help small-town residents, even if it means putting an internet café out of business, but her instant attraction to the owner's daughter, Janie Elliott, makes moving ahead with her plans complicated. (978-1-63679-293-4)

Between Takes by CJ Birch. Simone Lavoie is convinced her new job as an intimacy coordinator will give her a fresh perspective. Instead, problems on set and her growing attraction to actress Evelyn Harper only add to her worries. (978-1-63679-309-2)

Camp Lost and Found by Georgia Beers. Nobody knows better than Cassidy and Frankie that life doesn't always give you what you want. But sometimes, if you're lucky, life gives you exactly what you need. (978-1-63679-263-7)

Fire, Water, and Rock by Alaina Erdell. As Jess and Clare reveal more about themselves, and their hot summer fling tips over into true love, they must confront their pasts before they can contemplate a future together. (978-1-63679-274-3)

Lines of Love by Brey Willows. When even the Muse of Love doesn't believe in forever, we're all in trouble. (978-1-63555-458-8)

Only This Summer by Radclyffe. A fling with Lily promises to be exactly what Chase is looking for—short-term, hot as a forest fire, and one Chase can extinguish whenever she wants. After all, it's only one summer. (978-1-63679-390-0)

Picture-Perfect Christmas by Charlotte Greene. Two former rivals compete to capture the essence of their small mountain town at Christmas, all the while fighting old and new feelings. (978-1-63679-311-5)

Playing Love's Refrain by Lesley Davis. Drew Dawes had shied away from the world of music until Wren Banderas gave her a reason to play their love's refrain. (978-1-63679-286-6)